To PAM e Cedric
Hope you &
attempt at
with very best wishes
@bear S. Taylor .
alias - Susan xxx

Fixing
Flame *the*

ALESSANDRA S. TAYLOR

Fixing The Flame
Alessandra S. Taylor

First published 2021
Copyright © Alessandra S. Taylor

ISBN 978-1-5272-9491-2

Cover design: BespokeBookCovers.com
Editing: Alicia Street. Iproofreadandmore.

Contact Alessandra S. Taylor:
Facebook: www.facebook.com/Alessandra S. Taylor

For Steven.

TABLE OF CONTENTS

DREAMS AND ECHOES

I knew I was dreaming, but it wasn't like a usual dream, it was like being an actor in someone else's play, with all my senses alive to the surroundings. I was standing in a dark, and dirty room, the smell of general rot and decay filling the air. It was awful, but I knew being there was important. My heart was racing as I hurried to place a tray of make-up into a small battered brown suitcase. I could sense another person there with me and turned to see a dark-haired man peering out through the curtains into the street below. He was anxious, terrified, wanting us to get out, rushing me to leave, but I knew we'd die if we ran.

He bolted from the room yelling, "We have to get out now." Leaving me alone and petrified.

I needed to think quickly to save myself. I made my way out into a long bare corridor and realized there was only one way out. I was trapped. Shouting and heavy footsteps rose up from the floors below and absolute terror swept through me.

I awoke with such a jolt, my pajamas damp with sweat because of the dream. I felt the bed sheet beneath me, relieved I hadn't wet the bed this time. Then, like a snowflake in my palm, the dream melted away before I could hold on to it, and I was left with odd pieces, like a fuzzy mixed-up play. It was one of the many scary and intense dreams I'd been having lately. I couldn't quite fit all the scenes together to make a whole dream, it was like a puzzle to solve, but my mind was blocking me from doing it. I lay there trying to remember, then sighing heavily, resigning myself to not recalling for now.

I sat up in bed, but then remembered it was Saturday and no school, so no rushing about. I relaxed back onto my pillows and looked over to see Evelyn, my favorite rag doll. I knew I had to have her when I saw her in the store and pestered until Dad bought her for me. I didn't really see her as a doll; she was so special, like an old, trusted friend.

I gazed around my room as the morning sun filtered in. With four brothers and a dog, it was great to have some quiet girly space. I had chosen everything in it myself; the princess posters dotted around the walls, my dressing table with its heart-shaped mirror, everything. I sighed to myself at how perfect it all was, when my tummy rumbled in protest, and I realized I was hungry. With a flurry, I threw back the bed covers, and went out onto the landing. I tiptoed past Mom's room, as she usually slept in on the weekends, and I didn't want to be the one to wake her and get yelled at. Once safely past, I ran down the stairs, avoiding the one creaky step, and into the kitchen. Rocky, our German shepherd, was waiting by the kitchen table for any breakfast leftovers and barked when I came in. His usual greeting.

"Hi, Peanut," said Scott, my very oldest brother, who was eating his breakfast.

"Morning, Scott," I replied quietly, while shaking cereal into a bowl.

"Hi Chloe," said Mike, another brother.

"What's wrong with you, grumpy?" Scott said, noting my quieter than usual entrance. I could feel him watching me as I put milk on my cereal. I looked back at him, giving him my well-practiced, sisterly death stare.

"I'm not grumpy. I had a really, really bad dream last night."

"Oh no, not another one. What was it about this time?" asked Mike, as he munched on his toast.

"I can't remember, but I know it was scary."

"It's just dreams, Peanut," said Scott, always the sensible one. "We all have them, I've told you before, it's just your mind working overtime, trying to make sense of what you've been up to in the day and answer questions for you. Just forget it," he told me.

But I couldn't. It wasn't that simple. It was happening almost nightly now—flashes of different scary scenes and people, and places. It was leaving me tired in the daytime too, and I was starting to dread going to bed.

Unsettled, I shoveled cereal into my mouth. I was getting really frightened by them now, more so in the last few weeks, because they seemed so real. Not long back, when I had the most awful nightmare, I wet my bed. I squirmed at the embarrassing memory, and how the boys teased me about it. Mom got mad, telling me I wasn't a baby anymore, but I didn't do it on purpose and couldn't remember the terrible dream enough to tell her so she could understand.

Not remembering them was really maddening, like a name you want to recall, it's on the tip of your tongue, but you just can't find it. Then when someone tells you the name you think, "Oh, of course." If only I could tell the boys,

I bet they'd figure it out. Then maybe all the pieces would fall into place, and the bad dreams would stop. But I knew deep down they couldn't help me until I could remember enough to explain it. Until then I would just have to deal with it by myself. After all, I was nine now, nearly ten, not a baby anymore.

One after another, my brothers piled into the kitchen and sat around the table. My head was patted, and my hair gently tugged by each of them as usual. I loved them all, and felt safe and protected by them, especially Scott, except at night in my dreams where they couldn't help me. No-one could.

I loved weekends; it meant we would all be having dinner together too, since Dad was coming home today. I looked at them as they talked to each other and told silly stories. I smiled and laughed with them—especially after they'd explained Ryan's joke about a mushroom buying drinks for everyone, being a "fungi," or "fun guy" to be with —but deep down inside I wasn't happy. This unsettled feeling just wouldn't let me be.

Once breakfast was over and we'd cleared away the dishes, I followed as they went quietly up the stairs, everyone avoiding the creaky step. Each person had to clean up their room, it was one of the chores Scott insisted on. Scott was the boss of everyone, including Rocky, when Dad wasn't home. He was strict but fair, and in control of things, and that made me feel safe. He was a natural leader; everyone liked Scott. I listened carefully to every word he said to me.

'Peanut, if you fail to prepare, then prepare to fail,' he told me about my homework. He'd done that with all the boys and treated me the same as them, an equal, which I liked.

Scott had recently been given his own car and was dating his first steady girlfriend, Mia. I didn't like her much, even though she was pretty and nice to everyone. Going out with her meant he was away from me more. Scott used to take me out in his car alone on trips to the mall or the movies. I loved my time with him, just the two of us, when I could tell him anything at all, and he would always know what to do. He made me feel special and important and would make me laugh and tell me silly jokes as we drove along, getting take-out food to eat together. Secretly I thought he was my favorite brother, and now I had less time to talk with him about things because of her.

I made a flimsy attempt at tidying my room and then went quietly into Joel's room. At fifteen, Joel was the cleverest one in the family in my eyes. He was a computer wizard and read so many books and watched trillions of movies. His bedroom was like a library of books and DVDs with shelves of them from floor to ceiling. If you wanted to know anything for school, it was worth asking Joel first, before turning to your iPad. Mom asked him to find out about different things like diets and getting stains out. Everyone went to Joel for information. I stood there while he was folding his T-shirts and gazed at all the movies and books he had, all neatly organized. They were thrillers and spy films. I knew what I wanted to ask him.

"Joel," I shouted and jumped on his newly made bed.

"Shhh, don't wake Mom. What is it, Peanut?" he said, shutting the door and looking in horror at his neatly made bed being ruffled by me.

I lowered my voice and then just went for it with my questions.

"When you have a dream, is it real or pretend like a

movie? Where do you go when you dream? Do dreams come true? And can dreams hurt you?"

Joel laughed quietly and stopped his T-shirt folding.

"Whoa, that's a lot of loaded questions this early in the day. Where to begin... Okay, dreams are just that—dreams. It's your mind making sense of what you've seen and heard. You don't go anywhere, your mind wanders about, not you. You stay safe in your little bed while your mind thinks about things. Why, Peanut? Is this about the dream last night?"

"I can't remember the really bad ones," I said, shrugging my shoulders, which I hoped made him think I wasn't frightened. "I mostly forget them, or they're muddled in the morning when I wake up. One dream I can remember having several times though, is a beach dream. I'm standing on the sand and a big wave comes up the beach— it's huge—and it goes over my head, not anyone else's, but it doesn't crash down, it just covers me. It's like a water tunnel, like at Sea World. I can see you, Dad, Scott, Mike, and Ryan on the beach through the water tunnel. You all wave at me to come with you, and I'm shouting and waving at you about being stuck wanting to get out, but I'm trapped and scared."

He didn't say anything right away, only looked at me with a thoughtful expression on his face, and so I went on.

"I run along the tunnel of water to get to the end so I can get out, and I run and run for a really long time. There's a figure in the distance, but I can't see their face and I can't get any closer even though I keep running." I stopped and looked expectantly at Joel's face, waiting for his answer.

"Wow, that's intense, Chlo. But it probably just means you're watching us all getting older and we're not around as much as you want us to be. You feel distanced from us, as if you're being left behind because you're so young. The figure in the tunnel is maybe a goal you're trying to achieve or a puzzle you're trying to solve."

Wow, I stared up at his kind face and thought how wise he was. I liked his answer. If he knew what this one was, then maybe he could help me figure out the real scary ones.

"Thanks, Joel. Can I ask you if I remember any more?"

"You can tell me or ask me anything, anytime." he reassured me. "Come and play in the pool with us for a while. It's getting hot out there already."

Great, I thought, as I raced around the landing to my room to get changed into my swimsuit. Please stay asleep, Mom, I pleaded in my mind, and slowed down on tip toe to pass her room.

I found Rocky in my room. Rocky was my hero, a big soppy dog with huge paws. While he was always gentle with us, I knew if we were threatened in any way, he would protect us. I had the delicious thought he would protect me to the death. With that in mind, I went to the stash of cookies I kept in my closet for emergencies and gave him two, as a decent reward for being a hero. I also hoped he would remember me doing this in case I ever needed him to come to my rescue.

I RAN into the yard and made for the pool, kicking off my slip-on shoes, dropping my clothes in a pile, and sitting Evelyn carefully on top. All four brothers were already in, and I jumped in at the deep end with a splash. We did swimming races and then lazed about under the hot Florida sun. As I floated around in the water, with the boys giving my float a shove every now and again to keep me moving, my eyes fell on the sign Dad had found in a market somewhere. It said, "Welcome to our OOL. Yes, there's no Pee in it," which always made me smile. He'd got it as a reminder for when the boys had friends around playing in the pool.

A while later, I saw my mom, Helen, come out of the house and head towards the loungers by the pool. She was carrying her phone, a drink, and her cigarettes. She smiled and waved at us, then relaxed on a lounge chair, putting sun block on before lighting a cigarette. I waved back from my float, wondering why she lied to Dad about her smoking, which she made us lie about too, as he never got angry about anything.

As time wore on, the boys left one by one to their various plans. I watched as Scott's girlfriend, Mia, came to meet him. He swivelled my float around, stopped it and kissed the top of my head.

"Have fun, Peanut. See you later Ryan," he said, as he got out of the pool to meet her. A pang of jealousy ran through me, and I just waved at them half-heartedly as they went off hand in hand. That left just me and Ryan, my funniest brother. He threw me high up in the air, so I splashed down into the water one last time, and then he got out of the pool too, leaving me alone.

I sighed to myself at the loss of everyone and returned to playing in the pool. I loved swimming and jumping in the water, and I could still have fun, even on my own. I was a strong swimmer and could do most strokes and dives.

I decided to swim underwater, from one end of the pool to the other, as I'd done hundreds of times before. I counted the seconds as I went along, kicking my legs like mad and holding my breath trying to beat my record. I felt for the poolside with my outstretched hand. As my head came up at the side of the pool, I was met with Rocky on the poolside, peeing on the ground. A small amount splashed on my face and trickled into the water, and I froze. A feeling of terror swept through me, and I scrambled out of the water, breathless, upset, and not sure why. I'd seen Rocky peeing loads of times; he once peed on a picnic I was having with my friends. It had never bothered me before, but there was something distant in my memory about the pee and the water and it unsettled me to my core. It left me with the same feeling the real bad dreams left me with when I first woke up. The horrible feeling of death.

I looked over at Mom who was unaware of my distress. I knew she wouldn't understand and would only get mad if I made a fuss about it when she was trying to relax. I hurriedly showered and changed into my clothes, but I couldn't shake off that terrible feeling. I needed to escape and hide—from what, I didn't know. There was nothing to see to be afraid of. I made my way to my tree house, and sat there with Evelyn clutched to my chest, unsettled, and frightened. I looked at her and had the strangest feeling that if she could only talk, she could tell me everything.

My tree house was just for me; where I was supposed to feel safe, but today I didn't. Something...something I needed to remember, but I couldn't figure out what it was. Now it was as if my bad dreams had somehow made their way into my daytime as well. I knew I needed to remember whatever it was to figure it out and be normal again.

Then came a feeling of dread that I *would* remember, and that when I did, it would be so horrible I'd wish I hadn't.

$\sim$

I COULD HEAR Mom calling me.

"Chloe, come on, get ready, we're going to the yard sale."

Oh no, I'd forgotten about that. An old lady was leaving her house and selling her stuff. Mom wanted to go to see if there was anything she liked. I really didn't want to go, but there was no one at home to watch me, so I had no choice.

We pulled up near the house on the other side of Naples, and I saw people going through things laid out on tables outside and in the open garage.

Mom turned to me with her strict face on. "Behave yourself, Chloe. Remember this is someone else's house. Don't touch anything and don't embarrass me, okay?"

"Okay, Mom," I replied, but I wasn't sure what trouble she thought I could get into looking around an old person's stuff.

We got out the car and Mom made straight for an outside table, picking things up and inspecting them. I went into the garage since it looked cooler and more interesting. I gazed around and saw things piled on tables: ornaments, books, and lots of jugs which must have been someone's hobby. I went to the back and peeked through an open door to a hallway inside the house. There were large photographs in frames lining the wall inside. My gaze settled on a photograph of a man in military uniform which looked so familiar. Olive green and khaki colors. I stood there and gazed at it unable to pull away. *Where had I seen it before?* Maybe at Grandad George's house. A scene flashed in my mind of a different man wearing a similar uniform, he was stood by a truck with his hands on his hips and smiling.

I was jolted out of my thoughts when a voice came out of nowhere.

"Isn't he handsome, dear?"

I turned quickly and came face-to-face with an old lady. She must have been about a hundred. Her hair was completely white, and she had it half tied up and half down.

She had a sweet old face and wore heavy earrings that dragged her ears right down.

"He looks really cool in his uniform," I said, hoping that was the right thing to say.

"That's my father. He was killed in the Second World War. I was only little when he went."

I thought about that for a moment. "That's so sad," I said, meaning it.

"It is sad, but I know I'll be seeing him again soon. I'm moving from this house, you know. I'm too old to keep it going. My husband and I lived here happily for over sixty years, and now he's gone, I'm going to live with my daughter."

"I expect you miss him. Aren't you sad selling all of your things?" I asked her.

"They're just that dear—things. We don't need things. You come into this world with nothing, and you leave with nothing. It's what you do while you're here, how you treat people and who you love that really matters. Moving houses or giving up things doesn't change that."

I looked at her and thought she must be wise because she was so old, but then thought about my own things. Maybe it's just when you're old you don't need things anymore.

"As for missing him, even though he's gone, he isn't really. He's always here with me. Look."

She pointed at a corner of the garage, and I turned around warily expecting to see a ghost floating there, like Casper, but all I could see was a mower, a step ladder, and some fishing rods.

She got louder as she spoke. "We don't die, sweetie, none of us. We live, we get old, we pass on to the next world, which I can tell you is much better than this one. I've been there with him many times; it's beautiful. See, he's waving, telling me it's okay to move out of our house. He'll be coming with me wherever I go, waiting for me until it's my time, and we'll be together again. Wave back, dear."

She then walked to the spot she was looking at and started to dance and sing with her "dead husband." I was kind of scared, and not sure what to say or do. I was feeling awkward but fascinated, and wondered if I should join in, clap at her dancing, or run to Mom. I just decided to wave, even though I didn't know who or what I was waving at.

"Mother," a voice called out sharply behind me, making me jump again. "Stop scaring the child with your nonsense. Go back inside the house and make some coffee."

A younger woman had come into the garage. She had a warm, friendly face and a pretty blue headband in her light hair. She was wearing jeans and a tee shirt just like Mom.

"Don't mind Mother," she said, and then lowered her voice, adding, "She has something called dementia, sweetheart. Her mind isn't working that well right now and that's why she's coming to live with me. She makes things up in her head and sees things differently from the rest of us, so don't pay her any mind. She's harmless, she won't hurt you."

Mom then came into the garage; she was clutching a load of things.

"Chloe, there you are. What are you up to? Not causing trouble, I hope. Here, take some of these from me."

She handed me a cushion and started to chat quietly to the old lady's daughter. I watched the old lady still talking happily to her husband in the corner.

I thought dementia looked like fun. She wasn't upset at all about her things being sold or moving out of her home, so maybe dementia was a nice thing for her to have.

Her daughter then took my hand, and led me out of the

garage, saying, "Come with me. I have something for you to see; It's meant for a young girl and because I have all boys it's no use to us, but I think you'll love it."

My mother followed along as I was led to a table outside and the woman picked up the most beautifully painted pale blue wooden box. It had blue and yellow flowers carved and painted on the top and a little latch to open and shut the lid. It had dark blue velvet covering the inside. It was beautiful and I wanted it. I looked at Mom pleadingly.

"How much?" she asked the woman.

"Please, it's a gift. Mother has scared her with all her nonsense talk, I'm so sorry about that. She was supposed to stay upstairs and out of the way while this was going on."

The woman turned to me.

"I had this when I was young. I used to keep my little treasures in it, then it became my hope box, then a sewing box and then a photograph box for Mom. I hope you enjoy having it as much as we have, sweetie. The flowers are pansies."

She handed me the box which I clutched lovingly as we headed back to the car, our hands filled with our yard sale treasures.

Mom started to talk about what had happened.

"Did the old lady scare you, Chloe? She's gone a bit mad since her husband passed away and doesn't really know what she's saying, so don't let it worry you. I love your little box. Aren't you glad you came now?"

"She didn't scare me, Mom. She was kind of sweet." I told her.

Once we got home, I went straight up to my room and gave the beautiful box pride of place on my dressing table. It looked as if it belonged there.

I spent the afternoon in the tree house with my iPad

looking things up on the internet. Mom was on a lounger outside. I checked up on dementia, nightmares, night terrors, bad dreams, the meaning of dreams, but none of it made sense of what was happening to me. My dreams were so real, as if I were physically there, like being in a scary play.

THE SCARF MAN—CHLOE

The boys filtered back to the house and sat talking and laughing together around the pool. When the light started to fade, I heard a familiar voice carry through the house—Dad was home. Relieved, I watched from my tree house as the boys and Rocky ran to meet him as he came into the backyard. Each one got a manly hug, and they guided him across the yard to where Mom was waiting and smiling at him.

I noticed Mom had hidden her drink and cigarettes from Dad, so she knew she shouldn't be doing it.

"David," I heard Mom squeal, and I watched as he kissed and held her tightly, happy to be home. It was so sweet. My parents had been college sweethearts and had stuck it out so far, while some of my friends' parents had divorced or weren't living together anymore, but mine were, and I felt proud of them because of that.

Dad listened to each of the boys as they talked about their different issues and requests, bottled up since they last saw him. I wanted to be part of it all and scrambled down the wooden tree house steps and raced towards them. When it was my turn, he picked me up, squeezed me, and held my hand tightly as we all walked into the house.

I sat on his lap on one of the armchairs in the den. With my head on his chest, I could hear his heartbeat. I usually went to my dad if I were in trouble or upset, not Mom. When Joel broke his arm, she fainted. She couldn't stand the sight of blood or vomit. Once, Ryan brought an injured bird in from the yard and she screamed and vomited everywhere. She wasn't that good in a crisis and usually had to lie down and get wine to recover. As a result, we kids learned to manage things ourselves with Scott as the boss.

Once we'd all had our dad time, we sat down for dinner as the family of seven we were, not the usual six of us with an empty chair, and it was great. After a riotous time at the dinner table with lots of laughing and teasing, Dad spoke up.

"Listen up, everyone." A hush came over our noisy group and we looked at him expectantly.

"It's not another baby, is it?" said Ryan, who always found things funny, and we all laughed, except Mom who gave a curt, "No." I did think I'd like to have a sister though; it was tough being the only girl.

Dad looked slowly at each of us, making me more excited.

"I've booked a trip for us to Europe this summer. Two weeks of traveling seeing different countries and sights. What do you think about that?"

There was a boyish explosion around me. This was something big.

"We're going to Europe, Peanut." Scott said.

I joined in the hooraying, but I wasn't sure what they were all shouting about, and when things died down, I decided to ask.

"What's to see in Europe?" The boys all jumped in to explain and looked to Dad for confirmation.

"We'll be flying to London England first, and then on to Paris France." he said.

The noisy conversation went on among the boys, as they tried to outdo each other with their knowledge of famous sights. They talked over each other loudly about things like the London Eye, Buckingham Palace, the Tower of London, the different museums, the Loch Ness Monster, Sherlock Holmes house, Normandy, and the Eiffel Tower in Paris France. As I listened to them, their voices and the kitchen started to fade away, and I began to feel terribly ill. A sharp pain shot through the left side of my head, and a feeling of dread rolled over me like a thick, black wave.

"Chloe, are you okay?" Mom asked.

"My head hurts really bad, Mom."

Dad quickly got out of his chair and picked me up, kissing my forehead.

"Too much sun for one day, Peanut. Time for bed."

"Night," I said, peering over Dad's shoulder at the boys and Mom, as he carried me towards the stairs, and a chorus of goodnights came after me.

I heard them in the distance eagerly planning things as Dad tucked me in bed. The glowing moon, and hundreds of glow-in-the-dark stars he and the boys had put on my ceiling calmed me as I lay there. It was wonderful having my own night sky. Magical to look at. It usually soothed me to sleep as I imagined myself flying amongst the stars.

I had Evelyn by my side and my fairy lights, intertwined on the heart shaped cut outs of my headboard, were switched on, but when Dad went to leave to re-join the happy group downstairs, a feeling of panic flared inside me.

"Daddy, can you stay with me for a while?" I called after him. He turned and came back and sat on my bed.

"Okay, Peanut, but just for a short while. I need to make plans for the trip. Are you excited?"

"I think so," I said, not sure what the fuss was all about. We'd had family vacations before; we even went to Disneyland once for two whole weeks and swam with dolphins. This couldn't be better than that.

"You just think so." He laughed. "You're going to have a fabulous time sweetheart. We'll make sure of it. There are palaces, castles, and famous sights you've only heard of or seen on TV or at school. Now you'll have a chance to see them for yourself."

He sounded so pleased as he stroked my head and kissed my cheek. Flying across the ocean to Europe should be an amazing adventure, but I just felt anxious.

"How is your head now?"

"It's getting better. Can you read to me a bit?" I pleaded, not that I wanted him to, I was just desperate to keep him with me longer. He hurriedly read a part of one of my storybooks, but rushed it, not like Mike who always did the voices of the characters and took his time and made me laugh if he ever read with me. Once Dad finished, he returned the book to the shelf, said goodnight, closed my door softly and went back to join the others.

I didn't call after him to make him stay again, even though I wanted to. I didn't want to be alone, but he was super excited about this trip, and I felt mean keeping him from sharing that with the boys.

I was left alone under my starry sky, my headache fading as I looked around the dimly lit room, knowing this all meant something important, but didn't know what. The scary dreams, Rocky and his peeing in the pool, the man in his uniform, my fears about travelling to Europe—what did it all mean?

I looked at all the princess posters on my walls, all smiling and happy, not troubled by anything bad. All with their own happy endings and heroes to help them. But I was on my own.

Then an idea sprang into my head. I got out of bed and stood on my dressing table chair, reaching up to get the biggest book I could find from the shelf. It was a collection of stories that Grandma Irene had given me for Christmas. I struggled to get it down, but finally it gave way after a bit of pulling, and I balanced it on the floor against the bottom of my bedroom door. I wasn't sure why, but from somewhere distant, I knew if someone bad came in when I was asleep, the book would fall over when they opened the door, and the noise would wake me up. I got back into bed, pleased I had my own plan to keep me safe. If you fail to prepare, then prepare to fail, as Scott had told me repeatedly.

The other part of my plan was I would stay awake. I wouldn't sleep that night; I would sleep in the day. I might not have nightmares if I slept when it was sunny. The dark would be gone, and I would be safe. I knew I had nice dreams too. I had my flying dream, dreams about me and Scott driving along country roads in a truck and him teaching me to drive. There was also the beautiful place with blue flowers and trees with sunlight beaming through their branches. It was a peaceful safe place for me; nothing could touch me there. I hoped and prayed I would dream that dream tonight.

I thought about the answers Scott and Joel had given me about my dreams. I tried to reassure myself that you don't go anywhere when you dream. You stay in your bed. Your mind makes you dream about what has happened in the day and they were nothing to be frightened of.

"They're just bad dreams," I said aloud. "And dreams can't hurt you," I said louder, pretending more confidence than I felt. Thoughts twirled around and around in my head, and despite my best efforts and plan to stay awake, I drifted off into a deep and troubled sleep.

AT FIRST, I was having my most favorite dream, my flying dream. I could fly anywhere. I just had to stand on something like a chair or my bed and jump and off I went, soaring away. This dream took me to the most wonderful places. In this dream I found myself flying over the blue carpet of flowers I had dreamed about before. I was just starting to float down into the flowers when I felt myself being wrenched away. I tried to fight and stay but couldn't, the pulling was just too strong.

The beautiful scene dissolved around me, and I found myself in a room, looking out of a window. I saw my dad and brothers playing in a yard, waving at me to go with them. It was so clear, not at all like a dream. Then I saw *him* walking behind them. He was wearing dark clothes, and a hat. He had a white silk scarf around his neck. His eyes met mine as he looked up at me and smiled. I knew it wasn't a smile that meant anything good. I banged on the window to warn my dad and the boys he was there, to get away from him because he was dangerous and would hurt them, but they didn't realize anything was wrong.

I watched as he slithered the white scarf from around his neck. He smiled at me with his evil, piercing blue eyes and thin-lipped mouth. Then came flashes of horrific scenes in different places, rooms, fields, basements, and of being frightened and hurt with a smell of burning around me, and sheer terror overwhelmed me.

I awoke screaming. I heard footsteps pounding on the landing and Scott came bursting through my bedroom door, knocking the storybook I'd left behind the door flying. Rocky was behind him barking like mad. Scott looked at me with such a shocked expression on his face. I realized I was sitting up in my own bed, my eyes wide open in terror, my bed wet beneath me, and I couldn't stop screaming.

"The scarf man!"

Everyone bundled into my room, the main lights were turned on, and they tried to comfort me. Rocky was still barking furiously, not sure why, just barking along with the general upheaval. I watched as they checked my room all over—the walk-in closet, the bathroom, under my bed, out the bedroom window into the dark night, thinking it was an intruder. But I knew it wasn't. It was in my dream world, where only I could see. Mom cuddled me tightly and I could see the confusion and concern on Dad's and the boy's faces.

Mom released me from her grip, and having recovered from the initial shock, returned to her usual self.

"Thank God we have a detached house. Hopefully, your screaming didn't wake our neighbors' up or got anyone to dial nine-one-one. It sounded like someone was being murdered."

"The security alarm is still on," Dad reassured us.

I was breathing very quickly and had to concentrate real hard on slowing my breaths down. The realization I'd been in my own room all along, not the other places, washed over me. I was embarrassed at what I'd caused, feeling like a nuisance and ashamed I'd wet my bed again. The boys filed out of my bedroom one by one, patting my head before they went, reassuring me it was just a dream. Mom took the wet sheets off with a lot of huffing and wiped the plastic under sheet. I washed my tear-stained face and changed my night-dress in my bathroom in silence.

"I expect this is because of that mad woman at the yard sale talking about ghosts that set this off," said Mom as she went to make coffee for her and Dad. That left us alone and I lay down in my freshly made bed with Dad sitting beside me. He looked worried and I knew he'd once thought about getting a gun to keep in the house, concerned his being away left us vulnerable to intruders, but he'd decided against as he was worried about accidents happening.

I knew a gun wouldn't have helped the situation that night anyway.

"What scared you, Peanut?" he asked.

"I'm not sure," I said. "I dreamed a man with a white scarf was after me and Evelyn."

"Mom told me about the old lady talking about ghosts. Is that what bothered you?"

"I don't think so," I replied, but I hadn't told him the full dream. This one I remembered more about, and the flashes of scenes I saw were terrifying. Nothing to do with the old woman. Usually I told my dad everything, but this was something I couldn't share. The words and feelings for what I dreamed were just too grown up for me to feel comfortable telling him. I thought I'd caused enough upset without saying anymore. Dad sat on my bed and cuddled me, comforting me, and stroking my forehead until I went back to sleep. No more dreams came to me that night.

$\sim$

NEXT MORNING, I felt sluggish and not too good. I made my way down to breakfast, with my feet plodding one in front of the other. My right lower leg ached; I must have slept awkwardly on it. Rocky barked as usual as I went in. Mom, Dad, and the boys were there, and they all turned towards me.

"You okay, Peanut?" said Scott. I just nodded my head as Ryan tried to make me laugh about what had happened, joking about it as best he could.

Joel picked me up and swung me gently around, kissing me on my cheek and sat me down between Mike and Ryan.

"Never mind, Chlo. Worse things have happened. No one died," he said.

Mike took hold of my hand, and with an understanding expression on his face said, "It's okay. We all have bad dreams sometimes."

Their words didn't make me feel any better. I spent the day in a thoughtful mood, trying to make sense of everything, looking up stuff on the internet about dreams, but again finding no answers for what I was going through.

We had dinner together that evening; it was a quieter meal than normal. I didn't feel the need to say anything to anyone. I just watched them all individually, their habits, their features, how they ate, how they interacted with each other. How they all looked like Dad, tall with dark hair and dark eyes. I thought they looked like a boy band. But as I watched them all, for the first time ever, I felt a distance coming between us.

That night, I decided to talk to Mike and went into his bedroom. He smiled at me as I sat on his bed with its American flag cover. He was sitting at his desk making some model aircraft he'd just received in the mail. His room was full of model planes, some hanging from the ceiling, posters on his walls of every kind of war aircraft. It was his hobby, his passion.

"How are you Chlo?" he asked me in a concerned way.

"Better now, thanks. I'm sorry about waking everyone up. I didn't mean to. I just couldn't help it."

"Don't worry about it," he said. "It wasn't your fault. Lots of kids have bad dreams. You'll grow out of it, trust me, they'll stop."

I had a burning question I needed to ask him.

"Mike, can you ever be in two places at once?"

"What do you mean, Peanut? You can't physically be in two places at once because there's only one of you, but in your mind, you can be somewhere your body isn't. Like at school. You can be sitting at your desk, but in your mind, you're on a beach somewhere. The same as dreaming— you're in one place, but your mind is elsewhere. Is that what you mean?"

"Something like that, I think. I saw it in a Harry Potter movie when Hermione was in two places at once because of a magic necklace." Thanking him, I wandered out of his room.

"Sweet dreams, Chlo," I heard him say.

I went to get a drink of water and said goodnight to everyone, dragging out the time before I had to go to bed.

I had a feeling of dread as I slowly walked up the stairs, trying to delay the inevitable as I made my way towards my room. I saw the jeweled Chloe sign on my door glinting under the lights, no longer appearing pretty and fun. As I went in and stood in the middle of the room, my safe space now didn't feel safe at all.

I looked at all the princess posters on all my walls; they surrounded me. Their eyes were watching me, following me around the room. They seemed to be challenging me, questioning me, judging me and there was nowhere to hide from them. For some reason I didn't feel good enough for them; I didn't meet princess standard. I had a feeling of failure, worthlessness and of dread and despair. I wasn't brave.

I looked at the night sky on my ceiling, which usually calmed me, but now it just filled me with an awful feeling something bad was going to happen. I wanted thick clouds to come and cover them, but that was impossible, it wasn't as if I could just turn them off either. My only comfort was Evelyn and I held her very tightly that night as I plunged into sleep and another nightmare.

This time I was in a large, long room that smelled of animals, the floor was soft beneath my feet. There was very little light, just small shafts coming through the wooden slatted walls. I was walking slowly through it looking for someone or something. I heard a noise, looked up and saw a hanging man, his body swinging back and forth, his mouth was open, and his eyes were closed. Then his eyes sprung open, looking directly at me, and I heard myself screaming again.

The same family response, everyone piling into my room, the comforting, the reassurance. And I was hurriedly settled back to sleep.

∾

WHEN I AWOKE the next morning, my head still ached, and my right leg didn't feel right. But I was able to recall this dream and wrote it down on my princess notepad. I was determined to make sure all the dream details from now on were written down right away before I forgot them. I put the notes in my new box from the yard sale—it would be my dreams box. I hid it under my bed and then made my way down to the kitchen.

As I walked down the stairs that morning, I felt different in myself. Not nine-year-old Chloe Anderson, with a loving family and a wonderful life. Someone different, but who? And why? I was surrounded by family I knew loved me but was feeling so very alone.

"Are you up for school today, Chloe?" Mom asked.

I never liked to miss school, where I could be with my friends, not stuck at home with just Mom and Mollie the housecleaner.

"I'm okay," I replied, trying to look okay.

I was last to be dropped off at school by Dad, and as we drew up outside, he turned to me.

"Is anyone hurting or upsetting you Chloe? You can tell me, you know."

I shook my head in response.

"You must always tell me if anyone scares or hurts you and I'll take care of it. That's what Dads are for. I'm not always home, I know, but you have Scott, Joel, Mike, Ryan and even Mom and Rocky to help you. That's one hell of a team to have behind you if you're in trouble."

I thought that sounded great and felt a little happier than I did when I first woke up. When I thought of it like that, we were a team: Team Anderson, and I was meant to be part of it. They were all behind me, they loved me, and I loved them. We high fived, and I got out of the car, racing towards my friends.

I waved goodbye to my dad as he drove away, but I knew he'd forgotten the other team member in my life who was important—Evelyn. I'd tucked her into my school bag that day. Normally she stood guard in my bedroom until I got home, but not today. I needed her with me; she was part of my team too and should never be forgotten, ever.

Scarlett and Sienna Robinson were twins and we'd become friends when we started school together. They were fearless and stood up for me more than once when someone teased me or tried to bully me. I adored them. They lived near us too and came around to play or for sleepovers whenever they were allowed. We held hands as we went into school together and I was so pleased they chose me as their friend.

DAD PICKED ME, Mike, and Ryan up after school. I was still not a hundred percent well; my leg ached. Mom gave me painkillers and I went to bed early. Mike came in to see me and listened to me read a story from one of my school homework books about a beautiful princess saved from a monster by a handsome prince and living happily ever after in his castle.

"Feminist heaven," he laughed, sarcastically. I thought the ending was wonderful, a princess in trouble rescued by a handsome prince. I looked at my wall princesses and thought about that scenario over and over after Mike left me. Again, despite intending to stay awake I fell asleep.

I was standing outside a door, knocking furiously to be let in. Something was coming for me along a dark corridor, and I had to get inside to be safe. But when the door opened and I was inside, it was there with me. I was in a dark room with a desk and chairs, I knew I had to get out if I wanted to live, but I couldn't. My legs just wouldn't move, and blinding lights shone in my eyes. Then I saw him again. He walked across the room with his white silk scarf around his neck, smiling his evil smile. He slithered the white scarf from around his neck. It had blood on it. Terror took over once again, and I screamed like hell.

It was a repeat of the nights before—the family and dog responding to my distress with barking, reassurances, and cuddling. Once again, although much quicker this time, and in an annoyed way by Mom, they checked on me and I eventually drifted back into a light sleep.

The same routine happened on and off for the next few weeks. I had dreams about the scarf man with his evil smile. There was also a cross man who terrified me, a nasty man who cut off all my hair, and what I remembered as something like black running legs, hanging in the air and running in one place. There was a man with blood and brains dripping down his face. The hanging man and a horror basement haunted me, along with an exploding rat which showered me with its blood and guts. I found myself going through doors into different rooms, each one with its own horrors and feelings of fear and death.

I could see the effects my night terrors were having on everyone. Our family was suffering, and it was all my fault. I just didn't know how to stop it and make it better and I desperately wanted to.

I watched as my brothers became tetchy with each other, no more joking or teasing at mealtimes because they were so tired. They got so weary with it, especially Scott who was spending more time away from home with Mia's family. I knew he was doing it to get away from me and I felt so bad. Bedroom doors were shut and locked at night. Mom and Dad began arguing with each other, all because of me. I wanted it all to stop and for us to be back as we were before. No one blamed me directly, and they reassured me, but they were exhausted and helpless, and my screaming needed to stop. Screaming wasn't helping me anyway. I became quieter during the day, much more serious, and it took a lot more to make me smile or laugh.

I had the feeling I was different in myself, like I was half me. One half wanting to be happy, loving the family and life I had. The other half watchful, wary, mistrusting, frightened and alone. I felt the world was on my shoulders, carrying the responsibility for everyone in our family and everything that was happening to us. I began to watch everyone intensely, as if from a distance, looking for something in them, but I didn't know what. Clues? Comfort? Answers? There was nothing. Rocky wasn't himself either, probably picking up on the tension in the home. We all felt it.

AFTER ONE PARTICULARLY BAD NIGHTMARE, where I had jumped off something real high up and was plummeting helplessly to the ground, my screaming woke Mom up. Next morning, she wearily began the household chores, just as Mollie, our housecleaner arrived. Mollie had helped in the house since I was little. She was ultra-organized and efficient, unlike Mom. She knew the household routine well and knew where everything was meant to go in each of our rooms. As I left for school, I consoled myself, at least Mom had someone to talk to and help her after what I'd done. I hoped Mollie would still like me once she knew the trouble I'd been causing.

I heard my parents talking that evening when they thought I was asleep. The boys were either in their rooms or out with friends. I had a special spot on the upstairs landing where I could listen to what was being said downstairs without being seen. I used this spot if I were in trouble, or when my birthday was coming, to see what they'd planned. I also used it to listen for Santa, but I found out when I was six that Scott was Santa anyway, since I saw him one Christmas Eve carrying a big present and a sack down the stairs. Santa wasn't real, neither was the tooth fairy.

"We need some psychiatric help for her," I heard Mom say.

"I don't want my daughter labeled with some mental health issue on her medical files at nine years old, for heaven's sake," Dad said. "Let's leave it for a while longer and see if things settle down. She'll just grow out of it, I'm sure. It was probably that old nutty woman who set this off."

I scrambled back to bed, got onto the internet, and tried to look up the help word Mom said I needed, but I couldn't find it.

A few nights later I could hear someone screaming again and I half woke up. Dad was away and the boys didn't come running to me this time. Mom had already told me they'd taken to wearing ear plugs to block out the racket. Even Rocky didn't bark. Mom opened the door, and the storybook behind the door thudded to the floor as she came in. I knew she was there with me, but I could see I was also somewhere else too. It was like there were two of me in two different places at once.

Mom was tired and cranky and shouted at me,

"Stop this nonsense, Chloe. Go back to sleep."

I remember stopping screaming and words started pouring out of me, words I didn't understand. I knew my eyes were open, but I wasn't fully seeing my room—I was partly somewhere else, in a different house and talking with a different woman.

In my half-awake state, watching two scenes, I saw Mom snap. She grabbed me by my shoulders and shook me roughly, my head being viciously snapped back and forth. The minute she did it, a look of shock came over her face. She'd never been physically violent with us. She used time outs, taking away privileges and "telling your dad when he gets home," as ways of managing us.

I sprang fully awake from wherever half of me had been. I looked at this woman in front of me, shocked at what she'd done. I looked her straight in the eye and words spat out of my mouth.

"My other mother was nicer than you."

As the words came out, I wasn't sure where they'd come from. I only had one mom. We were both shocked. I knew I couldn't take the words back; I knew that moment was a massive one and she would be upset by it. She must hate me even more now. *Why did I say that?*

I didn't know what to say to make it right, so I just pulled the quilt over my head and lay very still. I could sense Mom was still in the room and I stayed still and listened until she eventually left with no more being said. She left my door open, and I could hear as she got a glass from the kitchen, probably for wine. That was what she did whenever she was upset. I heard the creaky step as she walked up the stairs and opened the door to her room. There was then the saddest sound of her sobbing. This was too much for me. I was the cause of all of this, and I needed to get away.

3

A MOTHER'S DESPAIR—HELEN

I wished David were here with me. I couldn't cope with this alone. I resented him being away from home again, leaving me to deal with everything, and it had been that way for most of our married life. Dear God, my daughter was talking about another mother. The sleepless nights and groggy tired days...*I just can't cope with it.*

I slugged my wine back wanting it to numb me. I'd always tried my best as a mother. I knew I wasn't a natural mother, but I'd always done what I thought was right looking after five kids. *Christ, when you say it like that—five kids.* That had never been part of our plans. It started when we met at the university, love at first sight supposedly. I gave up work when I was expecting Scott, and then the others quickly followed, Joel, Mike, and Ryan. I loved them all—my boys. We decided to stop at the four, and I was looking forward to a life after kids and diapers, but then God knows how, Chloe arrived. Probably the result of one of our drunken reunions when David came back from one of his long business trips.

It was strange having a daughter in the house, after

having all boys and being in such a fully established male household. We had our boy routine, our boy life, and the whole house had developed into a precious man cave that was ours. I even had my own hair cut short and dressed in a boyish fashion too, to fit in. The only girly spaces were Chloe's. *Where did it go wrong with us?* I asked myself, not for the first time. *Is it possible as a mom to dislike one of your children?*

Somehow David had known I was expecting a girl before she was born. It was as if he was desperately waiting for her to arrive, and when she was born, he became a doting father, not wanting to put her down. The minute she'd made a noise he was there, picking her up, soothing her. It had seemed so sweet at the time, and saved me doing it, but it could also be why I'd started resenting her intrusion into the family. His attention was focused totally on her. But she was my daughter too and yet we didn't really bond that well.

My life was put on hold to accommodate this little female person. I had planned to return to work and then she arrived and so that had to be cancelled. I'd also gained weight during my pregnancy with her, which just wouldn't go. It was as if I was being punished for having her, as my figure had always sprung back after each pregnancy with my boys. No matter what diet or latest exercise fad or medication miracle I tried now, it just wouldn't budge. I felt age creeping up on me as a woman, just as this new female was starting out in life, and I had to care for her and nurture her. Sobs racked my body over everything I was going through. Trying to be quiet so as not to let the boys or Chloe hear me, I put my head deep into the pillow.

I'd always loved David and still do. I trusted him with our lives. And I knew for certain he'd never strayed while he was away. I always checked his phone, computer, pockets, bank statements and receipts after each trip, to make sure my devotion and trust were not misplaced. I knew he had to travel for work. He was working so hard to benefit us all and give us a good life, I couldn't expect him to be here all the time. I realized I had to toughen up to manage this, and as the wine took its thankful hold on me, I vowed to be a better mom from tomorrow onwards. I would make it all up to Chloe in the morning and start managing this whole situation with her way better. *She's my only daughter*, I thought, as the wine guided me to sleep. *We should be so much closer than this, like the other mothers and daughters I know.*

I woke the next morning, feeling somewhat hungover, noting the empty wine bottle by my bed. But my resolve to make things better stood firm. I made my way towards Chloe's room with determination to be a better, kinder, more patient, and loving mother. I would stop smoking for one thing, cut down on the drinking, and would give more attention to my daughter until this problem she was having was resolved.

I gently knocked and opened her door....

4

THE CHANGE IN ME—CHLOE

"She's gone! Her bed's empty, the house alarm is off. Oh my God, she's run away, or someone's taken her." I heard Mom screaming in the house.

I was terrified at the distress in her voice. I was really in trouble now and huddled, fixed to the spot in my tree house. I didn't shout out where I was, something telling me I had to be silent, and hide. I heard rapid footsteps and prepared myself for a scolding or worse. I wrapped myself tightly in my blanket and clutched Rocky and Evelyn. Mom's head came into view through the tree house door. She looked shocked, relieved, angry, every emotion showing on her face. She went to grab my arm and Rocky growled at her.

Mom backed off and calmed down.

"It's okay, boy. Come back indoors, sweetheart," she said. "I found her," she yelled to the boys who were still search-ing. She helped me down from the tree house, and with Rocky padding along beside us, we walked back to the house. I made straight for my room and Mom followed me in and closed the door.

"I'm so sorry, Chloe, I didn't handle last night well. I'm

just an extremely tired mommy and shouldn't have taken it out on you. I'm sorry if I hurt you or upset you."

She looked so sad, and I saw tears form in her eyes.

"This will never happen again," she said. "It isn't your fault, we know that, and we want to help you with this. Please, sweetheart, don't switch off the alarm and leave the house again. Just wake me or Scott up if you're scared."

I just nodded, feeling strangely numb to everything she said, and my face must have been expressionless. She wrapped her arms around me, cuddled me tightly, her voice cracking with emotion as she said how sorry she was, kissed my cheek, and then left me.

Something happened deep inside me from that night. I began to feel tougher inside, as if things had shifted, and I was now more the other me. I managed the bad dreams better, even when the feared figures tormented me in my sleep. I learned how to control them and survive them. They were just bad dreams, I told myself over and over when they were happening.

I learned not to scream anymore. I knew I had to deal with this alone. Everyone was getting upset with me, and screaming wasn't helping me one bit. It was affecting Mom, but Scott and the others were becoming distant from me too, which upset me.

Let them then. I don't care, I don't need anyone, I told myself, but not really meaning it deep down. From then on, as I passed through my bedroom door at night, it was as if I was going to war with my dreams and prepared myself. That way I could focus and remember what the dreams were about. The book was always put behind the door, everything in my room was placed where it should be, with my pink princess notepad and pen within reach. When the dreams got too bad, I found counting to myself until it passed stopped me screaming, and if that didn't work, I could dream myself into the beautiful place with blue flowers and tall trees that guarded me and stopped anything coming near me.

I was getting more frequent headaches now. My right leg around my ankle still ached, causing me to limp at times, and now my left eye began throbbing. I hadn't had a fall or an accident and couldn't figure why they hurt. But at last, my family was much happier with me, and I was managing the dreams—but the reason for them was no nearer being solved.

OUR HOUSEHOLD RETURNED to some normality by the time Dad returned from his latest work trip. I heard Mom telling him briefly what had happened, apart from her shaking me, which she kept to herself. After dinner they went into the study to talk, and I positioned myself in my secret spot so I could hear what they said. I was becoming good at that, being able to listen to things without people ever knowing.

"I think there's more going on with Chloe than we think," she said. "She's not the same child at all. What if the house is haunted, like Amityville or *Chucky*? She's always with that doll," Mom said.

I heard Dad laugh.

"You're not going into the realms of the paranormal I hope, Helen. It doesn't exist. I think it's time to take Chloe to see her pediatrician. She told me this evening she's getting headaches intermittently, her leg aches, and now she says her left eye isn't right. Let's see if there is anything physical here first. It might also be worth speaking to her teacher at school to see if anything has changed that might have unsettled her. Please let's do all of that before we go off into the possibility of the body snatchers and the supernatural."

Once they'd finished talking about me and went on to talk about the vacation, I crept back to my room, avoiding any creaky parts of the floor. I wondered if there was really something wrong with me. I hadn't thought about that before. Was I dying? Was that the reason for the feelings of death I had in the pool? I'd also seen the film about a haunted doll, which terrified me at the time, but Evelyn wasn't haunted. I looked at her sitting on my bed, with her perfect kind face, and I felt total trust in her, more than anyone else in the world right now. With her blonde hair in a long plait, blue eyes, and a blue dress, she was perfect. I knew at nine I was too old for a rag doll, none of my friends had one, or any they admitted to, and so she was my secret.

I stopped swimming in the pool, despite the boys tempting me in. I really didn't like my head going underwater. I felt I would die if it did. I was pleased with how ultra-tidy I was too. I put things in ways which would tell me if anyone had been in my room. I studied people, spotting things about them I hadn't noticed before. I trained myself to behave as if nothing was wrong. I behaved as everyone expected me to: I went to school, played with friends, joined in family things, but deep down I was battling hard and coping by myself. I was living a secret life that no-one but me knew about. *What if I had dementia like the old woman at the yard sale?*

My dreams box was there with reminders of the dreams I had. Each time I remembered something, even the smallest detail, I wrote it down and stuck it in the box. I was hoping to be able to write enough down to put together the puzzle and solve it myself.

The boys quickly got back to normal with girlfriends

and hobbies. Mom gratefully went back to being how she'd always been. My parents told me they planned to meet my teacher and I was okay with that. I'd been good at school and worked hard. I hoped they would be happier with me once they talked with her.

~

ONE AFTERNOON, Mom was talking on her phone to Sienna and Scarlett's mom. I couldn't help but hear the conversation, the laughter and giggling. As I sat there reading my book, I heard her say,

"She's driving me to drink, but she seems to be settling down now at last, thank God."

I heard her planning lunches out, coffee mornings and exercise classes. I lost interest in what she was saying, put down my book and started to watch TV, flicking through the channels. I came across a film that was nearing the end, a war film with airplanes. It was night and a building had been bombed and was on fire. Bells were ringing and a man in uniform was watching it, upset. I knew immediately it meant something and concentrated on it. Mom then picked up the remote and switched the movie to one of her soaps.

"You shouldn't be watching war movies, Chloe; it will give you nightmares," she said in a hushed voice as she listened to her friend on the phone.

She drank some wine and continued chatting, while not really watching TV. She put the remote control on the coffee table, and I picked it up and tried to find the movie I'd been watching. I had to see it.

Mom was furious.

"Put that back right this minute, Chloe," she hissed, covering the phone so the other person couldn't hear.

I put the remote behind my back so she couldn't get it. "No, I need to watch that. Why don't you go in the den with your phone?"

"Will call you back in a minute, Hon," she said to her friend and then shouted at me. "Don't you dare tell me what to do in my own house, young lady. Especially when we've put up with all your nonsense. The trouble with you is you're spoiled, and you always have been. Just because your dad and brothers dance to your tune, it doesn't mean I have to. Change it back, now!"

I was so angry with her I stood in front of the TV screen with the remote behind my back.

"Hand it back now."

"No," I said, not really understanding why this argument was happening.

It was one of many rows that ended up with me going to my room. I needed to see that movie, I knew it was important, but it was likely to be over by now anyway. I didn't like my mother very much lately and I stood in front of the TV, not knowing what it was I wanted to happen. I didn't know why we weren't close. My friends all had fun with their moms and could talk to them, but not me.

I wanted her to know I was upset. I wanted to scream at her that something was wrong, but just couldn't, deep down for some reason I didn't trust her. Mom was counting very slowly to ten for me to move. I wasn't going to.

I knew she hated me; she told people I was a mistake whenever we met anyone. She blamed me for her being fat and how I was holding her back from returning to work. That made me laugh. I heard her saying once she hated her old job so much, she would rather eat her own liver than go back to it. I noticed her being annoyed with me more over the last couple of years and that was why we fought over something so trivial as a TV program, when what I really wanted was to talk to her about important stuff.

I heard her get to ten and I stood defiantly where I was. Mom was equally determined for me to move and for her to get her way.

"Right," she said, and shot out of her chair towards me. As she did so, she knocked over the large glass of red wine she'd balanced on the arm rest and the wine spilled onto the pale cream rug she'd recently bought. Mom screamed in horror, and I watched as she ran for cleaning items from the kitchen, to limit the damage the wine would do to her precious rug, yelling in fury as she went. I stood there gazing down at what looked like blood spreading on the floor inching towards my feet. A horrifying, violent scene flashed through my mind and with a feeling of absolute terror—I ran for my life and hid in my closet.

5

THE DRAWINGS—HELEN

David and I met Chloe's teacher, Miss Price, as planned. Miss Price, whom we'd met before on parent evenings, was very warm and had a friendly welcoming manner. She liked to be called Linda.

"First, I want to say how pleased I am you've come in to see me. I'd planned to call you myself anyway," she said. "Just to recap with you, Chloe is such a sweet child and fits into the class well. She concentrates on her work, is well behaved, and is way above her age range in reading and vocabulary. She is attentive and respectful in class, always inclusive and aware of people's feelings, and sticks to any rules we set. She's generally happy and laughs a lot and joins in with the others. I've had no worries from...."

"Is there any chance Chloe is being bullied?" I interrupted.

Linda laughed out loud.

"God no, she has two bodyguards in the Robinson girls who protect Chloe enthusiastically, and so that isn't an issue. I would also guess Chloe could more than handle herself if she were ever pushed."

"Have you noticed any changes in her recently?" David asked.

Her tone changed. "That's really what I wanted to talk to you both about. Chloe is usually a chatterbox and has her say on everything but is now much quieter. She has started daydreaming in class more and is more serious and cautious in her behavior. She also drew some pictures this week that caused me some concern, which is why I was going to ask you to come in."

"What sort of pictures?" David asked, looking worried. Linda took out a large brown envelope and pulled drawings from it. We looked down at them as she spread them out on her desk.

One picture showed what looked like birds flying in the sky, with stick people on the ground. Trees were drawn in a line and there was a thick, painted red line running across the page. The second picture was of a room with bare brick walls, a small window, a table and two chairs in the middle and a hat stand with a scarf hanging on it with red drops going to the floor; the walls had been colored in with red crayon. The third one was of a hanging man.

"Have you asked Chloe about them?" David asked, sounding worried.

"I didn't want to upset her and so just had a brief chat with her about them as I did with all the children about their drawings," Linda said. She shuffled the notes in her hands. "I wrote down what she told me. She called the person on the floor a vet, and the man was 'the scarf man.' The birds were what Chloe called 'Lizzies.' The red line she said was blood. The second picture was a 'bad room where the scarf man and cross man hurt people.' The third picture I didn't want to go into too many details about. It was after seeing this one I thought I'd call you."

We were both horrified; I was particularly concerned Linda Price was writing everything down. Did this mean children's services getting involved?

"Has anything out of the ordinary happened in the family recently?" Linda asked us, and we told her briefly about the nightmares. All three of us expressed concern for Chloe.

"Let's keep a close eye on her for the next few weeks." Linda said. "We should meet up again if there are any more concerns or things don't improve, if that's okay with you?" We both agreed.

David and I were both worried about children's services getting involved with Chloe, and when we returned home, we made an urgent appointment for her to see her pediatrician Mark Whitelaw. He had known Chloe since she was a year old.

6

NOTHING'S WRONG—CHLOE

When Dad told me that they were taking me to see Doctor Whitelaw, I thought it was okay. I liked him. He made me laugh and let me put the ear thing in to listen to my heartbeat and told me to call him Mark. He would know what was wrong with me. I would ask him about my leg, my eye, and my head.

I was taken to see him at his clinic, and he examined me while Mom was with me. He asked me loads of questions and I answered them in a way I knew Mom would want. I didn't want to upset her again. I told him where my body hurt, and he arranged a head scan and X-ray of my leg. He also took some of my blood and ordered an eye test for me because I told him my eye hurt still. I thought he had looked at me inside and out and if there was a problem, he would find it and know what to do. I might get medicine to stop it all.

A few days after meeting him, we were called back to get the results. I'd heard Mom and Dad talking at night about it. They were scared the tests would show something bad.

"Oh God, what if it's a brain tumor?" I heard Mom say to Dad.

I looked that up on the internet and saw the treatment and pictures. I hoped I didn't have it; I didn't want my hair to fall out. Dementia sounded like a better thing to have.

When we got to the Medical Center, Doctor Whitelaw called us in to his office. His files were in front of him on his desk and he asked us to sit down.

"All righty then," he said smiling. "Good news everyone. Everything's normal; the head scan, X-ray, blood, and eye tests are perfect. Chloe, you're in perfect robust health. Whatever is going on with you is not physical."

I felt my insides relax and saw my parents were both relieved, clinging to each other for a moment. I could see Mom was welling up as usual. Mark concluded I was under some sort of stress. I wondered to myself why my head, leg, and eye still ached if there was nothing wrong with me. It didn't make sense.

I sat quietly on my chair next to Dad and listened as Mark told my parents that as a girl in a household with five older males, there were a lot of their influences around me every day.

"Boys by their very nature watch horror movies, war movies, play scary and gruesome games and fight, which could impact on her at such a young age." He continued his questioning. "Does Chloe have any new teachers, new neighbors, new family friends or anything different happening that may have anything to do with the changes in her?"

My parents said they couldn't think of anyone or anything. He then summed up for them, and they talked as if I weren't there.

"In my opinion her nightmares are related to something

she's seen, read or heard that were not age appropriate and she didn't have the capacity to understand. It is now playing on her young mind, causing these dreams."

I hopped off my chair to go over by the window, while they carried on talking. It was then I saw the coat stand in his office in the corner behind a wall. The desk, the chairs, the coat stand—and a distant echo of fear surged through me. I felt dizzy for a moment but knew I couldn't show anything. My parents had just been so pleased after being told nothing was wrong and I couldn't spoil that. I steadied myself by holding tightly on to the window ledge and focused out of the window. There was a large tree at the back of the medical center, and I counted the branches on it one by one to gain control over the fear. This was scary. My dreams were now affecting me in the daytime more and more. There was no escape from them.

After a short while, Mark directed his questions away from my parents back towards me and I went back to my chair.

"Chloe, have you watched anything on TV or movies that scared you?" he asked me.

I replied without really thinking first.

"I saw a movie about a girl trapped on a rock with a shark trying to bite her if she ever got off, a ghost doll film, soldier Ryan, the war film, and one with white walkers. They were all scary."

I realized immediately I shouldn't have said what I did because my parents looked horrified. They glared at each other as if the other one was responsible. Mark asked me who had shown them to me.

"I saw them when I was playing on the landing when the boys were in Scott's room watching DVDs."

Mark then asked me, "What's the scariest one you've ever seen, Chloe?"

I had to think hard about that, not wanting to upset my parents any more than I had.

"*Beauty and the Beast.*"

I watched as my parents and doctor smiled at each other. Despite me seeing the most gruesome movies it was a fairy tale I'd rated as the scariest. I did think some of the fairy stories were kind of scary though. There were ones with princesses choking on poisoned apples, pricking their finger and being dead for hundreds of years until a prince kisses them. It was scary when you looked at them like that. You get told them at bedtime too. But nowhere in my storybooks could I recall a man with a white scarf killing people.

I heard him tell my parents to return if things didn't settle and he would make a psychology referral.

"Could she have some medication to help her sleep at night, Mark?" my mom asked.

"I'm not in favor of medicating children for this type of problem, Helen. These things eventually work out and resolve naturally. Try and distract her from anything inappropriate and get her more active in the day so she'll sleep better at night. Lessen her sugar and additives intake too. I would suggest you encourage her to play with friends her own age more and lessen the influence of the older boys."

When we got home, I went upstairs straight to my listening spot. I heard Dad say he would speak to the boys about being careful with what they watched when I was around and to start withdrawing from playing with me a bit. I was heartbroken.

"With Scott's room being next to Chloe's, she may hear or see things she shouldn't," Dad said.

"Thank God it was just that. Hopefully, this horrible nightmare is over with," said Mom.

We spent the evening as a family discussing the plans for our trip that was coming up in just a few weeks. The boys were especially nice to me that evening, they didn't tease me at all. Knowing what Dad had told them, I thought they were gently saying goodbye and wouldn't be playing with me as much. It made me so sad, but I showed nothing.

Each of the boys had something they wanted to see or do on this trip and Dad was trying to piece together a plan which would satisfy everyone. If I were being honest, I really didn't want to go at all.

THE NEXT DAY the boys were all out and I was left at home with my parents, who were sorting out vacation paperwork. Scarlett and Sienna were over to play, and we went to the tree house with nerf guns I'd taken from the boys' collection in the garage. We were sitting on cushions, each with our loaded guns, ready to play at hitting cardboard targets set up in the backyard. I'd grabbed apple juice and muffins for us from the kitchen. They were nice ones too because Mollie had made them, and she'd put frosting on.

Sienna took a bite from her muffin.

"Mom says you're having nightmares Chlo. What are they about?" She asked.

This was unexpected; I sipped on my juice thoughtfully, not sure if I should tell them. I was coping with my dreams much better on my own now.

I made my decision.

"I can't tell you because it might make you scared, and I don't want you two to be scared."

"We won't be scared," they said in unison. As twins they often did that. Knowing they were braver than me and shared a room at home so always had company, I decided to tell them. I sighed heavily, put down my juice and muffin, took a deep breath and began in a hushed tone.

"The scarf man, the cross man, and the nasty man in my dreams are really bad people. The scarf man has blood on his scarf, and he beats you, kicks you and pounds you. He knocks out your teeth, pulls out your nails, holds your throat tight, cuts off your hair and breaks your bones." I could see they were shocked, and I wished I hadn't said anything and stopped talking, not telling them the rest of the horrors. It upset me to see them scared and I wished I could take it back. *Why do I always have to spoil it by telling people things? Why can't I keep a secret?*

Dad poked his head through the tree house door to check on us and startled us all. As a result, he was hit by a hail of nerf gun darts from two automatic nerf guns fired by the now-terrified Sienna and Scarlett.

When he recovered from the attack, he yelled.

"What on earth do you think you're doing?"

"Sorry, Mr Anderson," Sienna said, embarrassed. "We thought you were the scarf man."

I was strangely pleased at my friends' efforts to protect me, it made me feel slightly less alone.

"This is getting crazy," Dad said loudly. "Group hysteria is kicking in now. You could have taken my eye out." He pulled his head away from the tree house door and left, mumbling to himself as he went. We looked at each other, with the seriousness of what had just happened hanging in the air and agreed to play quietly and not cause any more trouble. I didn't want him to stop them from coming over.

7

THE LADY IN THE MIRROR—HELEN

I was grateful my younger sister Beth, and her husband Owen were coming over to stay a while. I really wanted to discuss what was going on with someone I trusted, other than medics and teachers. I was also uncomfortable talking to David about other possible causes of Chloe's behavior, which was starting to worry me. She was definitely different, not in appearance, but in her mannerisms, likes, and dislikes, in fact her whole personality was changing before my eyes. She also seemed way older than nine at times.

We weren't particularly religious as a family, but I'd considered asking Mollie if there was someone at her church I could talk to. But as we were what David called a "hatch, match and dispatch" family, only attending church for christenings, marriages, and funerals, that was an avenue I didn't feel I had a right to pursue.

We agreed to keep the grandparents out of it all, as God knows, they would all four of them want to take charge and move in with us to sort it out. I couldn't cope with that and would end up being committed to an asylum myself. Both parents lived just enough of a journey away not to make unannounced visits but were happy to support us with the kid's college funds. I liked both sets of parents immensely. They were fun, warm hearted and generous, but I'd always kept them slightly distant from my family. I squirmed that this was partly because I didn't want my mothering skills to be judged too closely.

My own mother had been extremely organized. She'd worked full time and took good care of Beth and me. However, we never talked about anything in real depth— she was always so busy—which was why Beth and I got so close. I often confided in her. She worked in social services, and I respected her for being very grounded and sensible. I was sure she would have an idea of what to do about the Chloe situation. She couldn't have kids herself but seemed perfectly happy to be the naughty fun aunt to my kids. They adored her.

Beth and Owen arrived in time for dinner and once that was over, the younger kids went to their rooms and Scott went out with Mia. The four of us sat down to chat over drinks. We laughed at the most ridiculous things, as well as humorous incidents in their respective jobs, and the wine flowed. The mood in the house was lighter than it had been for a while. They were interested in the trip we had planned, which was now only weeks away, and David gave them a full rundown of the itinerary.

"That sounds awesome," said Beth. "I wish we were coming too. We're both jealous you know." She laughed.

I was thoroughly enjoying this adult only fun night but was hiding a guilty secret: I had given Chloe antihistamine tablets in her drink before she went to bed, to try and make sure she slept. Although the last few weeks had been rela-tively calm, my reasoning was she might be disturbed if we were up late talking, and it would spoil the whole evening for us if she started with her nightmares. Doing this meant I could relax and there would be no screaming to deal with. Just this one night and no more, I told myself. I was aware if David knew what I'd done he would throttle me.

The antihistamines had been another coping strategy I'd used if the kids wouldn't settle when they were little. David was always away when I did it and I found it hard to cope on my own. I'd seen the sleepy results in the boys when having them for hay fever or hives and had used it sparingly with them, for my own sanity. I also used the "small amount of alcohol in their juice" trick to aid their sleep. There had never been any side effects from it, and it never failed to work. This was the first time I'd used it with Chloe to get her to sleep, and I had always vowed to myself I wouldn't, even when her night terrors started. I knew Mark Whitelaw was against medicating her, but he wasn't the one having to deal with it. Desperate times called for desperate measures and my reasoning was I just needed this one night of worry-free relaxation with other grown-ups to get myself back on track.

We moved from the dining table to the couches, wine glasses in hand, and sank into the soft comfy cushions. It was then I mentioned the issues with Chloe. I'd already confided in Beth about some of what had gone on. I told them what she'd said to me about another mother. They all looked shocked at first but dismissed it.

"It must have been something she was dreaming about when you went into her bedroom. I wouldn't worry about it," Owen said. Which had occurred to me at the time, but they hadn't seen the look on her face or heard the mumblings from her mouth. We discussed different scenarios in our tipsy state, from the house being haunted, to Chloe being possessed by a spirit, a brain disorder, being plain naughty with attention-seeking behavior, one of the boys' playing tricks on her or just a very overactive imagination.

"Does Chloe ever stand in front of the TV and speak to beings inside it in the middle of the night?" said Owen with an inebriated grin. It made them all laugh, except me. That was a bit raw. We'd all seen that movie, but no, she hadn't.

"Does she see things that no one else can see?" asked Beth.

"Only in her nightmares," came the response from David.

"Does she have imaginary friends she played with?"

"No," was the response from us both. As the alcohol had loosened me up a bit, I told them what I'd been doing about it.

"I googled some stuff and it said young children were more susceptible to ghosts or spirits...." David tutted loudly, but then each of us went quiet, deep in our own thoughts. It was almost midnight and the lateness of the hour, and the amount of wine drunk had taken effect. As we sat in the candle-lit room in stupefied serious silence, a little voice came from behind us.

"Daddy," said Chloe, her voice sleepy.

We all shrieked in unison and jumped in shock as Chloe stood there in her pristine white silk pajamas, with her long dark hair hanging loosely down, holding Evelyn by her arm. Seeing us all jump in shock distressed Chloe, and it showed on her little face.

"There's a lady in my mirror," she said, and the four of us looked at each other wide eyed in terror.

David was first to respond. He picked her up and cuddled her tightly, wanting to stop whatever was happening, to keep her safe. He couldn't protect her from what we couldn't see, hear, or understand. I knew he was becoming distressed himself at each nightmare, feeling helpless as her father. He'd always been the stronger one in our relationship, and I knew deep down that if he wasn't coping, then things were really getting bad.

I decided to go with Owen and Beth to check out the offending mirror. We went in our very tipsy state, staggering up the stairs to Chloe's room. I gingerly opened the bedroom door and peered in. The others followed me in warily, and we gazed into the mirror on the dressing table, just to see three bleary-eyed, drunken faces staring back at us.

A voice behind us startled us.

"Goodnight."

We all screamed. Scott was home from his date. He'd sneaked up on us and thought it was funny, laughing hysterically, but I could have killed him. It took ages for my pulse rate to slow down, and we needed more drink to recover. That dose of antihistamines obviously didn't work on Chloe.

Chloe.

DADDY SAT TALKING with me on the sofa after the others had gone to bed.

"I want to try and get to the bottom of what's going on Chloe. Part of my job at work is troubleshooting, and so I'll figure out the reason for all of this and stop it," he told me. I could see he'd drunk a lot, because his words were foggy, his breath was like wine, and his eyes were sleepy. He asked me about the lady in the mirror.

"She's very pretty. She's got blue eyes and long blonde

hair like a princess or a fairy godmother. I saw her when I was floating in my room."

"Oh, so you were dreaming about the lady then," he said. "Does the lady say anything to you at all?"

"She just smiled. I liked her. She wasn't scary."

"That's a nice dream then, but don't worry, sweetheart, I'll protect you, whatever happens. You're not to be frightened. It will all work out, you'll see. I'll look after you." Daddy snuggled down sleepily into the cushions with his eyes fully shut and his arm around me as I leaned on his chest. A sudden clear realization shot into my mind.

"But that's it, that's right, that's why you're here, Daddy. You promised me, don't you remember? That's your job this time around."

"Yes, sweetheart, I suppose it is," he said as he drifted off into sleep.

I looked at his sleeping face for a long time, knowing he was here to look after me, and I fell asleep with his protective arm around me.

8

LOOKING FOR ANSWERS—HELEN

Next morning, Beth and I were clearing up in the kitchen, kids all at school. David at work and Owen off with friends at a local golf club. We were waiting for Mollie to arrive.

Beth looked at me intensely, hesitated, then finally asked; "Have you ever thought about employing a psychic to help with Chloe's problems?"

I was shocked. This was my sensible younger sister talking about psychics, something we'd never mentioned before. I'd already fleetingly thought about it myself but hadn't shared that with her for fear of being thought crazy. Beth must have seen the surprised look on my face at her suggestion.

"Just a thought," she mumbled and shrugged.

I initially dismissed the suggestion out of hand knowing David wouldn't buy it, but I began warming to the idea. Perhaps there was something in the house and whatever was here was affecting Chloe, causing her nightmares, and changed behaviour. I accepted I may be a bit of a crap mother to her but if the medical profession couldn't help my daughter, then it was my duty to step up to the plate and find something that could.

Beth also spoke about spiritual possession, but that was instantly dismissed. The mere thought of that terrified me. I'd seen the look in Chloe's eyes when she spoke of her other mother and was still reeling from that. I'd seen the exorcist films too and wasn't going down that route with Chloe. No way. David didn't believe in any of this. His approach to anything remotely spiritual was, "We're an accident of nature and once you're dead, you're dead. You live on in your children." A true nonbeliever, facts before fiction he always said.

I had thought about other reasons for Chloe's behavior and had secretly been researching metaphysical issues. I'd read animals were supposed to be more sensitive to ghosts and spirits. I had a thought and explained it to Beth, and she called Rocky in from the yard.

We both went upstairs to Chloe's bedroom with Rocky in tow to see if there was any reaction from him. We slowly pushed the door open and let Rocky in. I was amazed and briefly distracted by how tidy Chloe's room was, it was immaculate, not the normal state she usually left it. My focus went back to Rocky and saw he was looking intensely at the partially open closet. He made his way towards it, sniffing and looking interested as he nudged the door open with his nose. Beth clung to my arm, and we held our breath as the dog went into the walk-in closet out of sight. He then reappeared with what looked like an old half-eaten cookie in his mouth and trotted out of the room with his prize. We both exhaled loudly in unison, feeling totally stupid, and laughed as we followed him downstairs to rethink our strategy.

Beth searched the internet for a local psychic and came

across a warm, friendly looking face in an ad, and we both felt she would be suitable. She was an older woman, grey haired with a kind looking face. Her name was Maddie Groves. I immediately, under firm instruction from my sister, called her.

Being new to this, I explained to her on the phone the problems we were having. I arranged for her to visit and meet Chloe while David was at work the next day, and while I still had Beth with me for support. It would cost one hundred dollars for a home visit, and I was fully aware David would absolutely kill me if he knew what we were doing.

"He must never know," I told Beth.

We hurriedly ended the discussion about psychics, ghosts, and spirit possession when Mollie arrived. She was a fervent churchgoer and would wholeheartedly disapprove of anything like this. She would probably run from the house screaming and clutching her crucifix necklace never to return, if she knew what was going on.

9

THE SECRET GIRL CLUB—CHLOE

I was kept home for the day, Mom told me a lady was coming and so I couldn't go to school. My school had been told I was sick, which was a lie, but that was what I had to say to anyone who asked. So, she was telling me to lie, and it was all right. Mollie had been given the day off and I cleaned my room before the lady came. I hid my dream box in my closet and once I was sure my room was ready, I skipped down the stairs to be with Mom and Aunt Beth. All the others were out.

"It's just us three musketeers," Aunt Beth said, which made me giggle. "All girls together, no stinky boys," she said, and I really laughed at that.

We were waiting in the kitchen, and I could feel their nervousness as we waited, especially Mom, who was tapping her fingers on the counter. I wondered who this woman coming to our home was and felt a little excited. I wanted to ask questions; I knew Aunt Beth would tell me what was going on, as she was always honest. I told a lie about eating candy from the cupboard once when she stayed with us, and I got a telling off. She took me aside and told me a saying she'd heard from Grandma Nora when she was young. "Speak the truth, speak it ever, cost it what it will."

I remembered it word for word and knew to tell the truth no matter what the consequences. This meant I could never really keep a secret, I always had to tell the truth and the boys knew it, as I'd got them into trouble more than once because of it. Obviously, Mom hadn't heard that. She often fibbed about smoking, about telling us she made dinner when Mollie had, and now she was making me lie too. As I was about to say something about the unfairness of this, I remembered I hadn't told anyone about my real nightmares when asked, so was I fibbing as well? Maybe not telling something wasn't the same as fibbing, so it was okay.

We heard the expected knock on the door. I saw Mom shoot out of her chair to answer it; she didn't normally move that fast.

The lady was led into our kitchen by Mom, who was fussing over her. She was quite a large lady, with long grey hair loosely tied up with a ribbon, and a warm smiley face. She had flat sandals and a large skirt with a flowery blouse, dangly earrings, loads of necklaces around her neck and bracelets on her wrists. She swept into the kitchen with a large straw bag on her arm, as if she were queen of the house.

"This is Maddie Groves, Chloe," Mom said.

I said, "Hi," as Maddie sat on one of the kitchen chairs, and I listened in awe as she told us about her gift. She said she had her abilities since she was a child and was quite famous locally. *Someone famous in our home*—I was beside myself with excitement, but still didn't know what she did exactly. What were spirits, I wondered. I thought that was something to do with drinks.

Must be, since Mom then asked her, "Would you like something to drink?"

"No, thank you, Mrs. Anderson. If you would just kindly show me around the house, I'll get started." I saw Rocky looking at her curiously. He sniffed her straw bag, like he did when we brought groceries in.

"Has your dog been behaving oddly at all?" Maddie asked.

"Not really," Mom replied. "He barks at everything as usual, the door, the phone, the kids, the vacuum cleaner, stray cats in the backyard and food."

Maddie sniffed the air as if sniffing for something in particular. She straightened herself up as if going into battle and went with Mom to look around the house. I couldn't resist following, and so did Aunt Beth, even though Mom had told us both to stay put. We followed as Maddie looked in each room, including mine. I hoped I'd cleaned it enough if someone famous was going in.

"I feel something amiss in here," she said. I wondered what amiss meant but didn't want to interrupt. "If you could just leave me here alone for a few minutes, please," she asked.

We left her in my room, sitting on my bed, and I wondered what she was going to do in there. I hoped she wasn't reading my schoolbooks or looking in my dreams box. We waited in the kitchen, tension building. Mom gave me a cookie and looked at Aunt Beth nervously.

After about ten minutes, we heard the creaky step sound as Maddie came down the stairs and announced to us, "I think I've connected with the presence of an older woman who died near the house a long time ago. She seems to have attached herself to the young girl here," Maddie told us.

I was horrified but fascinated. A dead woman in my

bedroom with presents. Initial fear must have shown on my face because Mom tried to hush her, but Maddie was having none of it.

"Children are very spiritual beings, Mrs. Anderson. They can't be excluded from these things. They are in fact more accepting of them than we adults," she told Mom. Before Mom could argue back, which I was expecting her to do, as she got mad when people tell her she's wrong, Maddie went on.

"Your daughter, being so young, is more susceptible to sensing the spirit around. That's why she remains near her. The woman was murdered near this house and is in an unmarked grave somewhere. The spirit stays around here because it's such a happy home. She only wants to tell her story."

Mom looked at me, her eyes wide and her mouth open. Aunt Beth was quiet and looked very thoughtful staring into space. I was shocked, not just because there may be a dead woman in our house, but I'd never known anyone call our house a happy home. We were always arguing, teasing, fighting, and bickering with each other.

"The woman is in the room with us now," Maddie said.

Mom looked terrified and glanced around the room, as if expecting to see the woman. She reached out for Aunt Beth's hand and pulled me closer to her. Maddie came near me and patted my head. I could smell a scent like old dead flowers coming from her. Like when Mom kept flowers Dad had given her on special occasions until they were almost rotten. I wanted to see the dead woman myself and looked around the whole room, squinting, and blinking my eyes to see, but couldn't see anything, which was disappointing.

I wondered why Maddie and the old woman at the yard sale could see dead people but not me. *Maybe Maddie has dementia too*. I couldn't wait until the boys got home and I could tell them all about this, they'd be so jealous they missed it.

Maddie must have seen the horrified look on Mom's face.

"Don't upset yourself, Mrs. Anderson. It's not as bad as it sounds. I can perform a cleansing ritual to move on any spirits present; if you want me to that is. They're just people stuck between worlds, the physical world, and the spirit world and they need guidance to progress. It's an intense process, but I can do it now for you if you'd like. I do charge an additional fee to the house call fee, of one hundred dollars to carry it out because it's risky for me and makes me quite unwell. It exhausts me for days afterwards and I wouldn't be able to take on any more work as a result." Maddie explained with her nose in the air, as if daring Mom to challenge what she said.

I looked up at Mom and she immediately agreed. She was usually suspicious of anything related to strangers and handing over money, but this was blown away as she appeared to be caught up in it all. I wondered if I should ask her if we could keep the dead woman and save the money. I really wanted a new bike, one with a basket on the back for my iPad and Evelyn to go in.

"Are you sure, Helen? It's a lot of money. Do you want some time to think about it or discuss it with David first?" asked Beth.

Mom was adamant.

"No, let's just get this nightmare over with. Please Maddie, go ahead with the cleansing."

I watched as Maddie shuffled about, getting her stuff from the car. She brought it in and set it on the kitchen counter listing it loudly.

"Holy water, smudge sticks, crucifix, crystals and my bible. Yes, it's all here," she announced triumphantly.

We watched as she burned the sage, or 'smudge sticks' and waved the smoke around each room, talking as she went. Her bracelets rattled loudly with every movement of her arms. She waved the smudge stick over me and Evelyn, which made me cough and my eyes water. I thought she might set the fire alarms off with all the smoke. She splashed holy water in each room and on me and Evelyn. I saw her place different colored stones, or crystals, as she called them, in different areas of my room. I listened as she did what she called chanting, holding on to her bible and crucifix. She flung open doors and windows to let out any spirits, and the smoke, as she went.

It was so exciting; I'd never seen anything like it in my life. I was expecting something marvelous to happen and watched with amazement. No wonder she was famous. She went into our backyard, the tree house, around the pool and even the work shed.

After what seemed forever, she stood proudly and announced to us, "The spirit has moved on. She's now at peace. The home is clear of any negative energy."

I clapped my hands appreciatively, as if I'd just seen the end of an exciting school play.

She accepted the offer of coffee from Aunt Beth and seemed exhausted by what she'd just done. She was handed her fee by Mom, which she didn't count, just tucked it secretively into her straw bag. She smiled at me, patted me on the head, called me a cutie, and swept out of our home in the same way she'd swept into it, no longer exhausted at all.

Once she'd gone, we stood in silence, still taking in what had just happened. Mom told me what had gone on was our secret.

"The lady has made sure you won't have any more bad dreams, Chloe. Don't tell Dad or the boys about this, sweetheart. They wouldn't understand and would only worry. It's just our secret, yours, mine, and Aunt Beth's, okay? Do you promise?"

I nodded and she made a lip zip gesture firmly across her mouth, both me and Aunt Beth did the same. It was like belonging to a secret girl club and it did feel good, but then I realized it meant I wouldn't be able to tease the boys about it. I decided I could tell Sienna and Scarlett the next time they came over. They always kept our pinky promises.

Mom cleared away the coffee cups and wiped my cookie crumbs from the counter. She was smiling and humming a tune.

"The house feels so much lighter than it has for months. Can you feel it? I think our problems are finally over," she said.

Aunt Beth wasn't so sure.

"Helen," Beth said in a hushed tone, not really wanting me to hear. "Chloe talked about a man in her dreams and a young woman in her mirror, not an old woman. I think we gave an awful lot of information to Maddie Groves to identify Chloe and the room affected by a so-called spirit before she came to the house, and it's cost you two hundred dollars."

Mom appeared calmer than she had been, reassured by what had taken place. She turned to Aunt Beth.

"You're the one that suggested this in the first place, remember, and it's worked. It was worth every dollar."

Aunt Beth glanced at me with a look on her face that said silence might be the best option for now, as Mom was so happy, and arguing about it would spoil that. Mom even gave me another cookie without her usual lecture about me getting fat.

DAD, Uncle Owen, and the boys arrived home late afternoon and they made for the pool. The evening was warm, and they teamed up to play water polo while Mom and Aunt Beth rested on the loungers, gossiping together before preparing dinner. I spent time reading in my tree house with Evelyn by my side. I looked up ghosts on my iPad, and that was kind of scary, but Maddie had said she'd gone now, so it wasn't a problem. Not that I ever saw her anyway.

I really wanted to go in the pool when I heard them whooping and shouting. I loved swimming and wanted to be part of the fun, but there was still something stopping me. I watched from the tree house window as Mom and Aunt Beth went in to start dinner.

Once it was ready, they called us in. Aunt Beth and Uncle Owen were going back home that night and there was a lot of chatting, joking, and teasing at the table over our lasagne, which Aunt Beth made, not Mom, thank goodness. It was delicious. We all liked having our aunt and uncle visit. They always made the house feel like fun and gave us a few dollars each to spend when they left.

I was thinking over what had happened that day and was quiet at dinner. I usually had to talk a lot when we had visitors over to make sure my place in the family was noted; they all talked over me as if I didn't exist otherwise. I wanted to know what a "sidekick" was, as that was what they called Maddie, what "amiss" was and if "spirits" were the same as ghosts or different. Did I really have a ghost in my room? What presents did she leave?

I had been sworn to secrecy and so couldn't bring these things up over dinner, which was maddening. I watched the others intently while these important questions spun around in my head. I knew if I couldn't ask them, I would look it all up on the internet when I went to bed, but I really wanted to hear what everyone thought about it all.

"Hey, Peanut, what have you been up to at school today?" Dad asked me.

That came out of the blue and shook me out of my thoughts. I really wasn't expecting this question and looked at Mom and Aunt Beth, then quickly back at Dad. I really didn't want to give away our secret, and was torn between always telling the truth, but still wanting to be part of the secret girl club, which I couldn't be if I told on the three musketeers. It all flew out of my mouth anyway, despite my best efforts.

"I didn't go to school today. We had a sidekick in the house, and she burnt sticks and splashed me and Evelyn with water and put stones in my room and said a lady had died and her ghost was in my room but now she was gone. We paid her two hundred dollars."

I said it all in one breath, as if to get my betrayal over with as quickly as possible. As soon as I said it, I knew I shouldn't have. Everyone stopped talking and a horrible silence filled the air. I looked at Mom and Aunt Beth and put my hands over my mouth—about one minute too late. Dad looked at Mom, Aunt Beth looked guiltily at the floor, and Uncle Owen looked confused. The boys then all started talking at once, wanting to know the details, and I really wanted to tell them, but I also knew I'd said too much already.

"We'll talk about this later," Dad said, as he cast a furious look at Mom, who was blushing and giving me the same furious look. I realized I was in trouble as usual when I couldn't keep a secret. I did the lip zip again, slowly, to show her I wasn't going to say anymore and sat quietly.

Dinner was resumed with a cheesecake dessert and talk diverted to the European trip. The matter of the 'sidekick' wasn't over for my dad, and Mom and I both knew it. The tension between them was bad—we could all feel it during dinner—and I didn't know how to make this better. It was my fault again for doing something I was told to do, always tell the truth and then you don't get hurt or into trouble. That wasn't working this time, that's for sure.

Aunt Beth and Uncle Owen did their best to lighten the awkward mood over dessert. Once the ordeal for us was over and the clearing away was done, they packed up, said their goodbyes, and started the long drive back to their home. We waved them off and returned to our house to resume where we'd left off. I was nervous and dreading what was coming, knowing my parents were both fuming from different sides of the argument, and I was in the middle.

"How could you go behind my back with something like this?" Dad asked Mom in a controlled but angry way as we walked back to the kitchen. "How could you let some fraud-ster into our home to frighten our child knowing what she's been going through? Filling her head with stories about ghosts and then paying the woman two hundred bucks for the privilege." He shook his head and looked sympatheti-cally at me, then pointing his finger at me said, "This will probably screw her mind up more than help her, you know that don't you? As well as dragging her along to see some mad ghost woman at a yard sale."

He never shouted in the house, and he never shouted at Mom in front of us either. He wanted the boys to always be nice to girls. He always told them to talk things through where girls were concerned, to be respectful and supportive; girls were equals, simply different equals. He was still talking directly to Mom in the kitchen, stating his views on the sidekick subject through gritted teeth. Mom was quietly trying to defend what she'd done, but she must have known she'd been caught out. She looked embarrassed, and I desperately wanted to say how sorry I was and how I should have kept our secret.

Mom looked at me with fury in her eyes and I felt so ashamed I'd told on her and caused this trouble. I wanted to give her a drink of wine and a cigarette to calm her down. That usually worked.

We watched in shock as Mom broke down while Dad went on about his disappointment in her. She turned towards me, and all her fury and frustration came at me in a tearful, unstoppable wave.

"You're the reason for all of this. The fact I had to resort to psychics in the first place is because of you. The disruption you're causing this family is unbelievable. Everything we've built up here is being destroyed because of you. Look what you're putting everyone through now," she yelled at me as she waved her hand at all the boys and Dad. "None of us have been sleeping because of you. We're all on edge. I tried to help you and look what you've done in return."

I felt remorseful, worthless, a failure, and a nuisance to everyone. I couldn't keep a secret and look what happened. I felt everyone's eyes burning into me, blaming me for the horror that was unfolding in our house. I wanted the kitchen floor to open and swallow me down.

Mom then unexpectedly grabbed me firmly and shook me, shouting I was just plain trouble. I felt a hard slap on the back of my left leg. Rocky barked madly and growled at her; the boys looked shocked at what she'd just done. None of us had ever seen her this bad before, violence was not, and never had been, part of our family life. I watched as Dad pulled her firmly away from me and her grip on me released. I felt the walls of the kitchen closing in and the air in the room stagnate as long buried memories of being hurt thundered through me. I was panicking and needed to get out, far away from this daytime nightmare.

I bolted for the back door, running to get to the sanctuary of my tree house as if my very life depended on it. Scott was the first to react and I could sense him come after me. He shouted my name, but I wasn't stopping for anyone. I needed to reach my tree house, my safe space. He then did his usual sliding tackle on me to stop me running before I could reach it. This was a maneuver he'd performed on me hundreds of times. He would pretend to be a monster and I would run as fast as I could away from him. He would then run after me and slide his legs underneath mine as I was running, taking me off my feet. He always landed me softly on his chest, then cuddled me and laughed.

This time, once again, I felt my body being swept up and he landed me on his chest. He flipped me over from my back to my front and looked in my eyes. I saw a startled look on his face as he threw me off him and I landed heavily on the grass on my back, knocking the breath out of me. I was upset at first that he'd thrown me on the ground, then found I couldn't breathe, the air had been completely knocked out of my lungs. Scott rushed over and put me on my hands and knees and rubbed my stomach firmly until I got my breath back. I told him off as I gulped the warm evening air in. Scott still looked shocked as if he'd seen a ghost. Maybe he'd seen the one Maddie found in the house and she wasn't gone.

"What's wrong Scott?"

"Your eyes. Peanut, sorry it must have been a trick of the light or something. It startled me for a second. Sorry for throwing you. Are you hurt?"

I just huffed at him and stomped towards the back door where everyone was waiting. I marched defiantly past them all and made for the stairs to go to my room to be alone.

As I got to the bottom of the stairs, I heard Scott say to everyone.

"There may be something wrong with Chloe. Out there her eyes were blue, ice blue. For a split second she looked like someone else."

"For the love of God, I think we are all turning crazy here," Dad said. "There's nothing wrong with her. See what you've started?" He told Mom. "The boys are starting now. She's nine years old, for God's sake; she's just having bad dreams, it happens to kids as they grow up. If this carries on, we'll be screwing her mind up for life. Everyone should just calm down and be normal with her. No more of these nutty psychic episodes, or ghost talk or gimmicks. Just normality for once in this mad, dysfunctional, crazy house."

I crept up the stairs to my room and sat down heavily at my dressing table. I looked in the mirror, gazing deeply into my eyes. They were as brown as they'd always been. I blinked and squinted a few times, but they didn't change color. As I looked at my reflection, I had the feeling that as our lives spun out of control, whatever it was I needed to remember was coming. It was there just silently out of reach, but its presence was building like a storm, and I had a strong feeling that all my questions would soon be answered.

10

PAUSE AND REFLECT

Over the next few weeks, our family settled back into its usual routine. Chloe's teacher, Linda Price, told us Chloe was almost back to her old self. Helen said she felt justified in calling the psychic and I started to feel the same. Perhaps I'd been a bit harsh on Helen about it, as I knew deep down, she was only trying to help our daughter. I'd always felt guilty I wasn't home much to help her with the kids. She was doing her best and my attitude towards her was softening.

I knew about her limited coping abilities, which was why I'd employed domestic help and childcare when the kids were young. I also knew about the drinking and smoking, despite Helen thinking I didn't. All in all, I knew she wasn't that strong and accepted her weaknesses because I loved her, always have and likely always will. The sudden violence towards Chloe worried me though, and I'd spoken to her about it, reminding her that as Chloe's parents, if we couldn't be strong for her through this, she had no one.

~

HELEN

I FELT ASHAMED by my loss of control in front of everyone, especially David, I'd let him down so badly. This wasn't me and certainly wasn't how I wanted them to think of me. It was awful. I had grovelingly apologized to them individually and they were all so mature about it, forgiving and understanding. Except Chloe, who appeared indifferent. The boys were much more mature than me in every way and I was so proud at the way they'd all developed into such decent young men. *I must have done something right as a mom*, I reasoned, to justify my existence. It was a turning point for me, realizing how they were growing up. The one I needed to work on was my daughter and I was unsure how to go about it.

The excitement about our vacation overtook everything else for a while, as we made our preparations. I was still trying hard to repair things with Chloe. I took her on a shopping trip to get things for our vacation, and she chose the most awful clunky-looking lace-up boots and dungarees. I didn't argue about them, but she would have looked so much nicer in a new dress. We went for ice cream, and it was there I noticed Chloe kept looking intensely at the door of the ice cream store, watching who was coming in and going out with interest, which was very strange. We made small talk, but there was a chasm between us, and I knew it would take more than ice cream to put it right. I just didn't know how to make things better. I'd apologized to her so many times, but it was as if she didn't trust me anymore and was becoming more distant.

I knew as her mother I'd betrayed Chloe's trust by shouting and shaking her when she was in trouble and needed me, and felt so awful, irrationally so, for it. I knew it wasn't her fault and I should be more understanding and able to help. It was as if our whole lives together, we had been butting heads. She didn't trust me, always favored her dad, and I blamed her for things that had gone wrong in my life, which I knew really weren't her fault. As I looked at her serious little face, I felt so terribly sad and sorry for everything that had gone on between us. I desperately wanted to make it right.

We went home to finalize the packing for the trip with our new purchases. While we were packing in Chloe's room, I watched as she placed Evelyn gently on the bed. I was amazed to see her put what looked like a parachute on the doll. It was made of handkerchiefs and silk squares which she'd managed to sew together, badly, with large colourful wool stitches. I then watched as she checked the doll all over, inside it's clothes, shoes, collar, and hair until she seemed satisfied that all was in place. She caught me watching her.

"I'm getting Evelyn ready for the airplane."

I didn't want to upset her by questioning her about it and wasn't sure I wanted to know the answers anyway, so I just smiled, nodded at her, and left the room, perplexed.

11

OUR EUROPEAN VACATION—CHLOE

Departure day arrived and pandemonium had taken over our house from the early hours of the morning. Everyone was running around gathering things together, up and down the stairs, in and out of rooms. It was so exciting. Backpacks, suitcases, and all kinds of stuff were piled in the hallway. Dad kept listing passports, tickets, and booking sheets, triple checking everything. I made sure I had Evelyn with me for this adventure. I really wanted to take my dreams box too, but that would have been too much to carry. It was stuffed full of notes now, and I hid it at the back of my closet in a large, battered suitcase full of old stuff, so Mollie couldn't see it. Finally, Dad called us all together and we piled into the van. The boys were super excited, and it made me happy just to be with them and see the looks on each of their faces as we set off.

Mollie waved us off, she would look after Rocky and would check on the house, water the plants and collect the mail. Uncle Owen and Aunt Beth had our plans and hotel numbers, in case they needed to contact us. We had Skyped both sets of grandparents the night before, each of us spending time speaking to them. They were so happy for us, and Grandpa George had told us about his trips to Europe and the best places for us to see. He'd visited France and England himself and was telling the boys all about that. He wanted them to see Normandy, the War Museum, and the Royal Air Force Museum in London, as he'd been there when he was younger. They were to tell him everything about the trip when we got back and to take photos and videos.

When we arrived at the airport, Dad dropped off the van and we made our way through to the departure area. I was dragging my suitcase along on its wheels, wishing I hadn't packed so much stuff, as my leg was really hurting. We went to the check-in and dropped our suitcases off. That was a relief; just my backpack left now which I would take on the plane with me. Then we had to be security checked before we could get on the plane. This meant taking our shoes off, and I had to put my backpack on the rollers to go through the X-ray machine along with my iPad and Evelyn.

It was then I saw the man in uniform by the X-ray machine. I was terrified of him, and didn't want to go forward, not knowing why. I grabbed my stuff off the rollers and held back a while. What if I had something in my backpack I shouldn't have? Did I have candy? was candy allowed? I hung back further, dragging my feet, not wanting to be anywhere near him and I let people go in front of me.

All my family had already gone through, and I saw my dad turn around and call out, "Where's Chloe?"

Mom pointed to me from the other side of the security check, and they all started waving and calling me forward. I really didn't want to go anywhere near the security man.

The security man approached me smiling, and said softly, "Put your dolly on the rollers as well, Miss," and so I put Evelyn attached to her parachute in the plastic box to go through the X-ray machine.

There was a woman waiting behind me putting her things on the rollers too. She smiled down at me, looking in my plastic box.

"That's a lot of handkerchiefs for one young lady." She laughed.

"It's her parachute for when she has to jump from the plane. Have you got one?" I said as I looked up at her.

Her mouth dropped open and she turned to the security man, who was laughing. She gave a nervous laugh, giving me such a strange look as she did.

I made it through the security check, which wasn't as bad as I thought it would be after all. Then Mom let us buy drinks, candy, and magazines for the flight, and we boarded the plane. Our trip of a lifetime had begun, and the boys were beside themselves excited. Worried, I checked my seat belt, the TV and backpack again and again. As we soared into the air, I held Evelyn tightly. I looked out the window at the ground falling away below—and had a strange feeling we'd done this together before.

12

A FLIGHT TO FORGET—HELEN

O nce on the plane David and I sat with Chloe between us in the window seat row and the boys sat together in the middle seats a couple of rows in front. After take-off I noticed Chloe becoming anxious and fidgeting. She fiddled with the TV, the radio, the headphones and her backpack with Evelyn and her "parachute." She went to the bathroom about five times, causing me to move out of my seat each time, and wouldn't settle. She'd flown before and had been no trouble on any of those short flights, but this was different. She was extremely agitated and very, very annoying.

After a couple of hours of fidgeting, she began asking questions. How long was the flight? Are we there yet? Where are we going to land?

And worst of all—

"What happens if we have to jump? Who'll jump first? What if we land in the water or trees?"

I'd had enough. I'd been so patient with her up until then and finally gave her a small bottle of orange juice to drink. I'd put more antihistamines into it for her, doubling the dose, as the last one didn't work. I just wanted a peaceful flight; I thought Chloe might get bored on a long-haul flight, and I was also worried what she was coming out with might unsettle people around us. I felt confident Chloe would soon be asleep, and we could all relax and enjoy the rest of the flight. I did feel bad about it and thought what a dreadful mother I must be for doing it, but deep down I knew it was really being done for the good of everyone on the flight, not just me.

After a while Chloe duly dropped off into a deep sleep. I drank some wine and looked over at David who was resting with his eyes shut. It had been a horrendous rush that morning, performed like a military operation, and it was now taking its toll. We were exhausted. I reclined my seat fully back, hoping it didn't bother the person sitting behind me, but not really caring if it did. I was just too tired. I looked over at the boys who were amusing themselves playing computer games. I closed my eyes, tuned out the people noise around me, and gratefully drifted off to sleep to the sound of the humming of the aircraft.

After a while, a voice interrupted my sleep. Someone was talking loudly near me in a foreign language, which was irritating as I was desperate to rest. I shuffled in my seat to show my annoyance and tried to settle down again. The talking continued and grumpily I pulled my seat upright and opened my eyes. I then saw, to my horror, that the person talking in a foreign language was Chloe.

She had her feet on her father's lap and her head on mine. She was gripping Evelyn tightly. I was stunned. My little girl, in her sleep was talking in what appeared to be French. I tried to gently wake her up, but she was groggy and kept nodding off, still mumbling words. David woke up and tuned in to what was happening. He looked at Chloe and then me in astonishment.

I was panicking and looked around for something, someone, anyone to help and called to a cabin crew member passing us in the aisle and asked her if she could speak French. The woman looked at me strangely and said she couldn't, but knew another crew member who was French, and went to get him.

The young man came nervously down the aisle to my seat, and I pointed at Chloe.

"Can you tell me what she's saying?" I asked him.

The man knelt near Chloe and listened. He confirmed she was speaking French.

"It's a bit difficult to hear clearly, she's mumbling, but what I can make out she is saying is, 'Enough, please stop, please enough. How long do we have?' She's calling out a list of names, 'Evelyn, Yvette, and Sabine' I can make out, and is calling for her mother over and over with something about codes and a white scarf."

The crew member looked unsettled and embarrassed, as if he'd stumbled into something he didn't particularly want to be involved with. It sounded as if Chloe was talking about being abused. He used work as an excuse to escape, stood up and walked briskly away, leaving me and David in a state of incomprehension.

"A ghost wouldn't have followed us on an American Airways flight mid-ocean, surely," I mumbled to no one in particular. *What if she is possessed?* The horror of that thought chilled me as I looked down at my beautiful young child. I moved Chloe gently back into the middle seat as she stopped talking and picked up my handbag from the floor. I couldn't smoke and so the next best thing was gum.

David looked at Chloe and then me. His gaze fell on my open handbag, as I rummaged through it, catching a glimpse of the antihistamine box. I watched as he looked at his groggy, mumbling daughter, the empty orange juice bottle and again at me, putting two and two together. I must have looked guilty as I quickly zipped my bag closed. I knew David had suspected I'd given our kids antihistamines, Scott had hinted at it previously, but I'd always claimed it was only for hay fever or hives.

"Do you think it would be too much to ask you, as her mother, not to drug our child?" he said with an accusing look. I could feel myself blush with embarrassment. It was pointless trying to justify my actions to him at that moment. I would find the right time to explain, away from others listening. We both settled back uneasily in our seats, both deep in our thoughts about Chloe and what was happening to us.

13

LONDON CALLING—CHLOE

I woke up between Mom and Dad but felt sleepy, and not fully awake. Dad put a movie on for me, about a princess from another world finding herself in America by mistake, and he handed me a sugar free coke. I settled back to watch the film with my headphones on. Once my headphones were in place, and before I could adjust the volume, I could hear Mom and Dad talking over my head. It might be more interesting than the film and so I listened. Dad was talking about what Mom had done. I wondered what she'd done that had made him so angry.

"It's likely the drugs you've been giving her caused the problems she's been having at home all along." I heard him say.

Did he mean I was on drugs? I was horrified. He went on in a low voice. "I used to trust you totally. We've always been honest with each other, always. I'm not sure I even know you anymore, Helen. What with the psychic and ghost talk, the hitting incident, and now this medication crap."

I was shocked. I'd never heard Dad swear at Mom. I'd heard him swear when I was listening from my spot over the stairs, but that wasn't at her. He waved his hand towards her bag on the floor, which was now tucked under the seat in front of her feet. He left his words hanging in the air, slumped in his chair, put his headphones on and put on a movie.

Mom looked really upset, and again it was all because of me. She must hate me more than ever now and I felt so bad about it. I turned the volume up on my headphones and tried to take myself away into a wonderful world of princesses, handsome princes, happily ever after, and magical far, far, away places. But I was beginning to wonder whether they had ever existed at all.

The rest of the flight was peaceful, but I could feel the tension coming from my parents in waves as I sat between them. I felt terrible at whatever I'd caused, and I was on drugs. *Were they in my backpack? Was that why the security man wanted to check?*

WE ARRIVED at Heathrow and made our way to our hotel in central London via the shuttle. Strangely, as we got into London, I felt very alive after the long flight. We went in two taxis, and I had an odd sensation looking out of the car windows at the places we were passing. It was as if I knew some of them, but I'd never been here before. *I must have seen them on TV.*

Mom decided the time difference between the States and London would cause havoc with our sleeping patterns, and she said we should all stay awake for as long as possible the first day. This meant we would sleep better at night and jet lag would be less.

Once we'd unpacked, we went out to see the sights. We

saw the Houses of Parliament and Big Ben. As we walked close to Big Ben the clock chimed loudly startling me so much that I jumped, grabbing Ryan's arm. I shouted, "Good gracious," and everyone laughed. I couldn't remember ever using that term before. I must have heard it from Mollie, since she was old and said old things. Mom and Dad both said they were pleased I was enjoying myself, and to be honest, I really was.

We went on the London underground, which was the only time I felt uncomfortable. Being underground with lots of people shoving and pushing. It felt hard to breathe down there and I couldn't wait to get out into the fresh air. We stopped off at different tourist spots on our map, until we were exhausted and had had enough. We made our tired way back to the hotel for dinner and bed. We had fish and chips in the restaurant, with salt and vinegar. Joel said that was very British, and people used to eat them wrapped in old newspaper, which didn't sound nice. Mom and Dad had wine to try and help them relax after the traumas of the day, quite a lot of wine from what I could see.

THE FIRST NIGHT in London was terribly noisy. I could hear the traffic outside with police and ambulance sirens whizzing past. I was in a room with my parents. I had to sleep on a cot and the boys had an adjoining room, overseen by Scott. I eventually drifted off into an exhausted sleep and slept solidly that night. I remember visions of all the London sights swimming in my head. I also had the nice dream of being in the beautiful blue flower field.

The boys' list of attractions included Madame Tussauds, the London Eye, the Natural History Museum, and the

Tower of London. It was all organized well by Dad and the trip was going as planned. Mom was coping, as there was no cooking or housework to worry about; even our beds were made up for us.

It was just to be fun for us all as a family, as Dad said, "To put all our troubles behind us."

I was determined to do my part.

The boys wanted to see the Science Museum, the RAF museum, and the Imperial War Museum first. In London there were loads of war-related or horror-related exhibitions around, which excited the boys.

Mom was worried.

"I don't think Chloe should go to those sorts of exhibitions. She might be affected by it, making the nightmares worse. Perhaps she should just go shopping with me."

"We can't shield her from everything that's going on Helen. It's impossible and not really fair. Not all the exhibits are scary, we can just divert her from any unsuitable things."

I was on my dad's side on this, especially since I wanted to do what the boys did and not miss out.

Even though my wish list had Buckingham Palace, where the Queen and princesses lived, I was totally drawn in at the Imperial War Museum, which the boys desperately wanted to see. There was lots of information on something called 'The Blitz' and I was immediately absorbed by it. It was fascinating to read about. I saw funny posters from the war telling people to "Make do and mend," and "Dig for victory," "Loose lips, sink ships" and one that said, "Keep mum she's not so dumb." I saw the ration books people had for food and the gas masks and the shelters from the bombs.

I wandered towards a particular section, where there were radios used for wartime communication. One was in a suitcase labeled as a portable transmitter receiver. I couldn't stop myself from touching it, not sure if I were allowed or not, but was fascinated by it. I watched the short video of how they sent messages and then I studied the code called Morse next to the exhibit. I was concentrating intensely on it and tapped my finger on what was labeled, a Morse key, using the dots and dashes I'd seen on the poster.

A boy of about my age was standing next to me impatiently wanting to have a look, but I ignored him and continued concentrating on what I was doing. He was getting very annoyed and complained loudly to his friend.

"She's been on it for ages. She should let someone else have a go."

Joel, who was watching, called over to me.

"Let someone else have a turn, Chloe. It's more for boys than girls anyway. There's something over here for you to see."

That made me so mad, him of all people telling me it was only for boys. But he said he wanted to show me something and so I rushed the last piece of tapping, happy that despite all the interference, the tapping I had completed on the machine was accurate.

"At last," said the boy, and I gave him my death stare as I walked off.

The RAF Museum was another place on the boys' wish list. It was vast and had over eighty airplanes on display. There were 4D rides with the Red Arrows and a plane called a Spitfire you could sit in, which we all took a turn at. It was great fun. As I walked amongst the rows of planes, I was stopped in my tracks by one in particular. It was quite a small, stubby plane that couldn't carry many people, and it didn't look like a warplane at all. It was painted black and had two big, covered wheels at the front and a little one at the back. It had a glass cockpit and a seat at the front for the pilot, two seats in the back and a ladder on the side to get in.

Mike excitedly came to stand next to me looking at the plane, his face a picture of happiness. He loved airplanes and being in this museum must have been like heaven to him. As I looked at the plane it suddenly came to me.

"That's a Lizzie, Mike," I told him, pointing at the plane, feeling pleased with myself.

He looked at the name on the stand.

"I don't think so, Peanut. It's called a Westland Lysander MK iii."

I looked at it again, thinking I was right, but knowing Mike knew all and everything about planes, I said, "Oh, okay?"

He bent down to look at the card near the plane with its history and started reading it as I skipped off to the next exhibit. I looked back for Mike and saw him looking at me, at the plane, and then back at the card studying the plane's details and history. *Perhaps I'd found one that he hasn't got on his wall at home.*

We checked out the spitfires and went on the 4D Red Arrows ride again and then picked up things at the museum shop. I chose a spitfire key ring for each of the grandpas, and a poppy broach for each of the grandmas, from the 'Lest we forget' stand.

We were bubbling as we rode back on the tube train to our hotel. There was such a crowd on the train at first and we had to stand as all the seats were taken. Scott held my hand on one side, and Mom on the other, so I wouldn't get squished or fall over. When some people got off at the next station, we all managed to sit down.

There was a lady on the seat opposite us. She was staring and smiling at me. She had brown hair down to her shoulders with a jewelled hair slide and was dressed very neatly in a deep blue suit. She looked like a businesswoman. She had a kind face with perfect makeup and painted nails. She just wouldn't stop staring at me, and I didn't know why. She was concentrating hard at something around me and then looking through me. I just kept peeking back at her every now and again to see if she was still looking, and she was. We both smiled at each other.

The train was coming into a station, and she got up ready to get off. She stood right in front of me, holding a support strap to steady herself as the train slowed down. She then reached down and put her finger under my chin, tilting it up so she could look in my face.

"You've been here before, little one," she said to me.

Mom heard her and said, "No, this is our first time here, we're having such a wonderful time."

The woman nodded and smiled at my mother, and then said directly to me,

"Don't be afraid, little one. You're confused and frightened right now, but it will all be okay soon. Don't worry."

Before Mom could say anything back, the tube train doors opened, and the woman got off. As she left, Ryan made a face and waved his hand at the side of his head as if saying she was crazy. He laughed loudly, saying to Mom, "Weird." Mom and the others laughed.

I looked out of the window as the train started to leave the station. I wanted to see her again to wave at her, but I couldn't see her among all the moving people there. It was as if she'd vanished.

～

WHEN WE GOT BACK to the hotel, we had cheeseburgers and milkshakes for dinner, and as we ate, we all marveled at what we'd seen that day. The woman was only a vague funny story to everyone, but to me she wasn't. It was as if she could see deep down inside me and knew something was wrong. I let my feelings about her go though, because it was wonderful just being here with my family, sharing their enjoyment of the vacation.

We all had things to tell each other about the day and when it was my turn, I shared that I'd seen things made from parachute silk, ration books, and that people ate Spam and didn't have oranges, bananas, or candy. I talked about The Blitz and a film I'd seen of children being evacuated from their homes with gas masks.

"They had to leave their mothers and fathers and go and live somewhere else away from the bombs," I told them. What an awful thought that was. Children being sent away from their parents, not because they were naughty but in case bombs dropped on them. I decided war was a terrible thing. I looked at Scott and the others as they chatted, and I was so thankful we weren't in a war and were safe. I loved that evening together as a family. We were so close, and I knew I'd always remember it.

Mike then told everyone that I must have been studying the planes in his room back home because I knew what a Lysander plane was, and they all laughed. I really didn't see what was funny about it but smiled, not wanting to argue. My parents were happier than they had been for months, as if none of the bad stuff had happened, and I didn't want to spoil that.

But I did know what that plane was—it was a Lizzie. When I got back to our hotel room, I looked up Lizzie on my iPad to check. The first Lizzie that came up was a woman who killed her parents with an axe. I hoped that Lizzie was nothing to do with me and shut the iPad down quickly, not wanting to read anymore.

That night, I could hear way off in the distance an English woman's voice calling out: "Jump when I say." "Go there and don't move until I come for you." "Quick, start the truck and go." I could hear the voice questioning someone, "How long do we have?" "Do you have the torches and codes?"

I half woke up, again in two different places at once, and the words were coming from my mouth in a voice I didn't recognize.

As I jolted fully awake, I could hear my mom crying softly in the dark and my dad comforting her. Again, I knew I was the source of their upset and felt so sad. I wanted to tell them it wasn't real it was just dreaming, but I lay there listening silently in the darkness instead.

14

WHO ARE THEY?—HELEN

I tried my best to cry quietly. Chloe sounded so much older and like someone else in her dream state. I assured David that I hadn't given her any medication and didn't know where any of this was coming from. It was a devastating turn of events, especially since we'd been so happy the last few days. *David should have listened to me. I told him the sights and places we were visiting might cause this.* I didn't make a fuss about it with him; I had my own demons about my recent actions still raw between us. I wouldn't allow her to see or hear anything else that might frighten her on the rest of the trip though. I was terribly scared for her and couldn't help thinking of all the demonic possession movies I had watched over the years. There were illnesses I had read about too, where there is more than one personality in a person. Tears flowed down my face, and I had no wine or cigarettes to help me cope. I was lost. We were in a foreign country and totally out of our depth with this.

David listened and watched our daughter in utter astonishment. We were both witnessing something we were unable to comprehend or manage. Chloe in her deep sleep engaged in conversations with God knows who. Her final words before she stopped and went quiet were.

"Don't run, whatever you do. They'll catch you. We have to think our way out."

That freaked me out completely. Who on earth were *they*? We both just watched, listened, and waited until she settled before we discussed anything else, holding each other tightly for comfort in the darkness. I think it was then we finally accepted we needed professional help. We were unable to help Chloe with whatever problem she was suffering with and agreed quietly that she should see a psychologist privately. I knew being out of the States at least no one locally or from our family would know about it, and it wouldn't be on any of her records back home to affect her future.

David checked the internet for London-based psychologists to make a private appointment for her. He found one just a short tube ride away, a Doctor Niall Williams. We both agreed he looked perfect, although our experience of psychologists was zero and we could have just closed our eyes and put a pin in a list to pick one. David decided to get an urgent appointment first thing in the morning for an initial consultation, while the rest of us went on the London Bus tour.

CHLOE SEEMED PARTICULARLY calm and self-assured that morning, again appearing so much older than she was. She had meticulously tidied up the hotel room and put her things neatly away. I watched her intently as we rode around London on the tour bus. It was as if she were familiar with everything around her, pointing out certain buildings as we rode past them. She concentrated on what the guide was saying as they gave a commentary on the history of each building we passed. I looked at her sweet little excited face with its 'knowing' expression and had the most awful feeling in the pit of my stomach. It was as if someone else was jostling to be in my child and my child was disappearing. I was bereft and afraid for her and for the rest of us.

We made our way to see where the Sherlock Holmes Museum was and walked along Baker Street looking for the address. I was lost in my own sad, confused thoughts as I put one foot in front of the other, following the boys' lead as they used their phone maps to find the place. Chloe had been walking next to me, but when I looked down to my side for her, she wasn't there. I looked back down the road and saw she'd stopped quite a way behind us, standing right at the edge of the road—her gaze fixed intently on a building on the opposite side.

"Whatever now?" I said in despair. I walked back toward her, watching as she began to pace back and forth as if pondering whether to cross the road. It was almost ten in the morning and the traffic was quite heavy, with buses and taxis coming extremely near to the pavement where she was, and I started to panic. I began running towards her thinking she was about to step off the curb. My heart was pounding with fear as I ran, not taking my eyes off her for a second. I then saw Scott race past me at such a speed, plucking her from the curb, holding her in his arms. She was safe and a feeling of relief thundered through me.

"Thank God for you, Scott," I told my eldest son, so grateful to him as I reached them both. "What were you looking at, Chloe?" I asked her breathlessly.

"I think I need to go in there," she replied, pointing to a nondescript building on the other side of the road.

Scott, who had run so fast he was now trying to recover his breath, interrupted our conversation.

"No, Peanut, the museum is further up the road. That's where we need to cross, not here, not this time. Come with us." He grabbed her hand and rushed her up the road with him, towards the museum and the other boys.

I wondered what he meant by, "Not this time." Had I misheard him in my flustered state or was I just going completely mad? I would ask him later. I watched them walking together, the boys surrounding Chloe like a military formation, two of them holding her little hands, Scott one side, Ryan on the other, Mike in front and Joel at the back. I decided to cross the road to see what the building she'd been staring at was, but there was nothing there really. It was just a commercial building at number 64, with a small round green plaque on a wall dedicated to people in the Second World War in some outfit or other. There were loads of these plaques all over London. I'd seen so many on our walks around the place, and of course lots about Winston Churchill.

15

A FATHER'S ANGUISH—DAVID

I arrived at Doctor Williams's office and was shown in by a secretary. The doctor was about my age, athletic looking, wearing a gray suit. He and his office were expensive looking and immaculate, not a paperclip out of place. When he asked what he could do for me, I told him in a torrent of words everything that had happened. Not normally emotional, I did become so when I was telling him about Chloe.

"I just desperately want help for my daughter," I told him, bordering on tears in front of another man, a situation I'd never found myself in before. At work I was the trouble-shooter employees came to for answers to their problems. This was new to me, seeking out someone to help me.

Doctor Williams listened intently from the other side of his desk and let me finish speaking, before leaning forward and gently explaining,

"I tend to specialise more in adult psychology, not children, Mr Anderson. I don't think I'm the best person for your daughter's issues."

Having spent myself emotionally, I physically crumpled at his response, and he tried his best to reassure me.

"I do know someone I think may be able to help you and would probably be more suited to treating your child than me anyway. He's a doctor with an excellent, if unorthodox, reputation working with children, especially with the sorts of issues you are describing, and he works nearby. His name is Harry Mayfield."

He wrote down the address and telephone number for me to make an appointment and I thanked him gratefully for his help. I was now an emotional wreck, not thinking rationally at all. Rather than formally make an appointment, which I knew was the right and proper thing to do, I decided to go straight there in person. I thought this would save time, as I was acutely aware our time in London was rapidly running out.

I arrived at the address, having taken the tube, which I was getting the hang of, and rang the bell. A woman answered on the intercom and advised me to push the door open and come in. The woman greeted me with a beaming smile. She was young and stylishly dressed and introduced herself as Doctor Mayfield's PA, Debbie Marsh.

"Do you have an appointment?" she asked me, and I confessed.

"No. Sorry for coming in like this, but it was just to have a few moments with the doctor, if possible, to see if I could make an urgent appointment. He was recommended to me by another doctor, Niall Williams."

"Oh, okay. Is the appointment for yourself?" she asked me.

"No, my daughter," I replied nervously.

"To be honest with you, it's very unlikely he will be able to see you at such short notice. He's due to leave the country in two days' time and has two weeks of conferences in America with a whole load of work to complete before then. I'll ask for you, but please don't get your hopes up."

I nodded as I watched her enter the doctor's office and shut the door behind her, leaving me alone, nervous and pacing. She came back with the response.

"Doctor Mayfield is terribly sorry, but he just doesn't have the time to fit another appointment in before he goes away. He has asked for you to make an appointment for three weeks' time when he'll be back if you wanted to see him specifically, or he could recommend someone else who could see you sooner."

She walked back behind her desk to click on the appointments page on her computer. "Let's see what dates are free."

We would be moving on to France in a few days' time, so that wasn't an option for me. I felt myself unravelling, tired, scared, and desperate, not my usual self at all. I then did something I would never have done in my normal, rational state. I rushed into the office the receptionist had just come out of, with her calling after me.

As I entered, I found a man I presumed to be Harry Mayfield standing by a filing cabinet. He had a calm demeanour and an experienced, lived-in kind face. He looked to be about late fifties with gray hair, a beard, and wearing crumpled brown corduroy trousers, with a white shirt covered by a sweater. The very cluttered room smelled faintly of cigarettes and there was a bottle of whisky and a glass near a computer on the paper-strewn desk.

He was filing papers into an overstuffed metal cabinet, which was proving to be a struggle, and he turned to me when I rushed in. He didn't react, just remained really calm, and reassured Debbie who had followed me in, lecturing and warning me as she did so.

"It's okay, Debs," he said to her, and she rolled her eyes at him in exasperation as she left the room.

"I'm deeply sorry for the intrusion. Please don't be alarmed, I'm a professional executive, not some nut job. I don't want to frighten anyone. If I could just have a few minutes of your time, I would be so grateful. I desperately need help for my daughter, and I've been told you could help."

"I'm sorry," he said, adjusting his glasses further up on his nose, "I would if I could, but seriously I have no time available for a full appointment and treatment sessions before I go away. I have been forbidden to take on anymore appointments by Debbie, whom you've met already. I must complete work I am behind with or else I face her wrath. I could see your daughter as soon as I get back if that's any good. Or I know another person who may be able to help you."

I explained my circumstances of being on vacation and moving on in a couple of days. I stopped talking and just stood there, in front of a total stranger, a broken man with tears streaming down my face. He asked me to sit down in one of the two large brown leather armchairs and offered me a drink, telling me to call him Harry. I declined the drink, but that didn't stop him pouring one for us both anyway. He was looking at me with empathy, a distressed parent baring my soul in front of him. He must have dealt with many distressed parents in his time and gave me space to talk about it.

I watched him closely as he came over to sit in his large and very worn leather armchair, directly opposite me. I was so grateful to him and felt a tremendous rush of trust in this man for some reason.

"Tell me everything that has happened with your daughter up until now," he asked me calmly. "What sort of child is she? Her character, her likes, dislikes, habits, skills. We may be able to put strategies in place for you to use until she can be seen. Tell me what was going on in her life just before this change in her was noticed."

I told him about my Chloe, her brave, independent streak, how she battled for her equal place in the family with four older brothers. How loving, kind, and thoughtful she was. As for the change in her, I'd thought about that over and over in my head, and there was nothing I could think of that could have triggered this. Everything was normal, absolutely nothing different. I'd just come back from a business trip, she'd been playing in the pool with her brothers, we had dinner together chatting, all usual stuff.

"What I want you to do from now on is to write every-thing down as it happens. That will help pin down details like times of the occurrences, what she was doing before-hand, and what she actually says at the time. Can you describe some of the incidents to me?"

The words poured out from me in an unstoppable tsunami—the nightmares, the speaking French, and the conversations with people in her sleep. I told Harry about the headaches, the periodic limping, and the eye problem she had complained of. I reassured him we'd taken her to a doctor for tests and there was nothing physically wrong. I explained she'd seen movies she shouldn't have, one of which was a violent war movie. I described the drawings Chloe had done at school and what she'd said about them. The lady in the mirror was mentioned and Helen's use of antihistamine tablets to get her to sleep. The mad woman at the yard sale and the psychic Helen had used were mentioned too. Harry tutted, shook his head, and rolled his eyes at that piece of information, but continued taking notes.

He then asked specifics about the nightmares Chloe had told me about. I described what she had come out with over the last few months. The nasty man, the cross man, the man with blood on his white scarf who hurt her and the black legs that ran on the spot but didn't move anywhere.

A thought suddenly shot into my head. "Looking back, this all escalated the night I'd told everyone we were going on a European vacation."

Harry jotted that down. "Think back over Chloe's childhood—was there anything strange in her behaviour that you couldn't explain prior to all of this? Did she have any skills in her earlier years that couldn't be explained? Any unusual interests?"

I racked my brain about this and remembered she'd always been able to swim. I didn't teach her and assumed the boys must have. When I'd asked them, none of them could remember specifically teaching her, only with diving, the same with riding a bike; I knew I didn't teach her and again presumed the boys had; she could just ride a bike from an extremely early age. The name of her doll Evelyn was a mystery too. No one we knew had that name. It was one she just came out with from nowhere and was extremely insistent that the doll be called it. She'd learned to talk and read incredibly early and was way ahead in vocabulary at school. We had put that down to all six of us taking turns reading with her. Harry continued writing and then suddenly stopped me talking by holding up his hand. He looked surprised as if he too had remembered something.

"Back in a minute," he said, as he went into a small room leading off from his office, returning with a large battered-looking file. He started flicking through the pages, reading intermittently. He looked at me and then back at the file with intense interest.

After settling on one page in the file, he looked up at me saying, "This is remarkably interesting; I just may be able to help with Chloe after all. It would be a bit of a rush and will have to be tomorrow morning as an urgent session, as that's the only time I could possibly do this. I'll have to fight with Debbie about it later," he laughed. "The outcome of the session could still be that she's just seen or heard something frightening which has caused her current problems. If that's the case it will resolve naturally, and she'll grow out of it, as most of the children I see do. Whatever has disturbed Chloe, her current state suggests it's most likely stress related, and we need to find the cause of that stress, if possible, to help her resolve it."

My body just slumped in the chair with total relief. I closed my eyes and thanked whatever God there was out there for helping me, feeling guilty about my previous atheist viewpoint.

Harry was deep in thought for a minute or two and again looking intensely and wide eyed at a page in his file. He rubbed his beard thoughtfully. "This may mean possible regression therapy under hypnosis."

He explained that to me briefly, and told me his treatment usually lasted a few sessions before they got to the hypnotherapy stage and that was usually broken up into three or four sessions. His routine practice was that he held a session with the parents to get to know them and explain the process first. He then spent time just chatting with the child and interacted through play therapy.

"I don't have the time to do this by the book over multiple sessions, but if you agree, I'll see Chloe tomorrow and just see where that session leads us. I'll be directed by whatever she comes out with. This won't be cheap though I'm afraid." I dismissed that, happy to pay any price for this nightmare to be over.

"Bring Chloe in at nine tomorrow morning," he told me. "You do need to know beforehand that I work with children in a different way to others in this field and I'm currently experimenting with different treatments and methods."

That threw me completely, and I was a bit perturbed by what he'd said. He must have seen that flicker across my face as he sought to reassure me.

"Don't be alarmed, you'll be with her the whole time, and if at any time you feel uncomfortable, you can stop the session. I know hypnosis and regression therapy has received bad publicity in the press, which you may or may not be aware of. This was due to accusations of abuse, made under hypnosis, but I've always found it useful with children as a tool to determine the cause of their anxiety and stress. Of course, I may not need to go down that route, but just in case, you do need to be aware of it."

I was by now physically, mentally, and emotionally exhausted, and being new to all of this, had horror movie stills running through my head. "Does this mean her possibly being restrained, or levitation, crucifixes, green vomit, holy water or anything like that?" I asked in a hesitatingly, awkward manner.

Harry just roared with laughter. "Mr Anderson, this is hypnotism not exorcism, and in any case, if anything you just described happened, I'd be the first one out the door."

I suddenly felt totally stupid. I was in a senior position at work and managed hundreds of staff myself and here I was asking questions that might come from a ten-year-old. I put it down to being just extremely tired, emotional, and way out of my comfort zone. I was now, apart from being thoroughly embarrassed, feeling elated and grateful and left Harry's office with a spring in my step. I smiled at Debbie who nodded at me crossly as she tapped hard on her keyboard with her blood red fingernails. I'd broken the rules bypassing her as Harry's gatekeeper, and she hadn't forgiven me.

As I travelled back, I vowed to research the use of regression hypnosis and Harry Mayfield before our meeting tomorrow. I also promised myself to never again go unprepared or unresearched to any meeting whatsoever, with anybody or anywhere for the rest of my life.

I checked the internet for Doctor Mayfield that night and found articles on his work and the substantial number of books he'd written. I was satisfied he was a competent professional with a good track record, although not strictly mainstream in his approach to psychology. I told Helen I thought he would be perfect with Chloe, and I trusted him completely to help us. We discussed who should go with her to the appointment in a hushed tone in order not to wake her, agreeing it would be best for me to go.

"I would be hopelessly emotional and useless, David, and would probably fall apart in front of Chloe and everyone else." Helen said.

I didn't have the heart to tell her I already had. We all slept soundly that night.

16

HARRY MAYFIELD

A fter David left my office, I flicked through the file again. There were lists of cases I had taken on with children and their issues over a thirty-year period. I knew them all well, as I'd lived their experiences, the horrors, and terrors with them as they recited the details to me. I looked at the photos of their sad little faces, their trusting but fearful eyes, remembering them all personally. I normally would have declined David's request, as I really was pressed for time, but I was intrigued by this now with the brief details he'd given. It had stirred memories of my own.

I flicked through the details of the cases in the files. Most of the latest ones were about eating disorders, body image issues, divorced parent stresses, and social media issues. There were also nightmares about aeroplanes and cars crashing, torture, drownings, beatings, sexual assaults, starvation, gassings, falling from great heights, animal attacks, being shot, hanged, and being burnt. Phobias about heights, uniforms, spiders, snakes, water, and enclosed spaces. In several cases I had placed the child in a hypnotic state which usually confirmed they'd been scared by a specific incident, comment, or someone in their lives. Equally there were older cases where the child described a different life, albeit sketchy and with extraordinarily little detail. But a few were more specific, including one child from about twenty years ago I remembered so clearly as if it were only yesterday. The name had sprung to mind while I talked with David.

Robert, "Bobby" Harrington, aged seven from Bristol, had suffered persistent nightmares for years, from which he would wake up screaming. He was utterly terrified of uniforms and closed doors in his everyday life. He couldn't be in any room with the door fully closed without becoming distressed. He was an only child and was finally brought to me for treatment by his mother after she'd tried to resolve the issues herself with different therapies and medication from his GP. He was such a sweet boy, kind and thoughtful with such trusting eyes, eager to please, trying to protect his mum from his problem. He saw everything that was happening as his fault and was keen to get it resolved, eagerly doing anything I asked him to get it over with.

He had gone through about three sessions with me and appeared to progress quite well at first, but the damage to that family overall had already been done. Despite me drastically cutting the cost of the sessions for them, the parents struggled in their relationship, eventually separating. I saw Bobby one more time, he had descended into depression, blaming himself for everything and it was more difficult to hypnotize him or even reach him as he carried this deep burden inside. Periodically, he was still having nightmares and flashbacks, not as often but just as damaging. It was as if a door had been left open in the young boy's mind allowing the nightmares to return to haunt him at will. I hadn't had enough time to help him try and close off the nightmares so that he could live a normal happy life.

Bobby, under hypnosis, had given initial details of another life, being tortured during World War II in Poland. Investigations into this young boy's life, showed nothing that could account for the story he told about his other Polish life. I hadn't heard the whole story from him as I was managing it in brief, separate sessions. I thought reliving the whole story under hypnosis in one go might have been too much for him and so I was spacing the sessions out for an hour each time.

I had offered his mother more help by undergoing sessions with him for free, but she didn't bring him in again for whatever reason, and my calls went unanswered. Bobby had drawn a picture of his torturer from his dreams for me to see. This was what came to mind when David Anderson was talking to me about his daughter. Bobby was quite good at drawing, and on one of his pictures, he had drawn a man in a uniform with silver s's on his collar and wearing an iron cross at his neck. He had written the word 'Nazzi' and put a crude swastika on the page in thick black crayon above the man.

Looking at this through the eyes of a scared little girl, could this be the nasty man (Nazi), the cross man (iron cross) and the black running legs that stayed in one place (Swastika)? I was intrigued. If this was what I thought it was, then it may be something worth missing the start of the conference for.

I never forgot little Bobby and tracked him down when he would have been an adult. I was dismayed to find out he'd died at age twenty-two from a drug overdose. He had taken prescribed sleeping tablets, anti-depressants, and analgesics. Whether it was a deliberate act to end his life, or just desperation to block out the nightmares and flashbacks, I'll never know. I felt partly responsible for his death, as I didn't close off the route to the terrors that haunted his young life, and I could possibly have done with more time. He had no-one but his mother to look out for him and was alone trying to deal with his problem. Medication for him was never the answer. I felt guilty that I didn't pursue things with him more strenuously than I did. I hoped I could help another child avoid the life that Bobby had, feeling alone, isolated, and haunted to his death. This little girl, Chloe, may be another child, like Bobby, with haunting memories of a brutal past life that was 'bleeding' into her current life. Memories of that life were tormenting her, and I could help. I also knew Debbie would kill me for taking this case on.

17

OUT OF THE COMFORT ZONE—DAVID

Chloe appeared happy she was going with me and made sure Evelyn came too. Helen and the boys had gone to the London Dungeon and the London Eye for the day. I held Chloe's hand, as we made our way to see Harry Mayfield. I felt so intensively protective of her, like never before. I'd told her Doctor Mayfield wanted to help her with her bad dreams. I didn't want to say he would stop them because I didn't want her to feel disappointed if it didn't work.

"Is he like a dentist for your head?" Chloe asked me. "Does he just take the bad parts out?"

I couldn't help myself and laughed at her reasoning. "I suppose it is, Honey, but it doesn't hurt at all, and I will be with you all the time, so don't worry."

We were buzzed into the building and into reception. Debbie Marsh was there again and smiled at Chloe as she led us into a different room opposite Harry's office. Chloe appeared reluctant as we stood in his doorway. She was standing behind me holding my jacket, clutching Evelyn, and peering around at Harry who welcomed us in.

"Hello, Chloe," he said, beaming. "My name's Harry." He pointed at a large cream recliner or 'tv chair' for her to sit in if she wanted to, he told her it could go up and down and round and round if she wanted to have a go. Which of course she did, and clambered in. This room was different from his scruffy dishevelled office. It was clean and homey like a family den with armchairs, colourful soothing pictures, and a large screen on the wall. He showed Chloe how to work the controls of the chair and left her with Debbie. We watched as she was raised up and lowered down at the press of a button and was giggling. Once we knew she was settling, we discussed the session. He told me what might happen, and that it might be difficult for me to sit and listen to what my nine-year-old daughter may or may not come out with under hypnosis, if he were to go down that route.

"You will be looking at your daughter, but she may be speaking with a different voice and could possibly come out with things that upset or shock you. If it gets too much you can stop the session at any time, or just quietly leave the room, and I will continue with Debbie present. The session will be recorded, and you will be given a copy."

I nodded my agreement and signed the consent but worried what she would come out with. What had she seen and heard at home? What was that about on the plane, pleading for help? I'd read a disturbing case on the internet last night about this therapy which included memories of abuse leading to a court case. I sat in the armchair terrified at what Chloe might divulge, as Harry patted my back, put a glass of water and a box of tissues on the table in front of me and returned to Chloe's side.

He turned on the screen on the wall in front of Chloe and settled down in his chair and talked to her. He turned on the recorder and asked her to tell him about her family and her life. Chloe willingly told him everything including what made her happy and sad, as if she were talking with an old friend. She talked and talked on and on about everything in her life which, thank God, overall sounded rather pleasant, and was confirmed by Harry nodding his head. I let out a silent sigh of relief.

He gave Chloe a handheld control for the screen and showed her how she could put colors and shapes on it. She soon got the hang of it, and as she was playing, he walked around the chair to discuss what would happen next.

"I can't see there's anything in her life that would cause her nightmares. I have gone through all I can with her to determine what's bothering her and there is nothing obvious. Whatever is going on with Chloe, I believe it's at a much deeper psychological level. Undertaking a 'deep dive' into her mind under hypnosis at this point could possibly shed more light on where this is all coming from."

I agreed with him, not sure where all of this was heading, but feeling there were no other options. I knew I wasn't going to leave her side no matter what. I wondered if this was how Helen had felt about the psychic and empathized with her more now that I was in the same situation. You become desperate.

Harry returned to Chloe's side. "I help people with bad dreams, Chloe, and your dad tells me you've had some. Can you tell me about your dreams?"

Chloe looked up at him and then at me for reassurance. I nodded at her, and she began with a list of the dreams she'd been having, a beach dream, a blue carpet dream, a flying dream, and then she ran out of the nice ones. She then hesitatingly told of the ones where she'd been hurt by the man with the white scarf and the other horror dreams.

She described the lady in her mirror, and Harry asked her if she saw her when she had just woken up or when she was about to go to sleep.

"I only saw her once. I saw her in my bedroom mirror in the night when I was in a flying dream."

"Did the lady say anything to you at all, Chloe?" he asked her.

"No, she just had a smiley face."

"What do you mean by flying?"

"Just like in a dream but floating."

Harry asked her about the movies she'd seen that the boys were watching, and she said she'd just peeked at the screen every now and again while she was reading or drawing. She said she had seen and heard some scary things.

"But it's not real," she told him. "It's just movies."

He focused then on the man with the white scarf and Chloe described to him what he was like, and the horrors he had inflicted on her in her dreams in detail. He looked across at me, and all I could do was look back at him, wide eyed and shocked at the horrific story she was telling. This was the first time I'd heard her description of the "being hurt" she'd been so terrified of. I could have kicked myself then that I'd never really asked her about it before—and should have. I'd just dismissed it as dreams and didn't question her in any depth about them. I was now terrified that someone really was abusing my daughter and racked my brain as to who had access to her. Was it while I was away working? *Oh Christ, should I stop this session?*

Harry settled Chloe down. "You will feel a bit sleepy while we talk, Chloe, and that's okay. I'll be talking to you all the time and you'll hear only my voice. You must listen to my voice. Can you do that, Chloe?" he asked her gently, and she nodded.

"You're safe here with me and your daddy. He will sit quietly by your side, but he'll be here all the time."

She smiled and waved nervously at me with her fingers. I saw that she was clutching Evelyn tightly, *thank God for Evelyn*. I then fully accepted we had to go through this to help her, however hard it might be, but I had the most profound and overwhelming need to protect her that almost reduced me to tears.

"What's your favorite color, Chloe?" Harry asked her.

"Pink," she quickly replied.

She was asked to pick a shape from the screen, and she chose a heart shape. Harry asked her to concentrate on the shape while he talked to her. He dimmed the lighting slightly, tilted the recliner back a bit and asked her to concentrate on the pink heart on the screen, to look deeply into it, to tell him if she could see anything inside as it moved.

He went through a deep relaxation technique with her, all the time talking rhythmically, talking, and talking. I too was feeling a bit sleepy at one point and shook myself to stay alert. The pink heart shape was made smaller and larger intermittently on the screen, like a beating heart. Chloe's eyes were totally concentrating on it and visibly closing, as Harry's voice continued to carry softly, reaching every corner of her mind.

He told her his was the only voice she would hear and to listen to him when he spoke and repeated that she was safe. Chloe nodded when he asked her if she understood. He asked her to raise her right arm, which she did. She was then asked to lower it and she did. Chloe was to all intents and purposes hypnotized.

18

THE DEEP DIVE—CHLOE

I was getting very sleepy just watching the pink heart beating on the screen, coming near and then going far away. I was trying to look inside it because the man, Harry, said there was something in there, but I couldn't see anything. Harry was talking to me in a quiet voice by my left side. I saw my dad sitting next to me on my right and then felt myself sinking down into the chair between them. It was like floating slowly down wrapped in cotton wool and I couldn't move.

Harry asked me to think back to my eighth birthday and what happened on that day. A clear picture of it snapped into my mind. It was like watching a movie. I told him there was a big party at our house and my family and friends were there. There was a large princess cake on a table set up by the pool. I had a ton of presents put in a pile for me to open later. I remembered Ryan had eaten so much cake and ice cream he was sick everywhere.

Harry asked me about all the years since I was two and I could answer the questions so easily. My mind was crystal clear, and the memories just flooded into it. He then asked me if I remembered anything before that. How silly, of course I did. How could I not remember? It was as clear as anything. I remembered being dropped on the floor by my dad when he was looking after me one night and had fallen asleep on the couch. I was still just a baby, and he was terrified. I remembered him checking me over for weeks afterwards worried about brain damage and telling me how sorry he was.

I remembered Ryan feeding me bits off a candy bar when I shouldn't have had solids. Scott crying when he was the first brother to hold me when I was born and his salty tears dropping on my face. My dad rocking me for hours and singing to me in the night when I couldn't sleep, promising to protect me and about the wonderful life he would make sure I had. Mike accidently dropping his ice-cold cola drink on me when he peeked over at me asleep in my crib. It made me scream so loudly and terrified him. Joel helping to bathe me when my skin was very slippery and letting me slip through his hands under the water. I could sense his terror as I looked up at him through the soapy water. Rocky guarding me and licking food off my face when I was in my highchair and Mom getting flustered all the time about everything.

I remembered Scott teaching me to crawl and walk like he was training Rocky, Joel teaching me numbers and colors, Mike reading with me and Ryan making things with me, playing Play Doh and just making me giggle by pulling faces and doing silly things.

Harry then asked questions about my friends, my teachers and individual family members. He wanted to know if anyone had upset me, hurt me, or scared me. I couldn't think of anyone I was scared of in my life. They were all good to me. My brothers and dad protected me,

Mom tried to toughen me up, so I wasn't spoiled. I loved my friends and we had fun together, my teachers were nice. My grandparents were always kind and sweet, giving me presents and telling me silly stories and tales of when they were young. There was nothing bad to tell him. I then heard Harry say very quietly he would start the deep dive with me. I wondered what a deep dive meant but couldn't ask any questions from where I was. I could only answer them when asked.

He told me I was to imagine myself getting up out of the chair I was in and go to the far side of the room where I would see a door. He told me to describe it to him. I felt myself floating across the room towards the far wall. I saw an old, white painted door with two worn concrete steps and a silver handle appear. I told him what I could see, and he asked me to open the door and step inside. He said I would see a long corridor inside with doors on either side and I could pick any one I liked. I picked the first door on my right side, which looked like my bedroom door but without my name on it.

I mentally opened the door and went through, closing it behind me. Harry told me I was nine years old behind that door and asked me to tell him everything I saw there. I was confused at first and couldn't speak to him at that moment. I am nine now I know, but this was a different nine and what was in front of me wasn't clear at all. It was like looking through thick fog. I was trying to see and describe what I saw, but I was also trying to make sense of it all in my mind first and so couldn't say anything. The fog was clearing but I still couldn't see any clear details, then the foggy images in front of me finally lifted, like the tuning was at last correct.

And then I was the other me.

DAVID

WHATEVER WAS MEANT to happen appeared not to be working. After an awfully long period of absolute silence from Chloe, I thought we might as well wake her up and go home. It was disappointing, but I was secretly pleased, as my nerves were jangling, and I was wary of what she would say. If we left now, we could catch up with the others and spend the day sightseeing with them. I got up and moved towards Harry to talk to him, but Harry held his hand up to stop me and motioned for me to sit down. After what seemed like an eternity, Chloe began to quietly speak, and I looked at Harry totally surprised. I hadn't been sure what to expect from this session, but it was a shock. This wasn't my daughter speaking.

19

OVERWHELMING SADNESS

Once things became clear, I started to tell him what I could see, and he told me to speak in English, not French, which I did. I knew I was living in France with my mother, Elise, who was French and my father, Kurt, who was German. The man asked me what my name was, and I told him.

"Yvette Baumann."

I knew we had a small farm, that it was quite a long way from the nearest village. I collected eggs, helped with the animals, and had lots of chores to do on the farm. He asked me to describe myself to him as if I were looking in a mirror. I told him I was thin, had blond hair tied in a long plait, and had blue eyes, just like my father's and I was wearing grey dungarees. I could speak German, as my father had taught me at home, and French, as my mother was French, and we spoke that most. I described the farm and told him about the farmhouse we lived in. It was an old white building with small windows and wide ledges. It had a small kitchen with a fire in it, where my mother cooked, and there were two bedrooms, one for my parents and a tiny one for me. I had a small bed, a chair, and string tied up between the walls for me to hang my clothes on.

I didn't have any brothers or sisters, and it was lonely, as we lived quite a way from any neighbouring farms. I went to school as often as they could get me there. The house had a large barn and fields and trees around it. There was a large fast flowing river running nearby, with small deep still areas where my father had trained me to swim well because he didn't want me to drown if I ever fell in.

I remembered hearing my parents talking about the farm not making enough money. My father said because he was German, people didn't want to buy their goods. This made my mother sad, and I could hear her crying about it when I was in bed, which upset me.

Harry told me to move on to the next major event in my life. I remembered my parents were poorer now and were in debt. We survived on truly little. Local French people didn't like my father; I was teased about that by other children at school. He wasn't the most talkative man, and he was German and so they didn't come to his farm for their supplies. Our home was always such a sad one. We ate in silence, we lived in silence, apart from the rare conversation about the farm and money.

One evening, my mother asked me to fetch my father for dinner and I went to the barn to look for him. I opened the large, heavy barn door with a real struggle, and went in. It was dark and difficult to see. There were shafts of evening light coming through loose wooden slats in the walls which gave a tiny bit of light, but I couldn't see clearly. I could hear a creaking noise and went further into the barn and stood still, trying to see my father. I called out to him, but there was no reply. I felt something dripping on my head and could hear the rhythmic, creaking noise coming from above me. I looked up, and saw my father hanging from a beam, his body swinging gently back and forth with the rope making a rhythmic noise against the wood. His mouth was open, his tongue hanging out and his eyes were open and glazed. As I looked up, his urine dripped from the leg of his trousers onto my face.

Shock, horror, and grief overwhelmed me. My body stiffened and I screamed. Harry's voice cut through my distress, soothingly telling me to move on and my life rushed by extremely fast in different scenes, too quick for me to recognize anything. I was told I was now eleven years old and felt myself relax again, the bad memory fading away.

I could hear two men talking in a hushed tone around me with a final word "continue" and then Harry said to just tell him freely about my life from that moment. I then became the older me. I began to tell him my story.

I was now Yvette.

20

BREAKING THE FLAME

I was eleven when we had to sell the farm and land to pay off our debts. We were living in a small, rented flat in the northwest suburbs of Paris. My mother worked in a factory, and I went to school for a few hours each day. I felt distant from the other children, having lived in a mostly isolated environment in the country. We were living in poverty, like everyone else around us. Food and clothes were hard to afford, and I learned to live without things and without complaining, as I knew my mother was struggling hard to help us survive. I took to reading anything I could get my hands on to make up for the lack of schooling and to fill any spare time.

We'd been struggling for two years when my mother met an Englishman, Alfred Bradshaw, or Alfie as he liked to be called. They'd met while Alfie, a long-haul driver, was transporting equipment back and forth from the factory my mother worked at near Paris, to England. Alfie was a widower and lived with his son Gary. He started taking my mother on dates when he had a pick-up or delivery in France, leaving me alone in the flat, sometimes overnight.

When she dressed up, did her hair, and put makeup on, my mother looked so young and beautiful. I hadn't ever seen her like that before; she always looked so sad, old, and tired when we lived at the farm. He proposed to my mother, and she said yes. He wanted to take us both to England to live with him and his son Gary. I had then just turned thirteen years old. My mother was happy to accept his proposal and took great pains to explain to me that she was doing this for our future and security.

"We'll be much better off in England, Yvette. You can have nice things bought for you if we go, not the rags we're wearing. He has a respectable job and enough money to give us a good life and we will be safer there. Just think, you'll be able to go to an English school and learn English. Oh, Yvette, I really think we should go, but this is for both of us and if you really don't want us to go, then we won't. It's up to you, my darling."

I looked at her sweet expectant face and knew how happy she'd been for the first time since I could remember. I couldn't spoil that for her and so I agreed. After they married, we moved, with our pitifully few possessions, to Alfie's small, dingy, and dismal, three-bedroom terraced house in East London, near the docks. I was now Yvette Bradshaw.

∼

ALFIE'S SON, Gary, was older than me and was a large built youth. I disliked him from the moment we met. He always made sure his body pressed against mine as we passed each other in doorways or on the stairs. He sat next to me at mealtimes and when we sat on the settee, he kept his thigh tight against mine, making suggestive remarks, which my mother either couldn't hear or understand. I hated it but knew I mustn't complain, or our very security would be put at risk. I took to sleeping with a brick balanced behind my bedroom door every night, so I would wake up if he came in. I didn't like the atmosphere in the house; I didn't like my stepfather or stepbrother and lived under a feeling of threat. For my mother's sake I endured it silently, but I longed to be back in France in our old life on our farm, poor but safe.

Alfie was a bully and once we'd moved to England with him, his personality changed from the kindly, polite man, to a controlling, foul mouthed bully. He called mother Leese, not her lovely name Elise. He quit his driving job, not liking the travelling anymore, and worked as a foreman at a factory near the docks.

Alfie drank a lot and was a vile man, abusive to both my mother and me, even more so when drunk. Because of his drinking, money was always tight. He didn't like us speaking French and demanded we speak English all the time. I had to practice over and over in order to lose my French German accent to satisfy him. He thought nothing of slapping me around my head if I sounded at all French when speaking, and as a result I spoke less and less but learned English very quickly. He called me Eve not Yvette because it sounded less "foreign" and he hated the fact my father was German, or a Kraut as he called him. He viciously teased me, saying a dead Kraut was better than a live one at least. My mother did her best to comply with changing her accent, but her English wasn't that good, and she suffered abuse because of that when he was drunk. She was much more accepting of his faults than I.

To help with money, my mother took in laundry. She was also a cleaner in a large house in central London. She did what she could to keep us fed and clothed, but what came in the house was invariably spent on alcohol, cigarettes, and the odd gamble at the dogs. Apart from any money my mother could hide from him.

Alfie hit my mother and when I tried to stop it, I got hit as well. My schooling suffered because of our home life, and I felt on edge and jumpy most of the time. Thankfully, Gary got a job up North and moved out of the house, which should have eased the stress for me at home, but Alfie then rented Gary's room to transient workmates, dockers and ship workers, and a string of men ended up staying at the house for short periods.

I was used to seeing different men, with different accents, appear on the landing or at the breakfast or dinner table, and kept up the placing of a brick behind my door as a result. I never slept easily.

I managed to get a Saturday job when I was fourteen, at the local chippie, to help with money. I hated the smell of boiling fat and my clothes and hair stunk of it, but the free fish and chips which were left over for me to take home at the end of the day was a bonus.

I COULDN'T REMEMBER a time when I smiled or laughed. There was little to smile or laugh about in my life up until that point. I was such a serious girl who kept to herself and didn't make friends easily. I jealously watched from afar as girls my age flirted with boys and entered and ended relationships with ease. I had a list of chores after school as well as my job on Saturdays and so didn't have much spare time. Alfie didn't like me bringing anyone to the house either, not that I ever wanted to. I had no money left of my own once I had given my mother my wages to keep us afloat. Friends were not that easy to come by in my situation and I learned to be alone, reading anything I could find to occupy myself.

I was extremely mistrusting of people. I'd built an emotional shield around myself for protection, having been battered by life so far. I had hopes and dreams, which I kept to myself, but I couldn't see them ever being fulfilled in the life I was in. My future looked bleak. My mother became more sociable than she had been and now had several friends of her own amongst the neighbours. She embraced life as best she could, making the most of any opportunity that came her way. She had also acquired a taste for alcohol and was drinking more than she ever had. I assumed it was to numb the pain of life with Alfie. With her work and going out with her friends, I hardly ever saw her.

She met a nice French woman who had moved into a place a few streets away from us; Nancy Devereaux. Alfie tolerated her in the house as she usually brought some gift when she came. She knew there had to be some payment to allow her to visit her friend, and she, like mother, complied with speaking English until he was out of the house. She was an excellent seamstress and taught mother the same skill, so she could make more money for herself and clothes for us. I was now working full time at the chippie and Alfie then insisted I paid full rent for my room and board.

Nancy had a son, Ethan, who was older than me, and he started coming to the house with his mother. Alfie liked Ethan, as he was good at fixing things around the house. He also brought supplies of cigarettes with him. Ethan was aware he too had to ease his path into our house with gifts for Alfie. He'd replaced Gary as male companionship for Alfie to go for a pint with, which left the women alone at home to speak French and discuss Alfie's many failings and the France they loved.

I knew Ethan had feelings for me, which was why I thought he visited so often when not at work, but I really didn't feel the same. He was a genuinely nice man, kind, reasonably good looking, quite intense in his political views, but I wasn't in love, as I'd expected love to be. This was not the heart racing, magical, breathless romance I'd hoped for, read about, or dreamed of. Both our mothers had been matchmaking for a while, eager for us to get engaged. A marriage would cement the two families and the thought excited them tremendously.

ENGLAND AND FRANCE were now at war with Germany, both our mothers were desperately upset and fearful for France. That, however, didn't detract from their plans for Ethan and me. We were encouraged to go out on dates, and it dawned on me that this was destined to be a practical, safe, down-to-earth match-made relationship. I saw how happy my mother and Nancy were about a marriage, and against my better judgement and to my eternal shame and regret, I went along with it when Ethan proposed.

I presumed he loved me, and he treated me respectfully and well, taking me out and protecting me against Alfie's abuse. I was caught up in our mother's excitement, with talk of wedding dresses and cakes. I didn't want to upset anyone or let anyone down. *Perhaps this is love anyway*, I thought to myself. *It's what people eventually accept in real life when they realise that the fairy tale love you read about in books doesn't exist.*

Alfie was ecstatic at the prospect of a marriage, he would now have Ethan on tap if we lived nearby. He could still rent out my room to one of the dockers once I followed Gary out the door. All Alfie's Christmases had come at once.

Just as the war with Germany became more intense and bombs were dropping on England, we got married in a small ceremony. I was now almost nineteen, and Ethan was twenty-seven years old. I had the most beautiful lace wedding dress and veil made by the two seamstresses, but that couldn't make up for the feeling of deflation and disappointment festering deep inside me. In the absence of my real father, Alfie gave me away at the wedding in a manner that made me feel like a piece of property, owned by one man to be handed over to another. I was now Yvette Devereaux.

21

A MIX OF MARRIAGE AND WAR

We rented a small, terraced house near our respective mothers and started our married life. I found a part-time job in a local grocery store Monday to Thursday, and worked at the chippie Friday and Saturday as shops could only open certain days of the week because of rationing. Ethan continued working for his engineering company and began travelling with his job a few months after we got married. He was gone for long periods of time leaving me alone, and I filled my time working and supporting our mothers. He explained that because of the German bombing, his engineering skills were needed all over the country and he had to go where he was ordered to, usually where areas had been severely damaged.

He just wanted the war to end and for us to be safe. He was fearful for what was happening in France, now occupied by the Germans. But soon he became different, and when he came home each time after that he rarely discussed the war in detail, preferring to spend time on frivolous outings together. On one occasion he came home with a large amount of severe bruising on his face, arms, and body, explaining to me that he'd suffered an accident at work. He didn't want to talk about it, brushing off any questions, laughing and saying he was fine and for me not to worry.

Each time after that when he came home, he was even more distant, and we spoke less. When we did talk to each other it was mostly superficial pleasantries about family and friends, and he was guarded in what he said. Starting a family was out of the question for us at that time. I wondered then, if like me, he'd been press ganged into marriage by our respective mothers and was now regretting it. He was affectionate towards me but at times seemed to want to tell me something but couldn't. He told me he loved me, and I had no actual reason to doubt that, and in my own way I loved him too, but I was not in love with him. He was a good man, solid, kind, generous, and sweet, but I respected him more than loved him. He promised me things would be different after the war, when he no longer had to travel so much. We could go to live in France and start a family, move to the country, and live our lives in peace. Until then he said he had to use his engineering skills to repair and rebuild where bombing had taken place.

That made me feel so selfish, accepting his long absences was a sacrifice I had to make and shouldn't complain. He was good to both our mothers, who doted on him. He always made sure I had money and once he gave me an extra ration book for me and mother to use—God knows how, they were like gold dust and so restricted.

He was doing his level best to be a good husband, despite his absences, and I in turn did my best as his wife. The brief times he was home, his meals were on time, his clothes washed and pressed, and our marital bed was warm and welcoming, but he was seldom in it. I knew something else was on his mind when he was at home, but I wasn't sure what. He couldn't settle or be truly close to me and had difficulty sleeping. I tried talking to him about it a few times, but he just brushed off my concerns, telling me it was just the war, it was having terrible effects on everyone. I mulled over the possibility of him having an affair and had found a true passionate love with another woman while he was away working. He had the opportunity, and the justification and I was prepared for an announcement from him about that, but it never came.

THE WAR WAS in full cry by then—bombs were dropping on Britain in huge numbers, air raid shelters had sprung up in large building basements and underground stations, with smaller bomb shelters dug out and fashioned in back gardens. Barrage balloons flew high over London, sandbags were piled up against buildings and glass windows were taped up for safety. We heard sirens most days, and everyone was conditioned to run for cover carrying their gas mask when they heard it. Neighbours who had been sworn enemies and confrontational with each other, forgot their differences as they rallied in their efforts to "win the war." The blackout was in full force with an army of bossy wardens ready to shout at you if you didn't comply with it. Several times in our street I heard ferocious banging on doors and men shouting. "Put that bloody light out."

Several streets near us had already been bombed, and I was terrified being in the East End of London near the docks, where most of the bombing appeared to be targeted, and searchlights were active almost every night. I was eager to discuss this with Ethan when he returned. I wanted to know if there was anywhere at all we could go to be away from the deadly bombing raids. Maybe we could rent somewhere out in the country and take our mothers with us.

Ethan had been gone now for about eight weeks, the longest he'd ever been away from me in the time we'd been married. I hadn't heard from him apart from brief bland letters that said he was well, but terribly busy working long hours and weekends. He hoped I was well, and our mothers were well, and he would be home soon. I was looking forward to him being home, I was really missing his company and the outlet it gave me as he usually took me out and we spoke French together. I was becoming dreadfully lonely and even dreamt about him one night. I saw him standing alone in a field, near a river with a bridge. He looked so sad as he waved, turned, and walked away.

Christmas was coming and I'd received a pretty card from him that morning, so I knew he was well. I hoped he would at least be home for Christmas.

22

A WAR CASUALTY

One afternoon, a couple of days before Christmas, I was at my house with my mother. The place was small and barely furnished, but I'd tried to make it look welcoming for when Ethan returned. I'd put up handmade decorations, bought a cheap tree and picked holly for the mantelpiece. Ethan's mother had made the most beautiful handmade blue dress for me, as a present, which my mother had just delivered. I was admiring it when a knock came at the door. I answered it to find a well-dressed man I didn't know standing there. He was tall, clean-shaven, and looked to be in his late forties. He had a large dark overcoat on and lifted his hat saying he was from the War Office. He asked to speak to me inside. I was very confused, and a bit flustered, but invited him in and introduced him to Mother. He gave his name as Donald Peterson, as he sat down, put his hat on his lap, and declined the tea he was offered.

"I'm very sorry," he said solemnly, and my mind raced as to what this could be about. "I hate to be the bearer of bad news."

I was stood near Mother's chair, and he asked me to sit down and prepare myself, I was completely bewildered.

"Ethan was working as an engineer for us; there was a ferocious bombing raid in the area he was working in, and sadly he has been killed." He let that sink in and then said: "I hate having to tell you this, especially at this time of year."

I was shocked, my mind was spinning with what could have happened. My mother was hysterical. I then thought about what he'd said and was confused.

"How could he possibly have been killed? He was a civilian engineer, working up north in areas that had been bombed, so why are you from the War Office?"

"Ethan was killed in a bombing raid in Hull while his company was doing some engineering work for the government. We are certain it's Ethan who has died," he said.

He let me digest the news again, then watched as I began speaking fluent French to my mother to calm her down. She was crying and distraught. I was shocked but more composed, practical, and rational about the news, and could feel Peterson watching me and listening closely, to the point I felt uncomfortable. He gave me time to calm Mother down and then told me there was paperwork for me to fill out for pension payments and other payments due to me. There were also items I needed to collect. He gave me a card with an address written on it where I was to go for an appointment in two weeks' time in the New Year.

I was told to ask for a Colonel Steadman when I got there, as he was dealing with Ethan's effects. I could discuss all of this with him in more detail when I went to sign the documents.

He informed me gently that the memorial service would be paid for by his office. "Due to the extent of the explosion, there would just be a memorial service, no funeral as such."

This set mother off again, wailing and crying. Mr. Peterson was obviously uncomfortable with the female emotional outburst he had initiated. He again apologised for being the bearer of such sad news, deftly put on his hat and left. He left me confused, reeling from his message, and trying to console my terribly upset mother.

I had dreadfully mixed emotions. I was shaken and upset about poor Ethan. I hoped his death was quick, and that he wasn't aware of any of it. I felt for both our mothers' grief, which would be hard for them to bear, and the fact Ethan was gone would mean Alfie back to his abusive best. But I also believed deep inside I'd been legitimately freed from my marriage by this turn of events. I then felt such terrible guilt, shame, and remorse at my sheer selfish unkind thoughts.

"I'm so sorry, Ethan, we didn't really ever stand a chance," I said quietly, as I stood in the kitchen making tea for my mother.

TELLING NANCY about the death of her only son was the hardest thing I'd ever had to do; it was heartbreakingly sad, and I wondered if she would ever get over the shock. After the memorial service, I realised I couldn't afford to keep the rental house going by myself and moved back in with Mother and Alfie. A practical, necessary decision I wasn't thrilled about, but it made sense and I could keep an eye on my mother. Alfie wouldn't move out of London and my mother wouldn't go without him and so I felt I had to stay too. Alfie rented Gary's room to one of his workmates who was there, but the person renting my old room had left and so I moved back in. He told me gleefully I was to pay the increased rental rate for my room.

"Times are hard," he said.

WHEN I ARRIVED at the address in London I'd been given by Peterson, I found myself standing outside a rather bland-looking building. I wondered whether I'd got the address right. It didn't look like a War Office. I went into the reception area and gave my name and asked for Colonel Martin Steadman. I was led in silence to Steadman's office on the second floor and he met me at his door. He was a tall, thin, athletic looking man with a strict military air about him. His hair was short, and his eyes were what I could only describe as focussed. He invited me in and offered me a seat at his large desk.

The room was small and musty smelling, the ceiling quite high, and the furniture was large and made from dark wood which overpowered the room. There was an impressive bookcase with thick volumes of books, and a large window giving much-needed light. He said how sorry he was about Ethan and gave his condolences about his death, but it appeared this was a routine thing he had to say, rather than meaning it. He was quite business-like and gave me a file of papers to read and sign.

I read them briefly, seeing they contained pension payment details and Ethan's last will and testament. I realised quite quickly that it wouldn't be much money. It then dawned on me how organised and practical all of this seemed. Ethan was a young man, an engineer, with his whole life ahead of him, and yet had completed a last will and testament. *Perhaps all workers are asked to do that now we were at war.*

I signed everything I was asked to and started getting ready to leave, when Steadman came around from his desk and stood in front of me. He looked intensely at me as his business-like, efficient demeanour melted to a much warmer friendlier manner.

"It must be difficult for you, my dear, being widowed at such a young age. I would like to help you if I can. There's a possibility of a much better paying job than the one you currently may have. It would suit your skills and I would really like you to think about it."

I was quite taken aback, and it must have shown because he smiled at me reassuringly.

"I understand from my colleagues that you speak French and German fluently and we may have a position for you to help in the war effort if you feel you could work with us in this type of special employment. How would you feel about that?"

He must have seen the immediate flash of interest in my eyes; as a knowing look came over his face, as if a hunch he held was right. He didn't really give me time to answer his question but continued to talk to me, not really pushing too hard for confirmation right away. It was like he was fishing, dangling bait in front of me, reeling my interest in. I wasn't sure this was the most appropriate time for this conversation, having just received my newly dead husband's effects, but it certainly sparked my interest.

I was puzzled at first as to how he knew I could speak French and German, but then realised Peterson must have told him about the conversation in French I had with my mother. Maybe Ethan had told someone he worked with from the government about me having a German father and speaking German and that was how they knew. I suppose they had to keep an eye on things like that now we were at war with Germany, what with spies and whatnot.

"You don't have to decide now, my dear. Think it over and come back to see me on Friday if you want to pursue it further." He paused, looking at my face intensely. "There will obviously be training for this special employment if you take it," he said. "I would be grateful if you didn't mention this offer to anyone at this time if you don't mind."

I really didn't know what to think or say at that moment but agreed not to say anything about it. It was all so unexpected. He walked me down the stairs to the reception area, said farewell, turned on his heels, and walked smartly back up. I started my journey home and was walking toward the nearest tube station, past huge piles of sandbags, when the air raid siren sounded. I was pushed along to Baker Street tube station by the fast-moving crowd and sat underground while bombs rained down on London above. The bombing was quite intense and close this time. You could hear the droning of the aircraft overhead and the terrifying whistling sound, indicating a bomb had been dropped and was falling to earth. Everyone braced for the explosions.

When one fell nearby, the place rattled and dust and debris dropped down from the ceiling, causing people to jump and scream. Young children were crying, older people praying. Mothers clutched their babies close to them. Couples clung together waiting for what might be the bomb that ends it all. I felt so terribly sad for them all having to endure this, yet I was strangely detached from it as I thought about the wider war effort. With this job offer from Steadman I could be trained to do something useful, like a translating secretary. It would mean more money to support my mother and myself too. From that moment on I mulled over Steadman's offer until the appointment day, not discussing it with anyone.

23

WALKING INTO THE UNKNOWN

T he day of the expected decision about Steadman's offer arrived and I made my way nervously to the appointment. I stood on the opposite side of the road to the building, hesitating, still questioning as to whether I was doing the right thing. Working in a grocery store and a chip shop didn't exactly prepare you for much in life. I knew I was observant and had a good memory. I never forgot a face; I'd always been aware of that and could recall the most trivial of details and conversations, being more of a listener than a talker due to Alfie's brutal training. I could speak fluent French and German but had little else to offer. I couldn't type or do shorthand, which must be needed for secretarial work, and would need training on that.

I paced up and down the pavement a few times and then returned to the original spot opposite the building. I wanted very much to do something worthwhile, but the nagging doubts continued as they had done since the offer was made. I could walk away now, and settle for what I had, or embark on this new path that had presented itself. No-one but me would know. One door had shut, and another was opening tantalisingly before me, with the promise of something better. Torn, I stood opposite the building weighing up my options.

My appointment time was ten o'clock. At that exact time, another scene was playing out inside the building in front of me, although I was oblivious to it until much, much later.

STEADMAN

I was with Sergeant Adrian Jones, Sergeant James Hopkins, and Sergeant Paul Stapleton, watching Ethan Devereaux's widow from the second-floor office window. Each one of us summing her up and awaiting her decision as she paced up and down the pavement.

"We need female recruits like her," Sergeant Jones said. "Dual language, pretty." I agreed with him.

"Ethan told me she was perfect. He believed she would be a good asset and said he'd try and broach the subject with her after his next mission when he returned home. But..."

"Too bad we lost him," Stapleton said. "Ethan Devereaux was an exceptional agent. Able to speak both English and French, he had such good engineering and explosive skills too."

"His sacrifice saved many lives," I reminded the group. "She can't know that Ethan was working for us just yet, it might frighten her off knowing he has been killed doing it. We will have to tell her at some point."

Because he had engineering skills, Ethan had been sent to France to join a circuit working on the sabotage of buildings and railway lines in Lille, to disrupt German advances. On the second mission he was attacked as he parachuted in.

The group he worked with had been infiltrated, and the Germans were waiting. The French reception committee had tried to fight their way out, but were killed and Ethan, gravely wounded, had taken a suicide pill rather than be captured and tortured into giving away vital information.

"Young male agents are too easy to spot in France these days as most young French men have been called up," Sergeant Hopkins said. "Women are usually not working and wouldn't have to explain why they were not in military service. It's not unusual for them to be carrying handbags and shopping bags, she would be less likely to be stopped by the Germans when acting as a courier."

Sergeant Stapleton added. "Now that Ethan is gone, she only has her mother to worry about. There are no children I'm told. But I'm concerned she may be too young. If you ask me, she doesn't look robust enough for the sort of work she'd be expected to carry out. It's unlikely she'll even pass the physical training."

"I want her on board, Paul," I said. "Let's give her a chance. I trust Ethan's judgement about her, he thought she would be a good asset, put her through her paces in the training to test her."

Just as ten o'clock was about to strike, Hopkins said, "Look. Here she comes."

We were all gathered at the window and watched as Yvette Devereaux walked hesitantly across the road, and I couldn't hide the smile spreading across my face.

YVETTE

When I entered the building and spoke to the receptionist, I was redirected to an address further along the Street down a side road. Once there, an older man in a suit greeted me warmly and took me in a lift to the second floor, then along numerous corridors to what was basically a small flat. We walked along the corridor and glancing to my right into one of the rooms, I saw an odd black tiled bathroom. He asked me to make myself comfortable in the living room and told me someone would be with me shortly. The flat was decorated with heavy curtains and deep green settees. Steadman then entered and started talking rapidly, and in a matter-of-fact way about my future position.

"Firstly, you will need to be recruited into the First Aid Nursing Yeomanry, or FANYs, as a basic requirement for your job. You will go through an initial three weeks of basic assessment, training, and interviews to see what job we can best match you to for the war effort. You will of course need to sign an official secrecy agreement, as you will have sight of confidential information. I'm going to hand you over to one of our senior intelligence officers now who will fill in all the practicalities for you. Thank you for doing this, Yvette."

It was all so quick. I hadn't been able to ask any questions at all, and I had quite a few swimming around in my head. It was as if I was only allowed to know so much. After he left, a dark haired, smartly dressed woman in a suit came in, introduced herself as Patricia Ashcroft and started filling in the practical details, again leaving little chance for questions. She was warm and extremely organised and seemed eager to ensure the meeting was as easy as possible for me.

"Here is a list of what you need to take with you for your assessment and training Yvette," she said. "The assessment you will undergo is both practical and physical and this is where you have to report." She handed me a slip of paper. "You need to be fitted with a FANY uniform and you can go after our meeting to this local store that supplies them for us. Here's the chitty you need for that. Have you thought about what you will tell your mother about your three-week absence from home?" Totally bewildered, I hesitated, so she continued.

"Think of a basic cover story for the reason you'll be away. You mustn't arouse any suspicion that you will be working for the War Office. No one is to know, as it is paramount that your work is kept strictly confidential. Tell your mother you have joined the women's yeomanry. That will explain the uniform and the training. You will be paid for your time on the assessment. Do you have any current money worries or any other issues that need attention?"

I just shook my head, baffled, thinking they knew absolutely nothing about me at all, and yet were taking me on and talking openly to me about possible secret information. I didn't know at the time, but a full detailed security background check had already been carried out on me by MI5. They knew absolutely everything about me.

"Could you tell me some more about the job?" I asked.

"You will be briefed more about it on the assessment. It is basically how we can best use your language skills for the war effort."

I signed all the appropriate papers for my new role, as ordered, but it seemed a bit involved for just a translator-secretary job. I guessed that was just what war did, made everyone nervous and defensive about information. "Even the walls have ears" posters were everywhere.

I told my mother I was joining the First Aid Nursing Yeomanry and would be wearing a uniform for work. The job I'd been offered was much better pay and a chance to learn new skills. She was worried, but I reassured her it wasn't dangerous, just secretarial work. I'd be gone for a while for the initial training and would send money home to her. She reluctantly accepted my decision but was visibly upset. Alfie told me I still had to send my weekly rent home while I was away if I wanted to keep my room, as they couldn't afford to keep it empty.

"Times are hard," he reminded me for the hundredth time.

24

THE FLEDGLING RECRUIT

I t was bitterly cold, and I was well wrapped up against the snowy conditions in a thick old coat, scarf, and gloves. I travelled first by train, then bus, and then after a short walk was stopped at the entrance to the drive of the address I'd been given. The man checked my basic appointment letter and let me pass through. After a walk up a tree lined private drive, I arrived at an enormous, impressive looking, red brick country house. I was met by a man in uniform who showed me into a huge reception area. It looked awfully expensive to be holding a secretarial training course. It had ornate cornice around the edges of the ceiling, a huge chandelier dangling from the centre, and beautiful black and red mosaic floor tiling. I was led up a large, winding staircase with a deep red carpet, and then along a corridor into a bedroom to drop off my suitcase. I was instructed to report downstairs in an hour.

My bedroom was small and basic; the furnishings looked solid and incredibly old. The view of the gardens from the window, however, was stunningly beautiful and so peaceful looking, with its dusting of snow. The building was very private, being nestled in extensive wooded grounds away from any prying eyes. The curtains were heavy and lined and I sat on the firm bed, checking what else was in the room. There was a small fireplace with a black, and rich red tiled surround with a small mantlepiece above, a dark red wood chest of drawers, a desk, wardrobe, and a sink with a mirror above it, nothing personal or feminine at all. I unpacked my things and made my way back down the wide impressive staircase to the reception area. I passed under the incredible chandelier again, that twinkled with the light streaming through it. It did seem so out of place for a training facility.

The man who had initially welcomed me to the house came into the reception area and pointed his arm to guide me to the room I was to go to.

When I entered, I was slightly taken aback to be met by the stares of a large group of other people, who were also there for the assessment process. I really wasn't expecting this as a large group exercise. The room had an expensive air about it with its dark wood panelling, high decorative ceiling, and large windows with thick drapes. It had been adapted for the training, with long trestle tables and chairs set out. I took a seat near the back and waited quietly. Some people were chatting; others like me just sat and observed in anticipation of what was to come.

After a few moments, three uniformed men walked into the room, and everyone stood up. They introduced them-selves as Sergeant Hopkins, Sergeant Jones, and a senior officer Major Hammond.

The Sergeants talked about the process and tests we would be put through, both physical and psychological. After which we would be told if we could proceed or not. I was totally perplexed, and as they spoke further it dawned on me this wasn't simply basic training for being a translator or secretary as I had thought; this was a much more secretive complex role than Steadman had given the impression I was to undertake.

We were informed we couldn't leave the grounds during the course, and had to hand over any identity documents, cameras, and money. All mail would be censored, and no use of the telephone was allowed without permission. I was intrigued and excited, but I had the feeling they must have made a terrible mistake and sent me to the wrong place. I glanced around at all the others, who looked as if they were expecting this. I decided to keep quiet for now and just see how things developed, thinking they would soon notice they had made an error and cart me off somewhere else. I wondered if I'd missed something when Steadman or the intelligence officer spoke to me about this job. I recall they both mentioned "special employment for the war effort," whatever they meant by that. It could be that he and the intelligence officer assumed the other had filled me in on more details than they had. I then realised I didn't recall either of them ever mentioning secretarial work at all, that was what I had envisaged myself.

Hammond introduced himself and explained in general terms why we were there. That we had skills which could be utilised for the war effort. He told us we might end up working in different areas, depending on our assessments and our individual skills. I thought now might be a good time to say there may have been a mistake and was nervously about to raise my hand. But then thought it hadn't been a mistake at all, and this was Steadman's plan for me all along, this was the special employment. He must have assessed I wouldn't bolt once I knew what the training was. I kept quiet.

Once Hammond had given as full an explanation of our roles as he could, within the limits of his security brief he'd said, he informed us about the associated rules we must abide by. This included to trust no-one and never, ever acknowledge people from the training we might meet outside the facility in any capacity.

After he left, Sergeants Jones and Hopkins collected and bagged up our handed-in possessions. Both sergeants were consummate military professionals, both around mid-to-late-thirties and appeared to have a remarkably close bond with each other. They were about six feet tall, clean-shaven, and wearing immaculate uniforms. They'd been brought in to get us recruits physically fit and able to handle ourselves effectively for our future roles, whatever those were. They both looked as if they wouldn't stand for any nonsense from anyone. I had to admit I was a bit in awe of them.

We were each given a sheet of paper and asked to write down any phobias, illnesses, or any other issue that the team should be aware of before we took the first test. I had a mild fear of heights, but wrote nothing down on my sheet, in case it hindered my chances. We then had to report to a numbered room when we were called and hand in our completed paper.

I was in the second group called and entered a small, musty study, where a kindly looking older man in a tweed suit greeted me and invited me to sit down. He was sitting in a large deep red armchair, smoking a pipe. He looked jolly relaxed with his legs crossed, showing a hint of darned socks. He took my blank paper from me and asked me detailed questions about my personal life, past and present. I was very guarded in my answers but gave him enough to satisfy his questions. He asked me to complete written verbal reasoning questions and tested me on word association. He said one word and I had to say the first thing that came into my mind. I was shown pictures of different black shapes and asked what I thought they represented.

I only faltered once when I was asked what my happiest moment in life had been. I honestly couldn't think of one and had to really think hard before I came up with an answer that might fit—my wedding day. I noticed he made quite a few notes after that hesitant answer. Once that was over, I returned to the main room where the recruits mingled and chatted nervously with each other, all strangers flung together in this maelstrom of secrecy.

We had to have a meeting with a senior officer over the first few days. The officer I met introduced himself as Captain George Westmacott. He was a big burly man with an air of strong, solid military background about him. On this first meeting he was very pleasant to me, but I was still very wary of what I was getting myself into. He questioned me about Ethan and again I gave nothing important away. I kept my answers brief, being cautious and reflective. He asked what skills I felt I could bring to the organisation, and I mentioned my ability to speak both French and German, at which stage he asked that we speak totally in French together.

He asked probing questions about my motive for being there, my background in France, my German father and especially how I felt about the war and the German occupation. It was quite intense questioning about that, almost interrogating me for any discrepancies or weakness in my answers or character. I spent about an hour with him and summed him up as someone who liked women—his gaze and demeanour gave that away—but thought involving them in war was not a good idea; he was a man's man. Men were for war and women could do their bit by keeping the home fires burning. He likely had a wife and daughters, respecting women's equality to a point, but he tolerated women in the training programme not because he wanted to, but because he had been ordered to.

$\sim$

ONCE EVERYONE HAD UNDERGONE their meeting, we were gathered back in the main room. One of the other women, Valerie Cathcart, walked up to me to talk. She was attractive, in her thirties, with dark blonde hair and sharp well-made-up features. She was immaculately and fashionably dressed. I felt quite frumpy next to her, and to the rest of the women to be honest, as I was in my old everyday clothes, a skirt, blouse, cardigan, flat shoes, and no make-up. She asked about the interview I'd just had, but I was guarded in every-thing I said.

I wasn't one for social chitchat. I wasn't particularly good at it for one thing. I preferred to keep to myself but thought I should look as if I was taking an interest. I asked Valerie general questions about her life and then ran out of small talk. She told me all about her family, being brought up by her grandparents after her parents died, and what work she used to do before being invited to join this group. She could speak French as she had been taught at private boarding schools in France and Switzerland. As she was talking, I noted out of the corner of my eye that one of the male recruits was being quite loud and vocal about the process we were in. He was ghastly, and full of himself, with an air of upper-class superiority, as if this process were beneath him and he should just be accepted because of his family name. I took an immediate dislike to him.

Valerie continued talking to me about trivia, which I

acknowledged politely with a nod and a smile, not really interested. She seemed to want to be friends with me, but I was less than forthcoming in response. She eventually got fed up and left, telling me she should really go and mingle with everyone. I watched as she approached a couple of men and was quite flirty with them and they were flirting back like mad.

Another of the women recruits, who said her name was Audrey Turner came to chat and appeared particularly nervous and fiddled with her hair a lot. Another female recruit, Stella Wilkinson, was very bold and brassy as if nothing could faze her, and there was Alice Brewerton, who appeared much more socially elevated than the rest of us, and extremely confident. I just watched the others, smiled when necessary, and with difficulty made small talk as best I could.

In the short time I'd been there I had summed them all up by watching their interactions with each other. I knew about their previous jobs and their life histories by listening to fragments of their conversations. There was a mixture of backgrounds and ages represented: the old schoolboy network was well represented, but there were also engineers, servicemen, shockingly even a criminal element had been recruited. There were civil servants, electricians, housewives, policemen and refugees from other countries under German occupation. I was intrigued but had no burning desire to be close to any one of them during those first few days. Feeling a bit overwhelmed by it all, I sought solace in my room at every opportunity.

∽

AFTER MORE PAPERWORK and written tests, we were taken on a tour of the house and immediate grounds, the estate appeared vast. They showed us the temporary admin and supply huts where we could get any extra uniforms or equipment. Once we were released for the day, I went for a long walk around the grounds to see how far the boundaries to the estate went, and to enjoy the feeling of being in the countryside, alone. There were acres and acres of land, too vast for me to walk it all, with fields, small hilly areas, woods, a river, and ponds. It was quite crisp and cold but exhilarating to be walking through the grounds, my footsteps imprinted on the untouched snow.

Next morning as we gathered in the main room, Hammond entered along with the two sergeants. He informed us we had gone through the initial testing and then called out the names of two men and two women. They called the name of the loud man and another noticeably quiet older French man who had seemed lost in the whole experience. Audrey, the nervous one, was also called along with another woman, who looked furious.

They were asked to stay where they were while the rest of us went for the next session. Those four had obviously not made the next stage following the psychological testing and interview, and we wouldn't see them again. Four down, I thought, and I felt such utter astonishment and relief that I wasn't the first one booted off; anything else now was a bonus.

That afternoon we were given practical tests to do, working out how to make items out of bits and pieces of equipment we'd been given. We spent time looking for mistakes in written documents and were then asked to gather outside in front of the building. It was then a staged incident took place in front of us. I heard what sounded like real gunshots and shouting and then a group of men ran out from the side of the building towards the woods. They were followed by another man shouting in German for them to stop and more gun shots were fired. Everyone in the group jumped. I was shocked, but watched the scene play out, as did others. Some recruits hid behind their colleagues in fright, and one ran back into the building.

Once the incident was over, we were asked to return to the training room to answer questions about it. This was an observation test, and where I felt comfortable. I had good observational and memory skills from my years of watching people. I could describe it all as if in slow motion and answered the questions with ease.

Once everyone had settled down after that exercise, we were then given training uniforms and dismissed for the day. I went back to my room and thought over the day's events. This was a challenge, but I started to believe I could do this. I was awfully surprised I hadn't been the first one asked to leave. I then thought about the physical tests they had told us would start tomorrow, which I was dreading. I didn't think of myself as a particularly athletic person by any means and my confidence dipped. I was now certain I wasn't being trained as a secretary though, and secretly I was thrilled.

25

HATED CONFRONTATION

The first physical assessment was tough. It included a full obstacle course, a river swim, a three-mile run, sixty-foot climb and high rope walk, all over a three-day period. It was bitterly cold too. I managed them all but struggled on the obstacle course wall. The high rope walk terrified me too, but I refused to show it and no one observing me would have guessed I had a fear of heights. I clung on for dear life, praying as I did with every step, climbing gratefully back to earth, thanking God that I'd made it.

I used to swim in a river near our farm in France and was a very competent swimmer thanks to my father's intense training, so that test wasn't bad, just extremely cold, to the point my body was numb. As I sat on the bank of the river, trying to warm myself up with the flimsy blankets I'd been given, I saw my hair had icicles forming in it.

The next assessment was a group test. The main group was split into smaller ones, and all had the same mission to complete. We were shown items out of which we had to build a raft and get to the other side of a lake in the grounds.

We had to pick up a large box, plant an explosive device and get back across the lake as fast as possible with the large box. Every member of the team had to get back with the box for it to be successful. A man named Edward Cameron was named our group leader and I was extremely glad it wasn't me. I would hate to boss people around, especially men, who would just ignore me anyway. I preferred to work alone if possible. I did think we could just walk around the lake and collect the box, lay the explosive, and walk back but figured that wasn't the point of the exercise.

Cameron bossily gave us all orders of what items to pick up and what to attach where, to make a raft. Once it was built, I knew it wouldn't carry us all over and back. Unfortunately, I spoke up before I'd thought through any consequences and suggested maybe if we built it slightly differently and only half of us went on the raft and the others swam pushing it one way and swapped on the way back, that would give us a better chance. Cameron glared at me. He didn't like the challenge to his authority as leader, especially by a woman, and said crisply we were to stick to his plan.

He sidled up to me, out of earshot of everyone. "Just shut up and do as you're told. If you can't take orders, you shouldn't be here; just bugger off home and be a housewife."

I tried my level best to ignore him and just went quiet, hoping I was wrong, and he would be successful, which would lessen the impact of my intervention. As I feared, once the raft was fully laden and floated in the water it became unstable, broke apart, and we all ended up in the cold lake with the equipment floating about.

We returned to the bank unsuccessful failures, and from that moment, Cameron hated me with a passion. Sergeant Jones, having no idea what had gone on between us, asked the team to try again, with my plan. I really didn't want them to, as I already wished I hadn't spoken out. Unfortunately, when they tried my way, the raft was rickety but stable, and we were successful at dropping off the explosive and bringing the box back.

Cameron was utterly livid. He'd been humiliated in front of the sergeant and our small group and didn't like being outdone by anyone, let alone a woman. His contempt for me showed every time he looked at me or spoke to me after that.

I'd already noticed he talked over women when they were trying to organise things, indicating he thought they were stupid. He teamed up with another of the male recruits Bryan Garfield, who saw it as a bit of banter to tease the female recruits and make derogatory remarks to them, especially me. This behaviour was always done out of sight and earshot of the staff. In front of the officers, they were different people altogether.

The other females gave as good as they got and put the men down with humorous derogatory comments, scoring hit after hit to their male ego. Because of my upbringing, I couldn't respond like that. Instead, I retreated further into myself, and eventually the banter was just aimed at me. They accepted all the other females as equals, all doing the same jobs and were respectful and supportive of them. It became more vicious to me at each turn from both men and I couldn't understand why. We were on the same side after all.

To my sheer astonishment we were taught unarmed combat, including how to kill someone with our bare hands. Silent killing, they called it. We learned to pick a lock, handle a specialist knife, Colt handguns, and Sten guns. We were shown how to use grenades and explosives and, before

I knew it, three weeks had passed by, and the first phase was over. I had just drifted into the training without questioning my place and was reluctant to do so now. I was now more certain that this training was for a role in the war effort in occupied France. My language skills were not enough; I needed to be able to kill to protect myself if needed. I joked to myself it was either that, or I would be the most lethal translating secretary in history.

WE WERE ALLOWED one trip home that weekend before returning for the next phase, which was to be six weeks of what they said would be intense training in Scotland. After which we would undergo parachute training. This unsettled me, I felt this phase had in itself been intense. I wasn't sure how much further I could be pushed, especially with parachute jumping, something I'd never contemplated in my life. The thought terrified me.

We were told once these two sessions were over, if we passed, we would have a further placement at a "finishing school" to consolidate our training and go on to specialist job training our skills matched us to.

The final morning before we were allowed home, we were given a further talk about what the training was for. We were being trained to disrupt the Germans in their war effort and to create a link between England and the occupied countries. The work as agents would be dangerous and include espionage, subversion, reconnaissance, and sabotage.

Finally, confirmation of what I was meant to be doing and what the training was for. I felt a weird sense of relief. It all made so much more sense. We were reminded of the need for total secrecy. Anyone caught disobeying that order would be taken off the course immediately and held in a secret location or "cooler" until they were no longer able to pose a risk with the information they had gained. We were also warned about honey traps, this was explained as enemy spies or fifth columnists approaching us to start a relationship and glean information we had. We needed to be cautious with whom we met, and what we said at all times from now on. We were offered the opportunity to leave at that point if we didn't wish to proceed, now we knew what the job entailed. No-one left. I was quietly thrilled I'd been given this chance and wasn't going to leave voluntarily.

We had one more physical exercise before we broke off for the weekend, a five-mile trek with a map and compass, with several obstacles to tackle. One obstacle included being observed crawling on your belly through a small, dark tunnel with fast flowing water running through it. On the day of the exercise, it was incredibly cold, and the tunnel was so narrow that there was only a small gap between my head and the roof to breathe in. The rapid flowing water kept flying into my face, causing a feeling of claustrophobia, it was torture, but I persevered. I was then on the last part of the trek, exhausted, cold, and soaked, but I had almost done it, feeling relieved and satisfied with myself as I headed towards the finish point. My heels were raw and bloody from where my slightly small boots had rubbed, and I was just so glad it was almost over.

Cameron shot out from behind a tree and pushed me against it with his arm firmly across my chest. I was so exhausted I had no energy left to push him off.

"Do yourself a favour, Devereaux. Just leave. You're the weakest of everyone, just a little girl who doesn't know her limitations. I know it, you know it, and so do all the others. It must all seem so exciting, shooting guns and things, but you mark my words, when the shit hits the fan, you'll be captured and spill your guts. Brave people will die because you want to play at spies, do you want that on your conscience?" He took his arm down, releasing me. "Silly cow," he spat at me, and jogged away.

I was left there alone, feeling useless and worthless. Maybe he was right. It was one thing to do this under controlled conditions and playacting, but what about in real life? Was I honestly up to this? Did the others really think that way of me too? They all seemed so confident and socially adept. Did they know I had only worked in chip shops and didn't have the same experience as them? I was fully aware I wasn't the fastest runner, and I was a bit slow in other areas, but I was trying my level best.

And now parachuting? Oh god, what am I doing here, what the hell was I thinking? At the end of the exercise, I was met with a blanket, thermos, and a lift back to the house, retreating to the sanctuary of my room in despair to bathe my bloodied heels.

I mulled it all over and decided Cameron was just a bully who liked to be in charge. He wasn't a team player and had issues with women. Everyone in the group was going through this for their own reasons. I wondered what his reason for joining up was and why he had taken to hating me so. Cameron was average everything, average height, average weight, brown hair, nothing in his character stood out about him at all. I wondered if this training made him feel an importance he didn't feel in his normal everyday life. But what if he were right and could see a weakness in me the trainers couldn't? I made my journey home in a bit of a dejected and sorry state.

26

WELCOME HOME

I arrived on our street on the Friday evening, Cameron's words ringing in my ears, dragging my confidence down to the depths. As I walked up the street in the fading light, I could hear furious shouting coming from our house. A feeling of dread came over me. I knew I could walk away and not get involved, but my vulnerable mother was in there, and so I headed for the front door. I walked through to the living room to find Alfie bending over and hitting my mother who was cowering on the floor. He was in a drunken state and was shouting about her hiding money and pulling her hair. I physically dragged him off her and was then floored by a fierce unexpected punch to the left side of my forehead. I felt blood running into my eye from where my eyebrow had split open. Alfie staggered off and collapsed drunkenly on his armchair, calling us both frog bitches, shouting at us to leave him alone. I took my tearful mother to the kitchen and sat her at the table. I put together a cold compress for her cuts and bleeding mouth, and one for my own eye, comforting her in her distress as I did so. She sipped a glass of Alfie's whisky to calm her nerves. I wanted her to leave this foul brute, but she wouldn't hear a word said against him.

"He's always looked after me, Yvette. My life's here now, my friends are here. I can't leave just because he has a few bad days. Where would I go anyway? It's only the drink that causes his problems. He's a lovely man when he doesn't drink, and he loves me. Don't forget, he took us in when we had nothing, remember."

I just wanted us to be away from him. I couldn't understand why everything else was rationed but not beer, and how Alfie could keep getting hold of alcohol, which made his behaviour worse. Once our injuries had been tended to, I went to confront him. I found him in a drunken stupor flopped in his armchair in his string vest and trousers, his legs spread out, his trouser belt undone, and his fat beer belly exposed. His feet were bare, and I was disgusted by the very sight of him. I stood over him menacingly, looking down at him thinking what I would like to do to him with my newly acquired silent killing skills.

The next morning, I looked in my mirror at my bruised eye and cut eyebrow and knew I would have some explaining to do when I returned to the base. I covered the injuries with makeup as best as I could and went out shopping with my mother. I had a clothing ration book I hadn't used, and as I would be spending most of my life now in uniform, I treated her to a warm coat, which she was so pleased with and hugged me tightly. On Sunday we had enough food saved with my ration book added, for a lunch of lamb chops. My mother had invited her new neighbour, Maude Davis and her son, Gordon to eat with us.

As we gathered at the dining room table on Sunday, I was horrified Gordon had been placed next to me. He was in his late twenties, and his mother informed us that as much as he'd been desperate to join the army and serve his country, he was classed as medically unfit due to some ailment or other. He now worked at the factory near the docks with Alfie. I didn't really know them well, as they hadn't lived on the street long, but they had befriended my mother soon after moving in. Gordon helped with repairs in the house and went drinking with Alfie; Maude and mother went shopping together. Her contribution to the Sunday lunch was a ridiculously small bread pudding.

Maude could really talk, and it was with a strong Welsh accent which started to grate on me after a while, but I smiled politely and chatted with them about nothing much. Gordon didn't say a lot; just kept smiling at me, displaying yellowing unclean teeth. He also had cigarette-stained fingers and smelled not too great. Our chairs had been squeezed so closely together that our bodies were almost touching, which made my skin crawl. He kept asking his mother to pass things to him, and she was happy to run around when he ordered her to. All he had to say was, "Mother," and point at whatever he wanted, like the salt pot, and she responded immediately like a well-trained dog. This infuriated me even further. He was quite capable of getting off his backside to help himself and allow his mother to rest. He was a vile junior Alfie.

They asked what had happened to my face and after looking crossly at Alfie, who appeared to have forgotten his misdemeanours from Friday evening, I said I'd tripped and fallen.

Maude had obviously gleaned information about me from my mother and turned the conversation towards me. "It's so sad what's happened to you, and it must be so hard for you to bear, my lovely, being left all alone in the world with no man to look after you. Your mam has told us everything. Terrible, terrible shame. You're a pretty girl who should have a man to protect you in these harsh times. You're still so young, and you should think of marriage again, settling down and having a family. Nothing like a bonny baby or two to take your mind off things."

I saw all their smiling eyes drift from me to Gordon and back and then I knew why this gathering had been arranged, and where this was leading: Maude's bloody son, Gordon, who was single. I wanted to scream and was having none of it. I'd been down this road before.

"If you'll excuse me, I do have a pre-arranged appointment this afternoon. It was nice to meet you both," I said as I made my escape, grabbing my coat and heading out for a long walk, breathing in the smoggy London air. My life was now my own and the mere thought of going back to the sort of ghastly life they were plotting for me, with that excuse of a man, I would truly rather die. I would sooner face an army of Cameron's and decided to continue with the training. Sod Cameron.

THAT NIGHT I felt so sad saying goodbye to my mother; I just wanted to protect her and take her with me. I knew that was impossible with my current situation and I was also fully aware she wouldn't go with me anyway. I made the journey back to the base by train and bus with a mixture of sadness, trepidation, and excitement tussling inside me. Sergeant Jones was the first to meet me when I returned.

"What happened to your eye, Devereaux?" he asked as he walked towards me in the corridor.

"I walked into the wardrobe door, Sergeant," I replied.

He looked at me sternly and as he walked past, he said,

"The next time the wardrobe door does that to your eye, Devereaux, kick it in the testicles."

With each session from then on, my confidence grew, and this seemed to set Cameron off into another rant. He'd seen my cut eye when I returned from leave and said to me mockingly, "Late with his dinner, were you, Devereaux?"

I just ignored him. I was learning to absorb it and handle it more effectively. He really didn't let up though. At every opportunity he made a disarming comment, but I refused to take the bait. He wanted to knock my confidence so much I would fail or leave. His goading of me was so childish and unnecessary. He had an irrational hatred of me, and I really didn't know why, apart from that one incident and me being female.

27

EARNING MY WINGS

T he next six weeks in Scotland were gruelling and the survival tests were the toughest I had undergone so far, far worse than I expected. It was bitterly cold and difficult to concentrate when the cold seeped into your bones. More recruits dropped out at this stage; Cameron showed his disappointment that I wasn't one of them.

We found ourselves out on the snow-covered moors for days on end, trying to hide from pursuers or stalk others, and survive the rough terrain and the elements. We had to raid a protected building without being seen, burgle houses, cross icy rivers with equipment and climb up rock faces and abseil down. I was shouted at, sworn at, physically pushed, and moaned about but managed to scrape through it all. I was pushed almost beyond my endurance, and my body ached all over from the abuse it was suffering.

We were put through more advanced skills in the areas covered already, plus we now had to learn survival skills, which included trapping and butchering wild animals, Morse code, use of radios, interrogation techniques. We had to be able to undo handcuffs and locks with whatever came to hand and use explosives. We were taught to strip, reassemble, load and fire all the weapons we handled including German and Italian ones. I laughed at the thought of my life right now. I had worked in a chip shop and now here I was shooting guns, watching dead rats explode, having had explosives stuffed in them, throwing grenades, and learning to kill with my bare hands. I was revelling in every minute of it. I'd been brought to life by this training environment and felt very fit, stronger than ever before and much more capable.

One trainer, Paul Stapleton, was by far the most brutal towards me. He made me run carrying equipment and inhaling freezing cold air until I vomited. He hurled abuse at me in tests, trying to put me off when I should be concentrating. He was particularly hard on me on the unarmed combat techniques and advanced silent killing, and I always came away from any encounter with him badly battered and bruised. On one occasion, he slammed me down on my back onto the frozen ground so hard it totally knocked every wisp of breath out of me. I thought I was dying. I just couldn't breathe in. He looked deeply into my eyes as I struggled to regain my breath and must have been a bit worried by what he saw, as he grabbed my uniform, flipping me over onto my hands and knees. He rubbed my upper stomach firmly and I felt the breath coming gratefully back into my lungs. He was a sadistic woman hater, I thought, as I inhaled the bitterly cold air, making my lungs raw. He hated me with a passion, just like Cameron did. He too wanted me to fail, or worse - die.

The mere thought of them trying to make me give up made me more determined to get through it. I had suffered at the hands of men all my life. Even my own father had bailed out on me, which set my life on such a terrible path. I wouldn't give up now, and if they thought I would buckle from their abuse, then they didn't know me at all. It dawned on me then I'd never cried through any of this. In fact, for most of my life I hadn't cried. I just absorbed whatever came my way. I realised long ago there was no point in crying, it didn't help or improve things for you one jot. This experience was making me so much tougher; my self-confidence was growing daily. In the unarmed combat, which wasn't my strongest point, I was always told at every opportunity by one of the older soldiers when things weren't going well, "If all else fails love, forget the training and just kick him in the testicles and shoot him." I genuinely believed by the time we left Scotland, I could go into a dirty fight with anyone without hesitation and have a real chance of winning

WE WERE TAKEN to a Manchester airfield to make the necessary jumps for the course. We'd undertaken all the theory and practice of parachuting and landing and even been shown how parachutes were packed, now came the reckoning. We were each given a small spade we would need to have strapped to our legs, which we would use to bury the parachute on landing in occupied territory.

They were right. It was occupied territory and where I was born. They talked about the Germans in such derogatory terms, but my father was German, and he wasn't a bad man. He always treated people and animals kindly. It was Hitler and the German Army we were fighting, not civilians. That made me feel more justified in what we were doing, and I vowed in my naive way of looking at war, that women and children would be safe from anything I did.

We had been allocated a Whitley aircraft for the first drop. The usual stories had already gone around us recruits about the horrors of parachute jumps going wrong. Tales of parachutes not being packed properly and not opening when the person jumped out. Someone who jumped when his parachute was not even attached to the static line to pull open his chute. One landing in a lake and drowning, enmeshed in his parachute, some landing in trees and impaled on branches. One agent was said to have landed on the roof of a French police station. The other gruesome rumour we heard about was of a parachutist who got tangled with the plane as he jumped, hanging him. We terrified recruits were reassured that for every thousand parachute jumps only five went wrong. I thought that sounded rather good odds, unless of course you were one of the five.

The plane had a hatch in the floor for us to drop out of when ordered, and we were instructed to have our heads up straight, arms across our chests, and backs to be rigid when we jumped, or we would smack our faces on the far side of the three-foot hatch wall. This we were joyfully told was called "ringing the bell." Serious injuries could occur if that happened, including broken noses, jaws, and teeth.

The flight up was exhilarating, and even though I didn't particularly like heights, this was my first time in a real aeroplane, and it was incredible.

Each recruit, when called, had to shuffle sideways along the floor and put their legs over the side of the hatch and sit waiting on the edge. Their parachute was attached to the main static line, and they had to wait for the light in front of them to change from red to green.

Once the green light was on, they were tapped on the shoulder, given a slight push, and shouted at to go. The parachute would be pulled open automatically by the static line and they would float down to earth, hopefully.

I was fourth on the list. The first person called was the business friend of Cameron's, Garfield. They were like two peas in a pod and had become close in a short time. He sat at the edge of the drop hatch. The green light came on and the sergeant tapped his shoulder, but he didn't jump. He was shouted at to go, and given a slight push, but again he just wouldn't jump. He had frozen to the spot and looked absolutely terrified at the ground below, his face an ashen grey colour. He looked as if he was going to be sick. After the third attempt to make him jump he still couldn't do it and was hauled back from the hatch into the main body of the plane where he sat and shook in front of us, his fate sealed.

"Devereaux," shouted a voice unexpectedly, and I struggled awkwardly into position past the two other men who were listed to jump before me. My parachute was tethered to the static line, which I oversaw like a hawk, just to make sure, and I sat at the edge, the countryside far below me. I was suddenly terrified. *What the hell am I doing?* I thought to myself, as if I'd just woken up from a dream, and the actual reality of the situation was confronting me.

The plane went around again to come back over the drop zone, the red light on in front of me. My eyes were fixed on the light, waiting for the red light to go off and the green to light up. I hoped whoever packed my parachute knew what they were doing and had read the poster I'd seen in the packing room, "Remember, a man's life depends on every parachute you pack." Time seemed to stand still, but as I waited, a feeling of utter calm came over me. I'd never had such a feeling; it was as if my veins had ice water running through them. The green light came on and I felt a firm tap on my shoulder. I saw Cameron's face—his mocking eyes met mine, he had a smirk on his face as if to say I wouldn't do it.

They wouldn't let you do this if they thought you might die, would they? I thought to myself. My training would end here if I didn't jump, and I would have to return to my nothing life with Maude and Gordon Davies pestering me. I shut my eyes and with a slight push from behind I dropped out of the hatch, praying that the chute would open. The initial seconds of the drop were terrifying, and then I saw the canopy spread out above me and felt my body being jolted upwards and then float down to earth.

I just couldn't believe I'd done it and was euphoric, so pleased with myself. I enjoyed the float down, and looking around, I could see for miles. I landed as I'd been taught but was surprised at how fast I was going when I hit the ground. The staff helped me with my parachute harness, and I was driven back to the airfield hangar to wait for the others. It was here I heard about Ethan by accident. Two parachute trainers escorting us on the airfield came into the hangar to get equipment and were talking to each other, unaware that I was changing out of my jumpsuit out of sight.

"How many have we got jumping today?"

"Sixteen according to the list. Hey there's a Devereaux on the jump list. Is that a mistake? He was on the group from last year, wasn't he? Wasn't he the one who ended up injured after smashing into the hangar?" one of them said.

"No, it can't be him, they don't come here twice for training, let me see." The other one replied.

"No, this one's female," I heard one of them say as they left the hangar.

It then fully dawned on me that Ethan must have been an agent. All that rubbish from Steadman about him dying in Hull. Ethan must have given them information about me;

that was how they knew so much and why they contacted me directly about his death, rather than send a telegram, like they did with other families. I thought about his distant behaviour at home, all the hallmarks of stress, his inability to sleep and be close to me, his guarded conversations, the lengthy periods away, the bruising he came home with. How stupid of me to miss all of that.

I realised then, being dragged back to reality, that I'd been lied to, targeted, and manipulated. I'd been set up by my husband and the system. My trust in people nosedived more than I thought possible. It hurt, but I was still determined to complete the training, as the only other option was to return to my mundane, sorry, and sad life.

I caught up with the Sergeant who had been organising the jumps and asked why he asked me to jump second, ahead of the other two men.

"Quite simply sweetheart, if a woman jumps the men will jump too, bravado and all that stuff. If a man fails to jump, like that bloke did, it sends jitters through the rest of the jumpers."

"How did you know I would jump?" I asked.

"All the women jump, love." He laughed.

All the recruits who completed the first jump were given two more jumps, one from a balloon basket which was about three hundred and fifty feet from the ground. That was terrifying, as the ground came up to meet you in seconds, but I did it, screaming all the way down. The other was a night drop. Garfield was dismissed for failing to jump, and Valerie, who had broken her leg on the first jump, was in hospital.

My fear of heights vanished. I never dreamed I would ever do this sort of thing and found it exhilarating. I had two more successful jumps, but my success was tinged with sadness because I would never be able to celebrate it with anyone when I was given my jump badge or 'wings.' But I'd passed this test and secured my place on the next phase.

WE WERE down to twelve agents at this point. Some had failed tests; others had just thrown in the towel not wanting to continue. It was increasingly intense now and those of us left had numerous tests set for us—being split into groups to capture things, blow things up, send and receive messages under stressful conditions—and it was success all round. We were each becoming competent agents, not expert but competent. Cameron was finally easing off his abuse of me, I think he just got bored of it all as I didn't react. I liked my position in the group too, neither exceptional nor awful, just somewhere in the middle, muddling through.

All the tests and training were complete, apart from the final major assessment, to test the agent's ability to operate in the field alone. This was to take place from an army base in a rural area in the South of England. After this test, if we passed, we would be sent to "finishing school" to learn about disguises, cover stories, more interrogation methods, and life in the occupied areas we would be dropped in. I would be going to France as a radio operative or courier if I passed this test.

This latest exercise would be a lone parachute drop anywhere between fifteen to twenty-five miles from the base, with no money or equipment, and wearing civilian clothes. Local soldiers, police, and home guards would be on exercises hunting down pretend German spies—us, to keep them alert. We had to make a message drop on our way back, at the correct site and to the exact person described and return to the base by any means available.

The objective was to drop the message, avoid capture or talk your way out of being detained if stopped by local police, and get back to base within twenty-four hours. We could use any means necessary to achieve the objective, apart from assault, murder, or serious crime. We were assured repeatedly the people hunting us would not shoot us, but none of us were entirely convinced by the assurance. I knew we were up for a final review on our performance to date and this assessment was extremely important, as we could still be booted off the training if we didn't make the grade. I desperately wanted to stay.

It was just after transferring South that I had an appointment to meet the female intelligence officer, Patricia Ashcroft, for dinner at a restaurant in the local village. She told me it was a routine thing, to catch up, see how I was doing and if there was anything she could do for me. I was in my uniform, waiting at our table, when I had a message that she would be late and so I ordered a pot of tea. I wasn't too sure what she could do for me anyway, and it seemed a strange thing to do to ask to meet me here where people could overhear any conversation. I would be exceedingly guarded in anything I said as this should surely be done somewhere more private.

My mind wandered back to the exercise that was due to take place when I noticed a man at the next table on his own glancing at me and smiling. He was smartly dressed and seemed to be waiting for someone, looking periodically at his watch. The manager then came to my table to inform me that Patricia couldn't make it after all, and she sent her sincere apologies. The man on the next table then came and sat at mine.

"I'm really sorry, but I couldn't help overhearing, does that mean you've been left on your own for dinner? It's just that it seems my date isn't coming either. Do you mind if I join you? I'm starving, and dinner would be on me as a thank you for your company."

He introduced himself as Harrison Townsend and was impressively handsome, with intense, dark, smiling eyes and a non-military hair cut; he was what you might call dashing, funny, and very flirty. It was enough to turn a girl's head, but not this one. I found him smarmy, irritating and smelled a rat, too many co-incidences for my liking. I was hungry though and decided to make the most of the opportunity to have a nice dinner. I ordered the most expensive dish available, and as we ate, the questions came thick and fast from 'Harrison,' as he smoked his posh cigarettes and offered me expensive wine, which I declined. He intermittently touched my arm and patted my hand softly as we talked. His focus was entirely on me, his eyes intensely searching mine and hanging on my every word. He laughed loudly at anything slightly funny I said, which under normal circumstances would have been terribly flattering. I told him my name was Irene Davenport.

"Are you a local Irene? Where are you staying? What do you think of women being in the forces? What area of work are you in Irene? Is it dangerous? I think you are incredibly brave doing what you do Irene."

On and on the questioning went, becoming more personal and intense, but my answers were so bland and uninformative, despite him pushing hard for more. It must have been the most boring date he'd ever been on. Once dessert was over, and I declined his offer of going back to his nearby hotel "for a nightcap," I quickly got up from the table, thanked him for his company, and left him sadly protesting at my departure. Once outside, I waited in the darkness at the side of the restaurant. After a short while, he came out in his overcoat and trilby, and stood on the pavement smoking a cigarette. A car came to a stop to pick him up, the driver was Patricia Ashcroft.

I smiled to myself. His initials HT had alerted me, the dreaded honey trap we had heard rumours about. Even if it weren't a trap, and handsome and dashing as he was, he did absolutely nothing for me and I had no desire whatsoever for any relationship right now, my entire focus was on much more serious matters elsewhere.

28

STEADMAN

I travelled from London with Patricia Ashcroft, who was supporting the female recruits, to meet up with the main assessors. By all accounts there were only twelve recruits left out of the twenty-eight that started. *By Christ, not even half, we need more than that if we're going to make a difference.* I considered we would have to up the numbers on each group in the future or lower the benchmark to keep more in if we were to achieve anything of any note. We walked into the meeting room to find Hammond, Jones, Stapleton, Westmacott, and Hopkins waiting. All good solid men, exceptional servicemen. They all stood as I entered.

"Be seated, gentlemen."

Everyone sat, looking expectantly at me at the head of the table.

"Right. Well, we have twelve who've made the grade so far with the final test to go. Are we all set for this? Soldiers, home guards and all the others ready?"

A mumble of "Yes sirs" came back.

"Okay good, then let's look at the recruits we have left

and look at where the others failed. We will have to lower the bar a bit to get more through if they keep failing on minor details. It's costly to keep losing willing agents with skills we need, especially if it's only minor things they're failing on."

The first file handed to me was Devereaux's.

"Right, any thoughts on Devereaux?" I asked the group.

Sergeant Hopkins offered his opinion. "I think she's way too young for this. She isn't aggressive enough in physical activities and doesn't fight with the required killer instinct. As a young woman I think we all know she would be subjected to the most horrendous abuse if caught. I don't think she would survive for long without talking if captured and so would be a risk to others. She would be of better use working as a radio receiver in England because of her French and German skills. She's good with radio sets and has excellent Morse code skills. She is up to twenty words per minute now, which would suit that type of work, so her training wouldn't be wasted."

Hammond agreed: "I think we all have a lot of respect for her. She's tried hard in every test and never given up. She's passed all the standards set, but I have my reservations about sending someone so young into an occupied area with the possibility of capture, and its consequences. It's one thing performing these tests in a controlled environment and another completely where people are determined to kill you. I agree, I don't think she has a killer mentality."

Ashcroft had her say, "Devereaux has been cautious throughout the recruitment and training. We set up a specific honey-trap for her and she saw it a mile off. Having gone through what she has, there is no doubting her bravery for this. We have many female agents working effectively, they all bring their own unique abilities to enhance the circuits they join, and they have more freedom of movement than male agents. She keeps things incredibly tight; you just can't read her at all, and I think she is ready and capable to put into operation."

The room was silent, and then Westmacott gave his opinion. "Her bravery isn't in question, but radio operatives have a life span of around six weeks in the field and it's one of the most dangerous roles. We would be sending her to her death. She is too innocent and too feminine looking; she has no real-life experience to fall back on if things go wrong. She's worked hard and tried her best, there is no doubting that, but I believe she lacks the guile and inner strength needed for undercover work for any length of time. Those are my thoughts."

Sergeant Jones joined in. "She's been content not to lead others and so hasn't really had the chance to demonstrate leadership skills as such. I think her strength is in the fact she prefers to work alone and rely on herself, which would be useful for a radio operative. I may be wrong, but this will show up on the final test. She has a calm state of mind, she's not impulsive at all."

I looked around the room at each of them, got up and walked to the window to look out onto the English country-side to gather my thoughts.

"Gentleman, we send our young men to die in combat in all types of theatres of war and we expect them to fight for their country in times of threat. These young men are the same age, if not younger than Devereaux. We already have female agents working effectively abroad from earlier groups, so why not this one?"

I then turned to face them. "Britain expects that this day you too will do your duty" – that's what the posters say. Why do you think this woman can't do the same if she has the skills and willingness to fight for her country? There's something about her that makes me think she'll be a useful asset. No one knows much about her apart from what her husband has told us. She gives nothing away. She's a loner. The negatives you've listed could well be turned to positives under cover. Her looking young and fragile may play well in keeping her safer than a male agent. Women are needed as agents now, as young fit male agents can be spotted a mile away by determined and increasingly active anti-spy networks. It has to be a price worth paying."

Stapleton supported me. "She's come through the most brutal training I've ever put a female recruit through. She didn't cry or whine and just took it no matter how hard I pushed. She's a loner; she keeps things tight. She's passed all the tests set and I think she's proved herself good enough to be put into operation."

"Only just passed," said Hopkins.

"Only just is still a pass, and she still has the last test to go. That's where I think her strengths will come to the fore," said Stapleton.

Everyone had their say about Devereaux, and the majority, four to three, concluded it would be better and safer if she worked in England as a radio operator and translator.

I stood my ground, along with Paul Stapleton who tried to persuade the group.

"She tends to think her way through the training rather than just be led," he said. "She has an exceptional memory for faces and details, which she has demonstrated during the observational tests and that will be extremely useful as an agent. She doesn't drink, which some of the recruits have done from the deliberately well stocked bar and talked loosely about their roles because of it."

I threw in my support. "I accept that there are protective

concerns around her being so young and being female. I'm also acutely aware of the risk of who could be harmed and the damage that could be done if she were captured and talked. I acknowledge she is weak in unarmed combat, but it's easy to be lethal in other ways, which she will be more than prepared for. I fully accept your concerns believe me; they're all legitimate ones. But these are not normal times, gentlemen, they are desperate ones. My decision is that if she passes the final test, she will be sent abroad as a radio operative. If she doesn't pass this test, then she will stay at home and work as a radio operative."

They all agreed, and her fate hung on the final test. I was handed the next file.

"Now gentlemen. What about Cameron?"

29

A SECRET HELPER

We were settled in at the army camp in the southeast of England and told on the Friday to enjoy our long weekend, as on Tuesday we would be undertaking the final test. I watched as the others made their way to the canteen area to discuss what might be ahead of them. I chose to go to my room and read back through my notes and undercover story as Evelyn Bouvier. I was grateful I had my own room, even if it was so terribly small and cell like. The other recruits had to share, and I would have hated that. I heard a shuffling noise outside my room and saw a note had been slipped under the door. I picked it up and opened the door to see who had left it, but the corridor was empty.

I read the note which had a one-pound note wrapped in it:

"*The test is tomorrow. Get prepared.*"

I was both astounded and suspicious. Was this one of Cameron's dumb tricks or was someone trying to help me? The note stated the test would be tomorrow, Saturday, not Tuesday, and I had to quickly prepare for it. I thought long and hard about a parachute jump into an unknown area, no money, in civilian clothes, no map, no compass and twenty-four hours to get back here unseen, uncaptured, and I began to develop a plan. Even if it were a hoax, I would still be prepared for the exercise and was one pound better off. If it weren't a hoax then I would be more prepared than the others, which would give me a better chance. I destroyed the written note to protect whoever had sent it. I considered what I would need and planned to gather items from the main administration office block and stores at the base when they were unmanned.

My lock picking skills came in handy to get into the store and admin office to get what I required. As darkness fell, recruits and assessors made their way to bed and the camp settled down for the night. I made my way silently out of the building into the grounds, avoiding the guards. I went to a back wall at the edge of the camp, and once the perimeter guard had passed by, I threw my suitcase over it. I then climbed a tree and jumped to the ground on the other side, making off into the countryside with a map tucked into my jacket. I guessed they would be more alert to people breaking in than out. I planned to be back in the camp by dawn.

AT SIX A.M. we were woken up by soldiers shouting and banging on doors for us to get dressed. I had returned at four. We weren't allowed to wash, eat, or drink. We had to empty our pockets of any items and take off our watches. We were searched and told to put on clothes they handed us. I had a lilac flowery dress, and a light mac. I looked like I was wearing someone's curtains and it would make me stand out too much.

This was deliberate, planned chaos to disorientate us, but the other recruits, unlike me, were totally unprepared by the change of day for this test. We were taken to a training room and told to be back there in twenty-four hours. Each of us were given the message we had to deliver and details of who we were to hand it to and where. We were driven to an airfield and put our jump suits and parachutes on over our clothes, then guided in silence to the waiting plane. Six recruits were on each flight; Stella and I were in one group, with Sergeant Stapleton overseeing our jumps.

One by one we jumped from the plane at set drops; I was the last one due out and by now felt confident. I sat at the edge of the trap waiting for the lights to change and a tap on my shoulder. Again, an icy calmness came over me.

Sergeant Stapleton was in front of me watching me intensely and shouted, "Don't you dare let me down, Devereaux," just as the green light came on and I jumped.

I didn't have time to think about that comment because as my parachute opened, part of it became tangled. I didn't have full control over the drop, and as a result I was falling at a fair speed, going from euphoria to terror in seconds. This had never happened to me before. I knew the theory of what to do in these circumstances and twisted, turned, and pulled, grappling with the lines until the tangled area came free and the parachute spread welcomingly out. I thanked God that the danger was over, but I'd been dragged off my drop zone by the erratic descent. I could see a farm building below me rapidly coming up to meet me and I prepared myself for a very bumpy landing. I landed heavily on the roof of the farmhouse and tumbled over the side. My parachute became wrapped around the chimney stack, and I was left hanging at the front of the building with my feet about two feet off the ground.

"Good gracious," I said quietly to myself as two more roof slates fell off the roof, landing in front of me with a crash. "Holy hell," I exclaimed more loudly this time as another one came down. A man, whom I suspected was the farm owner, appeared menacingly in front of me with a shotgun, as another tile fell off the roof and landed with a crash at his side. I feared I would end up being shot by a belligerent Englishman, which certainly wasn't part of the plan.

The farmer looked at me, the parachute, and broken tiles. "Your another one of those bloody agents. Why can't they drop you lot off somewhere away from my bloody farm?" he yelled.

I stayed silent but thought things weren't as secret as they believed. He helped me out of the parachute harness and got his ladder to retrieve my mangled parachute from the roof, moaning as he did.

"At least six bloody roof tiles they'll have to pay for after this little escapade."

"Sorry," I said weakly in response.

He tutted and led me into the farmhouse and gruffly offered me tea. I took off my jumpsuit, which left me in the flowery clothes I had been given to wear. As I changed, I saw what looked like a cooling roast chicken on a shelf inside the cold larder in the kitchen; it was poking out from under some muslin, alongside a fruit pie and freshly baked bread. I hadn't eaten for quite a while now and was starving and the smell from the warm food was incredible. I looked at him and back at the food hopefully.

"You can forget that for a start. The wife's family are

coming to dinner. I'm not allowed to touch it; the wife would kill me."

I drank the tea and ate the bread and jam he gave me, warming myself by the kitchen fire before beginning my attempt at returning to the base.

The farmer joined me to drink his tea, in a more soft-ened manner after his initial gruffness, telling me his name was Reg Ogden. I studied him as he talked: he was a large man about fifty and had a ruddy outdoor complexion and a rather prominent nose. He was wearing very worn old farm-hand clothes, a cap, and boots. His hands looked gnarled and well used to hard work. When he took his cap off, I could see he had a badly receding hairline and he reminded me of someone I'd seen recently, and I started scanning my memory for details.

"Where's your wife?" I asked him.

"You've just missed her; she's headed off to the market stall for the day to sell our produce in the town."

"Do you have any children?"

"I've got two married daughters, but no son to carry on with the farm once I kick the bucket. The girls refuse to take it on, too much like bloody hard work if you ask me. It's just me and the misses now," he looked sad at that.

He then said, wagging his finger at me. "You're one lucky young lady do you know that? You've landed on your feet so to speak. I'm one of the local suppliers for the camp I think you've come from. If I'm right, and I think I am, then you, like the others before you must get back into the camp unseen. I'm going to make a delivery there this morning, in the next hour in fact. If you want, you could hide in the back of my lorry with the meat, fruit, and veg. I could get you back into the base without them ever knowing about it."

This sounded too easy, but very tempting, and an offer I couldn't really refuse. He noticed my slight hesitation.

"I'm not forcing you to. It's up to you, take it or leave it. No skin off my nose," he said gruffly, sniffing his disdain at the fact I didn't jump at his offer. "I have to get going soon and this is a very generous offer under the circumstances, so make your mind up quick."

I decided to go along with it, and fluttering my eyelashes at him, as I had seen the other girls do in their flirty way, I thanked him. "You're very kind, but I don't want to get you into any trouble by helping me."

"You'll have to be quiet once you're inside the lorry. I'm a regular supplier to the base, it's a good business for me. I don't want to risk that by getting caught helping you, so no noise at all. You mustn't tell anyone how you got back into the base either or I'll be in real trouble. Oh... and just because I am helping you out it doesn't let you off the cost of the roof repair. That still has to be paid for."

I eagerly nodded my full agreement.

Reg the farmer loaded up his lorry and I got in the back. I was buried between two pig carcasses and covered in sack cloth. He said to me in his no-nonsense way. "I don't want to hear another word out of you now until we get to the base kitchen door. I'll let you out when it's safe."

I nodded and lay there between the pig carcasses in my flowery frock and mac, as he went into the farmhouse to get the paperwork and security pass for the delivery. He returned to the lorry, getting breathlessly into the driver's seat and started the drive to the base.

REG OGDEN

At least she was keeping quiet in the back, which was a

bonus. This wasn't the first one and I doubted it would be the last that lands on my farm and I hand in. It was why they were so eager to give me the supply job, to keep my trap shut. It suited me and gave me a good income to boot. I could double the cost of the repairs to the roof, and they would pay it no question. Silence all the way to the army base, great. As I drove up to the gate, I saw Dan, one of the regular guards on duty. This would be a welcome surprise for him.

He approached the lorry.

"Alright, Reg," he said, looking bored.

"Alright, Dan?" I replied quietly, and motioned for him to come closer, "I've got another one of your lot hiding in the back. Landed on my bloody farm roof this time. The roof will need repairing."

"Just put the usual chitty in then, Reg. Who have you got in the back?"

"A dopey young blonde in a frock. You really are scraping the barrel now if that's the best you can come up with. She was so easily fooled by me. Hitler must be quaking in his jackboots."

Dan laughed loudly and made towards the back of the lorry. "Come out love. Time to go home. It's all over for you. Back to civvy street."

I moved next to him to peer in as he pulled back the lorry's rear canvass. I wanted to see the look on her face at having been totally duped by me and imagined she would be a bit tearful and upset. That would teach her a lesson for disrupting my day. Bloody woman, just like my daughters, bloody useless.

But there was no one there, just the pig carcasses, eggs, fruit, and veg. The pig carcasses had been positioned with a sackcloth blanket up to their chins, their trotters looped over the top as if they were sleeping in bed. I was flum-moxed at this unexpected turn of events and pulled at the sack cloth to check underneath. Where the hell had she gone? My mind flew back to my unprotected farm. *Oh Christ,* I silently screamed in my head. *The chicken, the fruit pie. The bitch. How am I going to explain this to the wife?*

Dan laughed at me.

"Not so dopey, eh?"

30

THE SHORTCUT HOME

I was riding a bike I'd found at the back of Reg Ogden's farm, wearing his wife's clothes and cap, under which I had my hair tucked up. A brown suitcase with my parachute, jump suit, dress, and mac, was tied on the back of the bike. I made my way cycling along country lanes towards my pre-prepared site. I'd taken the pound note I'd been given, small change hidden in the heel of my shoe for bus fares, and a tiny compass I had hidden in my hair, so as not to have it discovered on any search and directions with co-ordinates were hidden under the insole of my shoe. I now had to deliver my message before returning to the camp.

I was satisfied I'd done the right thing not staying in that lorry. I didn't trust the man, especially as he had so much to lose if he were found helping me, so why would he? He didn't know me. Also, I eventually remembered where I'd seen his face before. He was making a delivery the day we arrived at the camp. I remember he was smoking, laughing, and joking with the guards there. Too chummy by far to want to spoil that relationship for me, I was sure. What a swine.

I'd sneaked out of the lorry when he went to get his delivery papers and hid until he left. That's when I helped myself to food, his wife's clothes, a suitcase, and the bike and left a surprise behind for him, which might make him think twice about betraying women in the future.

As I cycled along, I approached a junction in the road and an army truck went past. The two soldiers in the truck must have been out looking for "German spies," as we had been warned they would be, and they slowed right down as they passed to get a good look. The one soldier looked at me intensely but must have decided I didn't fit any of the descriptions given: long blonde hair, lilac dress, no money, or equipment. I had a bike, a large suitcase on the back, dressed in worn farm clothes, and my hair looked short. They drove on, and as they did, I waved and smiled. The soldiers smiled and waved back.

After an awfully long and tiring bike ride using the directions and compass, I came across my pre-prepared site from the night before and opened the suitcase I'd left there. I stripped off the old farm clothes and put on a FANY uniform, polished shoes, and fresh underwear. I applied a small amount of makeup, did my hair, put on my uniform cap, and took the parachute and things out of the large suitcase from the farm and transferred it to the army supply suitcase. I took out an envelope, addressed to me using the name Irene Davenport on army-headed paper. I discarded the "borrowed" farm items behind a hedge and walked to the main road and along to the bus stop I'd seen the night before.

I caught a bus into a village, which was just three miles from the camp, and came across the Nags Head Pub, which

I'd been given as the site for the message exchange. I saw a small group of soldiers laughing with each other as they entered. Their army truck was parked outside, which gave me an idea. I was aware I was noticed by the group of men as I went in. I approached the bar and asked the bartender, who was wearing a fetching blue bow tie, which bus went by the camp I was due to go to. This was said loudly enough for the soldiers to hear and, sure enough, as I'd anticipated, the alpha male of the group approached me. I felt a "little girl lost" act coming into play when he asked me where I was meant to go. I fluttered my eyelashes at him, showing him an army headed letter stating I was to go to the army camp to take up the role of secretary to a Major Turnbull, a name I'd seen listed at the camp in the admin office I burgled yesterday evening. I asked him how to get there.

The soldier drew himself up to his full height and puffed out his chest. "We'll get you there, darling, don't you worry about it. You can come with us. We're going there after we finish here. No need for a bus, your one of us now."

"I really don't want to cause you any bother," I replied sweetly. "If you just tell me which bus goes there that would be lovely."

They all volunteered loudly that it was no bother at all and offered to buy me a drink, but I declined and pulled out the pound note.

"Please let me get this round as a thank you for the lift." I said to them.

They wouldn't hear of it and bought me a half a cider. The soldiers chatted with me, and I asked them about Major Turnbull, as I was due to start work for him on Monday. They all responded with terms like, "A bit of a bastard;" "Upper class twit;" "Thinks he's better than us, not one of the blokes, terrible Turnbull doesn't care for the ordinary lads, just officers;" sympathising with me about my future role working for him. I wondered if Turnbull had any inkling of his men's dislike of him.

Once they'd finished their drinks, they started to leave the pub and invited me to join them, one took my case.

When we were all outside, I stopped suddenly and said, "Oh my lipstick." I told them to carry on to the truck and I'd be back in a second. I could see the rolling of their eyes and tutting comments like, "Bloody women," being uttered as I ran back.

I went into the now practically empty bar, picked up my deliberately left lipstick, and approached the bartender. I thanked him for his help and shook his hand—at the same time slipping the message I had to deliver from my hand to his. He smiled and winked at me—my message had been delivered. I ran back to the group, waving my lipstick, and me and my suitcase were loaded safely on the truck by my unsuspecting helpers.

We were waved through the camp gates by a guard who obviously knew the soldiers I was with. Shouts of, "Thanks Dan," were made as we sped through. They dropped me off outside the admin building, helping me out of the truck with my suitcase. One of them, called Len, got out with me. He fidgeted a bit and then asked to meet up with me again at the same pub the following Saturday if I was free. I sweetly agreed to his request, thanked him for everything and smilingly waved him off, but I knew that meeting wouldn't happen. I cringed then that I was just a female version of Reg Ogden by doing what I'd just done, but concluded my actions were necessity; his were just mean.

I made my way quietly back to the residential block and my room unchallenged by anyone, as I was invisible in uniform like everyone else on the camp. I took out all the items that could give any information about my escapades away. I picked the lock to the admin office again and stored my parachute and other evidence in a box in there, out of sight. I changed from the uniform into the flowery frock I'd been wearing for the jump and hung up my uniform. I then headed towards the team room where I'd started my journey early that morning. It was now seven-thirty p.m.

∼

THE TEAM ROOM was empty when I entered, and I sat down and waited, then made myself tea. The first through the door was Sergeant Hopkins, who was shocked to see me there.

"Bloody hell, Devereaux," he said. "You did jump out of the plane, didn't you? How are you here so early? What did they do, parachute you directly over the camp?"

I didn't reply, just smiled.

He noted down the time, recorded it, and left, shaking his head. I had time to think back over the day as I sat there. I really wanted to be a fly on the wall when Reg Ogden got home. Not only had I borrowed a bike from his farm and his wife's clothes and suitcase. I also had a nice meal of hot chicken and fresh buttered crusty bread along with a decent slice of rhubarb pie. Naughtily, I had left him the gift of my army supply underwear in his marital bed for his wife to find. *Get out of that one,* I thought. But then realised the awful possibility, *oh my God, what if I'm wrong and he was genuinely helping me?*

As I pondered, and grimaced, over the possible domestic disaster I'd caused for Reg, another recruit came limping through the door. Alice. She'd been very capable through-out, and I thought she would make an exceptionally good agent. She was my height, with rich dark hair, dark eyes and a slightly plump, but pretty face. She was a well-travelled diplomats' daughter from what I had gathered. I was under the impression she came from an upper-class background because of her confident and poised air. This theory, however, was blown away somewhat when she spoke.

"Bloody hell, what a bloody, sodding nightmare that was," she exclaimed in a very course way, taking me by surprise.

"What happened to you?" I asked, concerned at the state she was in.

"I fell badly on landing, cutting my knee open on something in the ground. I managed to get near a road where an old man in a car found me and gave me a lift to hospital. I had stitches and a dressing put on my leg, and one of the ambulance men there, started chatting and made it obvious he fancied me. I cajoled him into offering me a lift to deliver my message and then onto the camp in his ambulance. He agreed if I went on a date. When we got to the camp, I told him to tell the guard that the hospital had received a call from a Sergeant Jones. He had instructed them to pick up one of their staff at the hospital who had suffered a serious leg injury and to deliver them back to this camp. I had forged a letter on stolen hospital headed paper, authorising the transfer, which he showed the guard. The guard, accepting the authenticity of the important-looking letter, let the ambulance in and instructed him how to get to the medical block with the casualty. So here I am," she said. "What about you?"

I just shrugged. "Uneventful really. A badly bruised backside from the landing, an awful lot of cycling and walking and then over the back wall into the camp. Would you like some tea?"

Having observed Alice over the training course, I concluded that she was like a chameleon, adjusting to whatever situation she was in, able to be whatever was needed at any particular time, from aristocrat to cockney. I was fascinated and hoped I could be as good as her at it. Over the next few hours, recruits like Cameron either returned by their own endeavours or were captured and brought back. Stella, the brassy, female recruit, came back quite late that night and told us she got into the camp over a back wall, helped by the local old boy's cricket club going home after a few drinks. Her escapade included stealing a milk cart.

"I was wearing the bloke's large overcoat and I just smiled as I went along." She laughed loudly. "One furious milkman will find his cart miles from where he last left it."

I was beginning to warm to both these women. They had proved themselves as good and brave as any of the men, and were both good at unarmed combat, much better than me. They'd become close knit, Alice, and Stella, drawing strength from each other to get through it all. I was a little envious still being very much alone, relying only on myself, but that's all I'd ever known in life. We all went to bed, knowing that people were still out on their mission, but we were just too exhausted.

31

INTERROGATION

At around three in the morning my room was "raided" by two people. I had a black sack put over my head and was roughly manhandled out of bed and down some steps, into a vehicle. My hands were secured in front of me, I only had pyjamas on, and it was freezing cold. The vehicle was driven over bumpy roads and then came to a stop. I was dragged out of the vehicle and up steps into an area with bare concrete flooring. I had nothing on my feet, which were now grazed, and bruised.

I went through this aspect of the training in my mind— don't panic, they will try and disorientate you, subject you to discomfort, humiliate you, make you feel as if they know everything already. They'll tell you there is no need to not cooperate, but never confess, deny, deny. Use your cover story and try and delay the interrogation to allow time for any other agents or resistance to get away. You should aim for not giving anything away at all, but certainly not for at least forty-eight hours.

I'd heard through the grapevine that the first fifteen minutes of torture were the worst and to have a strategy prepared, like reciting poetry or counting to fifty over and over to distract from the pain, ready for if it happened for real. There was a poem I knew off heart from my childhood, about a girl who told such dreadful lies, and had already decided that would be appropriate to use if needed.

They sat me firmly down on a hard chair and took the sack off my head. I was met with a bright lamp shining straight into my face. I couldn't see who was sitting opposite me due to the light, but I could see the Swastika flag on the far wall. I sensed someone was behind me and there was another person sitting at the far side on my right. As my eyes adjusted, I could see the person in front of me was wearing full German uniform and he asked my name. I stuck to my cover story which I had studied night after night of being Evelyn Bouvier and answered all the questions he put to me.

The "German" became very agitated and aggressive as he tried to break my story, shouting directly into my face, a fine spray of his spit landing on my hair. He was hysterically shouting now, and it then dawned on me the more this German got into a temper the more he sounded like a Liverpudlian German. I continued to answer the questions and stuck to my story, but I found it amusing. It broke any concerns I had about this play-acting, but my face showed absolutely nothing.

I realised that the multitude of men from the docks, coming and going at Alfie's house, had come from all over the country. I had picked up on their different accents and it was now paying dividends.

The person behind me came around to my left side and shouted at me in German, asking about personnel and training sites, but this time when he spoke, I could just make out a West Country German accent. They then spoke to me in English and started to play good German, bad

German roles. They tried to trip me up with my answers and made cruel jibes, threatening me with torture and death, still I didn't say anything. They brought in a trolley laden with torture implements and handled them menacingly in front of my face. They told me in detail what they planned to do with it all and how I kept a straight face I don't know.

The Liverpudlian grabbed my hand and put a metal pin lightly under my fingernail as if he were going to insert it deeper, but I didn't react. I was asked detailed questions again and gave the Evelyn Bouvier story to answer them. I was her now and could relay accurate information about her without hesitation. This was just too easy, and then the situation turned.

They dragged me from the chair and onto my knees, forcing my head into a bucket of freezing water. I thought I was going to drown, my lungs felt like they would burst as they held my head under. Using my hair, they pulled my head out of the bucket, and I coughed and spluttered on the water I had partially swallowed. They then repeated the head dunking; again, it was terrifying, I desperately needed to breathe, my lungs were burning. I was dragged up and pushed down hard onto the chair again. I stuck to my story. They forced me up against the wall after grabbing me by my hair and pulling me out of the chair and tore off my top. I was left wearing just a ripped bra and pyjama bottoms. They shouted in my face and kicked my legs, becoming quite menacing. If I hadn't known it was only an exercise, I would have been concerned.

I then decided to talk to them in fluent French, and as I did, they just looked at each other. They obviously weren't expecting that. Was it only English and basic German they'd been told? They looked confused and didn't appear to know what to do next. It was obvious they couldn't really torture me, that wasn't in the agreed plan. A bit of gentle hair pulling, clothes ripping, being dunked in water and the odd light slap and kick were all they were allowed to do, and that didn't have any effect. They kept me standing against the wall for a few hours with the light shining on my face, not giving me any drink or rest. They kept asking the same questions repeatedly and I didn't reply; I just recited my poem over and over in my head as the time ticked by.

The Liverpudlian turned off the light shining in my face and came to stand in front of me, staring intensely. His colleague joined him. *What the hell next*? I wondered. My feet were sore, my legs and backside ached from the initial parachute landing and then the cycling. I was thirsty and had a bit of a headache and desperately needed the lav.

I then asked them both, "Why are you wearing French insignia on German uniforms?" Their heads shot down immediately to check and slowly looked up to meet my grinning face. There was no French insignia there.

"Tea?" asked the Liverpudlian one, and I realised my interrogation had come to a natural end.

"Please," I replied as I put my torn top back on. The third person wrote down their observations and they drove me back to the camp in silence. It was now late morning, and I saw others with their heads covered being taken off for their interrogation. I went directly to my room and bathed the cuts on my feet, but I now had some idea of a strategy to manage under duress.

I checked my room, it had been searched while I'd been away, not that anything was out of place in a major way, but little things I had put in place on my desk and in my wardrobe in specific, subtle ways had been moved. They didn't find my illicit items, money, map, or compass, because I'd hidden them in their own admin office. Someone was on my side and had got me through this exercise. I thought about what Sergeant Stapleton had said before I jumped from the plane and considered it might have been him, but then I dismissed that, he hated me like Cameron did. I couldn't think of anyone else who would want to help me, but whoever it was I felt so incredibly grateful to them.

THE AFTERMATH of the exercise was reviewed in detail. Each agent had to report to Hammond and the three sergeants on Monday morning to discuss their route back. When it was my turn, Hammond read out to me several misdemeanours that had been reported in my drop section during my time on the run.

"Twelve broken farmhouse roof tiles, one stolen bike, one stolen set of women's clothes, one stolen suitcase, one half-eaten rhubarb pie, one half-eaten chicken." He hesitated and looked up over the top of his glasses at me and said, "Roast." He asked how I could account for this, and I denied any knowledge of it and didn't buckle under their intense questioning. They each rapid fired questions at me, Sergeant Jones asked how I had got back to the camp team room unseen, and I told him, over a back wall. I was then dismissed from the meeting. Part of the reason for this exercise was to look for weaknesses in the camp security itself and to me, the back wall was an obvious weak point.

Sergeant Jones approached me in the canteen for an impromptu chat; he wanted to clarify things. As he recounted it all, it amused him immensely. Firstly, that a local farmer had angrily returned a pair of woman's service underwear to security when he collected a bike and other items that had been stolen from his farm.

He also told me that at a local pub on Sunday afternoon, he heard a very chatty corporal talking about a blonde servicewoman he had taken to the camp in his truck to be a secretary. He was smitten and was looking forward to a date he'd made with her. He went to chat to the soldier to get more details and the soldier and his mates were more than happy to talk. The servicewoman's name was Irene Davenport.

He also recounted, laughing into his tea, that on the following Monday afternoon four soldiers were ordered to attend Hammond's office with him and Sergeant Hopkins. He asked them what they'd been tasked to do on the previous Saturday. One of them, a corporal, stood to attention in front of him.

"Sir, we were on exercise, tasked with being on the lookout for any possible German spies and to apprehend them and return them to the camp, sir."

"Exactly. Well done, Corporal, well done. Then perhaps you can explain to me why you brought one back into the camp in your truck, bypassing security." Hammond said.

He stood up and leaned across his desk towards the now confused Corporal, his voice getting louder and louder as he shouted at all four bewildered soldiers. "Having bought her a pint in a local pub. Then to top it all off, as the cherry on the cake, so to speak, carrying her suitcase for her and asking for a bloody date."

The soldiers were utterly floored and speechless and had no idea that the woman they helped was one they should have apprehended. The punishment meted out to them involved a lot of latrine duties.

"They decided all women were nothing but trouble, and your name was mud. I don't think they'll ever trust a woman again." He guffawed into his tea.

It dawned on me that this new friendliness might be a trick to soften me up and to let my guard down to reveal details of my return, "Trust no-one," was the rule. I kept a straight face and said, "I really don't know what you're talking about, it was nothing to do with me."

He laughed even louder and then abruptly stopped, stood up and said, "Well done Devereaux."

32

FINISHING SCHOOL

The final list of successful agents was complete, and I was sent straight to "finishing school." We were no longer using our real names and were allocated names to use from then on, I was given the name Ella. This was where I learned more about undercover work, disguises, interrogation techniques, forged documents, circuits, sub circuits and the resistance. I was taught how to find good landing sites for Lysander planes which could land and take off on a short landing strip.

We were updated about living in France, currently under occupation, and under intense bombing. We were advised on the rationing they were suffering and what could and couldn't be taken on missions, along with the German units in France we may come across. There were the Abwehr or German Military intelligence, Military police or Geheime Feldpolizei and the Gestapo or Sicherheitsdienst. There was the French Gendarmerie or newly formed Milice, some of whom worked obsessively for the Germans and others for the resistance. Finally, the main threat to us, the Radio Defence Corps who monitored illicit radio transmissions.

We underwent intense exercises in towns on how to lose someone when being followed and how to covertly tail someone. Once this was completed, I was directed to go to a camp in Oxford for advanced radio operative training.

I WAS GIVEN a few days to go home during that final part of my training, and then my flight out to France. I made my way home and noted how much bomb damage there was around the area we lived in. Whole buildings had been destroyed, streets had been shut off, and an air of fearful defiance emanated from the locals. The East End had taken a real battering. I arrived to find an unusually quiet home and was hugged tightly by my mother. I hoped Alfie had died, but unfortunately, no. He grunted at me when I went into the living room and told me I would have to sleep on the settee as my room was currently occupied but would be free from Monday. The swine had rented out my room again to someone from the docks, even though I'd been paying rent. My belongings had been bagged up and put in the shed next to the outdoor lav.

I opened my suitcase and took out the silk parachute I'd retrieved from the last exercise and gave it to my mum. I told her she and Nancy could make clothes to sell from the silk if they wanted. It would make them some money. My mother's eyes lit up at the sight of the silk and she began planning what she could make from it, murmuring about what good quality it was as she ran her fingers lovingly over it.

I really couldn't settle at home in those few days. I spent time with my mum, helping her about the house, but I was internally restless. I avoided Alfie like the plague as well as Maude and her son. Although I was relegated to the settee I couldn't sleep anyway. I was on edge, pacing, and I remembered Ethan being like this just before he left me for the final time. *Why didn't you tell me about your work? I could have supported you more than I did.* Then I realised I hadn't told anyone about my activities either and why. I was becoming distant from people, just like Ethan had.

I met up with Ethan's mother for tea and it was clear she had no idea what he'd been up to. I wasn't going to tell her, as she was still grieving his loss. The reality of his secret life and the fact he chose to risk his death, leaving her alone, may have been too much for her and so I kept quiet for now. At some point she should be told what he was doing, she would be so proud of her son.

I reflected on my new life. Even though I knew how dangerous it could be and it would mean leaving my mother, I was still committed to continuing. I had the sad, inescapable feeling, knowing what I knew about the return rates of agents, I may not be home again, but hope springs eternal when you're young, and you never think it will be you that fails or dies. That was always something that happened to someone else.

While at home the air raid siren sounded, and as usual we all hurried along the streets to the local community hall where we were led into the basement for the duration of the raid, my mother met up with Nancy. It sounded as if the explosions were happening quite a distance away, and apart from that it was all strangely uneventful.

On my last day at home, I gave my mother money and an excellently forged set of ration books. I had pleaded for them with a contact in the forgery team, who had obliged with a wink. I'd told her my job had been transferred to Sussex and so I would not be home for quite a while. I held her close, telling her how much I loved her. She didn't want me to go, and was tearful, wanting me to stay and be with her and not leave her again. Nancy arrived at that moment and handed me a brown paper parcel.

"It's a present from both of us for you, with so much love," she said. I unwrapped it and found the most gorgeous lingerie set, slip and nightdress I'd ever seen. It had been hand made by them in an amazing French design from the parachute silk I'd given them. They had attached lace and it looked stunningly beautiful. I was so touched that they'd done this for me in such a short time and I thanked them both. I was unsure when or if I would ever be able to wear it, but it was such a sweet gesture from them both. My mother started to cry again, and Ethan's mother signalled with her hand for me to go, as she put her arm around my mother and comforted her as I left.

33

THE PIANISTS

I made my way by train to my new base in Oxford where I was now with a new group of agents all being trained in the same thing. The bonus being that there was still no Cameron. The people around me were different from the groups I'd been with before. There were no uniforms and an innovative air and a jolly but serious nature around everyone. All the trainers were experts in their field and were producing new ideas all the time to be ahead of the enemy and keep agents safe. They were acutely aware we may die doing the work they were training us for, which made them more determined than ever that our preparation was the best they could deliver. It also led to a false light-heartedness in conversations with us, as if to rebalance the brutality of the training we had already undergone and what may come. They gave helpful hints and tips to us from experienced radio operatives who had returned from the occupied regions.

Our training was extremely detailed and specific around radio operating and lasted a few weeks. We had to have advanced Morse code skills to be able to send and receive messages under stressful conditions. I learnt about time limits on sending messages and set transmission times or "skeds" as they were known. I was taught how to identify detection vans and their triangulation techniques used to pin-point radio signals, and how to determine safe radio set-up sites. We were mentored on how to use a bluff code and true code system in our messages, so signals room staff would know that the message was in fact from us and not sent under duress if we were captured. The bluff code is one an agent would give to the Germans if captured, and they would leave out the true code, alerting the receiver that the message wasn't from them. We were given a call sign to use when sending messages to identify us—mine was Sabine. As we all tapped away on our Morse keys, they light-heartedly referred to us as "Pianists."

I was to be sent out to join a circuit in France as a radio operative. I would have a circuit organiser to answer to, a courier to help me obtain and distribute messages and resistance people to support us.

My head was bursting with information, I wasn't sure I would remember it all, but I believed I was as ready as I could be. In a few short months I'd been brutally taken apart piece by piece and rebuilt into a new person even I didn't recognise.

We had a final talk from Steadman who had overseen our progress. He stood in front of us all seated before him.

"You're going out to undertake one of the hardest roles to play in this war. You've been through a lot already to be prepared for this. But even now if you don't feel you're up to it, or if you don't wish to proceed, even at this late stage, you can still just walk away. No one will think any less of you. Just come and see me after this meeting."

He paused and was looking at the sea of faces in front of

him, appearing to have a flush of pride in the people in that room. It obviously brought a lump to his throat, and he couldn't speak any further. He gazed at each of us, our eyes met briefly, and he acknowledged me with a nod and left the room. Afterwards, we checked to see if anyone had left, despite the enormous danger we were going into and the strong possibility we wouldn't be coming back... No-one had.

We had to confirm we had completed and signed our last will and testament. I left anything I had to my mother. I wasn't concerned what happened to my body after death; I wasn't particularly religious. If there was a God, why would he allow such cruelty and suffering in the world?

I'd been prepared for my mission by very skilled staff. I had my cover story down to a fine art: I had become Evelyn Bouvier, my call sign was Sabine. My story was I had come to Arlaise, Northwest France, to look for work, with a plan to go to central Paris if I couldn't find anything. I'd left my hometown near Reims, as there was no work for me there after my husband, Andre, had been killed and I'd been left alone. I kept my simple wedding ring from my marriage to Ethan on a necklace as proof. He told me when he gave it to me it had been his French grandmother's ring and so it was authentic French.

This cover had been meticulously checked out and a man named Andre Bouvier had died in an accident a year previously in Reims. If the records were checked, this would be confirmed and give me time. I knew our address, his birthday, my fake parents' names, my in-law's names, where I was born, where I went to school, where I got married, where I went on honeymoon and all about the hometown I grew up in and had come from. I knew this well, as it was the nearest town to the farm where I grew up.

Every detail of my clothes, shoes and personal possessions had been checked for authenticity of a person living in
France at the time. My ration card, food coupons, identity
papers and travel card for France had all been forged to
perfection. My clothes had been miraculously aged or
distressed, as if I'd owned them for some time. They had
even sewn French labels into my clothes. Nothing was left to
chance. I was to be driven to a house near the airfield, to
stay until the next moonlit flight could take place.

I WAS MET at the precisely arranged time by a uniformed
soldier who was to drive me. He was in his mid-thirties,
around five feet ten with dark hair and extremely nervous
eyes. I saw his shoes were immaculately polished; I could
imagine him sitting up late into the night spit and polishing
them. I found this strangely comforting and it made me
smile. He held the car door open for me, inviting me to get
into the back seat with a wave of his hand. I remember
sinking into the worn leather seat as he closed the door. I
realised with a shiver there was no going back now.

He didn't initiate any conversation with me, which suited
me; I had no appetite for deep conversations. He looked
nervously at me from time to time throughout the journey,
and I wondered what details he had been given about me
that made him behave in such a way. Maybe he thought I
would suddenly produce a gun or something from my underwear, I laughed to myself. I had become quietly confident,
extremely able physically, with a challenge ahead of me that
might end my life. I had no time for female and male niceties,
which appeared entirely a new situation for the man driving

and I gave him no reason not to be nervous of me. I wish I'd been more like the new me at the beginning of the training. I would have handled Cameron so much better than I did.

As I sat in the back of the car, I remember looking at the driver intensely, just as you would gaze upon a goldfish in a bowl because it's there. I could feel his awareness of my direct stare and noticed him reddening on his neck and his left cheek as he looked intently ahead. I decided to let him be and turned my gaze out of the window at the villages we were driving through. I looked at the neat, whitewashed homes, the sandbags at either side of their doors, the taped windows and blackout curtains and the queues at the local shops. You could almost touch the fear of the people we passed, yet they were putting on a brave face, taking comfort in their daily routines. That's what I'd noticed about the soldier driving me, the polishing of his shoes, the routine, stability, security—that was what was in the back of my mind. There was to be none of that for me from now on and again it made me shudder.

We had driven for a much longer period than I'd expected, and I realised, as we passed the same village again, that he had followed a very convoluted route to confuse me as to where we were going. This, along with no visible signposts along the way, was to stop me giving information about airfields if I were captured.

"We're here, Miss," the driver informed me, and I gathered my things as we turned into a short gravel drive up to a red brick, ivy-covered house. It was well hidden from the road by a large hedge. The driver opened the car door for me, and I thanked him as I got out. I felt relief pour from his body as he was released, thankful that his ordeal was over. I watched as he hastily got back into his car and sped away, causing the rear wheels to shoot pieces of gravel at me as he left.

I turned around and found myself standing outside the front door with my case in my hand. As I went to knock, the door opened sharply, and I was greeted by an older, smartly dressed, trim woman. Her hair was neatly tied up, and she had a friendly wide smile with a very organised middle class English air about her. For some reason I was expecting someone with flour-covered hands wearing a pinny. I felt her take the case from my hand as she showed me into the kitchen.

"You must be absolutely exhausted," she said. "My name's Ann, if there's anything you need, just let me know." She spoke with an air of someone for whom this was now a matter of routine.

"Tea?" she asked, and I nodded as I sat down on a wooden kitchen chair at the small rectangular kitchen table with its cream lace tablecloth.

I was acutely aware I was one of many who had sat at this table and been given tea in front of the warm fire, others with their futures also perilous and unknown. I wondered how many were still alive. I quickly steered away from such negative thoughts and gratefully drank the tea, served in a fancy flowered print cup and saucer. All very civilised.

"You'll have a visitor later on this evening, to help you prepare for your trip," Ann said.

It sounded as if she were talking about me going on holiday, and I looked incredulously into my teacup. She appeared to not realise how those words sounded to someone like me with what I was facing.

"I'll show you up to your room where you can rest and freshen up before we eat. I will have to go through your suitcase at some point for last minute checks—routine you know," she informed me.

"That's awfully kind of you, thank you" I replied, grateful I could be alone for a while to gather my thoughts. I really wanted to go for a walk after the long drive, instead of being stuck in until the evening.

"Are there any nice walks locally Ann? I would really like to stretch my legs a bit after the car drive."

"You mustn't go into the village or meet any locals—security unfortunately," she said. "There are some nice walks on the base, large, wooded areas. The public don't have access to them, and if you want to go out for some fresh air, they're fine."

This was really happening; I was acutely aware time had flown by since that first meeting with Steadman and so much had happened to get me to this point. I sat on the small single bed, looking around at how someone had put effort in to making the room look pleasant and welcoming, but it still had the superficial feeling of a hotel or waiting room, which indeed was what it was.

I was desperate to get out of the confines of the room and left the cottage out the back door and across the fields towards the woods I'd seen in the distance.

I climbed over a small wooden stile and walked for about half a mile, ending up strolling into the woods where I came across the most amazing bluebells. The trees surrounding them were tall and strong and the bluebells were in the thousands. All standing together they looked like a magnificent blue carpet. The afternoon sunlight streamed in through the branches of the trees with beautiful butterflies flitting around—it was magical. The peace of the place, the stillness, the fragrance, the sheer beauty. I'd never seen anything quite like it in my life and I lay amongst the flowers, making an imprint of my body there.

The tall trees standing strong with their large trunks were like my guardians, towering over me, protecting me, but allowing the sun's rays in to bathe me. I felt so safe, so blessed in that moment. As I drank in the magic of the scene, watching the few white clouds pass overhead, I must have dozed off, as I awoke suddenly to the sound of aeroplanes in the distance. Sadly, I knew it meant I had to leave, but before I walked away, I looked back, breathing in the beauty of that glorious place, searing the image into my soul.

ANN WAS in the kitchen when I got back. She was chatty, all superficial stuff, and then she served her meal offering. It was basic: shepherd's pie and a jam roly-poly with custard. It tasted awful, the pudding tasting like cardboard. I had a few mouthfuls and thanked her. She looked surprised at getting any thanks at all for her cooking, it must have been a rare occurrence.

At six p.m. I was lying on my bed, with my thoughts all over the place. I heard a knock on my bedroom door, and I knew this was the "pre-drop meeting." I was hesitant to open the door, as every step I took now pushed me closer to what was waiting for me. I steadied my nerves and stood tall as I answered the door. I was met by a slightly rotund gentleman in uniform who was to be my escorting officer. He had a serious look on his face and a manner of having to get this done efficiently. His job was to support agents before they flew out, making the outgoing process as smooth as possible.

"I'm sorry, my dear, but I'm not one for frivolous conversations at a time like this," he said as he took his hat off and ran his hands over his thinning, slicked hair.

I was so pleased at his forthright manner. He was factual, clear, and precise in his instructions. He pulled out a map and put it on my bed, pointing to where I would be dropped.

"You'll be taken by a Lysander and landed in a field here." He pointed at a marked area on his map. "You will be met by a reception committee, who will keep you safe until you can meet the circuit organiser. He will then guide you as to what they need you to do as their radio operative." I nodded in agreement, but it was pretty much what I already knew, except the Lysander. That meant no parachuting, which was one less worry.

"You will have your radio to take with you. I will return to pick you up if it's a go tonight, weather permitting. We are awaiting the confirmation message, so rest yourself, my dear, anything you need, just ask Ann." He shook my hand, nodded respectfully, turned and left me. I was thankful to be alone again, to reflect on the task ahead. I looked out of the bedroom window into the fading light and saw figures going in and out of the back door to the kitchen. I knew the pilots had a separate cottage where they stayed on the base, and I wondered whether they ever knew anything about the people they were flying out and dropping off. I wondered if anyone had known Ethan. Had he sat at that kitchen table? Had he met Ann? Had he even stayed in this very room? He loved walking too—did he ever visit the bluebell wood? I really hoped so, as he would have taken such comfort from that place.

I knew all flights took off during a full or near full moon for navigation purposes. The planes had to fly exceptionally low as the pilots navigated not only by map and compass, but also by the moon's light. They needed to see the ground and specific markings below to guide them. The weather was said to be good for the next few days and so it was likely this would be my time.

～

I KEPT THINKING I should be writing a heartfelt letter to my mother, but didn't, as anything I wrote to her would have to be a lie. They would send her one of the dozen standard ones and a birthday present and card I had pre-written with my signature on anyway. I dozed on and off and sat in the dark on the flowery cushions of the window seat, looking out into the darkening evening. The time ticked by so slowly; every minute seemed to take hours. Finally, after what seemed an eternity, the time was upon me, and the escorting officer returned to pick me up to take me to the airfield.

He handed me the expected two standard pills. "Here is a Benzedrine to keep you awake should you need it at any time," he explained. "And the second pill..." his words hung in the air as he hesitantly handed it to me.

I knew it was a cyanide pill, or L-tablet, a pea sized capsule covered with glass and rubber which if you bit into it meant you were dead in under a minute. You could escape torture this way and not give away any information you may have on other agents, resistance, safe houses, or codes. I just thought it was their insurance policy, but I thanked him for them, God knows why. He gave me a small handgun and a commando knife that I'd trained with in Scotland.

I put the two pills in a specially designed lipstick case to conceal them and was taken to a building at the side of the airfield. I had my clothes and possessions checked again for the hundredth time. This was to look for any giveaway details such as British labels or English items, anything that would not be available in France at the time, like English cigarettes, and was then taken to another building. There were other agents also waiting for flights out, just like me. I didn't recognise any of them, as they were possibly from earlier agent groups and for some it was their second or third flight. They all chatted happily amongst themselves, no names or details shared, especially as to where they were being dropped. It was all very jolly in that place, a hive of activity for pilots, agents, and staff.

The ceilings in this house were extremely low. There was a large kitchen with whitewashed walls and a small dining table. The other two rooms consisted of a large dining room with two trestle tables and the other, a cluttered living room, had a large coal fire, a black beamed ceiling, and assorted styles and shapes of chairs scattered around. Detailed maps of Europe with areas of flak highlighted covered the walls and flying paraphernalia was all over the place. This was the ops room, which had two phones in for communication about flights. They had pilots who were decent cooks too apparently, which made me wish I'd stayed here instead of with Ann, but then decided her cottage was quieter, which suited me.

I heard the staff call us "Joes" rather than by any names; others referred to us as "Bods." We Joes or Bods were all offered a hot toddy to drink, but I just couldn't. I hated the taste of the stuff and it made me feel sick. I was sure the last thing they needed was me puking my guts up in front of them or in the plane.

I was handed a package containing a substantial number of used Francs to hand over to the circuit organiser when I met him. I split the package and put small amounts in pockets in a waist belt, which was then secured around me under my clothes. This was to help fund local resistance activities. Part of me fleetingly thought I could flee with my mum and the money and not go through any of this. I sighed deeply and looked at the others also making the same journey in a braver fashion than me and felt a bit ashamed of the thought.

The liaison officer escorted me to a car, and we were driven the short distance to where the pilot was checking the plane

I looked up from the car window and saw the beautiful full moon that was bathing the dark green and grey painted Lysanders on the airfield in its light. We got out of the car to find it was quite blustery out in the open fields.

"That's your Lizzie pilot," said the liaison officer pointing to the pilot near the plane. That was the nickname this type of plane had been given; others called it the "Air Taxi."

"Good luck, my dear," he shouted into the windy night air at me and handed me over to the pilot.

The pilot pointed to a small metal ladder, which was inbuilt to the side of the plane, and directed me to get in. I carried my radio case, and he passed my suitcase in. My seat was facing the back of the plane, and the pilot, a young man with fair hair and incredibly soft eyes, told me about the parachute and Mae West that was with me in the back in case we crash landed in the sea. God, I hadn't thought of that happening. Being shot, yes, being blown up, yes, being tortured, yes, but not drowning in the sea. It sounded awful, but at least he was prepared. He leaned over to show me the coffee thermos and gave me an idea as to how long it would take to get to our rendezvous. His uniform close-up looked well-worn and battered under a thick brown leather flying jacket.

He assisted me with putting on a flying helmet and told me to let him know by using the intercom switch, which he tested for me, if I saw anything he needed to be aware of I might see from the back of the plane.

"Like the Luftwaffe, for example." He laughed, but I didn't find that remotely funny.

He wasn't much older than me, and I thought how brave he was to fly in and out of enemy territory repeatedly, each time reducing his chance of staying alive. He told me to call him Whippet. The other pilots called him that as he was one of the fastest at the drop-off and pickup turnarounds, which made me feel some confidence. He was looking at me as if wondering what a young woman was doing in the back of his plane. On seeing his expression, I wondered whether he'd ever flown a woman into the war zone before.

34

THE MOON MEN

The plane took off from the airfield and for the first time I began to have doubts. Perhaps I wasn't ready. My stomach was in knots. I went through everything in my head over and over until the information was becoming confusing. I would be met by a reception party, my radio case was with me, I would be taken to a safe house and radio back at the first opportunity from a further safe site that all was well. I would blend into local life and be led by a senior operative who ran the circuit of agents and French resistance. I would meet the circuit organiser, courier and lookout and start sending and receiving information between the agents, the resistance, and England. It sounded so straightforward.

My nerves were starting to take over. This was finally happening, and for once I wished I'd accepted the alcohol offered at the airfield. I then went through my cover story again, how to set up the radio, my call sign, bluff code, true code and sign off. My mind was buzzing and fizzing with thoughts, my pulse racing, my heart pounding in my chest. I had never experienced such stress in my life.

Trying to calm myself, I gazed into the night sky. It seemed so peaceful out there. I could see how much light the moon gave off and as we were flying so low, I was able to see landmarks and things like rivers and streams below. I had always loved moonlight, I found it so magical and exciting. There were millions of twinkling stars above me, and looking down, I saw that as the light shone on the English Channel, it magically turned the cold, muddy water into what looked like sparkling diamonds tumbling over and over on the waves as they broke.

My teeth started to chatter loudly, and my body was shaking with the cold. Inside the plane was incredibly noisy too. The package of money was becoming extremely uncomfortable around my waist and back. It did cross my mind as the plane flew on that if I were going to die, they could at least have made the final journey a bit more pleasant.

Whippet flew over the channel and into searchlights and light flak from just beyond a beach area of France. The plane was rocked a bit from side to side, but that soon passed. The weather wasn't as good as it had been in England and became cloudier as we flew nearer to the landing zone. I couldn't see anything below us now and felt sure Whippet couldn't either. I thought we should be landing soon but couldn't see any code lights on the ground. We circled around and around, and I began to feel terribly nauseous.

"We're going home," Whippet said quietly over the intercom, and he flew us back to the airfield.

This was a major blow, as I'd been mentally prepared. I was in severe adrenaline fight mode and now had to calm myself down until the next opportunity to go. It was so frustrating.

After landing, Whippet led me back across the darkened field to the pilot's cottage for a cup of tea, with a plan to try again tomorrow night. I was in a bit of a state, and over numerous cups of tea and pieces of toast and jam he tried to take my mind off things. He told me fascinating stories about his flying and about the different moons during every month of the year. Most of their flights were by some degree of moonlight and as a result the pilots were called the "Moon Men." All the new moons had names, there were also eight phases of the moon.

"There's the flower moon, the pink moon, the wolf moon, snow moon, the strawberry moon. There is one named for every month of the year," he told me.

I was utterly mesmerised. It was something I'd never thought about before and had truly little knowledge of.

"What moon are we under at the moment, Whippet?" I asked him as I sipped my tea.

"The flower moon; it takes its name from the myriad of wildflowers that bloom in the late spring months, bluebells and violets for example." I loved every detail and was impressed with how informed he was about it. This wasn't really a manly subject, but he held me captivated by the fire-light as he described every different new moon and its meaning.

"I studied it because I spend so much time flying under one, I felt it only right to know about it and respect it." He then went on to tell me about his own life. He was engaged to his childhood sweetheart and had plans for after the war. Marriage, children, and take over the family business when the time came. Until then, he loved being a pilot and the camaraderie with the other pilots.

A string of pilots and other staff came in and out of the cottage that night. They laughed and joked with Whippet, patted him on his back, shook his hand, and ruffled his hair. It was obvious they liked and respected him very much. I could understand why; he was such a good man, risking his life with such youthful bravery, good humour, and thoughtfulness. He was a true gentleman. I couldn't really tell him anything about me and as the professional he was, he didn't ask.

When the last person had left the kitchen and we were alone, he surprisingly took my hand across the table and unsettled me by saying, "I've been brought up to protect women, and here I am about to land one into danger. I've seen the faces of the people I've picked up from over there, haunted, in shock. It goes against everything I know, it's not the natural order of things. I know I can't change your mind and wouldn't dream of trying; things are what they are. But I want you to know I think you are beautiful and brave, and if I'm ever called on to get you out of there, I promise I'll do my damnedest to get you safely home."

I was stunned at this turn of events. He'd completely thrown me. Not once had I considered the stress on people working with me. Beautiful and brave he said—was that just tea he was drinking? He obviously didn't realise how scared I truly was, and no one had ever called me beautiful before, not even Ethan; that was far too frivolous a word. It wasn't how I would describe myself either. I'd always looked at things from my bleak perspective and this was something new and unsettling. I thanked him for his kindness and started to get up from the table, releasing his hand from mine.

As it was late, he showed me to a bedroom in the pilot's cottage and wished me goodnight. He was a brave pilot but had a softer side to him too, which came out while we talked. I'd never come across a man like him before. He was utterly charming, and I had an overwhelming feeling I would come to no harm if he were with me. I didn't feel romantically linked to him in the slightest, knowing he was engaged and happily so. I just had a feeling of sheer respect and deep trust. He was a kind, gentle hero, and his fiancée was so lucky to have him.

I really wished he hadn't said what he did though, as it made a small chink in the emotional shield I'd put up for protection. He treated me as female and vulnerable, which wouldn't help me at all where I was going.

After he left, I couldn't sleep. I was terribly wound up mentally and physically. Being in a room with a choice of three beds, all packed in tightly for pilots and their guests, I lay on one but couldn't settle and crept down the stairs to make myself more tea. I sat most of the night at the kitchen table going over and over my training. As dawn broke, the kitchen had become frightfully cold with the fire having long gone out. I made my weary way to bed, as exhaustion finally took over and the adrenaline rush subsided.

I SKIPPED breakfast and geared myself up for the next attempt. I couldn't cope with any more chit-chat or deep meaningful heart-to-hearts and so I just rested alone. That evening, I was told it had been confirmed that we were game on again and Whippet came to collect me. He looked a bit sheepish, as if he wanted to take back what he'd said the night before in case it had upset or unnerved me. I brushed it all off and reassured him as much as I could that everything was fine. It was no big issue; in fact, I was glad at least someone cared.

The dining room was crowded with pilots, and we ate

the most marvellous bacon, sausage, and eggs. The pilots had other skills than just flying and one had made a beautiful treacle sponge. It was such a treat. Whippet had recovered his cheeky charm and I was relieved at that, as we made our way out to the plane together. The sound of the remaining pilots and staff singing jolly French songs and larking about rang in our ears as we went out into the night.

We followed the same routine as the previous night, flying back over the Channel. After a while, I noted clouds drift beneath the plane and despaired. I'd heard sometimes weeks or months went by before a successful drop was made due to the weather or some other catastrophe, like not finding the drop zone. Agents dropped out completely because they lost their nerve after so many abandoned attempts. I couldn't take another failed flight and my anxiety permeated the plane.

We were over the landing point and Whippet indicated he could just make out a light below, a Morse code letter being sent to us from the ground. Whippet answered with the response code with his own light. Five lights then came on from a field in an inverted L-shape below us to guide him to the landing point, and the plane landed incredibly smoothly. We landed in the field between two groups of trees. He kept the engine running as expected and slowly turned the plane as I was getting out.

"Good luck. See you on the return journey," he said quietly over the intercom.

"Safe journey back," I told him, really meaning every word.

I got up and out of the plane as quickly as I could, as six figures emerged from their hiding places, five men and one woman. Two of the men were being taken back to England and started to run towards the plane.

The leader of the welcoming group was from the French resistance. He was a very thin, short-statured man with a moustache and thin lips, and what remaining hair he had was slicked sideways. He was acting in a very strange manner. He didn't say anything to me, just kept looking at the soon-to-depart plane and back at me, behaving more manic as the seconds went by.

He then mumbled in a low voice, "I'm sorry, I'm so sorry, that's it for me. I can't do this anymore. I have to get away."

He started sprinting after the two men and squeezed into the small back area of the plane with them. The plane had been on the ground about three minutes now and Whippet wouldn't have time to argue. He needed to leave and took off with three passengers instead of two.

I watched this happening in stunned silence, this man was meant to support me to get to the circuit leader and had suffered some sort of mental collapse and left. This wasn't in the training manual. *What the hell do I do now?*

The others were also aghast at this turn of events. One of them, a dark-haired, muscular young man, took control and grabbed my arm. He took my suitcase and led me into the woods away from the landing site, his gun slung over his shoulder. The older French man took my radio case and the woman joined us. The four of us made our way in silence through the moonlit fields and woods. I followed their lead, my mind filled with questions. *What would happen now? Who would I be working with? Why did he bolt like that?*

The first two, the woman, and the older man, left the trees we were in and motioned for us two to wait where we were. They had to cross a field and a road, to get to their truck on the far side which had been hidden. Once on the other side of the road near the truck, they would signal if it were safe for us to go as well.

Just as they were almost at the road, and before they were under any cover, they started signalling for us to stay where we were. The sound of a motor vehicle racing our way could be heard and I saw headlights coming rapidly along the road. The German patrol must have heard the noise of the plane, or seen it's lights at the drop off, and were coming to investigate.

We stayed where we were hidden in the woods, the other two were very exposed and it was too far for them to run back and still a distance to get to cover. We watched in horror as the older man tripped as he ran, sprawling on the road with my radio case. They were caught in the headlights as she rushed back to help him up.

A shot rang out from the vehicle and the Frenchman grabbed my arm and pulled me further into the deeper cover of the woods. We couldn't see anything but heard German voices shouting and the vehicle staying put with its engine running. The soldiers shone a bright light into the surrounding fields and trees. The searchlight waved over us, but we were well hidden in the undergrowth. The thorns on the branches of a bush pierced my skin painfully as we waited, and my hair was tangled in the brambles. We stayed as still as we could until we were sure we hadn't been seen, and after a while, we heard the vehicle move slowly off along the road towards where the drop-off had taken place.

I desperately wanted to check if the older man had managed to throw my radio in the undergrowth, but I was stopped.

"No, it's too dangerous to be around here now or use the vehicle. I must warn the others those two have been captured. We have to leave and get you to an alternative safe house to the one planned, in case they talk," he told me.

"We can get another radio dropped for you to use, don't worry."

I can't work without a radio. Damn blast and hell. How could it have all gone so wrong so quickly?

~

WE WALKED BRISKLY for a couple of miles through the countryside, moving silently in the darkness. My shoes were becoming clogged with mud by this time, and I felt like a complete failure having lost my radio, something I'd been entrusted with. They had lost two resistance fighters too.

The man I was with introduced himself as Lucien and told me the other two were a father and daughter and I despaired; this wasn't supposed to happen. I needed time to think and get my bearings. I wished I could turn back the clock and start this all over again.

I was becoming incredibly tired and at last could see a farm in the distance and started to eagerly make for it. Lucien firmly grabbed my arm, stopping me from going any further. He looked at the farm and surrounding area through binoculars, and only when he was satisfied there was nothing out of place, did he signal for me to move.

We reached the farm and Lucien gave a coded knock at the front door. A man greeted him with a huge bear hug and shook my hand. He then took us through to meet his wife in the kitchen.

Marion and Daniel Roussel were both long-term resistance fighters. They were in their early forties; Marion was slim with thick dark hair and such a beautiful smile that drew you to her. Daniel was solidly built, rugged, confident, and welcoming. Their farmhouse was used as a safe house for escapees or agents, they also stored ammunition and supplies for the resistance. Everything relating to them went through Lucien and a couple of other trusted people, to protect them from being caught. The small farm was a fair way from the main town and up to that point hadn't really been checked on by the occupying forces or local police.

I was led into a barn and straw bales were moved to uncover a hatch in the floor with steps down into a darkened room. Marion gave me a torch and wine and food to take with me. She took my shoes to clean off the mud and I went hesitantly into the underground room to await the next move. Lucien started to lower the hatch above me.

"I have to warn the others of the arrests and will come back for you. If I don't return, Daniel will arrange for you to be picked up. You can trust them both, they are good people. Try and get some rest." He closed the hatch, leaving me in darkness.

This was not what was meant to happen. I knew I was extremely vulnerable, and incredibly tired, crashing down after the adrenaline rush. I was sitting on a single camp bed and shone the torch around the small space and saw with absolute horror that with me were piles of different types of guns, ammunition, and German grenades. There were also several German uniforms of differing rank. This was a bit disconcerting—there wouldn't be much left of me if the explosives went off, but I had to ignore it all and get muchneeded sleep. I'd be even more useless than I had been if I became too exhausted, and I needed to have a clear head for what was coming.

I ate the food and stretched out on the camp bed, wondering how I could make the best of this dreadful situation. I covered myself in a blanket and two German thick overcoats to try and keep warm. I didn't feel in control of things and, if anything, I liked to be in control. I didn't like being dependent on people I didn't know for my safety. Lucien, Marion, and Daniel had been kind, and I was beginning to realise that my life from then on would be reliant on others as much as myself. I had to learn to be dependent on people, and I hated the idea.

I then had the most awful thought sweep through me— what if this was a set-up? What if Lucien and the Roussels worked for the Germans? He knew about the drop-off; he could have planned the capture of the two resistance fighters. It could be that when the hatch to this basement opened, a load of Germans would flood in, and my mission would be over before it had even started. Cameron would love that.

I quickly dismissed that thought; he could have had me captured at the landing zone if he'd wanted to. What good would come of having me captured now? I knew nothing and was pretty much useless. I still took out my gun though, just in case.

I slept fitfully, with the gun under my pillow until next morning, when thankfully Lucien opened the hatch. I came up the concrete steps warily into the early morning light. Lucien explained this wasn't my designated destination, just a trusted stop off until they could get me to where I was supposed to be. They had arranged an apartment for me to use in Arlaise itself, which would be my initial base. I would need to move from place to place to avoid detection and set myself up with safe sites where I could use my new radio when it arrived. The two captured resistance fighters knew nothing of these new plans and so it was considered safe to continue, even if they had talked.

Marion handed me my now perfectly clean shoes and we had breakfast together in their charmingly decorated kitchen. The food was marvellous; it certainly paid to be on a farm during a war. Daniel and Marion were such committed resistance, they were very jolly about what they did, accepting of the risk it entailed. They were very much in love, which showed in the way they spoke to each other and touched tenderly, giving the other support. They didn't have children and so it was just the two of them, which they said made it easier to risk their lives. They hated the Germans passionately and wanted France to be liberated and the war to be over. I envied them their marriage—they worked well together, their love and protection of one another obvious. It was heart-warming to watch and made me acutely aware that it was a world away from my own short, dismal marriage.

They knew where the German headquarters were and places they frequented and their bases. The German navy had a base in a large local chateau because of the deep port nearby and Marion described their uniforms to me so I could differentiate them from regular forces. They pointed out on a local map the areas where roadblocks were set up and where soldiers mostly patrolled. They warned me that while a few people in the French police were known resistance, I shouldn't trust any of them. Lucien told me the address I had to make for and gave me extra money to tide me over until I was settled into the system.

Daniel led me to his truck for the drive to the station. "It's easy for people like me with businesses and farms to move around locally through roadblocks to make deliveries. I've been stopped and searched so many times now that most of them manning the local roadblocks know me and just let me through, I give them food gifts like cheese to soften them up. It's more difficult for cars now as there is much less petrol around and the Germans are comman-

deering the good cars. They have a preference for Citroens."
He laughed.

"Once in Arlaise you will be contacted by a member of
the circuit to arrange to meet up with what is left of them.
They need a radio operative badly, as the last one had been
shot."

"Oh God," I muttered under my breath as I got into the
truck.

I waved goodbye to Lucien and Marion, thanking them
for everything. We drove through a village and then into
open countryside where I felt more at home. The more I
looked at the countryside, the more I grew in confidence I
could do this work. We were both lost in our own thoughts,
and as we neared our destination Daniel broke the silence.

"Your papers will be checked on the train as they are
suspicious of anyone travelling. They will also be checked at
both stations when you go in and when you leave, so have
them ready. Make sure you aren't left fumbling for anything.
They watch everything and everyone, they are not always in
uniform so be careful."

I nodded, knowing I had to show confidence and an air
of being a seasoned, local resident: otherwise, I would give
rise to suspicion.

He wished me good luck as he dropped me off outside
the station then quickly drove away, leaving me to my fate.

I CHECKED the train routes and timetable and bought my
ticket. I had my papers and suitcase checked briefly by what
the uniform indicated were French police and made my way
onto the platform. It was there I had my first sight of the
"enemy." I saw a small group of German soldiers gathered at

one end of the platform and local people spread out along the length of it. It was unnerving, but the soldiers didn't seem interested in anything that was going on, they just looked bored, chatting to each other waiting for a train. I took up a seat in the middle of the locals and sat down to wait. The train was awfully late; it was likely the war was disrupting the railway schedules.

Once on board I sat in one of the carriages near a window and pulled out a book I had taken from the Roussels' farm to use in situations like this. It was an old, well-thumbed book and I opened it pretending to read, while all the time acutely aware of what was happening around me as the train moved off. While glancing out the window, I saw signposts of places were now in German as well as French showing the true occupation of France.

A short while later, I heard the carriage door open behind me. I looked up and found myself looking into the face of a German soldier standing over me.

"Papers," he said loudly down the carriage, and I handed over my ID, ticket, and travel permit. This simple interaction was inexplicably such a shock, my pulse rate soared. I could feel my insides contracting in fear. I put on as calm and innocent look as I could, knowing I appeared incredibly young and vulnerable with no makeup. He stared at the documents and then back at me, then looked again at my ID and looked intensely back at me. I wondered if he'd spotted anything wrong and was panicking inside, but he then handed the documents back and moved on. I thanked God for the skill of the forgers, but I didn't show any signs of relief, as I knew what might come next.

Exactly as I'd been taught, the door behind me opened again and I saw another man in a long coat and hat following the soldier through the carriage. He might be

Gestapo looking for signs of relief from people once the soldier had checked their papers, indicating they had something to hide. He glanced at me as he passed, but didn't stop, and I continued to "read." My first real close encounter with the enemy. No one realised that on the train with them was a young agent, carrying thousands of used Francs in a belt around her waist, along with a gun and a knife.

I GOT off the train and handed in my ticket at the exit, where my papers and suitcase were checked again. I headed towards the general part of the town I'd been told to go. I didn't ask for directions as that would have singled me out as new to the area. I had a short walk, and after a few wrong turns, eventually found the apartment block I was to stay at. I waited to see if any activity was taking place around the building, and once I was satisfied it was safe, I entered. I knocked the door of flat ten and a young, serious-looking brunette woman opened the door and ushered me in.

This was my cover address for now and once the keys had been handed to me by the young woman, she said sternly, "You'll be contacted within twenty-four hours from now. The code to this door is one loud knock and three soft knocks. If you don't hear that, don't open the door. Don't leave the flat until contact has been made." With that said, she left, closing the door quietly behind her.

I was left in the tiny one-bedroom apartment. There was odd-looking dark bread, cheese, sausage, and coffee left out, as well as a forged rent book, local ID papers and coupons for food. Newspapers had been left for me to update myself on national and local issues. I was suddenly overcome with exhaustion. The stress, tension, and fear had begun. I was disappointed no one had really prepared me enough for this aspect of being an agent. This would be my life from now on, waiting for knocks on doors, possible capture, constantly being checked, taking risks, always looking over my shoulder. I would be living on my nerves, being reliant on others for my safety and sustenance. That feeling of dependence gnawed away at me. I absolutely hated it.

As I looked around, I caught a glimpse of myself in the bathroom mirror and was alarmed at my reflection. I had dark circles under my eyes, my face looked strained, and my hair was a mess. I initially thought I wouldn't last five minutes looking like this, but in fairness, I realised with rationing, intense bombing, Germans everywhere and lack of supplies I fit in quite well with the current state of the locals. I washed my hair, nibbled at the food, and went to bed with my gun under my pillow. I put a jug on the floor behind the door to wake me if someone opened it. Then slept deeply for the first time in days.

35

ARCHITECT

W hen I woke next morning, I felt refreshed and energised, eager to establish myself. I heard the coded knock on the door about nine. A tall, middle-aged man was standing there in a suit that looked too big for him. He was carrying a case and I let him in. He said in a deep, funereal voice that his name was Lombard, and he handed me the case, which I realised was in fact my new radio.

"This is a spare one from our previous operator." He looked heavenward and made the sign of the cross on his chest as he said this, to indicate they'd died. I really wished they wouldn't keep referring to the demise of the previous radio operator. It was unnerving. I let him continue.

"You need to be at this address at nine tonight. You must be back here before the curfew at eleven. They are strict with this, and if caught outside you will be arrested or worse." He handed me a slip of rice paper. "Memorise it and destroy it. Don't carry anything written with you when you go out."

He went to the kitchen cupboard under the sink and got

on his knees. He opened the cupboard and pulled away a false backboard revealing a space that had been constructed in the back wall.

"This is for your radio and anything else you need to hide," he said, putting the case inside. He closed the door and stood directly in front of me, a serious look on his face. I wondered what on earth was coming next, but he merely put on his hat, nodded to me and said in his deep tone, "Welcome to France. Good luck." And left.

This meant I had the rest of the day to recce the area and get my bearings. I took my ID papers, a local newspaper and ventured into the town. As taught, I'd positioned items in certain ways in the flat for me to know if someone had been in there while I was out.

I walked around enjoying being outside and in the fresh air. Like London, this area had been bombed, but not as badly yet. Buildings had collapsed under the onslaught of the German advance and the people again had that quiet air of defiance about them as they went about their damaged daily lives. Arlaise had a port and railyard, all of which were targets for the resistance and Allies. The river running through the town had a temporary bridge going over it. The French army had destroyed the original bridge when they left, and the Germans had constructed the temporary one when they arrived. The architecture of the place was glorious to see but had suffered from both German and Allied assaults, which was such a tragedy. Buildings that had stood for hundreds of years destroyed in seconds—heartbreaking.

I sat outside a cafe drinking coffee, which looked and tasted awful, not like any coffee I'd ever had before. German soldiers were walking around, some seated in the cafe area I was in, but they didn't bother me at all, just glanced now and again in an indifferent manner. There were a lot of German soldiers and sailors just visiting the town from surrounding areas. It appeared to be a bit of a social gathering place for them; they were there to relax and have fun, not look for spies.

By the afternoon I had established where main buildings were, where Germans were stationed, and places I might be able to use my radio. I noticed how austere the town looked. The people had pinched thin faces and almost all wore ill-fitting clothes and repaired shoes. There was rationing and food coupons as in England and it looked like a black market was running for some goods. You could buy restricted things if you had the money, or you were collaborating, or knew the right people. Alfie would have loved it.

I saw long queues of people outside bakeries standing for hours on end for bread of any sort. It was strange because the shop fronts were full of luxury goods, but not basics, you couldn't get things like toothpaste. I noted how the women were dressed and made sure my clothes didn't look too out of place. My hair was also fashioned in the same style as theirs. I returned to the flat, satisfied I blended in well, and finished off the cheese and by now stale bread. The rationing was much worse than London, possibly because the Germans were now transporting agricultural goods from France to Germany to support the German population.

WHEN EVENING STARTED TO FALL, I made my way to the address given to me. It was a long walk through the town then over the river into narrow winding streets, but I eventually found the address, a small church. I looked around the outside and watched as civilians entered before I went in. I looked through the doorway and saw a small number of people dotted around, praying, and crying quietly by candlelight. I sat at the back, drinking in the sheer reverence of the place, and waited, and waited, but nothing happened.

It was well past nine-thirty now and I was becoming increasingly concerned, things had gone wrong. I was about to leave, when the serious young brunette woman I'd met at the apartment came and sat next to me nodding for me to follow her. She led me around to the back of the church and in through a door leading down to a shadowy basement. As I went inside, she positioned herself outside smoking a cigarette. She was stood against a wall which had a pavement level window, appearing ready to warn those inside with a knock on the window with her foot if anyone approached.

I could just make out a few people in the minimally lit room and as my eyes adjusted to the light, a man approached me and said in clear English, "Welcome, welcome, my dear, we've been waiting for you." He explained he had taken over the circuit, and to be referred to by his code name: Voltaire.

"I do apologise for the chaos at your arrival. I must tell you sadly, that the two people who were with you when they were captured, have been killed. We're as sure as we can be they didn't talk."

He looked directly at me as if expecting an emotional reaction, but there was none. Inside, however, my guts were churning at this news. I was truly shocked at the death of two of the first people I'd met, who had been tasked to help me. The possibility of my own death made me quiver, even though I was aware it was a strong possibility.

"No German raids have taken place since, but we have

moved key people and changed our meeting places and message dead drop sites, just in case. We are all to be extra vigilant," he announced to us all.

He turned to me again and put both his hands on my shoulders. "Forget everything you were taught in England, the training manual, what the trainers have told you. This is real life not textbook stuff and the theory you've been taught doesn't always match it in practice. You must think on your feet here. We all rely on each other to do that for our very survival."

"Of course. Oh, I have something for you," I said, taking the money belt from around my waist and handing him the valuable package from England.

"Thank you, my friend. Now let me introduce you to Ava. She will be working with you as your courier. She knows the area really well." We shook hands. She was English, middle aged, rather thin and a plain housewife type. She blended in well locally.

"I'll take you to see the current dead drop tomorrow. Meet me here at this address at eleven in the morning," Ava informed me in a warm voice. She handed me a slip of paper to memorise. My temporary lookout, and radio support from the resistance, was a young man, Louis, who would also keep in close contact with me. He had replaced the previous lookout, the man who had met me at the Lysander drop and been shot.

I observed Louis closely. He was a dark-haired, lanky, early thirties male with a bit of pock mark scarring on his face. I didn't feel confident in him and wasn't sure why. He had a weak handshake for a man for a start. I wondered why he hadn't been called up for army service. I found out from Ava that he was in a protected service as a mortician's assistant, which explained an awful lot to me. He was also useful as they used his coffins and hearses to transport people, and equipment around unseen and stored ammunition in false empty graves.

The meeting went ahead with talk about the latest news, movements of Germans in the area and what actions they had been asked to carry out by England. They talked about the new BBC message service, which they had to tune into increasingly now to hear updates on the resistance and personal messages for individual resistance groups. This put them at risk because anyone found using a radio by the Germans, was shot, but it gave them answers to questions they had sent messages about and confirmation of actions they were to take, all in code.

Louis didn't like to be told what to do and argued about everything that was said in the group. *That might be a problem.* Discipline was a must in this job, and I had to trust him to watch my back while I was messaging. He was trying to assert his authority in the group, and this wasn't well received.

I concluded it must be because he was used to working with the dead and they weren't able to give him orders or argue with him. He had difficulty being around living, tetchy, opinionated human beings. He had an inflated opinion of himself and his abilities as a resistance fighter too. This made him dangerous in my opinion and he would need to be handled carefully, or I could insist I work alone.

The circuit itself consisted of an organiser, radio operator, and courier, local resistance people were included to use their local knowledge, ensure their co-operation, and foster good working relations. Louis was one of those. There had been initial reluctance from the French to work with English agents in a circuit, but that had improved, out of mutual necessity. The circuit I was part of was named Architect.

I was told not be at any further meetings with Voltaire unless strictly necessary, contact would be through the courier system to protect us both. There was no need for me to know people's names, as most of my time would be spent picking up and sending messages which didn't need a lot of local face-to-face activity. The less we knew the safer we were, and it would protect people if I were arrested. More importantly it would protect me if others were caught, as radio operators were not that easy to come by.

"Just one thing to mention before you go, we have sub-circuits, foreign agents and other groups working in this area. Some of the groups are purely French resistance and others are a mix of foreign individuals and resistance. Communication is a bit erratic and leads to some risky chaos as to who is doing what and when, but we are working on it."

I was dismissed, as they wished to talk without me there. I noted a spiral staircase leading from the basement which must go up into the church. They were using the side entrance to lessen the excessive comings and goings into the main church entrance which might arouse suspicion.

I looked at my watch and was startled at how the time had flown. I had less than half an hour to get back before the curfew. It was quite a long walk too. I hurriedly went up the basement steps to the back road, saw the brunette who nodded it was safe, and went out into the now much darker night.

The places looked so different from when I'd walked past them earlier. There was an eeriness about the place, especially where buildings had partially collapsed or been burnt out. There was hardly any light to guide me and not many people around. A sense of panic started to set in, and I wasn't sure I would make it back in time. I couldn't go back to the group and say I was lost; that would hardly instil any confidence in me. I took deep breaths to calm myself and tried to re-trace my steps back, staying close to walls of buildings, picking out landmarks I'd passed on the way there. At last, the river came into view, and with ten minutes left, my pace quickened and so did my heart rate.

Finally, I turned a corner and with utter relief recognised my building. I rushed through the door and up the stairs two at a time, slamming the door behind me, gasping for air, and trying to steady my nerves. I realised then I'd just broken every rule of being an agent that had probably ever been written. I brought attention to myself by running, not checking if I were being followed, or if the building was secure before I came in and was almost caught outside after curfew. I'd made a complete arse of myself, putting myself and others at risk. Once I was sure I was safe, I did what I imagined all agents do in such stressed times, I burst into hysterical laughter.

I MET Ava the next day and we walked to a small square where we sat on a low wall rather than the benches. Ava informed me the telephone system was being tapped and you couldn't be sure if any outdoor seating had a listening device attached.

"In the back row of the church on the left-hand side, there's a bible tucked under the bench near the wall. The bible has a cut-out section in which messages can be left or picked up. That's the dead drop for now, but it will change again soon. No one ever sits there, it's too far back, and everyone is in front of you, so they can't see what you're up to, except the priest and he's in the resistance." She paused for me to acknowledge I understood and then carried on. "I'll leave any messages there for you to pick up and send back for now and you can leave messages or replies for me. If it's urgent give the message to the priest, he has good reason to be going to people's homes at all hours. If you think at any time you're being followed, use the stairs in the vestry to the basement and get out that way, the door in the building opposite is always unlocked so go in there to lose anyone following, and lock yourself in."

We split up and I went for coffee at my local cafe, which I'd chosen to use from now on. A lot of German servicemen favoured it and I considered they may talk loudly about work, troop movements and general gossip. This sort of lazy relaxed chat could be useful, and I would be hidden in plain sight listening. The coffee was much nicer too; it didn't have the horrid chicory taste the other place's coffee did. It was close to my current apartment, which was satisfactory for now, but I would need to move soon. I wouldn't give my new address to anyone; I preferred people didn't know where I lived. I also wouldn't use my apartment to send messages from; I would find other sites. Ava told me the agent before me was caught because he only used two designated sites to message from and stayed on the radio too long sending very lengthy messages at specific times. This was picked up by the Germans who were monitoring the sites, leading to his arrest. They knew he'd been shot a few weeks after his arrest, but no further arrests were made, and they presumed he hadn't talked.

36

NO WAY OUT

I prepared my radio set to send my first message. The suitcase had a tray of French make-up inside to cover the radio beneath in case it was checked. Louis had identified a safe house just on the outskirts of town to use and I sent my first message to England three weeks after landing, keeping it short. They might have thought I was dead, not having heard from me, and I knew the name Sabine would have come up on the radio receiver's board for the first time. I remembered to put in my bluff code and true code and signed off with just a straight goodbye.

I gave them information about railway lines being used for troop movements; this had been supplied by the resistance working in the railways. I also passed on information about activity at the port. The messages confirmed which German troops were in the area and the seniority of the troops seen. I asked for specific equipment requested by the resistance.

Louis had started getting panicky after ten minutes and was trying to rush me, telling me to hurry up. I had to ignore him to ensure the message was coded accurately and received; otherwise, there would be no point in sending it at all. I would receive the reply to the resistance question on my next transmission.

My set-up and message send took thirteen minutes in total and Louis and I parted company as Louis went out the front of the building first, then me five minutes later out the back.

I hoped my message got through and the decoders could read it. I thought about a joke I'd been told by one of the radio receivers in training about an army message being sent out as, "Send reinforcements we're going to advance" which ended up as "Send three and fourpence we're going to a dance," to indicate how badly things could go if we weren't accurate.

I walked back with my radio in its suitcase, which was quite heavy, making my arm ache after a while. It must have weighed about thirty pounds, they really needed to make this lighter to carry.

I SETTLED into a steady routine sending and receiving messages from different sites and safe houses. Louis remained edgy during messaging, which was a distraction. I lived like a local—with ration coupons, and quite a bit of money. I had secretly taken a wad of the old francs I'd been given to bring from London to the resistance and adjusted to my undercover life. I figured I'd be more at risk if I had no money. It's amazing what people would do if you paid. It also meant I could buy decent food if I wanted. There was no reason for me to starve if it wasn't necessary.

I was handed an urgent message to send from Ava and met up with Louis to go to a site he had checked out. It was an abandoned top floor apartment in the town, which he assured me would be safe to use as a one off to send a message. It was four floors up so would make transmission easier; it also had a balcony for the aerial. I picked the lock and entered the flat, which was a stinking, festering mess. It was fully furnished and there were piles of household items strewn around inside, the contents of every drawer and cupboard having been thrown to the floor. On the balcony was a huge pile of rubbish tipped on it, including rotting food and the remains of a dead dog. The dining table was set up for a meal and the food had rotted. God knows what happened to the occupants, but it didn't look good for them.

I ignored the surroundings and the awful smell and set up the radio. Louis attached the aerial to a washing line stretched over the balcony. The first message sent was short but then I had to wait for a response from a previous message, which was taking its time coming back. Louis was agitated, pacing behind me, rubbing his hands together, clicking his finger joints and whistling gently through his teeth. He was making me incredibly nervous. He was looking out the window for anything to alert us that we'd been targeted, but I wouldn't be rushed. The Germans, like the British, were watching every wireless wavelength and it usually took them about twenty-five to thirty minutes to triangulate and pinpoint the area where the message was being sent from. We still had time.

Louis became alarmed when from his elevated position he thought he saw a butcher's truck moving slowly between buildings, quite a way in the distance, identifying it immediately as possibly a radio transmission detection van.

"They're in the area, stop and pack up now."

The message was incoming; I just needed a few seconds more. The confirmatory message came through and I shut the radio down and started packing up, putting the make-up tray into the case. Louis told me that the van was still in the area, but I knew they would have lost the signal now and we would be okay if we just sat it out. Louis raced towards the door.

"Their moving closer, we have to move."

"Don't run, Louis," I called to him. "The radio's off; the signal's dead. They'll catch you if you run. We have to think our way out."

He wouldn't listen and ran out, clattering along the corridor and down the stairs. I opened the balcony door and peered out from behind the curtains into the side street and saw a car and trucks slowly turn into the main street at the front of this building. I heard shouting and doors slamming. They were just patrolling and must have met the running, panicking, desperate looking Louis.

I heard a loud German voice directing men to go into the block to search. I went to the door and heard heavy footsteps rushing into the entrance and loud knocking on doors on the floors below. Fear rose in me like a flame when I heard footsteps making their way up to the next floor.

I hid the radio case and aerial under the rubbish piled up on the balcony. I went into the corridor and then realised Louis had stupidly picked a transmission site with only one way in and out, no lift, no fire escape, back stairs, nothing—I was trapped. I knocked on the apartment door opposite. There was no answer and no sound coming from the flat. I went further along the corridor and knocked on another of the doors, my heart hammering in my chest. The occupant was taking forever to answer. I hoped they were in. I could hear soldiers coming up the next flight of stairs, getting nearer to me, and thought I might pass out from the fear. My mind racing, I formed a plan of what I would say if they found me, although it would sound very weak.

I knocked again. I was breathless, perspiration oozing from every pore of my body. Eventually the door opened, and an old woman in her seventies answered. I asked her if she knew of a random named person that came to my mind, who used to live in the empty flat. I told her I had come a long way to find no-one there, and could I please get a drink of water. The elderly woman pointed to her ears, indicating she was a bit deaf and invited me in to listen to what I was saying properly. I went in, took off my coat and sat down, trying to recover my composure. The elderly lady walked about with a stick, which was why it had taken her so long to open the door. She offered me the water and I gratefully drank it, my hand shaking uncontrollably as I held the glass. We heard heavy footsteps in the corridor outside and shouting. The woman opened her door to see what was going on and then quickly shut it.

"There are German soldiers making their way along the corridor." She said in a hushed tone, "They're searching for something or someone, you'd better stay inside here with me until they've gone." She stood in the middle of the room, like me, waiting for the expected knock on her door.

"Boche bastards," she spat. "God knows what they're up to, vicious swine. They dragged two of my neighbours away, and I haven't seen them since. You'd better stay away from them, a pretty young girl like you."

The dreaded loud banging came on her door and the old woman walked slowly to open it. I could hear her being asked in poor French if she lived alone. They asked her if she'd seen anyone suspicious around that day, or at any time recently and she replied crossly. "No."

I'd moved to the kitchen to return the glass, just as an

older soldier pushed past her to get into the flat, she shouted as he almost knocked her over. He found me washing up the glass in the kitchen.

"Who are you and what business do you have here?" he yelled.

I desperately thought of what to say, and just as I was about to give an answer, the elderly woman came to my rescue.

"She's just a girl from the church who volunteers to help me with my housework from time to time. Leave her alone."

He asked to see my papers, and again the forger's work was passed as authentic. I then playacted the helpless victim and asked him if we were in any danger, as I had to leave soon to carry out my next visit. A second German soldier, whom I noted was particularly handsome, entered the flat as I asked about my safety. He smiled at me reassuringly.

"You shouldn't worry Mademoiselle. We think we've found the person we wanted and so you shouldn't concern yourself. You'll be safe."

Both soldiers left, and as their footsteps continued along the corridor, the old woman shut the door, turned, and winked at me. Raising her stick in the air, standing on wobbly legs, said quietly, "Vive La France."

I left the building after thanking the woman for her help. I watched the handsome young soldier getting into a truck and he saw me. He waved and smiled, and I waved and smiled back, grateful to have escaped, and planning how to get my radio back if they hadn't found it. I turned away and saw Louis being driven past in the back of a car with men sitting either side of him, and I covered my face discretely with my scarf as they passed me. He looked like a trapped, wild animal, wide-eyed and desperate. He didn't see me and that was the last I ever saw of him.

I knew he didn't know my full name or where I lived, and my apartment remained safe. Only three people knew where I lived: Voltaire, Lombard, and the brunette woman I first met there. What was the saying from my training? Oh yes, that was it, *"Three can keep a secret as long as two of them are dead."*

Three knowing my address was too many, and that would have to change following this incident. I would look for somewhere else to rent. I watched the soldiers, closely noting markings on their uniforms, their ranks. Once the troops and vehicles left, I turned to leave, and as I did, a woman marched out of her front door, slapped my face, and spat at me.

"German whore," she shouted, probably because she'd seen me waving at the German soldier. *Vive la bloody France,* I thought, as I wiped the spit from my face. I left an urgent message with the priest at the church to pass on about Louis.

I WENT to visit the block of apartments next day, to see if I could retrieve my radio, if it were even still there. As I approached the block, I saw a man standing in an opposite doorway, pretending to read a newspaper, but watching the people going in and out of the building. He was also oddly shaped, a thin small head and a large 'fat' body. I knew this was one of the radio detection team we had been warned about. They had devices attached around their waists, linked to a watch which indicated where radio signals were coming from. He was there monitoring if a radio signal came from this block. I pulled my collar up and pulled my headscarf a little around my face and went up to the top floor. No-one was around. I looked at the empty apartment, the door had been broken in, so no lock picking required, and I chanced it. I entered through the broken door, checking as I went, listening for any footsteps coming up the stairs, but there was just silence.

I crawled out onto the balcony and couldn't believe my radio and antenna were still there, covered in foul-smelling debris and the remains of the dog. Maybe that was why they didn't look too closely, or they'd deliberately left it to see who came to use it or collect it and would arrest me when I left the building. I dragged it back into the flat, but now I had to get it out of the building past the person watching outside.

I spoke to Madame Blanchard, the old woman who'd helped me the day before. She was very eager to help and brought out a wicker shopping basket on wheels her deceased husband had fashioned for her to carry shopping in. The radio fitted neatly in it, and we covered it with a thick scarf. She got her hat and coat and walked out with me. I gently carried the trolley down the stairs and then pulled it along as Madame Blanchard walked with her stick while holding on to my arm. We laughed as if we were sharing a joke while we passed the watching man. He didn't acknowledge us, apart from a very brief dismissive glance. I took the radio out and hid it in my apartment, while Madame Blanchard waited outside. I walked her to the cafe for a drink and then took a tram back home with her wicker basket on wheels. The watching man was still there, but with a second man now. They both looked at us briefly and again dismissed us as if we were of no importance whatsoever.

I was more alert to danger now than at any time. I had moved radio sites and been working flat out for weeks, feeling lonely, isolated, tense, and aware of betrayal from Louis or others. I felt unnerved and jumpy, but nothing happened—no raids, no arrests, and so it was assumed he hadn't talked. I later learned Louis had tried to run when they got him out of the car and had been shot dead. That's probably what he had wanted them to do, shoot him, rather than go through a brutal interrogation.

37

IN PLAIN SIGHT

My replacement lookout was a man called Dubois. He was so much more suited to the job than Louis, unflappable and supportive. He was in his thirties, taller than me, muscular, with a full head of thick brown hair and such twinkling smiling eyes. He had a dry sense of humour and could make people relax and laugh in the most challenging of times. He was a carpenter by trade but knew quite a bit about radios and was very handy with any equipment. He could mend anything and could also strip things down to their basics and rebuild them. I was grateful to have him supporting me. He had a calm manner, didn't like disagreements, and had a soothing effect on me, which I desperately needed at the time. He also saw amusement in most things about the war —the French, Germans, British, the Resistance, nothing was off limits—it was quite refreshing and lightened my mood somewhat, which gave me a bit of strength to carry on.

There were long, boring, periods with nothing happening which were hard to deal with. We'd been warned that agent work would be ninety percent boredom and ten percent action. Agents had been caught because they'd become too relaxed during these periods and then made silly mistakes. I had a quiet spell with not a lot happening and went to my usual cafe and sat for a while in the outside seating area, just observing. There were people dotted about on different tables. I noticed a young man sitting with a coffee looking incredibly nervous and gazing around furtively. He didn't fit in as a local, that was for sure. There was something about him that was wrong. He looked well fed for a start and his shoes looked new, and new shoes were difficult to come by for locals at that time. The German soldiers sitting at the outside tables didn't appear to give him any thought as they chatted and joked with each other.

The cafe owner, a smartly dressed, slim young woman with blonde hair tied up fashionably with an ornate hairpin, approached him and topped up his coffee cup for free, which was unheard of. I wondered if she'd given him more coffee because she wanted him to stay where he was for longer for some reason. Was she resistance? Was he waiting to be picked up? She then went back through the door of the cafe.

I followed her in, under the pretence of ordering some-thing and saw her talking on the telephone at the back. She turned and raised her finger to me to indicate for me to wait, and I smiled at her as she continued her conversation in a hushed voice with her back to me. She finished the call and served me with a beaming smile. She'd seen me quite a few times now, acknowledging me like a regular customer. I smiled back and returned to my seat outside with a crois-sant, periodically watching the nervous young man seated there. He stood out too much, and I feared for him but knew approaching him now was too risky. I believed he was already doomed, and he'd been there a while already.

I then saw an older man go and sit with him. *Was he resistance? Did the cafe owner call him?* I wondered. They talked very briefly and then both stood up to leave. As they did so, a car roared up and screeched to a halt with several men piling out. The young man, seeing them all too late, began quickly walking away, tripping over a chair as he went, and in his panic, started running and jumped over the wall at the side of the cafe. They shouted at him to stop, but he didn't and was shot at. He fell on the pavement, screaming in pain, holding his shoulder. He was grabbed roughly, bundled over the wall, dragged across the fore-court, and put in the car. The older man was held at gunpoint against a wall by the soldiers who had been seated at the cafe and was then hauled away. The civilians sitting around, and walking past, screamed, and shouted as the incident unfolded before them. I was still sitting at the outside table when the owner came out to calm everyone down.

I feigned shock and distress at the incident and asked, "What's happening?"

"Those men are just dangerous criminals. Don't worry about them, you're safe. Have more coffee and calm yourself."

She went in and out of the cafe with pails of water, which she threw over the blood pooled on the pavement and forecourt where the young man had fallen. She seemed to want to urgently erase any sign of the incident happening at her establishment.

I had a plan forming in my head. I needed a deeper cover than I had at present, as I was incredibly vulnerable if questioned, as to how I could support myself. Also, the long boring periods of inactivity were frustrating. I could go a week with no messages or interaction, and it was driving me mad. I needed to keep active and alert to protect myself. I could afford to work part time while still managing to do my messaging in my sked times as needed. I had seen the new 'help wanted' sign on the door at the cafe and approached the owner, Adelle, asking if I could work part time there. I showed her my ID papers under the name of Evelyn Bouvier, and she eagerly agreed.

"You will of course be paid off the books for any work you do. No need for lots of paperwork these days," she informed me sweetly. "Can you work mornings from eight until two in the afternoon?"

I just couldn't believe my luck. I could listen to conversations and observe at the cafe in the mornings and at lunch when most people came in. I could also arrange to have messages handed to me from Ava under everyone's noses. I was aware the owner was collaborating, and I could find out more about that and would still have time to carry out my messaging work as needed. It was dangerous but bloody perfect.

I WAS SERVING tables one afternoon when I encountered some loud, obnoxious German soldiers on the cafe forecourt. There were usually disturbances when young soldiers were in and had been drinking, but this was getting out of hand. They were foul mouthed and grabbed me and the other waitress, making lewd gestures as they pulled us on to their laps, slobbering kisses on us. I acted distressed and cried as I tried to push them off. To my absolute astonishment, I saw a German officer get out of his car and march towards us. The soldiers tormenting us froze where they were as he strode onto the forecourt in his crisp Nazi uniform and reprimanded them.

"You are not animals," he shouted. "Behave like soldiers when in uniform, not schoolboys. You bring shame on your uniform. Leave now." He apologised profusely to me and the other girl, bowed his head and snapped his heels together in his smartly polished boots as the soldiers bolted. He then got back into his car ordering the driver to continue. I was completely stunned and then Adelle came out.

"Who was that?" I asked.

"Stay away from that one, Evelyn. He's an SS officer, newly posted to the area. His name is Schaefer."

"Why, what's wrong with him?" I asked her.

"I hear the soldiers talking when they're in here. He's known for sadistic torture of anyone taken into custody and his reprisal against local French citizens if any resistance activity takes place is so awful. He's a brute. Just stay away from him," she warned me, as her eyes watched his car intensely as it disappeared from view.

"Someone told me even his own men are terrified of him," she paused. "The German Abwehr, who have been here for a while now, have a strict military code. They don't do torture as such. They tend to threaten, reason, or blackmail to get information, but they're not vicious, and brutality is a last resort for them. The Gestapo, however, arrived here as well, and they are brutally ruthless with him in charge. They have no code of honour; anything goes to get results. Schaefer is happy for his men to torture and kill anyone they suspect, with impunity, and that causes friction between the two groups. The Abwehr and Gestapo don't like each other, I've seen that animosity and I'm always on edge when they're in, waiting for trouble."

ADELLE APPEARED to have grown very fond of me, as I'd planned. I was hardworking, respectful, efficient, polite, and always on time for work, not missing a day. I was okay to look at too, which helped in this type of work, especially with young soldiers frequenting the establishment. I went out of my way to ingratiate myself with her and earn her trust, biding my time until my chance came. While working there, I was just a lowly invisible waitress, sweetly serving German soldiers as they chatted over their drinks and food. I noted their insignia and rank, listened to any names and any loose talk about troop movements, which I then reported back to the circuit on notes handed to Ava with her bill, when she stopped in for a drink. She put messages for me folded in local newspapers or napkins on one of my allocated tables as she left. It was a smooth operation.

After a few weeks of working together, Adelle invited me back to her flat for a drink. She lived directly above her cafe, and I thought my hard work on her was paying off as I made my way there. I needed to get information without arousing suspicion, and this was the perfect time. I felt nervous and hesitant as I approached the flat, needing to take deep breaths to calm myself at the top of the stairs before knocking on the door. One mistake here could be my undoing.

Adelle opened the door and smiled warmly. "Come in, come in, Evelyn, my darling." I smelled expensive perfume as she hugged me tightly, as if we were old friends. "Sit down, make yourself comfortable. Let me get you a drink. Coffee? Wine?" she asked.

"Just coffee, please." I responded, knowing I needed to keep a clear head. Her flat was colourful and dreadfully cluttered, with all sorts of antiques, lamps, large paintings, cushions, and ornaments galore. A lot of money had been spent to make it look like this. There was a collection of antique porcelain dolls with weird looking eyes placed on a long shelf that looked more suited to a young girl's room than a grown woman. I listened patiently and tried to look interested as Adelle talked and talked for ages about her life and general things. I watched her laugh and grimace as she told tale after tale of visitors to her cafe, the odd ones, and the regulars. I found myself nodding in agreement as she complained about the difficulties with rationing.

"I need to update my wardrobe with some new clothes now the weather is getting warmer, you should too, we must both take a trip into Paris together," she said.

I agreed and was then shown expensive perfume she'd been given, which she ostentatiously sprayed on me.

"That's so beautiful," I said, looking suitably impressed, as the perfume wafted around my face. "You really are lucky. How do you get such gorgeous things during these awful times? You must know some especially important people— or thieves." I laughed and so did she. "Could you get some for me? This miserable war shouldn't take all the enjoyment from our lives. I probably have enough money saved to pay for some if you know where to get it."

I looked expectantly at Adelle for an answer, and as the long afternoon visit was drawing to a close, I got the breakthrough I was after.

Adelle lowered her voice and said to me in a hushed tone. "Don't tell anyone what I'm about to tell you, Evelyn, or we will both be in danger. Do you promise? Can I trust you?" she said looking incredibly nervous.

"Yes," I said. "Yes of course."

"I have an understanding with one of the local German

Abwehr officers who helps me with my cafe. He has asked me to look out for anyone behaving oddly in or near the cafe, or to tell him if I hear things from local gossip that I think he needs to know. They also use my place as a location for people to be guided to so they can be watched, then followed to see who they meet with, and arrested. He makes sure my cafe and I are looked after. He also encourages his colleagues and staff to favour my business to improve my profits. He gives me stamped, signed papers that give me access to any goods I need from the produce at the port, which ensures the place is always well stocked."

I nodded at her with my eyes wide open. So that's why her coffee was much nicer than others. She looked at me intensely for any negative response to what she'd just said but there was none. I just showed concern for her.

"Don't people realise you're working with the Germans, Adelle? If you're well stocked and others aren't, they might think you're a collaborator. Aren't you worried they would punish you?"

"Goodness me, there are no concerns about that my darling. I tell them I've been forced to do this by the Germans who have commandeered my premises. The man I work with makes sure I get 'arrested' every now and again and taken in. But it's just to get the necessary business supply papers and local people think I'm taken in for questioning. I get lightly raided by his soldiers every now and again too, and a few plates and bottles get smashed. That shows I'm suffering just as much as they are. They trust me because of it. Don't worry, I'm quite safe."

"You need to be careful, Adelle. I've heard from the other waitresses there might be foreign agents and French resistance in the area and if they knew what you're doing…"

"Really, Evelyn, don't worry. I'm very protected. The

Germans look after those who help them. I've also met so many others with businesses doing the same. I'm as safe..."

I stopped her mid flow. "You see, Adelle, there are those of us who just want to live a nice life. We didn't start this awful war, did we? We're just the victims of it and why shouldn't we make the best of it? We're just young women, but this war has stolen our lives and it makes you feel so old."

Adelle readily responded, as if she had been terribly lonely and had at last found a kindred spirit who understood her and didn't condemn.

"I do agree, and people like me are doing what we need to do to survive, and so must you, Evelyn." She shifted to a more serious tone. "There is another side to this...." She paused as if wondering whether to tell me or not, but then carried on.

"The arrangement means I have quite a personal relationship with him, if you know what I mean. That's where this perfume came from," she said, as she picked it up and admired it lovingly in her hands. "He's quite handsome, you know, and highly intelligent. I wouldn't go with just anyone. I think it may lead to marriage after the war, as we've become so close." She laughed girlishly.

I nodded, suppressing my revulsion. "So, he's handsome, intelligent, obviously loves you and brings you beautiful things, you're a lucky girl" I responded laughing, playing to her vanity.

"He works with the intelligence unit, very, very secret apparently from what he's told me and what I've picked up from him when he's drunk and talks in his sleep. He is well travelled and even studied in England for a while and has English contacts. He needs people like me who know this area and the people well and can supply information. The

Germans are going to win the war, we all know that. They're unstoppable and are sure to look favourably on those who helped them. France would be much better off just working with them now and fighting them is just delaying the inevitable, causing more unnecessary suffering. People like me could shorten the war by years and save hundreds of thousands of women and children's lives just by helping the Germans." She stopped talking to get herself another glass of wine and continued.

"You should find yourself a nice officer like mine. They're in abundance here. It will improve your life during this dreadful war too and make sure you're protected and survive it. It would be wonderful for us both, and safer to have each other for support, and we'll be together at the cafe. I could promote you, which would pay you more."

My suspicions were confirmed. Adelle told me again not to tell a soul about what we had talked about, and she would see if her officer friend knew of anyone nice for me so I could reap the benefits as well. I just smiled and feigned a thankful response but wanted to kill this woman there and then, but I needed her as my cover for a while longer and to find out who else was collaborating like her.

Just as I was considering her demise, someone knocked at the door. Adelle looked through the spy hole and back at me wide eyed in utter panic.

"It's him, Evelyn. You must hide," she whispered. "I wasn't expecting him to visit until much later. He doesn't like people in the flat when he's here."

She rushed me into her bedroom and bundled me into a large ornate wardrobe. I pushed her dresses and coats back to make room and was balanced precariously on a pile of shoes as I strained to hear what was going on.

I heard him thank her for the men they'd recently

caught and what a helpful girl she was. Her reward was an evening with him for which he would pay her well. I could tell by his slurred speech he'd been drinking.

"I've brought some excellent coffee for you, as a gift."

I could just about see through the narrow slats in the wardrobe door as he guided Adelle backwards into the bedroom where I was hiding. My view was limited, and I could only see him from his chest down. I tried to bend down slightly to see if I could see his face, but quickly realised I couldn't move without making a noise. I was perilously perched on a pile of shoes, with every muscle straining to keep me stable. If I moved an inch, I feared I would fall off my perch and tumble out of the door.

He took off his jacket and shirt and laid them on a chair and started to kiss and manhandle Adelle. He tried to pull her dress up, but she must have been embarrassed, knowing I was in the wardrobe and could see and hear everything going on. She resisted him, which I could hear in his voice was making him increasingly angry and he then persisted forcefully.

As she was trying to push him off, looking for ways to distract him from his obvious intentions, she said, "My darling, I have to tell you I've found someone else to help us in our work. She wants to join in what I do for you and meet an officer too; do you know of anyone? She's a pretty girl and an officer like you would be perfect for her."

The man pushed her roughly away from him and went into a rage.

"I told you not to tell anyone about our arrangement. I told you!" he yelled in her face. "The people you talk to could be resistance and could identify me if they know my name or position." He slapped her hard across the face. "Stupid whore," he hissed at her, any semblance of romance gone. Adelle clutched at her face, looking furtively towards the closet, and then tried to kiss him again, to no avail. I could hear her voice faltering nervously, she probably hadn't ever seen this side of him before and didn't know how to handle it. She had dug a hole for herself and just didn't stop digging.

"She's a wonderful girl. She's just like me and wants to survive the war until you win, that's all. She could help you." I started panicking inside the closet now. Balanced on the shoes, my thighs and calves aching like hell, I was trying to breathe quietly. *Please, please don't lead him to the closet to meet me in your panic*, I prayed.

But he was now so furious, he couldn't contain himself or take any notice of what she was saying. I knew what was coming from my own sorry experiences. He would want to teach her a lesson she wouldn't forget, after which, bruised and battered, she would know to keep her mouth shut and do as she was told without question. I cringed inside and waited for the inevitable.

He called her a French whore and punched her hard in the ribs. She doubled over with a loud groan, and when she tried to stand up straight and catch her breath, he punched her hard on the side of her head. She fell to her right side, hitting her head on the metal bedhead, and fell to the floor. She lay there silent and still.

I saw the back of him as he bent down over Adelle. He shook her roughly and yelled, "Who have you told about me? Who is this woman? What's her name? Did you tell her my name? What does she know?"

There was no reply. I could see the back of his head and his back as he reached under Adelle's head to lift it up off the floor. He let go of her head allowing it to crash to the floor, leaving her sprawled there, he started backing away from her towards the wardrobe I was in. He was so close; I could hear his heavy rapid breathing and smell his alcohol-filled breath. I then heard muffled noises of him getting dressed. I began to believe this nightmare was over as I heard his retreating footsteps, and finally the main door opening and closing.

I waited a few seconds to make sure he'd left, but just as I came out of the closet, breathing a sigh of relief, I heard the front door open again; it hadn't locked. I quickly positioned myself behind the open bedroom door, gripping the knife I had in my skirt belt in case I needed it. There was a shot of iced adrenaline running through my veins now preparing me for a fight. He was shocked and drunk, and I believed that gave me a chance.

My brutal combat training whizzed through my head as I waited, remembering to aim for his carotid artery. But thankfully he'd just forgotten his hat, which I saw his hand grab from the dining room table as I looked through the gap in the door frame. I had a quick glimpse of his lower arm which had a large mark, possibly a burn, or birthmark, but it happened too quickly to see properly. I listened as he fled the flat in panic, slamming the door behind him.

I realised I'd been holding my breath and took in great gulps of air as the front door slammed shut. My muscles ached from being cramped in one position in the closet, and it was a relief to stand up straight and stretch out. I knew ultimately, he would have killed me in a straight fight, even if he was drunk.

Rushing over to check on Adelle, I lifted her head and saw that the fall against the metal bed had caved the right side of her skull in. She was dead.

I gazed down on her face, despite such a violent end she looked so peaceful. The perfumes, the new clothes from

Paris, the cafe, none of it mattered anymore. Her life was over. *What this war has done to so many people. None of us are who we were before it started.*

I shrugged, accepting that her death was an inevitable consequence of her choices, and watched as her blood seeped out from under her head, pooling at my feet. I needed to get out. I quickly looked around the flat for any clues as to names or other contacts that could be useful. I took Adelle's address book to give to Voltaire, pocketed a substantial amount of money I found in a box, grabbed the decent coffee, and left. I didn't take the perfume—I couldn't stomach the smell.

I TURNED up for work as usual on Monday, having left a message about Adelle and the cafe at the church. I opened the cafe with the spare keys kept under a flowerpot in an outside window box and took in the food deliveries, working the shift as usual.

When the afternoon staff turned up, I told them worriedly I hadn't seen Adelle and didn't know why she hadn't come to work. "There were no messages and no answer when I knocked on her door. I'm very worried about her." I told them all.

Adelle's body was found three days after her death. One of the waitresses had reported her missing after discussing it with us all, and we expressed concern about our missing manager. We were gently interviewed by the local police, and we all said the same thing; we had last seen her at work and didn't know anyone who would want her dead.

I continued with both my waitressing and agent work, organising more equipment drops and allied servicemen pick-ups. The circuit had helped to carry out explosions on train tracks in other towns, with explosives I'd requested. Certain buildings were identified and blown up, documents from the town civic headquarters, which could be used to create forgeries were stolen, and I met with a Lysander drop to hand them over to the pilot to take home. The circuit was now working effectively under Voltaire, a tightly knit group who trusted each other with our lives, working more collaboratively with the French resistance than before. The circuit was expanding too, and they now had a second radio operator and courier along with more local resistance people.

I played my part in the group, but was working mostly in isolation, the fewer people involved with me the safer I was. I remained tense, stressed and very, very lonely. My radio and all the spare parts for it were now stored in the cafe basement, right at the back where no one ever ventured. It was dark, dusty, and full of cobwebs, with old unused or broken equipment from the cafe stored there.

I was nominated by the other staff to take charge of the cafe after Adelle's demise. I now had the keys to the front and back doors, and the flat. I used Adelle's flat a couple of times to send a message and I could come and go as I pleased. If I were ever stopped anywhere near the cafe, I had a good excuse to be there. That soon changed.

38

HECTOR THIBAULT

A few weeks after Adelle's funeral, her uncle Hector Thibault took over the running of the cafe. He must have established a working relationship with the officer Adelle had been killed by, or another one, because the place was left alone and was still patronised by the Germans. He either had no idea the German had killed her or didn't care. I decided to stay on working there, as it was still proving to be a good cover for me.

The new owner was a lazy devil and I found him repulsive. He had filthy habits and a hacking smoker's cough. He took to spitting on the pavement over the side of the low cafe wall onto the side street when he was outside smoking. His standards of personal hygiene beggared belief and that transferred into his cafe. He leered at me and the other waitresses and made suggestive remarks, he was detestable but harmless.

He ordered me to open the place up every morning and take delivery of goods. He always, without fail, lit up a cigarette to smoke outside the cafe at seven forty-five on the dot before coming in, and then smelled of cigarette smoke as well as sweat. He did little serving and less cleaning. He was always doing what he called 'the books' and took over a small back room off the kitchen as his office and stayed there. He had his newspapers and bottles of wine, shouted now and again for food, and then just collected the takings at the end of each day.

Hector was trying to rent out Adelle's flat above the cafe, but once people knew it was where someone had died, they declined it. I offered to rent it as it was. I said it would be a good arrangement as I could keep an eye on the place out of hours and would be early to open up and receive the daily deliveries. He agreed but said he would take the rent out of my wages and charged me the full rate, which left me working for nothing. Thank goodness I had plenty in reserve from the resistance money and Adelle's substantial contribution.

EARLY ONE MORNING, after the place had only been open a short while, a young man came in and sat in the forecourt in an agitated state. I went to serve him, and he asked for coffee. I went to get his order, which had been given in quite simple French. I returned with his coffee, and he said as clear as day in his nervous state, "Thank you, Miss,"—in English. Realising his mistake, he looked at me with terrified eyes. I felt desperately sorry for him, as he held the menu upside down as well.

I looked around; Hector was nowhere to be seen. The other waitress and the new chef were busy inside, and it was too early for German soldiers to be in, there were just a couple of regulars. In case we were being watched, I pretended to write an order on my pad while I spoke to him quietly in English, smiling as I did so. "Go immediately up this road to your left and up into the third side street on your left. Wait for me there in a doorway. Don't move or speak to anyone until I come for you. Leave once I've gone back into the cafe."

I walked back inside and watched as he got up nervously and walked away in the direction I'd said. I went to find Hector, who was in his office smoking and reading a paper.

"I'm not feeling too well, Hector. I need to take a break and lie down for a little while in the flat to clear the most horrible headache. If you don't mind of course. I'll work extra at the end of my shift to make up for any time I take. I'll come straight back as soon as I feel better."

He made a terrible fuss about it being so inconvenient, even though the place was quiet at the time. The telephone started ringing and he picked it up, practically standing to attention for whoever was on the phone. He waved me away telling me to be quick.

As I left, I heard him say, "Yes sir, three of them you say sir. Alright, I'll call if I see or hear anything."

Just in case I was being watched, I went out to the forecourt with a croissant, looking around theatrically, as if wondering where the young man had gone. I then put on my coat and went out of the delivery door at the back and made my way to where the young man was waiting, checking all the while I wasn't being followed. I hoped I was right, and he wasn't a German agent, but my gut instinct told me he wasn't.

When I found him, he looked desperate, and panic stricken and started babbling information.

"I was part of a bomber crew that crashed. I was helped by a couple who also had two other escapees with them, an Englishman, and a Pole. This French couple gave us money and civilian clothes and dropped us outside a church where we were told to go in and wait, and we would be picked up and helped. None of us could speak French well and for some reason I had a gut feeling and didn't feel safe entering the church. I decided to walk away to try and find someone else from the resistance. The others followed me, and we ended up near your cafe thinking we could approach the owner for help."

"Where are the other two?" I asked him.

"Hiding in a shed down the side road next to the cafe. I was to go back for them if I found someone to help. I drew the short straw to go first," he said anxiously. "I need to go back for them."

"Impossible," I told him. "They may well have been picked up already, it's too risky."

I thought sending them into the church was done to use them as bait, to see if any resistance came to their aid. It wasn't the church Architect used, but it might mean they had an idea a local church was involved with the resistance. Only he had sat at the cafe, and they were looking for three people and so he might have gone unnoticed. I hoped no one had been watching me, but my cover as a waitress was helpful to explain my interaction with him. I'd left by the delivery door at the back and so wouldn't have been seen from the street. I could say I was in my flat all the time. I knew for certain I hadn't been followed.

"Christ," I said quietly to myself. I wondered where I could take him. *Think, think*. I grabbed his arm.

"Come with me." I walked with him briskly through the back streets to a block of apartments. I checked no one was watching the entrance and took him in. I knocked on a familiar door to be met by a smiling Madame Blanchard who happily welcomed us in.

I gave her a limited explanation as to why we were there and asked whether he could wait with her until I came back. She was more than happy to help the young man and started fussing over him. I left him and went to find the other two. As I turned the corner to the back entrance of the cafe, I saw a German truck parked further down the side street and darted into my flat. I ran up the stairs and looked out as two men were being dragged along the road into the truck. They looked as though they'd been beaten. I saw one of the soldiers pat Hector Thibault on the back as the truck drove off. I realised then his "office" overlooked the side street they'd been hiding in, and he must have seen them acting suspiciously and gave them away.

I waited until the truck and Hector had left and rushed through the back door to the serving area. While putting on my apron I asked as Hector came in, "What's going on out there?"

"More patronage for the cafe is what's going on, and you won't be paid for your time away this morning." He said gruffly.

He called both of us waitresses to his office and told us sternly. "From now on you're to look out for anyone behaving oddly and to let me know immediately if you see anything."

"What do you mean by behaving oddly?" I asked him, pretending not to fully understand.

He huffed and rolled his eyes at my stupidity, pulling out a piece of paper and read from it. "It will usually be men with poorly spoken French, new clothes, or shoes that don't fit in with what we locals wear. People asking for English-type drinks or food in French which they should know we don't have if they're local, like butter with croissants for example, or café noir, café au lait. Mostly look for well-fed young men on their own with large bank notes, who don't understand the currency. Look if they are nervous when you serve them. Watch if they leave their cutlery the English way with knife and fork together. Observe when you are on the forecourt as people approach the cafe from the road, do they look right when crossing the road? That may mean that they are used to drivers being on the left side of the road like in England." Hector looked up. "That sort of thing. It means they may be spies here to damage our beloved France. Also watch who comes to meet them and write down their description before coming to see me."

Thank you so much for the tips, Hector. If only you knew.

I RETURNED to Madame Blanchard's apartment after work and found her trying to teach the serviceman French. She'd also shown him loads of photographs, cards, and letters from her collection, and the young man looked at me, begging for mercy with his eyes. I asked her if I could speak to him for a minute and she reluctantly let him go.

"Tell me about the people who helped you."

"It was all a bit rushed, to be frank with you. They were just your average French man and woman; I didn't hear any names mentioned."

"How did you come into contact with them?" I asked.

"We crash landed in a field after coming under heavy fire. My pilot was seriously injured; the others were dead. I had broken ribs but left to try and get him help. I walked through the fields to find someone and came across a farm building which was where I met these people."

"How did you get to the church?"

"The farm people were incredibly kind and went to

check on my pilot, but the Germans were already there swarming around the plane. After a meal and a short rest, I was taken to another safe house to wait. The other two were already there and we were told we would be driven to a place to be picked up by the resistance and returned to England. They drove us to the church and dropped us off at the entrance and told us to go in and wait together. They couldn't stay with us they said, because of the risk, and they had to get back."

He paused as he thought over the details, "None of us were happy with the plan. We were left exposed and vulnerable, we thought we would be taken to another safe house to hide or physically handed over to the resistance. We didn't want to make a fuss as they had helped us already, but we didn't know who would be waiting inside the church for us and that's why we decided to walk away and find our own help. We thought we might be being followed and so briefly split up and met each other again near your café, which was the only one we found open. I drew the short straw to go in to approach the owner. That way at least the two others could get away if I were captured asking for help. I was summoning up the courage to ask for the owner when you came along."

I asked about the location of the farm he'd crashed near, and he described it to me as best he could. It had been quite a long drive and the three of them were laid down either on the back seat or floor and couldn't see anything on the journey. The second safe house the three men had stayed in was a lot nearer and could have been one of several we used intermittently, which was a worry. I told him he had to stay put for now while arrangements were made for him, and it might take time. I told him about his friends capture which visibly upset him, and then left him in the capable and coquettish hands of Madame Blanchard, who returned enthusiastically to volume five of her Blanchard photographic, mementos and postcard collection with the captive young man.

I left a message for the circuit about the airman, the church, and the cafe. I didn't give away any information about Madame Blanchard because I didn't trust anyone. No one locally knew of my relationship with her, and I wanted it to stay that way to keep her safe.

A week later, I received a message to bring the man to the church at a set date and time and they would assist him. I dressed him in Madame Blanchard's dead husband's suitably worn shoes and coat which she'd kept after his death, and we walked like boyfriend and girlfriend, arm in arm to the church. I could feel him physically shaking with fear through his clothes. He looked as if he wished he were back in the safety of the flat with the old woman looking at her family photographs. Once inside the church I handed him to the priest and wished him good luck as he was secreted away into the safety of our new, hopefully secure, escape lines.

39

A PROMISE FULFILLED

I was now starting to feel very unwell. The constant tension, sleeplessness, threat of arrest, betrayal and torture were taking their toll on me, and I was living on my nerves. I had broken out in a rash on my arms, which was likely related to the stress hammering my body at the time. I had documents I had to hand personally to the pilot at the next pickup, which I'd arranged. The air crewman and another pilot in the escape line were being picked up and a specific night was identified as being suitable. I was to join the team taking the air crewman to the pre-planned pickup site, which I would help to prepare with torches.

I met the group on the outskirts of a small village a mile or two from the pickup point. I hadn't seen the young serviceman, Peter Holmes, for a couple of weeks now and he'd been well looked after. He'd been spruced up ready for the return, although his French was still dreadful despite Madame Blanchard's best efforts. We were to gather at a safe house for a half hour at most, collect the second escapee, and then move to the pickup point. The safe houses were all being used intermittently and for the shortest times possible now to avoid any patterns being established. With each arrest the Germans were more likely to be aware of them and could be waiting. Some of the safe houses had been taken out of use because of the owner's arrest and our choices were becoming very limited. I was surprised to see Voltaire there as he, being the organiser, didn't normally undertake the practical side of jobs. He told me he was a last-minute replacement as an urgent message had come through that the person due to collect Peter had been arrested. There was no one else available.

We drove through back roads, Voltaire, me, Peter, and another of the resistance, named Laurent. He was a thick-set man with black hair, small eyes, and a large bushy moustache. He hardly spoke, tending to grunt his responses, and seemed terribly grumpy.

We stopped a short way from the farmhouse, and I was sent on ahead to check for any traps. they would follow once I signalled it was safe.

I had a small knife and gun tucked in my waistband. For whatever reason I had such a bad feeling about this. It should be so straight forward, but my gut instinct told me otherwise. The place looked vaguely familiar in the darkening light. However, I'd seen so many farmhouses in the last few months, at the different sites I used my radio, it was difficult to tell them apart. I stopped near the farmhouse, hidden from sight of the people inside by a large wooden cart.

I saw the silhouette of a tall man come out of the barn and go into the house and shut the door. I sneaked around the outside of the barn and silently slipped through the barn door. Looking around, even though it was dimly lit, I knew where I was. I opened a trap door in the floor after moving some hay bales and my worst fears were realised. I closed the trap door and replaced the bales of hay and then saw a radio set, the aerial still in place. I dismantled it so it couldn't be used again.

I made for the farmhouse and looked through the window first to see how many people were there. I gave the coded knock on the back door, and a plump dark-haired woman in her early forties answered the door, welcoming me in.

She talked in French as she led me through the farm-house. "We've only just been told you were coming, but there's enough food for you all if you want to signal the others. I'm sure you have time to eat before you leave. How many of you are there?"

"Two," I replied, lying for some reason.

"Do you have far to go to the pick-up?" she asked.

"It's probably best you don't know that for your own safety," I informed her.

She nodded in agreement as we entered the kitchen. I saw her give a quick glance at the tall thin man standing by the kitchen sink and then a subtle nod. There was another man in the kitchen for the escape to England, a young American. He was heartily tucking into the stew the woman had made, eating chunks of bread, and drinking wine. He smiled at me with his mouth full of food and raised his glass. He looked very calm, considering the danger I knew he was in. I smiled and made small talk with them in French, pretending to sip the wine they'd given me. It smelled foul.

"My name is Daniel Roussel, and this is my wife, Marion, and this young man here is Nathan," he said, still talking in French, smiling, and indicating the American.

As soon as he uttered those words, I put my glass down.

"I'll go and get the others so they can eat and then we must get going."

I walked behind the woman, who was now sitting at the table organising the food, and pulled the gun out of my waistband, levelling it at her head. Firmly grabbing hold of a large section of her hair. I asked the man, "How long do we have?"

He looked surprised. "I don't know what you're talking about. Let my wife go."

I told him icily, "I won't ask you again—how long before the Germans get here?"

"You're wrong; we don't work for the Germans. We're here to help you; we work for the resistance. You're mistaken. You must trust us."

The American airman began yelling at me as if I'd lost my mind. "Don't be stupid. Put the gun down. They're here to help, they're resistance. You've got it all wrong. What the hell are you thinking? Put the gun away." He got up from his chair and started to come around the table towards me.

I firmly but calmly said in English, "Go back and sit down, there's a good chap." Nodding to my gun, I added, "If you want to live, don't move again until I tell you to."

He fled back to his chair; his appetite clearly deserting him, his dinner ruined because of the antics of this mad woman. I kept a firm hold on the woman's hair; I could feel her struggling hard under my grip as she tried to reach for a knife on the table.

"So, you're Marion and Daniel Roussel."

"Yes, that's right, that's right," the thin man said.

"Are you sure about that? Because Marion and Daniel are both lying dead in the barn basement, so I'm asking you again, how much time before they come?"

The man started blustering a denial and I shot the

woman I had hold of through the head. I only needed one of them to tell me what I wanted to know. She went face down onto the table with a hard thud. Blood sprayed across the table splattering the bread and stew, dripping off the table onto the floor.

The airman shouted in shock, not understanding the French conversation at all.

"What the hell are you doing? What the hell have you done? you murderer, you shot her in cold blood, you evil murdering bitch?"

"Stay there," I ordered him, gesturing with the gun. Then I pointed it at the man pretending to be Daniel. "I won't ask you again."

He hesitated and stuttered and as he was about to talk, the door flew open, and Voltaire and Peter rushed in, alerted by the gunshot.

I looked at the man who appeared to realise the game was up. "You have about fifteen minutes. I'm sorry. I was forced to do this; they have my wife an—"

I shot him square between the eyes before he could finish the sentence. He was dead before he hit the floor. I again had no feelings other than I was doing the job I came to do. He'd cost lives by his actions, he was no longer a person, he was a traitor. We couldn't take him with us, and we couldn't leave him, he'd seen my face and could identify me, so he had to die.

I bundled the very shocked and confused American pilot out through the door with Voltaire leading the way, dragging Peter with him. We headed for the truck.

I shouted at Laurent. "Get us out of here as fast as you can and make for the pickup point. Keep the headlights off."

We jumped on board the truck and sped off away from the farm, using only the moonlight to guide us. Looking back, we could see vehicle lights way off in the distance speeding towards the farm we had just left.

"Fifteen minutes, the lying traitorous swine," I muttered to myself. The road was incredibly bumpy, and we were all thrown around in the back as Laurent sped away.

Once near the pickup point, we parked and hid the truck in an outbuilding, quickly checked the area in case the pickup had been compromised, and once satisfied it was still safe, arranged the landing lights ready to guide the pilot in. This had to be a quick pick up because the Germans were in the area now and would be guided to us by the sound of the plane or it's lights. Laurent had the landing code sign for the pilot, and we waited out of sight in the trees until we could hear the plane.

When it was almost directly above us, Laurent went into the open and sent the agreed code with his torch. The pilot responded with his confirmation code, the prepared landing lights made up of bicycle lights and torches were switched on, and the plane came in to land. The pilot turned the plane ready to take off again and kept the engine running waiting for his passengers. The two servicemen sprinted towards it. I had given Peter the papers to be taken to England and looked longingly at the plane, its silhouette bathed in moonlight, my chance to get home away from all this horror and back to a safe normal life so close, just feet away. I felt so incredibly old, tired, and lonely. Any reserves I had left were gone.

In the distance we could hear a vehicle. It was coming rapidly in our direction, probably the Germans coming from the farm. Voltaire glanced at me and must have seen the look on my face, a look he'd seen before on people at the end of their endurance. I'd worked flat out under the most enormous stress for months and he shouted at me to go, pointing at the plane. I nodded gratefully at him, any argument in me gone. They had a second radio operator now and still had communication if I left.

He and Laurent started to make their own getaway towards the other side of the clearing towards the truck. I ran after the two escapees getting into the back of the plane. The pilot waved at me encouragingly to run and get on board. As I reached the plane, I recognised Whippet, the pilot who'd dropped me off what now seemed like years ago. I felt so relieved as I threw myself into what was a very tight squeeze in the back of the plane for the three of us, very intimate indeed. The plane started to rumble across the bumpy ground as German vehicles burst into the clearing and the plane veered slightly when a couple of bullets shot through it as Whippet opened the throttle, soaring the plane into the air.

I'm going home, I screamed inside. I felt such desperate relief, my spirit soaring with the plane as tears coursed down my face. I asked the two men if they'd been hit by the bullets, but they indicated they were okay, and I breathed a sigh of relief. I felt guilty the take-off had been delayed slightly to make sure I got on board, and I'd put them all at risk by being selfish and weak. If anyone had died, I would never have forgiven myself.

WE FLEW BACK low over the English Channel; the weather was deteriorating and drizzle beginning to fall. The flight had been a bit bumpy and uncomfortable as we were all squeezed in together, but it was a small price to pay for our escape. We were all lost in our own thoughts as the plane started its descent at the airfield. I then realised we were coming in too quick. The rescued pilot in the back also said something was wrong. There was no response from Whippet via the intercom and the ground came up at speed. We crash landed heavily going through two hedges before we came to an abrupt stop. The plane landed with its nose down, in a field near the airfield. We were cut, battered, and bruised but alive. The American had a broken arm; Peter had a bad head cut and what looked like a broken nose and his already broken ribs had taken a further battering. I was lucky, they had both cushioned the landing for me when I fell against them, and I only had minor cuts and bruises.

The three of us scrambled out of the back of the plane as fast as we could, worried it might explode. We pulled back Whippet's cockpit hatch and saw his head slumped forward, blood running down his right side and splattered on the map on his thighs and pooling at his feet. He must have been hit by a bullet at the pickup point but hadn't said anything. He had flown the plane, gravely injured and in terrible pain, to get us home.

We hurriedly unstrapped him and pulled him out of the plane, laying him carefully on the ground, and pressed on his chest where the blood had come from. It was all too late.

I looked down at young Whippet's dead face, unmarked in any way, and got on my knees next to him and held him in my arms. I began sobbing, quietly at first, as I held him tightly, and then louder and louder. I felt my heart breaking.

"Not Whippet, please, please, not him," I screamed into the night air.

I thought of Ethan, then Whippet the young pilot dead in front of me, with his whole life ahead of him snatched away. I thought of all of those I'd seen captured and finally the two people I'd murdered, without hesitation, and for what? I hugged Whippet's body close and sobbed. From somewhere far away I could hear someone howling like a wounded animal, not realising at first it was me. I looked at Peter and the American who sat injured on the grass watching the scene before them. They had tears running down their faces, their own stress from the horrors they had also witnessed being released. The rain started to pour down on this tableau of tragedy. I could see vehicles and torchlights in the distance making their way hurriedly towards us across the fields.

40

BROKEN

At twenty years of age, I, Yvette Devereaux, came apart mentally and physically. My body and soul broken into a thousand pieces. I was ashamed and full of guilt I'd lived and others more worthy had died. I knew Steadman was aware of my return and instructed I should be sent to the cooler in Scotland to recover. I had a fair idea what the plan for me was likely to be as I would be considered a security risk if I were just allowed to go home. In the current, vulnerable state I was in, I may talk loosely about what I'd been through and give details no one else should have access to, and they couldn't risk that. I would be looked after and helped back to being "normal." A personal supporter would help with my physical and mental recovery and return to health. I was aware of the routine.

I'd been there about a month, and they had reviewed my case at least twice. I'd been given a full medical on my return and been told I was physically well. Mentally, however, I knew I was far from well. The constant stress I'd been under for such a prolonged period and the horrors I'd seen had taken a major toll. I'd been given appointments to meet psychiatrists but didn't turn up for them. I didn't see there was much point. They couldn't take away what I'd seen and done by getting me to chat about my feelings to someone wearing a tweed suit and smoking a pipe.

I was told in a solemn tone by a uniformed soldier, that a Sergeant Stapleton had been tasked to work with me. He informed me Stapleton had experience working with traumatised soldiers. So, that absolute swine of a trainer had been ordered to get me better. *Just as I thought my life couldn't get any bloody worse.* He hated me, he'd put me through hell in the training, and now of all people was tasked to "fix me."

Stapleton was a rugged and fit man's man in his early forties. He had volunteered from the regular army as a trainer for the agents. He had the ability to get the most out of any recruit and was not a "do as I say" man but a "do as I do" one. I remember the other recruits commented on how much they'd learned from him and wanted to earn his respect. Praise from him was worth having, they said. I couldn't ever remember him praising me, not once during training. He just about tolerated me, and would no doubt feel justified in his initial assessment of me, seeing me as I was now.

I had taken to my bed since arriving at the large, isolated house I was staying at. I didn't mix with the others there, preferring to be alone in my room. I would go down for meals every now and again, and could feel their eyes cautiously watching me, fearful, seeming to expect me to do something terrible. I merely picked at my food, as I had no appetite, and went back to my room with alcohol, the taste of which I was becoming rather used to. It was the numbing effect from it I craved.

I'd been handed letters which my mother had sent while I was away, and I knew she had been sent back pre-signed cards and letters from me in return, telling her all was well, and I would be visiting soon. My mother had been receiving these letters for months. I had no desire to be at home in that ghastly environment at present. I was numb inside, neither angry nor sad, just existing. I was like a wounded animal that needed nurturing back to health, to be loved and gently cared for, but the world I inhabited didn't work that way. I found, after the tears I shed the night of Whippet's death, I couldn't cry. There was no release for all the pent-up emotions and feelings buried deep inside, and oblivion by alcohol was proving to be the answer.

The failed recruits waiting to be sent home were nervous and jumpy around me. If they came across me by accident they always panicked. They must have assumed I was just another failed recruit, a madwoman who had suffered a mental breakdown. I didn't care about my appearance, I didn't care what people thought about me, I just didn't care full stop. My emotions had gone from being unbelievably, unbearably raw to completely non-existent. I could neither cry nor laugh. I was as far down as I thought a human being could go and there seemed no way out of this bottomless pit of despair. I must admit ending my life of misery at this point was seriously considered.

EARLY ONE MORNING there was a loud knock on my door, and someone just walked in, not even waiting for me to reply. *The cheek of it.* The room was a bit dark with the curtains partly drawn and I was fully clothed lying on the bed on my side, with my back to whoever it was. I knew there were wine bottles strewn on the floor and the room smelled none too pleasant, but I wasn't bothered. I heard a male voice and recognised it immediately. *Oh God, it's bloody Stapleton, already. That's all I bloody need.*

"Right. Out of bed, Devereaux. Stop moping around feeling sorry for yourself. You need to get back to some structured work. People can't run around after you anymore. You can't just lie there for ever. It just won't do."

"Bugger off," I told him without moving an inch.

"So foul language now, is it? I've never heard you swear before, is that how low you've stooped from your training? That's not very professional, is it? Come on, up and out of it. We have work to do, for which I might remind you, you're being handsomely paid for by His Majesty's government."

I stayed in the same position, not willing to move an inch or even acknowledge him by looking at him.

"I outrank you now, Stapleton, and so I'm ordering you to bugger off."

There, that should show him things are not the same as when I was just one of his recruits. I heard his footsteps leaving the room. *Ha! So there, Stapleton, take that, you swine. I'm in charge of me now, not you.* I settled back down into blissful nothingness lying on my bed, satisfied with my small victory. I heard the door open again and someone taking steps towards me. Before I could fully react, freezing water was tipped over my head. I felt the mattress being picked up from under me and I was hurled onto the floor.

"You absolute bastard," I yelled at him in shock.

"Yes, that's me. Now stop sodding about. Get your arse in gear, get changed, and come with me."

I was soaking wet from his childish water throwing and needed to get changed.

"Wait outside while I get changed," I ordered him.

"No, I'm not budging. You'll just go back to bed. I'll wait right here. Thank you."

"Stay there then. I don't bloody well care," I yelled at him as I dragged myself up off the floor, holding on to the chest of drawers. I then caught sight of my reflection in the mirror above it and was absolutely devastated. I looked like a wild animal and had aged thirty years. My hair was matted, and straw like, my skin sallow, and my eyes were sunken. I had lost so much weight my bones were prominent, and it was weight I couldn't really afford to have lost. It wasn't me looking back at me, but I knew it was and it shocked and distressed me.

I turned to Stapleton with my mouth hanging open and what I imagined was a distraught look on my face. I couldn't speak; the words just wouldn't come.

He must have seen how bad I looked compared to when he last saw me in training. He must also have come across this look before on soldiers he'd tried to help after they'd been traumatised by war.

"I'll run you a bath and get you some soap and towels," he said quietly as he left.

He brought back soap, toothpaste, a toothbrush, and clean towels for me to use. He had also found makeup that had been discarded by women when they had left the base. He walked with me down the corridor to the bathroom and left me to it.

"I'll see you downstairs when you're ready, Yvette, take your time."

I bathed, washed my hair, untangled it, and tied it up off my collar. I brushed my teeth, such a simple pleasure which felt wonderful. I put basic make-up on, not out of vanity—I really didn't care how I looked—but in order not to frighten people in my haggard state. I looked like an asylum patient without it. The makeup proved a handy mask against how I really looked and felt.

I went back to my room to find all the alcohol bottles had been removed and someone had tidied up. I dressed in my FANY uniform, which hung loosely on my thin frame, and went downstairs to meet Stapleton. He made no comment about my appearance and led me into the dining area where he had prepared a bacon sandwich and a mug of tea for me, which he made me eat. He then drove me to where part of my nightmare had begun, where I'd undergone intense training with him.

We hardly spoke on the journey. He knew I was damaged emotionally and would have to go at my pace. To wait, according to the mythical 'handbook for the traumatised,' for the moment I broke, when it would all come pouring out of me one way or another.

We arrived at the training base, and I had flashbacks of myself doing my best to pass all the tests, not knowing then the full horror I was letting myself in for. *If I'd known then, what I knew now, would I have gone?*

I watched indifferently as Stapleton put the recruits through their paces. I noticed more how the instructors worked. I identified the same tactics they had used with me to get the most out of recruits and find their weaknesses. *Did they identify any weaknesses with me?* I wondered. *Did they suspect that I would suffer mentally under intense stress? If so, why did they let me go?*

I watched dispassionately as the recruits went through more detailed psychological assessments than I had. My training had taken only a matter of weeks, the training was now much longer, and agents were being prepared much more carefully. I thought even the new system wouldn't have helped. *It all goes to rat shit when the intense stress and killing starts.* After a while Stapleton came back to me and offered me the chance to work with the recruits with him for a while if I wanted.

"You have experience that could help them and may save their lives," he told me as he tried to lure me in. Again, recovery handbook, probably page ten: "Have something to occupy the person, distract them, or the time spent without anything to concentrate on would be filled with the horrors they had experienced." Yes, textbook stuff. I had ceased to be a person. I was his job, a thing to be fixed by the book, chapter by chapter.

"Think it over, Devereaux. You could do some good here. Now drive me back to the base."

I looked at him as if he were mad. "But I can't drive."

He laughed loudly. "You mean you can shoot guns, blow things up, parachute out of a plane, but you can't drive?" He shook his head in sheer disbelief and threw me the keys. "Get in."

My intense driving instruction began. They had assumed I could drive when I was a recruit, because I was enrolled in the FANY's, and no one ever asked me if I could. I'd always been driven from place to place, usually by a man. On the exercises it was usually a man, especially Cameron, who took control and drove, although Stella did once I recall. I don't remember ever being asked to. In France it was either a bike, bus, tram or train, or some man driving me. The car groaned and strained as I crunched the gearbox, but very quickly I got the hang of it.

"Treat your car like a man, Devereaux," he said laughing as I struggled with the gears. "You control him, not the other way around. Make it do what you want it to do."

Over the next couple of weeks, he taught me to change tyres, check water, oil, and general car maintenance. I became quite competent and was taught to drive several types and sizes of vehicles. We drove hundreds of miles enjoying the English countryside. I concentrated intensely on this newfound skill I'd acquired. He taught me to drive at speed, how to evade people chasing me, and how to keep control of the vehicle on different terrains. We stopped off at out of the way places for lunches, talking about general things and gradually, bit by bit, I began to feel better.

I enjoyed his measured and even-tempered way with me. He didn't flirt or treat me like a weak female. He respected me for what I'd done and treated me more like an equal, just with different skills and abilities to him, and I liked that. I didn't need anyone falsely mollycoddling me or feeling sorry for me or constantly harping on about me being a female, and he fitted the bill perfectly.

He had a wife he obviously adored, "her indoors" he called her. She was the only person on earth allowed to tell him what to do outside of the army. He had two children, a girl, and a boy whom he doted on. With such a loving grounded homelife he was able to focus on his job. He was a very capable man with a sensible down-to-earth approach to his work; he carried out his orders to the letter. He'd told us recruits of the importance of that.

"If you don't follow orders, then others die, and wars are lost."

I began to trust him.

I started to feel more in control now, not a hundred percent, but a turning point had been reached in my recovery. I certainly couldn't have gone any lower. I'd gained weight from having regular meals and began to relax more with Stapleton. We even started sharing jokes when working together. He let me know more about his family, something he tended not to discuss with recruits. I shared snippets of my experiences with him, to enable him to understand me better.

Stapleton knew what he was doing and as we drove around the countryside, I was aware he was subtly counselling me. He knew I'd been badly traumatised, and had taken to drinking to blot things out, along with the self-neglect, and the feelings of despair I told him about. They were all textbook responses to trauma. But I couldn't tell him I'd killed people in cold blood; that was a step too far even for me at that stage. My guilt by admitting to it would have been too much.

I knew he was expecting me to burst like a dam at some point with everything pouring out, but I thought I'd already passed that point. I was much more in control of myself than I had been and knew it was partly down to him. I knew I was just one of his jobs to complete, but I genuinely began to think he had started to care about me as a person, just a little bit.

41

MISPLACED TRUST

I was transferred to a base in Southern England and Stapleton came with me. I was given a job as a driver and thoroughly enjoyed it, as I was mostly alone, either dropping something or someone off or picking them up, and didn't have to talk to them at all if I didn't want to. I joined in as a stooge for the new recruits on their tests, when I felt up to it, and gave my observations as to how I thought they would manage as agents. I updated the instructors on the mistakes being made by agents in the field I'd noted during my time in France, along with my own disasters. I gave them Hector's list and updated their information on the rationing and austerity, the problems with drop sites that had been encountered, to prepare the next set of agents. I was then moved to another base, which was unsettling. I wasn't being allowed to remain anywhere for any length of time and that troubled and destabilised me.

I was sent a message that Steadman wanted to see me in London about my progress and my future role. I wasn't fully recovered yet but thought a discussion about my future was needed. Stapleton gave me an update on my progress. I had improved enormously, just needed more time and that's what he would tell Steadman.

He had encouraged me to go running, take gun practice and even do the odd parachute jump with the recruits. A healthy mind in a healthy body, he kept saying as we joined in long runs, but he cautioned me, from his experience I wasn't fully recovered. I was still vulnerable, and unpredictable, and he was worried that any pressure would spark a reaction, either depressive or violent, which took me by surprise.

I genuinely thought I'd gone beyond all of that; I was on a much more even keel and was more like the old me, not drinking or swearing anymore, which I'd never done before. I was far more in control of myself. He told me I still needed support with regular meals, exercise, sleep, and peace for a few months more before I recovered enough. I thought of asking Steadman for a driving job or radio receiver role when I met him. Either one would be good.

I WAS PERMITTED to drive myself to London to meet with Steadman, which I appreciated, and I was greeted unusually warmly by him at the flat and offered a seat. He asked me general questions—how I was feeling, how my recovery was coming along—and was pleased I looked so well. He asked after my mother, and then seemed to run out of trivial questions. Neither of us was any good at small talk and both just wanted to get down to business.

He explained to me the problems they were having in France. They had concerns about messages coming out of a particular circuit. It was thought an agent might have been captured and their messages were being sent under duress.

The other possibilities were that an agent had been killed and their codes were being used, or worse, were working as double agents. Either way, it was causing a real headache.

The radio message receivers had noticed some agents had stopped using their true codes, not sure at first if this was just a mistake, or something more serious. They weren't sure whether to believe what was coming out of that area and needed to be certain about the source and the general integrity of the circuit. This was to protect any agents being dropped in and secure the precious supplies they were sending.

Several agents had recently been parachuted straight into German hands. The Abwehr, German military intelligence, had infiltrated the resistance group somewhere along the line and the whole system was compromised. They had pilots, Allied servicemen, resistance, and agents waiting in the numerous escape lines and safe house systems in that area. They needed to get them back to England quickly and safely, but the system was blocked, people paralysed, too frightened to move. The number of resistance sabotage attacks had also dropped off to the bare minimum in the last two months, which was another indication all was not well.

"A list of five agents has been drawn up of those who had worked near that area previously. Those agents would know and trust some of the resistance and could hit the ground running, unsupported and alone should they agree to return." He then said, "Your name is one of them, Yvette."

He quickly put his hand up to stop me responding. "I know this is a lot to ask, but we need you to return if you will, and help find out what's going on. Not as a courier or radio operator this time but working as a lone agent, to review the two circuits and the agents working between Arlaise and Drayville, to look for signs of infiltration and rogue agents." He stopped talking as my mind tried to ratio-nalise what he'd just said.

"You needn't answer now, my dear. Go home, have some time with your family, and think it over." He studied the expressionless look on my face and went on. "It's now Thursday, if you could get back to me on Monday by ten with your answer. If you're willing to help us, a planned drop would be arranged during the next moon phase."

I felt my guts quivering, my mind racing with pictures of the horrors I'd seen, all still brimming underneath the surface of my calm exterior. Just talking about it made my nerves jangle and my pulse race. I had flashbacks of some of the worst incidents, but nothing showed on my face as I fought hard to maintain a fragile control. I wasn't expecting this at all. I'd done my time, only just getting out alive. I was expecting him to tell me I would be a radio operative in England or a driver, for which I believed I was now much more suited.

I maintained my composure. "Thank you for updating me, sir. I will consider it carefully and get my answer to you by Monday."

"Thank you, Yvette, thank you. We're enormously grateful for what you've done already. I know what you've been through, believe me I do, but the war isn't over yet, not by a long shot, and we desperately need experienced agents like you to help. The other four agents have already agreed to return," he added, piling more pressure on me. He then dismissed me from the meeting and started preparing papers on his desk. I stood up, turned, and left.

I got into the car and started the drive back, stopping when I was out of sight of his building, in a side street. I opened the door of the car to vomit as the stress raged at me. I desperately wanted to get back to the sanctuary of my room, to numb myself with alcohol. Every nerve in my body was screaming, exposed and raw. My mind kept wandering back to what I'd seen and done in France. The dead bodies, the tension, the loneliness, and stress that ate at your very soul. And then Whippet's face flashed into my head.

At the same time, I wondered where it had gone wrong, and if the people in Architect were okay. I was completely disarmed and unsettled by this, emotions I thought had been deeply buried roared to the surface once again. Confusion, grief, empathy, anger, despair, and helplessness all raged at me.

I began to think of those poor souls who were living under the stress I had and who were still bravely risking their own lives every minute of every day to help end the war. I then had overwhelming feelings of selfishness, uselessness, and guilt to add to all the others. I wasn't brave and I'd survived when better people than me, like Whippet, had died.

Cameron had been right all along, and people had died because of me, and by my own hand. I then started arguing with myself, *I was just one person, for goodness' sake, and they could always find someone else. They were training agents all the time. It shouldn't just be down to me; I was only twenty-one.* I then realised, yes, I'd just turned twenty-one—my birthday had gone by this year in a fog of despair, and I didn't celebrate it or acknowledge it, and neither did anyone else.

I STARTED the car and drove out of London with the burden of this decision hanging heavily over me. I wasn't sure if I would ever be ready for the intensity of agent life again, despite Stapleton's support. The loneliness, perpetual terror, and dependency were something I had not been prepared for on my first mission. Now that I knew what was waiting for me, and had only just escaped it, I had real fear about ever attempting it again.

I took a detour off the main roads, preferring to drive along the almost empty country lanes. The sky was blue and cloudless, and I wound the window down to smell the cold country air. I remembered the bluebell wood and the magical feeling that gave me. I imagined myself there to give me comfort.

Life should be so simple—there shouldn't be wars, and horror. You should just enjoy life, be kind to one another and live peacefully. As I argued with myself, weighing up the pros and cons of returning as an agent, a crushing thought roared into my head that evil starts wars and if good people do nothing then evil wins. The horrors would be much worse for all of us down the line unless it was stopped.

I felt raw and exposed as I drove, desperate to get back to my sanctuary, and was driving a bit fast in my haste to return. I came to a bend in the lane, and as I drove around it, I was confronted with a large truck coming head-on towards me in the middle of the lane. It forced me to swerve to avoid hitting it and I ended up in a deep drainage ditch at the side of the road.

I was stunned for a few seconds, having banged my head, and then got out, immensely angry with the other driver. Stapleton would kill me if the car were damaged, and it wasn't even my fault. I crawled up the ditch on my hands and knees and was met at the top by a pair of army boots and trouser legs. I looked up further and came to face to face with an American serviceman in an olive and khaki uniform, looking concerned, with his hand outstretched to help me up.

We looked at each other, our eyes met, and I felt my insides weaken, my legs turning to jelly. My heart raced for a different reason other than fear this time, as he helped me to my feet. This was a totally new experience for me.

I was still very cross with him though and told him off. "What on earth do you think you were doing? Driving like that in the middle of the road. You could have killed me."

"Are you okay? I'm so sorry. It's a large truck and I'm not fully used to it yet. I've only been in your country a couple of weeks. These roads are real narrow round here, there is just no room to maneuver and pass at all."

I was still cross, as my car was stuck in the ditch and I vented my feelings on him, waving my arms madly as I spoke, like some demented windmill. "Why were you driving in the middle of the road? Why on earth are you on a country lane instead of the main road with a vehicle this big? they're not made for vehicles this size."

"As I've already said, it wasn't the middle of the road." He argued back. "It's a narrow road and I have a big truck and so the whole road was taken up. There is no middle. I didn't realise until I turned onto this road, that there was nowhere to turn around."

He then tutted, raising his eyes heavenward. "Women drivers. You were going too fast and so it is partly your fault."

I took the bait. "This is England, not America. You should have been more careful on roads you don't know. It has nothing to do with women drivers. It was your fault."

We then started arguing over each other at the same time, blaming the other for what had happened, not allowing the other to speak. We were getting nowhere near resolving it when he pulled me forcefully towards him and kissed me full on the mouth in mid verbal flow and stopped me talking.

"What an absolute bloody cheek," I said, slapping him.

He laughed, "Don't read anything into the kiss. I only did it to stop you yelling at me. There was no other way." He laughed.

I felt myself blushing and huffed furiously at him as I went down into the ditch to check the car. I examined it, feeling his eyes watching me as I did, and then I stood by it and told him bossily he would have to pull me out. At which point he came down, grabbed my arm, and started pulling me up the side of the ditch.

"Not me, you idiot, the car!" I said, waving my arms furiously at my vehicle.

He just laughed so loudly at me, and I rolled my eyes at him, finding him infuriating. He was completely gorgeous and funny. This was something totally new to me and in my guarded state I didn't know how to react. I was experiencing feelings I'd never, ever felt before in my life. Once my car was out of the ditch, having been towed out by his truck, he asked me my name.

"I don't give my name to strangers," I said haughtily, still struggling with my feelings for this stranger.

"I've kissed you; we've been intimate. We're not strangers anymore." He winked at me suggestively.

"How impertinent, 'oversexed, over something and over here,' as the saying goes," I said sarcastically.

He looked at me and laughed loudly again, "I think the term they're using," he said, "Is 'overpaid, overfed, oversexed, and over here. Our take on that is you Brits are underpaid, undersexed and under Eisenhour." He looked deep into my eyes. "I am obviously annoying you."

"You most certainly are," I said.

Then, with the naughtiest twinkle in his eyes, he said,

"But look me in the eye and tell me you don't just love it." And winked at me again.

I wanted to scream at him, but finally gave in, fascinated by him. We walked to his truck to return the tow rope and as he opened the truck door a pamphlet fell onto the road, and I hurriedly picked it up. He tried snatching it back, but I held him off.

"What's this then? Aha, 'Instructions for American Servicemen in Britain.' How jolly interesting. Hmm, let's see what it says about British women. I flicked through the pages, well, well, it says here, and I quote, 'When you see a girl in khaki or air force blue with a bit of ribbon on her tunic, remember she didn't get it for knitting more socks than anyone else in Ipswich.' So very true." I indicated the ribbons on my tunic.

He looked heavenward and hit back. "I think it also says you are meant to be nice to me being a guest in your country, and we should get along." He grinned annoyingly and laughed.

I'd never met anyone like him before in my life, and in full blush now I laughed with him. His name was Cole Eastman and he asked to meet up for a drink to make amends for the crash. He had a forty-eight-hour pass from Saturday morning, and he and some friends were going into London for the weekend. He suggested getting together on Saturday afternoon. I told him I had to take the car back first and wasn't sure about it. He wrote the name of a pub he knew in the West End on a piece of paper. They had been there on their first weekend pass, and it was a decent place.

I decided, in a rather childish fashion, not to make it that easy for him. "I might be there, and I might not be. I really don't know. I might be working. I will have to check my diary and any other commitments first."

He moved closer to me, lifted my chin up so his face was looking down on mine, looked deeply into my eyes, then winked. "You'll be there." I was blushing again because I knew he could see right through me, and infuriatingly, he was right.

I told him there was a turning spot for his truck about three hundred yards further along the road and got back into my car with an incredibly strange feeling. I was infuriated but enthralled by him and I felt lighter than I'd ever felt in my life. My mood lifted, my soul was singing, and I kept imagining his gorgeous face, his green eyes, his sandy hair, his broad shoulders, and his six-foot-tall body. I had to stop myself imagining more.

I watched as he waved and drove off, and as he did so, another car came around the corner and veered off the road to avoid a collision with his truck. There was a lot of arm waving going on, and he was having difficulty explaining to the very cross elderly home guard, who had been driving the other car and was also waving his arms like a demented windmill, how it had happened.

I laughed to myself as I watched that scene unfold behind me. *Try twinkling your eyes and kissing your way out of that one.*

~

I DROPPED the car back to Stapleton and he looked curiously at me.

"What happened to you?" he asked.

"I met with Steadman, and he's offered me work," I told him.

"Not that. What's happened to give you such a lift? You

left here such a misery this morning and have come back like a flighty, grinning teenager."

I trusted him fully now and let him in on what had happened in such a joyful way and the fact I had a date. He asked about damage to the car, and I reassured him it was only minor.

"What pub are you meeting at? having visited so many in my time, I can probably tell you if it's any good," he said, laughing.

The rule "Trust no-one" was screaming in my head repeatedly, but I had an overwhelming need to tell him my decision. "I won't be returning to France, which is what Steadman asked me to think about. I'm only twenty-one, Paul, and surely now after everything, I deserve a chance to live. I think I've done my bit. I will continue working in England as a radio operator or driver, I don't mind which."

"I'm happy for you," Stapleton said. "Maybe that's the right decision for you now." I was so pleased he could see it from my point of view, and I believed he had truly given me his blessing to say no. I trusted him totally and told him which pub I was going to. Little did I know how misplaced that trust would be and how far "following orders" would go.

I skipped into my room to get packed for my trip back to London, while he checked the damage to the car. I just couldn't take the smile off my face or settle down the excited feelings I'd been left with. He gave me a lift to the station; I was relieved that he drove, and I made the rest of my way home by train.

STAPLETON

I watched Devereaux skip out of the room. *Bloody hell, how did this happen? This wasn't supposed to happen.* My orders were to get her combat ready as soon as possible to return to the field. I was ordered to report any problems in her recovery directly to Steadman. I told him she wasn't ready yet, but a few more months and no doubt she would be. He couldn't accept that and wanted her ready now. I'd started to feel quite protective of her. I liked her; she was gutsy and decent and had done her bit for her country, she deserved to be left alone to work in a safer role.

I knew they were having problems and wanted any experienced agents not currently in the field back as fast as possible. I'd prolonged it with Devereaux for as long as I could. Given a bit more time, I could probably have arranged that she stayed in England to work with me training new recruits. That would have kept her safe, but Steadman's insistence on the new urgent timetable for her return, meant that my chance to protect her had passed. The added problem of her new-found romance couldn't be allowed to stand in the way of the war effort either.

I gave her a lift to the station and saw how excited and happy she was. I'd never ever seen her like this; it was so refreshing, and she looked so young and pretty. It dawned on me then she was only a few years older than my own daughter. Her whole life was ahead of her, and I felt torn at what I was about to do. *Dear God. I had my orders and orders had to be followed.* I waved her off, drove back to the base and, after a period of tortured thought, reached for the phone to call Steadman.

"Sir, I think we've developed a problem with Devereaux."

After giving all the details to him, I was told. "Do whatever you have to do, Paul. Just bloody fix it and quick."

Several phone calls were made. She would be tailed and

any "interference" to her life was authorised from on high. I was suffering dreadful pangs of guilt and regret at what this might do to her and where it might lead. I knew we were at war, and I had to follow orders, but I also knew deep down, somewhere along the line I would come to regret my dreadful betrayal of this young woman.

42

A CRUEL BETRAYAL

I arrived home and was greeted tearfully by my mother, who was pleased to see me after such a long absence. Alfie just grunted at me until I produced a bottle of whisky for him. I had "obtained" it from the army base storeroom, from where it wouldn't be missed. My lock picking skills were still useful. He grabbed it and grunted his thanks, at least it would keep him quiet for a while. I had my old room to use, as no one was currently in residence, and started planning for my date.

I didn't tell my mother where I was going when I left that Saturday. I was so accustomed to lying and she thought I was going out to meet an old friend. I chose the light blue dress with three-quarter-length sleeves that Ethan's mother had made for me. I hadn't had the chance to wear it yet. It hung a little bit loose on my frame due to the weight loss, but it was still okay. It had small blue silk buttons all the way down the back and had a flattering flare. I had an old rich blue coat to wear over it and had my hair out of its usual tied up no nonsense fashion, in a softer loose style that framed my face. I applied makeup and perfume from my mother's dresser and went excitedly on my date.

My stomach was in knots on the bus. What if he didn't turn up? What if I'd read more into this meeting than was meant? What if this was just his usual routine with women and it meant nothing, just flirting? What if he was engaged? Married? What if he was married with kids? What if he couldn't be released and his pass was revoked? What if he only liked me in uniform? I was driving myself mad. It wasn't even a firm date, just an "if you are there" type of conversation. I felt stupid for the way I was behaving. It was totally out of character. I was a hardened murdering veteran agent, for goodness' sake, not some love-struck teenager. This was all new to me. A new world had presented itself and I struggled to understand my behaviour and innermost feelings, all the while knowing I had to confirm my decision to Steadman. I knew he wouldn't take a negative response well.

I stood outside the pub where I was due to meet Cole and steeled myself to go in. *Would it look bad, a woman on her own going into a pub?* I suddenly wondered. It was so much easier in uniform, no one thought anything of it. I decided to enter the pub following the next people who went in and managed to sneak in behind an older couple. It was quite crowded, very noisy, and cigarette smoke was thick in the air. I was being stared at by men in different uniforms at the bar and civilians in small groups on tables and felt jolly uncomfortable. I noticed thankfully there were other women there too, including the barmaids, which lessened the embarrassment.

I looked around, but couldn't see him anywhere, and panic started to creep in. I thought about a tactful retreat out of the doors, pretending that coming in was a mistake.

Perhaps this was the wrong place, the wrong date or maybe we had just missed each other. Then out the corner of one side of the pub pushing through the crowd came Cole. He had a huge grin on his face and looked incredibly pleased I was there. Relief washed over me.

He took my hand and introduced me to his small group of friends, who looked like fun, and they asked me if I had any friends they could meet. I only had Stapleton at the time and was quite sure they wouldn't want to meet him. They squeezed me into a booth with them and we had a couple of drinks. His friends were flirty, and funny, and I could feel him watching my reaction as they each animatedly tried to impress me with tales of their exciting lives.

Cole was acting nervously as his friends chatted with me. He then told them how he had been yelled at by a very bossy woman in uniform and this couldn't possibly have been me; he didn't recognise me out of uniform. He told them the tale of the crash from his own amusing perspective. They'd already had quite a bit to drink when they started telling me about Cole. They all agreed he was a real catch; he could have any girl he wanted in New York where he lived. His dad was loaded, girls fell all over themselves to go out with him, and I must be something real special for him to be the one making the effort. I'd knocked him sideways apparently. I just laughed.

I could feel his unease and embarrassment as they spoke, and he was worried about what else they might come out with.

"Okay, we have to go," he said, grabbing my hand and almost dragging me away. They all cheered us off loudly and he put his arm protectively around me as we made our way through the pub and out into the streets of London.

Cole was new to London, having only been here twice briefly since coming to England and it usually resulted in him and his friends getting lost and going to a pub. We took the bus to see the usual sights everyone wants to see: Big Ben, Buckingham Palace.

We were standing in front of Big Ben when it chimed, which startled us both. I jumped, grabbed his arm, and exclaimed, "Oh good gracious," and he laughed at me, which made me laugh too. Startled by that bloody clock, I'd heard it thousands of times and was used to it like background noise, but my nerves were still so incredibly raw and exposed. Then the air raid siren started. What a bloody nuisance, I thought. That's just typical. *When will this war give me a moment?* I silently screamed to myself.

He was lost as to what to do during a raid away from his base and I led him down into the nearest underground station. We sat on one of the benches as the station filled up around us with frightened and annoyed people. The bombs then started falling above us. He hadn't experienced bombing this close before and looked at me trying to hide his obvious fear. He put his arm around my shoulders in a manly protective gesture, but I could see he was nervous, and could feel him jump slightly and squeezed me extra tightly whenever a bomb dropped.

I pulled him towards me and kissed him to take his mind off things and he responded as if he were trying to absorb any bravery I had left.

My guard was fully down. I was vulnerable as never before, and had I been in France this would have been my undoing. Had I been in full agent mode at that moment, I would have seen a pair of eyes fiercely burning through me from further along the station platform, watching my every move.

We sat there in the underground, talking about nothing much. I got him to talk mostly, and he told me how long he'd been in England, what he'd done since his arrival. He talked about his family in New York, his father's financial investment job, his mother, whom he adored, his younger brothers and sister who were all still at home. He was also in finance like his father and was keen to get back to his life. He wanted the war to be over quickly. He reasoned that once all the Allies get together, they could just take the guy out, meaning Hitler. I admired his enthusiasm and optimism, but I knew it really wasn't that simple.

I was still an agent deep down and gave little away about myself. We sat in silence for periods and just held hands. The chatter in the station became louder, and shrieks and cries reverberated around the station at each bomb exploding. We were by then oblivious to the people around us, lost in the moment in our own world—war was something that couldn't touch us.

Eventually, the all-clear siren sounded to confirm the raid was over, and we all filed out of the station. It was getting late now, and our date was practically over. I felt bitterly disappointed our day had been ruined. I could hardly take him home to meet my mother; Alfie would have an absolute fit and throw us both out. I resigned myself to the date ending, with the possibility of another date at some point.

Cole then turned to me and unexpectedly took my face in his hands and kissed me as the crowd of people bustled passed us on the pavement. It was such a loaded kiss, full of emotion, passion, longing, and love. One I'd never experienced in my life. It completely floored me.

"I want to spend as much time with you as I can," he told me. "We don't know how long we have together with this war. Let's go to a hotel, make a weekend of it. I just want to spend any time I have left with you."

I must have looked shocked, still reeling from his kiss, as he hurriedly continued, "I don't want you to think I'm disrespecting you in any way and I would understand it if you slapped me again, probably more than once, for suggesting it. Forget what the guys said in there, they were just messing around. That isn't who I am." Again, he faltered slightly. "This isn't something I would normally do, and I'm without doubt sure you would never do this usually or have ever done so, and I'm digging a hole for myself here suggesting you may or may not have done anything or would do anything."

He stopped speaking, the look on his face showing that he realised he was getting himself into a terrible knot, but then went on. "These aren't regular times for us. I feel stupid saying this, but in the few hours we've spent together I've fallen in love with you. I will understand if you say no, but I hope you don't. I would think no less of you if you do say no and we could still spend some time together tomorrow if you still want to, if you don't hate me too much now, that is."

He looked at me as if expecting a slap. I was taken aback at the suggestion at first and it was something I would never have considered for a second. In fact, I would have turned on my heels and left him standing there in normal times. But these weren't normal times as he'd said, and having experienced what I had, having seen how fragile life is, and any happiness being in such short supply in my life, I threw caution to the wind, went with my gut feelings, kissed him, and agreed. I was now in love with him too, whatever "in love" meant. I had by then, in my tortured mental state, lost all sense of such things in reality.

∾

WE WENT by train to a hotel I vaguely knew of; I'd been to a base near there once and thought it looked okay from the outside. As we got off the train, rain started to drizzle down, the sky was dark and miserable, but neither of us felt that way. Anything could have been thrown at us at that moment and we wouldn't have cared.

We walked a fair distance to the hotel and rushed the last fifty yards into the reception area as the rain started to get heavier. We burst in breathless, wet, and laughing, and were met by a middle-aged, large-bosomed woman behind the reception desk. She had her dark hair piled high on her head and looked up from what she was doing, peering at us over her dark-rimmed glasses with uncontained disgust.

"We'd like a room please," said Cole.

"Two single rooms will that be, sir?" said the woman in a Scottish accent. I decided I would name her "frosty face," as she looked disapprovingly up and down at Cole in his uniform. We both smiled at each other, desperately trying not to giggle.

"No, a double room please, under the name Mr and Mrs Eastman."

She tried to look at my ring finger, for any evidence of a wedding ring, but my hand was firmly tucked in my coat pocket much to her annoyance. We were signed in and taken to our room on the first floor by the junior reception-ist. She was a young girl with red hair and freckles, who told us her name was Abby. She handed us the key to room thir-teen and told us to go to reception if we needed anything.

She then coughed theatrically and gave us her important prepared speech.

"Breakfast is between seven thirty and ten and check out time is eleven. Don't forget the blackout rules and if the air raid siren starts, come to reception and you will be taken to the nearest shelter," she told us. We thanked her and she smiled as she left.

Once inside the room I looked around at the décor and furnishings. The hotel looked much better from the outside, and the room we'd been given was incredibly small. There was a tiny bathroom with a sink and toilet, and thick curtains in the bedroom to ensure they met the blackout regulations. The patterned carpet was worn, and the bedspread looked gaudy, with the bed being just about a double size. The whole room looked in need of refurbishment, but at least we were alone, and it wasn't as if we were going to live there.

The curtains were closed, and I quickly peeped through them out into the darkening night before closing them again. I took off my coat and turned to look at Cole. It suddenly hit me that without my coat I was absolutely freezing. I tried not to show it, but wondered if you could be equally romantic with your coat on and perhaps gloves?

We looked at each other nervously, as only people who hardly know each other and find themselves in an intimate moment would. He walked towards me and took me in his arms and kissed me. He told me I was the most beautiful and enchanting woman he'd ever met. He was captivated by me, he said, and I blushed deeply. I had no memory of ever being told that before in my life and was unsure how to respond. I was speechless. Ethan had always been so practical about our lives. It was more about where we would live, work, eat, and the war... I was so unprepared for this onslaught of passion on my emotions.

He undid my dress, taking time to undo each of the buttons, kissing me gently as he did. That was no mean feat, especially with the number of buttons that had been put on by Ethan's mother. The dress finally dropped to the floor, and I thanked the trainers sincerely for all their fitness regimes which had left me with a toned, taut body. He flipped the straps of my parachute silk slip off my shoulders, which slithered off to join my dress on the floor and, again, eternal gratitude to Nancy and my mother's sewing skills with lingerie. Part of me had secretly hoped my date might lead to this and I'd worn the beautiful lingerie set and packed some overnight things in my handbag. If my agent training had taught me anything of any value, it was always be prepared. With that thought in my head, I was picked up by Cole who cradled me in his arms, kissed me passionately, and took me to bed.

The night was a revelation to me, and Cole was much more experienced than me. I was reserved, nervous and unsure, and he took the lead where I was more than happy to go. I had gone from dutiful wifely lovemaking to raw passion with someone I desperately wanted and who loved and wanted me as well, repeatedly. All the horrors I'd experienced started melting away as I gave myself up to this man. I was entrusting him with my heart, body, and soul like I'd never done with anyone else. He began to wash away the horrors I'd seen and began to nurture and soothe my lonely, traumatised soul.

We dozed off in the early hours of the morning and when I finally woke up, I found him lying on his side facing me, his head resting on his hand, gazing at my face as I opened my eyes. He smiled at me and gave me a very naughty wink, and I blushed again. *How on earth does he keep doing that to me?* I wondered. I wasn't the sort of person who blushed at all. He made me feel wanted, loved, beautiful, protected, and a bit naughty all at once.

"I think we just crossed the line in the instructions for relations in the American servicemen in England booklet," he laughed, as he kissed me lovingly.

He suggested that after breakfast we should go for a walk and for me to tell him all about my life and family as I'd heard about his already. I was genuinely fascinated by America; having heard everything he had told me about it.

"We must promise each other that once all the warring is over, we will meet up again and I'll take you to America, so you can experience it for yourself."

It sounded wonderful and what I desperately needed to hear at that time—the promise of a future.

"I'll get dressed and go and scout out breakfast while you get ready," he said. Let's book a room for tonight as well, not at this hotel, a better one, if you agree."

I most certainly did and smiled at him, nodding agreement. He pulled the covers back to get out of bed and squealed, as the room was bitterly cold, and I laughed loudly. He picked up a pillow and hit me playfully with it and then wrapped the covers tightly around me on the bed and kissed me tenderly.

"I love you. This is all so new to me, but I know I love you. I've never felt anything like this before. It's crazy. I can't wait for my folks to meet you; they'll love you too. If only the war could be over, and we could just get on with our lives." He sighed, then hurriedly washed, dressed, and left the room, kissing me warmly one more time before he went.

I heard the door close as he left and sighed. I looked at my watch, it was eight-thirty and I thought I would have just five more minutes. The warm bed, the delightful exertions of the night and the scent of him on my pillow, along with his last loving kiss, encouraged me to drift back to sleep. Just before sleep enveloped me, I confirmed to myself that my decision on Steadman's offer was made. I would not be returning to France. I would seize the day with Cole. I loved him and genuinely believed he had saved me from the broken spirit I had become. I hoped we both survived the war and could build a good and peaceful life for ourselves in America once it was all over. Even I, after everything terrible I'd done, deserved some happiness.

I WAS AWOKEN a while later by the door opening, and realising I had nodded off, said to the person I thought was Cole, "Oh God I'm so sorry, I fell sleep. Getting up now. Have we missed breakfast?"

But it wasn't Cole. It was the room maid coming into the room to clean. She looked at me in bed, terribly embarrassed.

"Sorry, Madam, I thought you'd left. I'll come back in a while."

"What time is it?" I asked.

"Nine forty, Miss."

Gosh, I'd slept for over an hour.

"Just give me ten minutes and I'll be out of the room."

The maid nodded and left. I washed and dressed double quick, shoving my things into my bag. I thought Cole must have come back to the room, seen me asleep and left me to sleep a bit longer. I grabbed my coat and handbag from the back of the door and skipped down the large circular staircase to the breakfast room. I was expecting to find him there, but there was no sign of him. Breakfast was no longer being served and so I sat down and asked for a pot of tea. I went to reception to find frosty face behind the desk with Abby beside her.

"Can I help you, Miss?" she asked, letting me know she knew I wasn't married after seeing my naked ring finger.

"Are there any messages for me at all—room thirteen?"

"No, Miss," said frosty face.

"Have you seen the gentleman I was with this morning?" I asked her.

"You mean your *husband*," she replied sarcastically, emphasising the word husband, and looking pointedly at my empty ring finger.

"Yes. Mr. Eastman."

Frosty face then said with a glint in her eye, "He was here this morning and was met by some soldier friends. They looked like they were having a jolly good laugh about something as they left."

"Did he book a room here for tonight?"

She checked her booking sheet slowly, obviously taking a delicious pleasure in doing so. "No."

"Did he say anything to you at all before he left?"

She shook her head, looking theatrically pitiful at me as she did so.

I went back to sit in the breakfast room. How did other American soldiers know we were here? Did he telephone his base to check in? Perhaps he'd been called back urgently. Maybe he'd gone to find another hotel and was on his way back. I thought of all the reasons for him leaving suddenly —an accident, death in the family, being called up to move out. I asked for more tea and sat for another half hour waiting, hoping, and praying. I realised I didn't know where he was based, and he knew nothing about me at all, as my training had stopped me giving him any real information. That was to be today's conversation.

I waited for another fifteen minutes and then remembered when I'd grabbed my coat from behind the bedroom door, his coat and cap weren't there. Gradually the horrible heart-breaking truth dawned on me. I'd really known deep down since I woke up the second time and was alone, I'd been used, and he'd gone.

My heart and soul sank into depths I never thought possible. I guessed he was married as well. That was why he wanted to get away from his friends in case they drunkenly told me things he didn't want me to hear.

I went to reception at eleven and asked to leave a message for Mr. Eastman if he came back, and frosty face handed me a hotel notepad which I wrote a brief note on. She took the message and as I turned to leave, she coughed loudly.

"Excuse me, Miss, the bill for the room has to be settled. The American gentleman didn't pay for you."

"Oh, good gracious, yes, of course. I'm so sorry."

Her revenge taken so viciously; she was enjoying every second of this. I fumbled for the money in my handbag and handed it over and she then took a deliberately long time to count it.

Frosty face, Abigail, along with a small group of people waiting to check out, were in the reception area now. It was as if everyone around me was silently laughing at me. The excruciating embarrassment of my situation flooded through me, and I could feel myself just dying inside. I wanted the ground to open and swallow me whole. I would have happily taken an L pill at that very moment if I had one.

I walked out of the reception area, and stood around the

corner out of sight, to regain my composure. As I did so, I heard frosty face in the crowded reception area say in her thick Scottish accent. "That woman, young Abigail, is a trollop, and trollops don't deserve to be treated well. Any unmarried woman who turns up to stay at a hotel with a Yank she hardly knows deserves to be treated like a trollop."

I heard a tearing sound, probably my note.

I slowly made my way back to the train station in a very dejected state, upset, confused, and utterly humiliated.

I CAUGHT the train back to London. I was so pleased I had a carriage to myself, as I didn't want people around me at all. I realised I didn't really like people that much. I sat down and looked out of the window, watching the world pass by as I cried silent tears damning him. Tears of rejection, humiliation, embarrassment, and despair flowed down my reddened cheeks. I'd opened myself up totally and trusted him fully as never before with anyone, and the resulting betrayal of this final act had destroyed what was left of me. I was totally broken now, and, in my mind, there was nothing and no one that could ever fix it.

When I thought I could cry no more a strange feeling came over me, as if my heart had frozen in my chest, and an emotional iron shield snapped firmly shut around me. I vowed never to be hurt like this again by anyone. Any remaining trust I had in human beings had gone. I mentally and emotionally returned once again to full agent mode. I would now do what Steadman had asked of me and return to France a much more dangerous and determined agent.

43

THE RED MIST

I made my way up the familiar street to our house, hardened by this betrayal and planning to see Steadman on Monday. I opened the door and went into the living room. Alfie was standing there in his trousers and vest with a furious look on his face. He seemed to have been waiting for me. I saw my mother looking anxious and worried. I could also see Maude Davis sitting on the settee looking very smug for some reason.

Oh God what now?

Alfie started shouting, "You cheap whore, staying out all night like some alley cat." He yelled directly in my face, his foul breath filling my nostrils. He wasn't finished. "Your husband's not even cold in his grave, and here you are lying on your back for some Yank. You've brought shame on this family, in front of our friends and neighbours. Don't try and deny it. Maude here saw you with him kissing at the station yesterday. I won't put up with it, not under my roof, do you hear? You had a chance to be decent with Gordon and you chose to be a whore. Now get out of my house and out of my sight, you filthy, dirty, French whore."

I was disorientated at first, and slow to react after what I'd just been through emotionally, and then felt a full slap to my face. The momentum knocked me off balance and I fell against the large wooden side table, slightly knocking his gramophone. I felt groggy for a few seconds and then the second blow came from Alfie's belt across my backside.

The moment Stapleton had predicted from his well-thumbed broken agent handbook finally arrived. Agent Devereaux emerged, and the red mist descended. I hit Alfie with a full blow with the side of my hand to his throat, and then gave out a firm punch to his solar plexus. Once he was breathless and defenceless, I finished off with a full-bodied kick to the groin and he doubled over vomiting. He struggled to breathe as he slumped down the wall to the floor, dragging his framed picture of the King from the picture rail with him.

None of them were killer blows, I knew. I was still in sufficient control of myself to make this revenge linger. It was enough to disable him for now and for him to understand what was happening to him and who was doing it. I looked down venomously at him: he was just another person to be eradicated from my life. I picked up his leather belt and went in for the kill. As I did so, I caught sight of my mother's terrified face looking at me and stopped abruptly.

The red mist lifted, and I looked at the pitiful sight of Alfie on the floor, the big man, the bully, the shit that had tormented me and my mother all these years. He'd been put on his arse by me and was now whimpering for mercy, covered in vomit like the coward he was. He was nothing, and certainly not worth my trouble or time anymore, I threw the belt to the floor.

I glanced back at my mother who looked so shocked and afraid, it tore at me. I needed to protect her from any repercussions my actions might bring from Alfie and turned back to him, he had made no effort to get up.

"If you ever hurt my mother again, you bastard, I'll kill you. Even a shit like you has to sleep, and believe me, if you touch a hair on her head, you won't know what night I'm coming, but come I will, and I will bloody well finish you off."

It was said in such a low, deadly, ice calm manner, I hoped it would make him think a bit before he hurt my mother again, and it would certainly give him sleepless nights.

I turned to the now petrified Maude Davis, with glazed, vengeful, raging eyes. She must have been in the crowd in the underground during the raid when I was with Cole and told Alfie. All because she wanted me to be handed over to her son like a piece of meat. She looked terrified as she fled past me out the door screaming blue murder and wailing to high heaven. My prospect of being her future daughter-in-law diminished somewhat. My mother was now tending to the injured Alfie. He was snivelling and telling me to leave him alone, he was an ill old man.

My mother looked up with such a horrified expression on her face; she couldn't believe that the foul-mouthed, mad-eyed, aggressive animal in front of her was her daughter.

"What's the matter with you? What has come over you, Yvette? You'd better go now. Go, go on, go. You're just making things worse here, with your foul language and violence. Why did you stay out all night with another man? How do you think poor Nancy will feel when she finds out about this? How could you do this to Ethan and to poor Alfie, after all he's done for you? He looks after me while you are away doing God knows what with God knows who for months on end. You're selfish and are never here for me. Alfie is, he's all I have and look what you've done."

I looked at my mother's face filled with disgust and fear, not because of Alfie but because of me. The realisation of what I'd just done becoming clear. It was never my intention for her to be subjected to agent Devereaux, and I was ashamed, but her words stung. I was selfish, she said, and "After all he'd done for me"—was she mad?

It dawned on me then my mother had always tolerated this abusive relationship when she didn't really have to. She could have left him but didn't and I despaired. There was only so much you could do to help people and I looked at my mother sadly, resigned to the situation she had accepted in her life. I said a heartfelt goodbye to her as she struggled to help Alfie up off the floor.

I packed my things in the grim little bedroom, leaving behind the blue dress and lingerie, the reminders of my betrayal and humiliation, and walked out of the front door. Knowing my mother would rather stay with Alfie than leave with me hurt dreadfully. She had become his 'Leese,' drinking with him rather than try and stop him. I'd offered on numerous occasions for her to leave with me and been swatted away. The resulting rejection used to cut me like a knife, but not now. It was just one less worry to have hanging around in my head.

I USED ALL the money I had left to book into an expensive hotel for the night, soaking myself luxuriously in a beautiful grand bath, and on Monday visited Steadman. I agreed to return to France as soon as possible and he looked pleased at the news. He indicated the bruising on my face, the result of Alfie's slap.

"Wait a few days until that has resolved and then we can discuss your brief fully."

I knew it would mean a blind drop, with no reception party, and to find safe houses based on whom I trusted. I was booked into a hotel for a few days to prepare myself for my next mission, paid for by Steadman's office. There were fearsome bombing raids during those few nights. I had ventured out for a walk one evening and the sirens sounded, which resulted in me spending hours in a communal bomb shelter, with loads of people—it was absolute hell.

I was forced to listen to them talking drivel about winning the war, with old soldiers discussing tactics on how to beat Hitler and fend off any invasion. Angry conversations were held with people complaining about conditions, queuing, rations, the lack of daily items, family trivia galore. There were kids being yelled at for playing and running around, husbands and wives arguing, and it drove me mad. I heard knitting needles clacking, a man was smoking a pipe and clicking the pipe with his teeth from one side of his mouth to the other, a little boy was bouncing a ball on the concrete floor repeatedly, and babies were crying. People were coughing and sniffing repeatedly, and everything sounded so loud and grated on my raw nerves. I was on edge, and once they started singing the dreaded morale boosting songs, I wanted to silent kill someone. "Roll Out the Barrel" and "Knees Up Mother Brown" were being sung with gusto.

Dear God, let this torment end, I despaired. I tried to tune out of it all, but it was getting worse when they got to "Run Rabbit Run." As I looked at the people around me, with their laughing, shouting, crying, and swearing, I was acutely aware of all their annoying habits swamping my head. I began teetering on the brink of violence and knew I had to get out. The smell in the shelter was awful too, with so many people packed in tightly together. I needed fresh air and solitude. I made my way through the crowded shelter saying "sorry" over and over to the tutting, complaining people having to move to accommodate my passage through to the stairs and the exit, where I was stopped by a warden.

He refused to open the door to let me out during the raid. "It's against the rules, Miss. There are lights on in the shelter and if I open the door, I will break the blackout and let the bombers know where we are."

I thought the chances of some sodding German, thousands of feet up in the air, seeing a light for a split second and dropping bombs directly on this dingy little shelter were pretty slim, but nevertheless, respected the rules the warden had been asked to follow.

"Please, sir," I said, with what I hoped he saw as true respect for his position and authority. "I know you have a heavy responsibility for this shelter and rules to follow and I'm really sorry, but I feel terribly sick, and I'm about to vomit everywhere. If I do, all the others packed in this shelter will follow suit, and it will get messy and even smellier in here. I'm just trying to avoid it, that's all."

He thought about that, his eyes were darting from the large crowd at the bottom of the stairs, to the door and then back to me, obviously imagining the horrific results of mass vomiting in the already fetid shelter. He turned one of the main lights off, to the groans and annoyance of the shelter occupants, pulled back the thick blackout curtains, opened the door, and quickly shoved me out into the cold dark night, slamming the door behind me.

I was alone at last, amongst the searchlights, flak, and

bombs, with the heavy smell of explosives in the air. I felt myself physically and mentally relax.

As I walked along the deserted streets, I reflected on the situation with Alfie. I really needed to make things right with my mother and apologise before I went to France. If anything happened to me over there, I didn't want her to be left with fearful memories of our last meeting. I accepted I had to respect her decision to stay with Alfie and live her life the way she wanted, alcohol and all. She was still my mum and I loved her dearly, but I could no longer live with her. My new life meant I would be away from her anyway and she would be with Alfie. I had to accept that my place in her life now was second best to him. There was a deep, sad realisation then—it always had been.

I MADE my way to my mother's house early the following day, preparing myself to deal with either a belligerent or sheepish Alfie. There had been several bombs dropped in our part of London the night before and a lot of damage done. There were sirens wailing in the distance as I walked up our street, steeling myself for my first encounter with Alfie and my mother after our last brutal interaction. The house was eerily quiet, no-one in the kitchen, living room or dining room. I checked the rooms upstairs, nothing. My room was as I'd left it, with the dress and lingerie thrown on the bed. The rented room was in a bit of a state, but no-one there. Perhaps Alfie had been more injured by me than I thought and been taken to hospital.

I checked downstairs again. No-one was there or in the outside yard or lav. My mum had cooked their tea and it was left cold and half eaten on the dining room table, along with

Alfie's half-drunk beer. Her precious sewing machine which she always put safely away when not in use was left out. Where could they have gone?

I went outside looking around, it was not usually this quiet in our street, there were usually kids playing, neighbours chatting or rowing.

One of the neighbours from across the street came out of his front door and called over to me. "If you're looking for Alfie and Leese, love, they were in the community hall basement shelter last night for the raid. It's been bombed, half the street was in there, kiddies' 'n' all. They're still pulling people out. There are survivors. I'm not sure who or how many. I've just come home from there for some tea and a fag before I go back to help."

I was stunned, the man seemed haunted by his experience. "It could have been us and our own kids in there, but the wife had such a strange feeling about the shelter last night, and so we stayed at home and sat it out. Thank Christ we did or..."

I began running to the community hall before he'd finished speaking. It was a place I'd been many times before during the bombing raids. Before I even reached it, I could hear the sirens blaring louder and saw smoke billowing in the sky over the rooftops. I got as near as they would allow me, the acrid smoke filling the air, stinging my eyes. I couldn't see properly and clambered up onto a wall where I had a clearer view of the site from a distance. All the noise around me faded, as I looked in shock at the site in front of me.

Where the building had once been, lay a huge pyre of concrete, wood and rubble, smouldering. It had been destroyed, along with the buildings on either side and had buried the people gathered in the basements of all three buildings. It was absolute chaos. I was stunned that people had survived and had crawled out unscathed, shocked but alive; others were being dragged out severely injured and put on stretchers. Some were so severely burned, and others had limbs missing. It was horrendous to see. The screaming, crying and sirens from the site which had been silenced by my acute shock suddenly roared back to life around me.

I was still hopeful and scrambled down from the wall, forcing my way through the crowds to get to the site, fiercely pushing aside one of the wardens to get past. I desperately searched the crowds and injured for my mother, or Alfie, but after checking the dead under the sheets I knew they weren't there. I was told there was a list of the survivors at the hospital and a list of those of the dead identified so far. I went as fast as I could to the main hospital. If my mother was injured, I needed to be with her. I also needed to say how deeply sorry I was for everything I'd put her through over the last few months, how selfish I'd been, and how much I loved her. I wanted to tell her what I'd been doing so she would understand and forgive me.

Once at the hospital I took directions to a room off the reception area. There was a crowd of people there, some sitting on chairs, a few on the floor, some crying loudly, some weeping gently, some covered in dust and injured, some holding each other and looking for loved ones, while others were just in total shock and sat silently. There were a couple of FANY'S in uniform seated at a trestle table trying to answer everyone's questions about missing or dead relatives. People queued in front of the desks to take turns to speak to them. *How awfully bloody British, to queue in such an orderly fashion when all around was chaos and death.* I nevertheless took my place in the queue waiting patiently like everyone else, expecting to hear that she was injured but alive.

My mind was in turmoil, absolutely raging. *That's my mum; she can't die in a war. That isn't how it's meant to happen. I was the one risking death, not her. I should be dead. She should be safe at home with Alfie, cooking, sewing, meeting her French friends. She should die when she's old, happy, and safe in her own bed, preferably in France.*

When I reached the front desk, I gave them my mother's name. The woman who was sat in front of me ran her finger agonisingly slowly down the list. She lifted her head, looked at me sadly and said how sorry she was. My mother was listed as dead. I asked about Alfie. He'd survived but had been left severely injured; he'd identified my mum. I enquired about Nancy Devereaux, and they checked the list again and gave me a sad acknowledging look, she too was dead.

I needed proof of my mother's death. I was aware of all the cockups that could happen with chaos and mass casualties. It could be a mistake and she could be somewhere confused, worried, and drinking tea, or injured and being treated somewhere alone and frightened, waiting for me. I asked to see her body to confirm it.

I was taken in silence by a shocked-looking porter into the bleak basement of the hospital, where there were multiple trolleys with bodies covered in sheets lining the walls on either side. The bare lights dangling from the ceiling created an eery glow against the old white tiled walls. The porter gently patted my shoulder called something to a colleague and left me there. Some bodies had relatives around them crying and there was a vicar in full regalia comforting the bereaved with passages from the bible.

I was then led into a room and to a trolley at the far end. There was a body covered in a white sheet with a large tag around its foot. Before I even reached it, I could see the body was misshapen on its right side under the sheet which had dried blood on it. I didn't want them to fully uncover her; I just needed to see the face, to be absolutely sure. I began imagining all the horrors of what a bomb explosion and resulting fire could do to a body and started to fear what I would be subjected to when the head was exposed.

I wasn't sure my mind could absorb anymore horror and could feel my heart hammering in my chest as I waited. I was holding my breath preparing myself for the worst, but when the orderly pulled back the sheet, it was just my mum. Her hair was full of thick dust and her face had a couple of grazes, but she looked so serene and peaceful, as if she were sleeping and all the worries of the world had left her. That was some comfort to me at least. I could finally breathe out and then kissed her forehead thanking her for being my mum. I told her I loved her so very much and how sorry I was for anything I'd ever done to hurt or upset her in any way. I covered her back up with the sheet and left, avoiding the rapidly approaching vicar.

My mother's death was the final blow. I consoled myself on the way back to my hotel that at least she was safe and being alone would make my mission much easier to undertake. I had nothing and no one to live for. It did cross my mind that I'd killed a man and woman in France and had lost Cole and my mum since then. Seeing the vicar made me think—*Was this the 'eye for an eye' that is preached about? Had I brought this all on myself? Had I caused my own mother's death? Was this my punishment?*

44

ROGUE AGENT

The bruising on my face had faded, and that night would be a full moon for my flight out. I didn't report my mum's death to anyone before this mission; there was no point in them knowing and it would only delay things. I was taken to a different waiting place this time, a large country house full of different nationalities of agents, but again I didn't want to interact with any of them.

I went through the usual pre-mission checks. I had with me a small metal tube of toothpaste. I'd scraped off all details about manufacturers, hoping to take it with me, my one luxury, to be able to brush my teeth in France. This was taken and binned at the final inspection. It was unallowed on the grounds that it wasn't easily available in France and would raise suspicion as to how I obtained it.

I didn't argue but laughed to myself. *Is it me or are they all completely mad? They're making a fuss about a tube of bloody unmarked toothpaste raising suspicion. Do they not think that having thousands of francs tucked in your knickers, a gun in your bra, knife strapped to your leg and a transmission radio in a suit-case might raise even the slightest question?*

I was shown on a map where I was being dropped and was offered alcohol, which I accepted this time. The pre-drop procedure was much briefer, thank goodness. I had the usual pills and equipment handed to me. I had a locket fashioned to hold the two pills in. This was to be a blind drop and so my parachuting skills would be tested again. There would be no welcoming party—no one knew I was going. I had a bulky jump suit and parachute strapped on me and the small spade on my outer leg. My radio would be dropped with me to collect after I landed.

There were two other agents being dropped on the same night and we were grouped together to await our flight out in the pilot's cottage. I didn't really want to meet any of the pilots this time around; Whippet was still too raw for me; I was still harbouring the incredible guilt of his death and I avoided any chats with anyone. As the three of us sat in the plane, it was obvious to me by their behaviour this was the other two agents' first drop into occupied territory. I gazed at them, knowing what they would be facing, and felt numb.

The plane was incredibly noisy and had a full crew on board. It was hit by fierce flak on the way over. The pilot took evasive action to avoid it, causing us to be jolted all over the place in the back. The flak eventually eased, and they signalled we were near my drop zone and to prepare. I had specifically asked for this area, as I knew it gave me the best chance of staying safe. I was first out of the plane with no hesitation, and the moonlight, my only companion, gave off enough light for me to make out the land below. I landed textbook style, far away from the trees, collected my radio, buried the parachutes, and melted into the trees, alone once more.

I knew where I was going as this was part of my plan. I had a new cover story prepared and memorised: I was now Camille Janvier. Memorising the background details of this new life was harder given the short space of time, but I was confident I could keep it up under questioning. It wasn't as strong as my first one, as I had lived as her, but it would have to do.

I found the farmhouse I was looking for. It was now abandoned, and once I'd checked the surrounding area, I went in. The place had been looted and ransacked, but apart from that it was as I remembered, except for the bodies being removed from the kitchen. I banked on the fact no one would be eager to live there knowing what had happened. This would be my base for the night while I gathered my thoughts and planned my mission in detail. It was going to be much more dangerous now, as there were people who knew me with my previous cover name. I checked the barn basement hopefully, but it had been totally cleared of all guns and ammunition.

There were people I was sure I could trust—Dubois for one, my radio support. I would contact him first. I was glad I was alone in a way. No endless chitchat or talking over and over about stupid plans I knew wouldn't work. A lot of hot air and little action summed up the chaotic approach of some of the people I'd worked with, on both sides of the Channel. The sheen of mystery and awe had been taken off an agent's life for me and could never return. I had one job to do and would do it to the best of my ability, and then get the hell out.

In the dark, I fashioned a bed on a torn sofa in a downstairs room. As usual I placed a large piece of wood behind the front door as my early warning system. I had my gun and knife with me as I settled down to sleep. I thought about the four people who'd died here, two at my own hands. Was there such a thing as ghosts? They would be very annoyed ghosts with me having shot them, that was for certain. I wondered if there was an afterlife, would I have to face them there? The saying, 'Vengeance is mine sayeth the Lord,' came to my mind. I did wonder what vengeance I would face for killing these people, even if it was in a war.

Whose side would God be on anyway? Wouldn't he want us to fight evil and cruelty? Were some people born evil? What if there was no afterlife? no God, no nothing; we just ceased to exist, dust to dust. I pulled my coat tightly around me, worrying about possible ghostly retribution for a while, but then drifted off into much-needed sleep.

AFTER A FULL NIGHT'S undisturbed rest, I got up and disguised myself as I'd been taught. It was small subtle changes that put people off recognising you, and I chose to dress in a more boyish fashion and was wearing glasses. I found an old battered but workable bike behind an outbuilding. That would do for now.

I cycled to the station to catch the train and noted how many more German troops were around now than when I was last here. The place was flooded with them. I also saw the evidence of severe and sustained Allied bombings which were becoming quite extensive. I watched as people went through to the station. They were only checking ID not luggage. I discarded the bike and after showing my ticket and ID, went through unchallenged with my radio in its case. It had been modified, and thankfully weighed much less than the old style one and had been disguised as a small gramophone inside.

There were an awful lot of Germans travelling on this train, but no-one bothered me or my radio, not the soldier who sat next to me, or the grinning one opposite me.

Dubois worked at his carpenter's workshop in one of the villages outside Arlaise, which was on the train route. I got off at the stop nearest his workshop, hoping he was still alive. There were just civilian ticket staff at the exit and so again I strolled through unchallenged. He recognised me standing outside his shop after a few seconds and smiled. He seemed really pleased to see me and took me into the back of his workshop, so we could talk.

"It's much more dangerous now, Evelyn, they're all over the place. There are German intelligence working in civilian clothes, trying to infiltrate the circuits. Several resistance people from a neighbouring circuit between Drayville and Paris have been caught, and we can't be sure if any of them have talked or have been turned into double agents. The Germans have more information, which shows in their activities and arrests. People are waiting to see who will be picked up next. Some have fled, and the rest are living in fear of being captured."

There was still a small section working on sabotage in my old circuit. They had been trying to build up the numbers of resistance and agents for when the Allied advance eventually came. They had new people join the group and still had a radio operator and courier.

"I need to urgently meet up with Voltaire," I said.

"Voltaire's dead. He was killed on a mission with the resistance. He shouldn't have even been there, he was filling in because of lack of numbers. There's a new circuit organiser running things now, code name Boden."

I was shocked about Voltaire, but he was supposed to be the organiser not a foot soldier and had put himself at risk.

Dubois went on, "Boden's a bit of a loose cannon, he likes blowing things up. He doesn't understand that when the resistance blows something important up, the Germans shoot civilians in response. We've lost good people because of it. I want to keep the group focussed on returning downed air crew through the escape lines and safe houses, pilots in particular, as they are desperately needed. The Allies are now carrying out so many more targeted bombing raids around Arlaise. The railyard and port have been bombed and has led to civilians being killed as a result. There are more planes being shot down, with their crews on the run, so they should be our priority." I agreed with him.

Dubois listed the meeting places for the Secretary circuit I was to check on and gave me the keys to a house he was doing carpentry work in. "It's a safe house, the family are away for a few days, you can stay there overnight. It's safe for you." I gratefully accepted, and he took me there and settled me in.

As he was leaving, he turned to me and said sadly, "Concentrate on being more your French self from now on. There's bad feeling amongst the resistance and locals because of the Allies killing women and children in their bombing raids."

THE NEXT DAY Dubois took me in his carpentry van to meet the organiser of the second circuit in Drayville, that had possibly been infiltrated. A few arrests had been made locally already. The new organiser, Segal was a young man in his thirties, but looked so much older, his face lined and his eyes wary and nervous. Like everyone else living there at the time, he was very thin, his clothes hanging loosely around him. He was as satisfied as he could be that those remaining with him could be trusted. He told me one or two resistance fighters and agents were now working between the two circuits Architect and Secretary, which I thought was incredibly risky. If one group was compromised, then the other one would be very quickly too, meaning two circuits lost as a result.

He thought some of the people captured, agents and resistance, had already talked, as the Germans seemed to know in advance what they were planning. I told Dubois to leave me with Segal and go back to his workplace in case someone came looking for him. I didn't want him taking unnecessary risks. I hugged him tightly as he left. My trusted group of contacts was now incredibly small.

Segal then took me to a farm out of town where I could fit in as a relative of the farm owner for a brief time. The family were happy to have me stay and knew me as "the lady" to ensure their children could not give away any names. They had been visited by the Germans just once recently, but overall were left alone to manage the farm on the condition they delivered the correct farm supplies to the Germans as ordered.

Theirs was a large working farm and so they had good reason to be travelling around in delivery trucks and moving between villages and towns. The farmworkers were all trusted locals, mostly women, but all were kept away from the main farmhouse, and so would have no idea what went on there. The Bissett family included Margot, Aaron, and their children, Theo, seven, and little daughter, Mathilda, aged four.

They made such a fuss over me, and in my emotionally bruised and battered state, it was difficult to accept and adjust to such a caring environment. I watched them when they were together and the obvious love and good humour they shared, even in these difficult times, was a joy to behold. Little Mathilda adopted me and followed me everywhere I went, whenever I looked behind me, there she was striding to catch up. She collected eggs with me from the chicken shed and showed me all the farm animals, each of which she had names for. She wanted me to read books to her, which I happily did. I thought wistfully how I wished I'd been born into and nurtured by such a loving family; how different my life could have been. With her large smiling eyes, and light brown curly hair, she was the one beacon of hope for the future, reminding me there is some innocence and goodness in this terrible, evil world.

If I ever had a daughter, I hoped she would be like this little one, so cheerful, so full of life, taking joy from everything she saw. I would love her intensely and protect her from evil with every fibre of my being, until the day I died.

The food they served was wonderful too, such a change from the constant supply of potato soup, sausage, and black bread I'd survived on. Once again being in the countryside showed there were benefits. The German occupation had taken its toll on farms with a lack of fertiliser, workers, and petrol it was hard to get by. The resistance secretively helped the Bissetts maintain theirs as an effective farm, providing them with supplies, which were all kept well hidden.

I would happily have frozen time and stayed on their farm forever if I could, but I knew the horrendous risk they were taking having me there and I planned to move on as soon as possible.

～

One evening I was reading a story to Mathilda as she was settling down in bed. When I finished reading and tucked her in, she sweetly kissed my cheek and asked me my name. It was such a simple question from an innocent child, and I had by then been deeply overwhelmed by the normality of the family and surroundings I was living in. It was so alien to everything I'd known up until then. Being lost in the moment, without thinking about security risks, I told her, Yvette. Mathilda couldn't say my name properly and called me Avette. No matter how many times she practiced it, that was what came out.

Mathilda announced at breakfast next day that the lady's name was Avette, and they all laughed as she tried repeatedly to get it right, Avette, Avette, after which, for security, I went back to being called "the lady."

I was driven by Aaron to a nearby village, as he had deliveries to make there and knew a resistance meeting was taking place. He pointed to a clothes shop where he said Segal and others were meeting in the apartment above. He left the truck parked where I could observe the entrance, as he delivered to local shops and customers. The meetings were now all arranged last minute to stop anyone informing and were held in double quick time. They were also keeping the meeting groups as small as possible for safety.

"Don't wait for me. If I'm not in the truck when you finish your deliveries return to the farm. Don't take any risks," I told him.

He nodded and started making his deliveries in the village, leaving me to watch who went in and out. I saw people trickle out at differing intervals. First, a group of mostly older men, followed by a few younger men and women and then nothing. There had been no one that sparked any interest, and I resigned myself to having to attend the next meeting to assess the individuals there.

I was waiting for Aaron to return, when I saw a face from my past coming out of the building. Valerie, the agent who'd broken her leg on the parachute jump. She must have returned to complete the training and been dropped in months after me. As she came out of the building, she turned the corner out of sight. I left the truck and followed her as she walked quickly through the streets and into the train station. She looked nervously around as people passed her or walked behind her. I'd been trained well enough to stalk someone and keep myself unseen. My blonde hair was completely covered by a hat, and I was wearing trousers and glasses. I bought the same destination ticket to Bourselle she had, which was a short train ride south near Paris, and entered the train carriage behind hers. Our papers were checked on the train and at the station, but I was more confident in the British forgers now, and they didn't let me down.

Out of the station, we walked for about ten minutes, and down a small side street. I watched as Valerie knocked a door and went into a building. I waited and after a noticeably short while, she reappeared with a man in civilian clothes, he said something to her, and they split up. She started walking back towards me and I slipped into a shop and watched her go by. I decided to follow the man. I knew I could follow Valerie anytime I wanted to in the future, as she attended the circuit meetings, so the man would be my target. He walked down the opposite end of the street and strolled quite nonchalantly along a few more streets. He had an arrogant swagger about him and didn't appear to even consider for a second that he might be being followed. He just skipped up the steps and strolled into the entrance of a large building without a glance anywhere. The building had the German flag and swastika flying outside.

I needed to get my radio from the Bissett farm and find a safe transmission site to urgently let London know what I'd seen. They should discount any messages from the compromised agent Valerie and the 'Secretary' circuit.

I TRAVELLED BACK, collected my radio, and once I was safely away from the Bissett's farm, sent a message about Valerie. I thought long and hard about my next move, as it would be incredibly risky. I needed to get close to her and find out what she had informed the Germans about, who she was working with, and then kill her.

How easy that sounded, how dispensable and of little value human life was to me now. What a cold-hearted, unfeeling bitch I'd become in such a short space of time.

I kept my thoughts about killing Valerie to myself. But this was a traitor who had to die to stop her putting other brave people at risk. I would join in the next meeting with Segal, knowing others in the circuit might also be compromised like her. I knew I could be captured, but as Stapleton once said: "You can either die on your knees or make a stand and do something useful," which meant taking risks. I would leave the Bissett farm immediately to protect them from any further risk relating to me.

They seemed incredibly sad to see me go, especially Mathilda, and they handed me a package of food as a gift. They let me have one of the farm errand bikes and I put my radio in the large basket on the front. I covered this with the food parcel and put loose farm vegetables on top. I then covered it all with my coat and tied it with string and made my way from village to village back to where I knew Valerie was staying. I didn't particularly want to get on a train with my radio again if I could avoid it and the train systems timetables were becoming so unreliable, partly—I laughed to myself—because the resistance kept disabling trains or blowing up the tracks with explosives. Explosives I'd been providing through organised air drops.

I must have cycled hundreds of miles in my time as an agent, I was almost sure I did that and Morse in my sleep too, but at least the area was flat, and once again I cycled methodically along the lanes making quite a bit of progress. I then saw a German patrol ahead—and they saw me. I had been cycling fast and didn't have time to get off the road, or turn around, without it looking suspicious, so I continued cycling towards them. Some were on foot, and a car was being driven slowly behind them. I was shouted at to stop and was asked for my papers. I was asked simple questions as to what I was doing and where I was going, and I told them I'd been to collect vegetables and was going home. I lifted the coat on the basket to show them potatoes and carrots underneath. They handed me back my papers and I prepared to cycle on.

One of the young soldiers who'd been walking behind the car approached me, grinning. He ordered me to get off my bike, and I laid the bike carefully on the ground so as not to dislodge the radio tucked in the basket under my coat. Some of the vegetables rolled out, but not enough to completely expose the case. He then grabbed me and pushed me up against the car. He started kissing me trying to lift my blouse and cardigan, pawing at me. I made a feeble attempt to push him away and feigned tearfulness at his actions, crying at him to stop. I acted like a maiden in distress, and that usually worked where a group of men were together and someone started misbehaving, especially if you were just an innocent-looking young girl.

Sure enough, as I'd hoped, one of the older soldiers stepped in and ordered him to leave me alone. The younger one didn't listen and continued his assault on me but was eventually dragged off by two of the others, who told me to leave quickly. I grabbed my bike and cycled as fast as I could away from them. My back was hurting like hell; it had been badly bruised by the gun I had stuffed down the back of my trouser waistband and had slammed into my lower spine when he pushed me against the car.

45

A TRAITOR AMONGST US

I was put up in a house in a small village by trusted friends of Segal. They were a very sad-looking older couple called the Fourniers, their faces aged and ravaged by war and sadness. They'd lost two sons to the war and had a further son they hadn't heard from for quite a while, presumed dead. They willingly shared with me what little food they had and gave me their sons' room to sleep in.

The house reeked of sadness; misery pervaded every nook, their never-ending grief hanging heavily in the air. I knew they were behaving just as I had when I wasn't bothered if I lived or died. They just didn't care anymore, they had nothing left to care about. From my experience, talking to them about it or saying how sorry you were was utterly pointless, it wouldn't bring their sons back.

I hid my bike and radio in their cluttered, run-down tin garage, amongst all the other equipment and family items they'd stashed there over the years. I saw their sons' possessions from when they were young boys boxed up. I picked up some family photos taken in happier times—mother, father and three handsome healthy-looking boys, which was heartbreakingly sad to see, knowing two, probably all three were dead.

I ATTENDED the next circuit meeting as planned and was welcomed by the few attending. Valerie smiled, but we didn't show any recognition of each other as our training had taught us. Segal introduced me with information we had agreed to in advance. I'd already told him, as the circuit organiser, that someone was collaborating from his group and to be guarded in what he told them. We also agreed that any meeting sites would be changed last minute to avoid them being raided.

"Camille is new to the area, and I've given her the role of liaising with existing safe houses, finding new escape lines, pickup and drop-off sites," he informed them, and they welcomed me into their group with a mixture of grunts, and hello's.

This general role gave me plenty of scope to be out and about and keep an eye on Valerie. I considered she might give me up straightaway, but gambled she wouldn't until I'd gathered much more useful information for her to spill to her German contacts. No one knew, apart from Segal and the Fourniers, where I was staying, and I wanted to keep it that way. Wary of being followed I took evasive measures whenever I left or returned there.

There was an equipment drop-off due in two days' time, and a pickup of personnel arranged for seven-days' time. Two groups were organised: one to set up for the equipment drop and one for the pickup. Valerie and I were on the pickup group. There were four people being taken along the escape line, to the final safe house. They would be taken to

England by a double Lysander pickup from a site I had identified and told them about, deliberately including Valerie. Once the meeting was over, she left in a rush and didn't stop to talk, but I had a good idea where she was going. I wouldn't attend any more meetings from now on, for fear of being ambushed.

I gave myself seven days to find out what Valerie had been up to and what information she had passed on. I would then be on the pickup out of here and back to England. I would inform them in London what I knew and then that was it for me. No more agent work at all. I was done.

I FORMED a plan for the equipment drop-off site, as I was sure she would inform them about that. I couldn't "out" her or kill her, until I had all the information that I could get from her. If she informed about the drop and it didn't go ahead, she would become suspicious of the group, thinking they knew someone was collaborating. That wouldn't end well for them, and they needed protecting, as well as those at risk at the equipment drop.

Segal and I checked out the equipment drop site twenty-four hours before it was due to take place. We set up an excellent observation spot to conceal me in the wooded area surrounding it, and a secondary site to escape to. Segal had given me all the equipment I asked for and helped me set it up without question. It was all in place, ready for what was coming.

When I assumed my position, you couldn't have seen me unless you tripped over me; the cover was that good. I had dark clothing and had covered my blonde hair and face with a black balaclava. I was dug in and covered by a natural mat of foliage. I could see the whole of the area from my slightly elevated position and waited—as the hours ticked by. I took the Benzedrine tablet I had with me to keep me awake, panicking at first that in my very tired state I'd crunched on the wrong pill.

Thankfully, I didn't die, and settled in the same spot, only getting up when necessary, vowing never to pee outdoors again after my stint there—it wasn't that easy to do and was very undignified. I had uncomfortable short seconds of light dozing but the buzz from the Benzedrine held up and kicked me back into alertness. I had brought water and food to keep me going. But oh, how I longed for a bag of soggy fish and chips smothered in salt and vinegar. I sighed looking at the meagre offerings I had to eat. My mind started picturing the longed-for food as I waited, my mouth watering.

Lost in thought, I concluded that the war could be won by having an army of Maude Davis's working as agents. Nothing and no one would be able to be kept secret from them, and the War Office could save a fortune on parachute silk as they could use their own Maude Davis witch's broomsticks. I giggled to myself.

Again, I started imagining the taste and smell of roast dinners, gooseberry pie and custard, but was brought sharply back to earth with movement in the clearing below me. As darkness fell, a small group of German soldiers began positioning themselves, hiding opposite to where the landing lights had been prepared and where the resistance would emerge from. I was positioned slightly above them, and they had their backs to me. One soldier was less than twenty feet away. I didn't have the usual nerves, which was strange, especially when you consider I was close to several

German troops, who would shoot me on the spot if they found me.

It was clear they had been warned by Valerie about this drop and were settling down for the event. After about two hours I could hear the droning of the aeroplane in the distance. The resistance group began to leave their cover on the far side of the clearing to signal to the plane. The Germans in front of me readied their guns; the group would be cut down and captured once they'd signalled to the plane it was safe to drop the equipment. Equipment which usually included guns and ammunition, money, explosives, and food would then be seized, and the resistance couldn't afford to lose it.

I held back until the plane was nearer and readied myself. I twisted the switch on the box I'd been clutching for hours, and as I did so, an area in the middle of the clearing where my pre-placed explosives had been set, blew up, dirt and grass flying high into the air.

I took my leave while all the soldiers' attention was focussed on the explosion site and resistance in front of them. The resistance fled back into the cover of the trees and the Germans opened fire. No equipment drops took place that night as the pilot, seeing the explosion not the normal code, had left, and the plane could be heard droning away in the distance. I buried myself deep into my secondary hiding place, waiting until it was all clear for me to escape. Just as I'd thought, they had no dogs with them, as the dogs barking would have given the game away. There was no need for me to run, just hide.

A German officer went into the middle of the field where the explosion had taken place. He grabbed the wire protruding from the explosion site and followed it back to where I'd been hiding originally. He shouted and raged expletives into the night air as he realised what had happened.

THE RESISTANCE GROUP were summoned to an urgent meeting late afternoon the following day to discuss the previous night's incident. I didn't attend. I was waiting where Valerie would head to after the meeting. The group were to be told only two men were slightly injured, the rest got away, and they didn't know who had set the explosives, possibly a rogue group. They were going to issue a warning to be vigilant with whom they spoke with outside of the group, indicating that the people involved weren't amongst them, hopefully reassuring Valerie.

I watched as she left from her meeting with the same man and knew I had to act now before the correct details of the Lysander pickup were fully known. She looked anxious as I followed her to her home and watched as she went inside. Peeking through the windows I saw a man in uniform sitting at a table with his back to me. He had a drink in his hand and appeared quite at home. He looked vaguely familiar, but in fairness, they were all starting to look the same with their strict haircuts and similar uniforms. I realised I wouldn't be able to do anything with him there and left.

I returned to the Fournier's, or bleak house, as I now called it, and slept fitfully thinking of ways to get Valerie alone, find out what she'd done, and then finish her off.

I met with Segal, and we went through the group members and their history, discussing if there were anything unusual or concerns about any of them. He came to Valerie, code name Roxanne.

"She's been with us for about three months now after being parachuted in. Her reception party had been compromised, but she managed to get away and hide for a few days before she was picked up by the resistance. She's a good courier and researched the area well."

"Anything unusual about her?" I asked nonchalantly, as I had about all the others.

"Not really, she's always willing to help with anything and seemed happy to take risks when asked. She is calm, friendly, a good courier, nothing is too much trouble." *I bet it isn't*, I thought. What I knew about her was kept on a need-to-know basis as I figured she might not be working alone in this group.

I HAPPENED TO "BUMP" into Valerie a couple of days before the pickup of escapees was due to take place and we chatted. I'd been following her now constantly to confirm to myself I was right in my assumptions about her. What I'd observed confirmed it. The Lysander pick-up point had already been changed without her knowing

"We shouldn't really be seen chatting in the open. Come to the house I'm staying at to talk." I offered.

She readily agreed, rather quicker than she would have liked. I explained to her I needed to protect the people I was staying with, but as she was a fellow agent, I knew I could trust her, and she nodded so very eagerly. You could see on her face she couldn't believe her luck. This would be useful information to hand over to prove her worth following the disaster at the failed drop, and what a stupid security lapse I was making.

The trap was set, and the bait willingly being taken, by this very, very inexperienced agent.

We travelled a convoluted route to the Fourniers' house with Valerie's eyes eagerly trying to memorise every feature along the way. I opened the door and let her in, knowing the Fourniers were out that afternoon visiting a friend and would be gone for a while. I pulled out a chair for her to sit on at the kitchen table and made her coffee. We continued to small talk to each other, laughing about certain instructors and recruits from our training and I felt her easily relax in my company.

When she appeared to be as relaxed as possible, I reached under the table on the chair positioned next to me and produced a gun, pointing it directly at her. Her face was a picture of utter surprise and she tried to get up and run, but I was quicker and shot her in the back of the left leg, dropping her to the floor. She shouted in pain, but I icily told her to be quiet or I would kill her there and then. I dragged her back to the chair and tied her to it with rope from the Fournier's garage. She was moaning in pain as I wrapped a towel around the bullet wound in her leg and put pressure on it to stop the bleeding, I didn't want her dying just yet.

I took time questioning her and after initially denying everything, when faced with the evidence I had, she tearfully confessed. I untied her and gave her one of Mr Fournier's cigarettes and she puffed nervously on it, tears staining her face as she told her story.

"I was parachuted in with another more experienced agent to support me and they were waiting for us. We were captured as we landed. The reception committee had either been captured or shot. I was tortured by an SS man, and I couldn't bear it. He was brutal; it was horrendous what he did to me, Yvette. I had to tell them everything I knew and agree to work for them, or they would have killed me. They tortured the other agent too. I could hear it all happening, it was dreadful to listen to, the screams of agony I can still hear in my head. They told me they knew about my family in England. They said they had German agents in Britain who could harm them if I didn't do as I was told. I have younger sisters and parents to protect. If anything happened to them because of me..." She left that information hanging in the air between us for sympathy.

"I was told to meet up at an address with a man if I had information. It was more beneficial to have me stay as part of the circuit to tell them about plans and hand over messages, and as a courier I had a lot of messages. I was told to offer to work between the two circuits to increase the information I could supply. I only ever told them the bare minimum to try and protect everyone involved. I had no choice but to do what they said," she snivelled.

"Did you tell them about me?" I asked her.

"No, Yvette, for goodness' sake, I wouldn't do that to a fellow agent. Never, never. I know what's at stake for any agent caught here. Trust me, I wouldn't wish it on anyone." I had an idea she was lying but continued playing the game.

"Thank you, Valerie. How much do they know about the circuit and the pickup? Is there anyone else collaborating in the group?"

"They're everywhere, Yvette, they know an awful lot already. They know about the pickup, when and where it will take place, everything. I honestly didn't tell them much; they'd already heard a lot from another source about it, not just me. I don't think the source is from our group, but they get information from somewhere. It could be someone's neighbour, friend, or family member, some are doing it for financial rewards. Their plan is to learn as much as possible about the two circuits, capture as many resistance fighters on the ground as possible. If they can get the addresses of all the safe houses and those involved in the escape lines, they can then smash two circuits in a vital area."

She paused for effect then continued. "We have to change the plans, Yvette," she said, trying to reinvent herself as a British agent again now she'd been caught.

Thank God she'd been fed false information about the pickup and the circuit had moved sites again. They would be safe even if she had talked since the last meeting. I immediately thought of the Bissett family, and the horrendous risk Valerie was to people like that. I couldn't bear the thought of them being harmed in any way, not that lovely little family. My mind raged at her and what she'd done, and I started dismembering her body in my mind. However, despite my pure hatred of her, I softened my manner.

"It must have been really hard for you being tortured, Valerie. None of us know how we'd react to it, and I really don't blame you at all," I reassured her. "It's not something they really prepare you for with their stupid play acting. We all have our breaking point. You obviously need to go back to England on the pickup to explain what has happened and get your leg fixed. I think the war is over for you now anyway. You can go home, make some sort of life for yourself after all this horror."

"Yes, thank God, and thank you for your understanding, Yvette. I've got myself into a right pickle, haven't I?" she giggled, and that infuriated me more. She then shocked me by saying, "I was planning on escaping to England on the next pick up anyway if I got the chance, to get away from all of this."

"Really? You will be on it now anyway and so you'll have

to stay here with me where you will be safe until then. I'm sorry I've been so rough with you. I do feel awfully bad about your leg."

"Oh, I understand perfectly. No hard feelings. I'm sure I would have done the same." She smiled at me, appearing happy she'd been let off the hook with her heartfelt explanation and the promise of returning home to the safety of a country she'd betrayed. She willingly then wrote down names of people she had worked with on the German side, and collaborators on the French side. I wrapped a clean towel around her leg and offered her wine and another cigarette.

"It'll help with the pain," I said, as I went to get it for her. "It will also settle your nerves a bit as well after all of this."

"I'm glad it's all out in the open to be perfectly honest. I'll go back and explain to them how it happened. I always knew I wouldn't make a good agent. They should have known during training. I barely scraped through the tests they set. I even think I failed one and so it's their fault really," she argued. "They were so desperate for women who could speak French and had lived in France to work for them, and it all sounded so exciting. It was stupid of me to get caught up in all of this. I should have just told them at the start I wasn't up to it. Not all of us are cut out for this. They should know that. You don't fully understand until you are actually here how horrendous the reality of it is."

I handed her the small glass of wine.

"It's not a good old English cuppa," I said, laughing, "but it's the best I can do in the circumstances, and it will help numb the pain a bit. We can then get you out of this mess. Bottoms up."

Valerie knocked hers gratefully back in two gulps.

"I'm so glad we met up again, Yvette, I really liked you

from the first time we met, you looked so calm and graceful amidst all the turmoil at the recruitment. I really hoped we could be friends. There is something important you really need to know though, and I'm not proud of what I've done; I am not the only one—" And then she must have sensed the burning sensation in her throat. She clutched at it, looking quizzically at me. I just watched dispassionately as she struggled and writhed in agony. She had about twenty seconds to live.

The lethal L pill does work then, I thought, as I watched her death throes. It wasn't just more codswallop to make you feel you had a way out when you didn't. I carried on watching as she convulsed on the floor, foam and blood surrounding her mouth.

"Traitor," I spat at her.

She then stopped moving. I wondered about the last unfinished comment, did she mean to say she wasn't the only one collaborating? Another agent had been caught with her she said. Damn, I should have waited a bit longer before giving the wine, but it was too late now. I had to figure this out quickly, knowing someone else we trusted was working against us.

I looked down at her body. I knew she wasn't being threatened at all. I'd seen her with her German lover, and she was more than a willing partner from what I'd observed. She must have been hedging her bets. If they won the war, she would be looked after, and if we won, she would also be okay.

Why was she planning to go home? There is no way on earth the Germans would allow her to escape their clutches that easily, they wouldn't give her any opportunity to be near a plane, unless—my mind then came to the awful realisation as to why she would return home with their blessing.

To be a good liar you must have a good memory and unfortunately for Valerie, she didn't. I remembered the small talk in training on those first days when she had gone on and on about her family. No siblings were mentioned, just her being brought up by grandparents as her parents were dead. She had been sent to finishing schools in France and Switzerland, hence the recruitment as an agent. I was thankful my memory was still as acute as it had been.

I was dragging Valerie across the kitchen towards the garage just as the Fourniers returned home. They found me hauling a dead female body across their kitchen floor by the legs, blood and foam trickling from its mouth and nose, with a bullet hole in the leg. There was a trail of blood across their flagstone floor. I looked at them in horror and they looked down at the body and then back at me expressionless, as if they'd found me washing my hair in their sink.

"Traitor," I said, nodding at Valerie, and they shrugged. Mr. Fournier helped me with the body and Mrs. Fournier got water and started removing the blood from the floor. We stashed the body, wrapped in tarpaulin, beneath an old broken car, in the garage.

"Leave the rubbish with me to get rid of," said Mr Fournier.

46

FIGHT OR FLIGHT

I finally managed to get a message to Boden to confirm the alternative pickup site and their radio operator sent a message to London. The information was kept strictly "need to know" and very last minute for those involved. This was to ensure the Germans didn't find out and the safe houses remained just that for now.

The night of the pickup was so clear. An amazingly large moon and thousands of stars lit the sky as we waited under cover for the Lysanders to fly over. The four people being transported out were being driven to the site. Dubois was one of the vehicle drivers dropping off two of the escapees. We hugged each other tightly, a great bond of respect between us. Laurent grunted and nodded at me, but I was used to him by now and knew even grunting meant he liked you. He had picked up the escapees from the Bissett farm where I'd stayed. One had been there for a week, and the second one, the air crewman, had arrived that morning.

There was a feeling of intense fear amongst the group of escapees and resistance as we waited in the moonlight. The recent events and thoughts of being captured terrified everyone. I and two others had scouted around the area for hours beforehand making sure it hadn't been compromised and lookouts were strategically positioned. Valerie had told the Germans the original pickup details she had been fed, which was safely miles away from here.

I was determined to be going home on this flight. I'd really had enough. I'd done everything asked of me and had murdered another person in cold blood. Segal and Boden would have to figure out who else was collaborating and deal with them. I'd given them Valerie's list and as much information about her as I could. I was finished and started to relax a bit at the thought of finally leaving this place.

The codes were exchanged between pilots and resistance and the landing torches lit to guide them in. The two Lysanders rolled majestically onto the landing site, turning around, ready to take off again. The passengers started getting on board and the first Lysander took off into the clear night sky.

I was waiting anxiously behind the returning air crewman climbing up the ladder in front of me. I was desperate to leave this life of horror behind, and yet this man didn't appear to be in any hurry to get on board. I thought it strange he kept looking around as if expecting someone to be there. He was in civilian clothes and eventually got in to join the other escapee already in. He smiled and reached out his arm to help me get aboard. As he did so, his jacket sleeve slid up slightly, partly revealing a large mark, a mark I'd seen before. It was a burn, quite clear now, the one I'd seen on the arm of the man who killed Adelle in her flat.

He was German intelligence going to England to infiltrate the system. He had studied in England Adelle had said, and would be enormously dangerous, especially if he were working with someone in intelligence on the other side of the Channel to pass him off as a legitimate escapee. I don't know why, and I didn't really consider the consequences, when I firmly shut the canopy over him and jumped off the ladder. I indicated for the Lysander to take off without me.

This man was one of the people who had been staying at the Bissett farm. He must have had help to get to that safe house. He had been involved with Adelle but was he also linked to Valerie? I wondered if Valerie had meant to say, "I'm not the only one who shouldn't be going to England on this pick up." Was she the one who had passed him off as a genuine escapee and would support his story back home? Did she know he was in the escape line? Had she supplied documents for him to be accepted back in England? Was he the man sitting at her dining table that day? He would be lethal to our intelligence, and a danger to any female in our intelligence he could charm.

Oh God. I needed to make sure the Bissetts got away before any raids on their farm took place. I also had to send an urgent message to alert them of the German agent making his way to England before he could message back any details about his safe house trail and the people involved.

I knew he would be held for a few days in debrief with no outside contact, so I had a bit of time to work in, but not much. I watched despairingly, as the second plane flew through the moonlit sky, carrying its treacherous load to England, without me. *What the hell have I done?*

～

DUBOIS AND LAURENT had long gone, and I stayed the night in a barn near the pickup site with another of the resistance who had a car. The curfew had long passed and would mean we would run the risk of being stopped and shot if found outside. I had to get my radio from the Fournier's' garage and gratefully accepted a lift there as early as I could the next morning. I was dropped off two streets away.

My mind was working overtime as I walked through the streets to their house. I wondered how deep the infiltration of this group and our own services in England went. How long before the German agent with his forged papers would be released? And when was I likely to get home again once the Bissetts were safe? My mind was in turmoil as I approached the turning into the Fourniers' road.

I was brought to a sudden halt as I turned onto their road and saw the Milice and Gestapo outside their home. I ducked into a deep doorway of one of the houses further down on the opposite side of the road. Peeking out, I saw Mr and Mrs Fournier stood outside their home at gunpoint. Mr. Fournier was trying to protect his wife, with his arms tightly around her. They had been savagely beaten but looked incredibly brave and defiant as they stood there facing the Gestapo. They were then both shot, Mrs. Fournier first so her husband could watch her die as he lowered her gently to the ground, and then Mr. Fournier. They were crumpled together on the ground outside their home. The home where they'd brought up three sons and lived a happy life until war came along to destroy it, as with so many others.

I peeked out again and saw more vehicles slowly approaching from the other end of the road. I was effectively trapped in the middle—whichever way I went I would be stopped and questioned. Were they looking for me? I realised I was now in a desperate situation, and this could be it for me. My pulse rate rocketed as I tried to think of a way out. I formed a plan. I would behave as if I were leaving this house rather than entering, the porchway was quite deep to allow me to do so. I had my papers. I would wave to an imaginary person as I went and then try and bluff my way through the soldiers on the left, not the Gestapo near the house who would have more information on me.

The soldiers were getting closer, it was now or never, then the door behind me opened and I was pulled silently in by an older man who made a shush sign at me with his finger against his lips. He bundled me up to his attic to hide. I could see the road from a small window in the attic and watched as they carried out Valerie's body and my radio case, which they took with them. They left the Fournier's behind on the road as a warning to others. I knew I'd only trusted a few people with where I was staying. *What if I'd been betrayed by one of them and that was why they were at the Fourniers' house?*

Thinking rationally, it could also be nothing to do with me at all, and they were just known resistance being rounded up and interrogated. They might have found Valerie's body and the radio by accident on a search. *Why hadn't they got rid of her body sooner?* It was desperately urgent I get to a radio now.

I then remembered the one at the cafe in Arlaise where I'd been working. It might still be undiscovered in the basement. I'd left it there when I returned to England the night Whippet was killed.

After a while, the man who had rescued me knocked on the attic entrance indicating it was safe to come out. He explained he was a friend of the Fourniers, and they helped each other out if they were ever in trouble. He would not give his name or any details about himself, but was angry they'd died, and their bodies left in the street.

"I've seen you at the Fourniers. They must have been

helping you. What can I do to help you now on their behalf?" he asked me.

"I urgently need to get to Arlaise. If you could get me to a station, I would be so grateful."

"Don't worry. I can drive you all the way there. You mustn't take trains if there is any possibility at all they're looking for you. Don't tell me anymore about your business; I don't want to know. What I don't know I can't tell, and what you don't know you can't tell either."

True to his word, he took me in his small, dilapidated van via back roads and country lanes, avoiding roadblocks, to the main town where the cafe was. His van made the strangest noises, which he appeared to be oblivious to as he drove along, and I did begin to wonder what it was being fuelled with and whether we would make it at all. Miraculously it did and he dropped me off wishing me luck in the process. I thanked him profusely for all his help. This had been incredibly dangerous for him.

I WAITED until the cafe was closed on Saturday evening, watching from the shadows as Hector locked up, and walked down the side street and into the entrance to the flat above. He must be living there now. I waited until I saw a light go on in the first floor flat and went to the back door. Using a thin piece of metal which had been left in a pile of odds and ends, I fashioned a tool, picked the lock, and let myself in. I went down into the basement and was astounded to find my radio exactly where I'd left it, along with its spare battery, dusty and untouched. I grabbed it and went quietly into the main building and in the rapidly fading light helped myself to some food. I was starving. I couldn't remember when I last ate and wasn't sure when I would again. I grabbed a large old coat from the staff coat rack and left a surprise for Hector which I thought he might appreciate if he had any sense of irony. I slipped through the back door into the darkness.

I was extremely vulnerable now, carrying a radio in a suitcase out in the open in the evening. If I were stopped, that would be it for me, there was no excuse I could come up with to explain it. I made my way cautiously out of the town, and knowing the place well, I avoided patrols and roadblocks, and headed towards the open countryside. My hair covered, glasses on and wearing trousers and a large coat, I didn't look like the Evelyn who had been there before.

Once away from the main town, I climbed a tree to set up the aerial and started my message. I knew this was risky and easier to be pinpointed by the German detection team, but our listening team were now also working twenty-four hours a day. The operators who usually picked up my messages would recognise my "fist" or style of messaging confirming it was me. I transmitted the information about the German agent in their midst, Valerie's death, the information about the Bissetts safe house and to get them out as fast as possible. I asked for a pickup, as we were still in the moon phase, and gave the details of the date and location to be used. It was one I knew would be suitable and to my knowledge hadn't been used for some time.

Once that was completed, I hurriedly packed away the equipment and ran from the area, planning how I could stay uncaptured until I left. I hoped and prayed I'd been in time with my information. It was out of my hands now and I had to just trust the system. The thought of that family being captured filled me with absolute horror. I'd heard dreadful stories of families tortured and shot, their children first, in front of their parents, babies killed by being smashed against walls or bayonetted or dropped from high buildings. Groups of people had been locked in barns and the building set alight as revenge acts by the German army, evil and depravity knew no boundaries and it was terrifying. That couldn't happen to the Bissett family, not little Mathilda. I desperately needed to make sure they were safe, nothing else mattered now.

I HAD SOME MONEY LEFT, enough for a hotel room for a night at least, and decided to risk it. I approached a run-down place and entered reception. I filled out the necessary card with my details, which the hotels were obliged to collect for the Germans and paid in advance for the room. The manager matched the neglected air of his hotel and didn't even glance at my completed card, just added it to a batch in a basket on the reception desk. He gave me the key; told me which room I was in and nodded grumpily to the stairwell. I went up the winding, worn wooden stairs into the room on the first floor, which was as run-down looking on the inside as it was outside. I thought no self-respecting German would be seen dead in this place. I hid the radio case from sight and did the automatic placing of my things.

I went down to the hotel restaurant. They called it a restaurant, but it was just six bare wooden tables and chairs in a dingy room, and they served the same old rationed food and awful chicory coffee. I looked at the food being served and decided against eating. It indicated they probably weren't collaborating, and I went back to my room, put my radio case behind the door, and lay on the bed. The full realisation hit me as to how truly exhausted I had become. All the walking, cycling and perpetual stress had dragged me back down, and with my mind questioning my sanity at not leaving when I could have, I dozed off into a fitful sleep.

ON SUNDAY MORNING I started down the stairs to check out and stopped abruptly when I heard German voices below in reception. I glanced down through the wooden stair spindles and saw two men standing at the desk with their backs to me. They were checking the guest admission cards. I realised this might be because of my recent radio use in the area. The owner saw me, and while the Germans had their heads down checking the details on the cards, he indicated with his eyes and head for me to go back up the stairs. I crept back up and heard something crash to the floor and him telling the men he would get a maid to clean it up. He came up the stairs, grabbed my arm and dragged me along the corridor to the second stairwell, which was hidden by a thick curtain at the back of the hotel. He handed me my completed registration card and silently shoved me out the door. I knew he risked being shot if I'd been found at his establishment. I checked no other Germans were around and then "borrowed" a bike from a number that had been left leaning against the back of the hotel and made off along the dirt road. I would wait until nearer the time of the pickup and would prepare the site myself. I knew there was a farm with outbuildings nearby and considered the owners might be resistance. I would have to chance it.

I reflected that despite me not being happy with it, most of the time as an agent was spent relying on the locals for help, and this was becoming increasingly dangerous as a number of them were now collaborating. I cycled as far as I could and then walked through the countryside off the road behind hedgerows and woodland, and by late afternoon I reached the farm. I was incredibly tired, hungry, and thirsty and needed to rest. My mission here was done, my inner reserves gone. I went into one of the outbuildings to rest and my thoughts drifted to what I would do when I got back to England.

I would move out of London, to the country or by the sea and find a little job to sustain myself and live the rest of my life in peace. I wouldn't return to France as that had too many reminders of the horror of my life. I realised I didn't feel like I belonged anywhere anymore. I may even go to America, as it sounded nice, the men weren't to be trusted from my experience so far, but I thought the country sounded fascinating.

I dozed for a while and then buried my radio far away from the farm and outbuildings. I didn't need it anymore as I was leaving never to return, but if it were found it might compromise the people living there. I headed to the farm not sure what sort of reception awaited me, but having little choice left.

My hunch was thankfully right—the farm owners were working with the resistance and after a swift, but intense and frightening interrogation of me at gunpoint, they linked me up with members of the local circuit, who came to collect me. One of them was Lucien who had helped me the very first time I landed in France. I felt choked seeing him again, as it brought back so many memories, and I hugged him tightly.

He told me how the Roussels had been betrayed by a local man they had employed to help with deliveries. He had asked for their farm and land as his reward for collaborating. That man had been "taken care of" but a lot of damage to that whole escape line was done by him before he was identified and stopped.

Dubois also joined the group and told me they were on their way to an equipment drop and asked me to go with them. Once they'd finished at the drop, they would take me to a safe house to wait for my pickup tomorrow night. I was handed a Sten gun and ammunition to use on the drop-off, just in case.

I spoke to Dubois when I could get him on his own, and for the first and only time in my life, I asked someone for a huge personal favour.

It was about an hour to curfew now and the area for the drop was set, the torches ready to switch on, and the resistance waiting. The droning of the plane was heard, and everyone took their positions. The Morse signal was sent, and the return response from the pilot seen. We saw several parachutes floating down with their desperately needed loads.

The plane could be heard moving away, and the group started collecting the large canisters on wheelbarrows to be loaded on the trucks. Unfortunately, the parachutes had been blown over quite a large area, which slowed us down collecting them in and put us at risk. Just as I feared, we were only halfway through, when shots were heard, and vehicles burst into the area. Lucien grabbed my arm and we made for the woods, followed closely by Dubois and two others.

I chanced a glance back as I was running and saw a small group of resistance fighters being shot in the legs as they tried to get away. The Germans continued firing and I knew we only had a short time to get away ourselves. We made off through the woods, bullets whistling past us, slamming into trees and foliage as we ran. We flew through to the far side of a clearing where the truck had been camouflaged. Dogs could be heard barking in the distance as we ran.

I scrambled towards the truck and in panic clambered into what I thought was the passenger seat as it would be in England, but of course it was the driving seat in France. Lucien jumped in next to me, Dubois and the other two resistance men jumped in the back. I started the truck and drove away as fast as I could, barrelling out onto the road.

We were making incredibly good progress along the bumpy roads, but we were soon being chased by two German vehicles and being fired at. Lucien and the men in the back returned fire. Dubois grabbed the back of my seat and slotted a panel into place he had fashioned himself. It was made of solid wood and metal, and it slid up behind my seat, designed to protect the driver from bullets. It came right up behind the back of my head and curved slightly either side of me.

We saw a truck join in the chase after us and continued along the road towards the river. I knew we wouldn't outrun them for long.

I could see a chance ahead and I shouted at Dubois, "Two of you need to jump out. When we come to the winding road ahead, I'll slow down as we go around the bends. Once out of their sight, you two must jump when I say. We will carry on in the truck to distract them. That way some of us might escape alive."

I could just make out in the lights a long bend ahead with foliage along the side where we would be out of the pursuing vehicles' sight for a matter of seconds—this was the place.

I shouted at Lucien, "When they jump, fire at the vehicles as they come around the corner. That will focus them on us not the others."

The bend was coming up Dubois and a younger man got to the side of the truck ready to jump. I tried to get some more distance between us and the chasing group. I knew I had to time it perfectly.

I veered the truck to the right and yelled at them, "Jump!" and both leapt out of the side of the truck into the hedgerow together. Lucien and the older man still in the back, fired as soon as the chasing vehicles came around the corner drawing their attention to us, as I floored the accelerator.

Lucien continued firing, and I was driving the truck as fast as it was able to go. The road was uneven, throwing us around, and my knuckles were white from holding the steering wheel so tightly, trying desperately to keep control of the vehicle. I didn't have time to be scared as adrenaline flooded my body. The vehicles were still following; they hadn't stopped, and so I presumed Dubois and the other man had escaped.

"Watch the smaller one coming up on your right!" Lucien yelled. I swerved the truck to the right and forced that vehicle off the road. There were still two others chasing us now, a car and a truck. They fired a fierce hail of bullets at us, some thudding into the wooden panel at the back of my seat.

Lucien and the other man stopped firing and Lucien slumped across me—I could see he had been shot in the head. He fell across my thighs, and I had the sensation of his warm blood and brain fluids seeping through my trousers. I felt nauseous; I shuddered from head to toe at this horror before me but knew I mustn't slow down or stop.

I continued to throw the vehicle about to stop them from

overtaking me and felt Lucien's body partially slump into the footwell. I could feel bullets continue to slam into the defence shield Dubois had fitted around my seat. Bullets were whistling past me, shattering glass, and taking chunks out of the seat Lucien had been in because there was now no-one firing back. I wildly thought how Stapleton would have been proud of my efforts at evasion from my lessons with him. I also knew this chase couldn't go on forever and I desperately needed a plan.

I quickly formed one. We were intermittently running almost parallel to the river. I would look for an area where I could drive the truck into it. Once in the water, I would push Lucien's body out as a distraction and swim underwater away from the body and the truck to the bank area and hide. I hoped they would think Lucien had been the driver, and the other man had been the shooter. It sounded like a reasonable plan.

Just then the truck took on a life of its own, and the steering wheel was violently ripped out of my hands. They had shot out my tyres and I lost control of the vehicle. The truck tipped over and Lucien's body and mine were thrown together over and over like in some horrific, macabre dance. Everything appeared to go in slow motion with blood and glass flying around me. It then came to a shuddering stop upside down in the dirt.

I knew as my head cleared from the crash I'd injured my right wrist, my ribs hurt, and I was cut and dazed. I was covered in blood but quickly realised I had no major injury and thought it must be Lucien's blood. I got out of the vehicle from under the tarpaulin and quickly crawled towards the hedgerow, dragging Lucien's gun with me.

My right hand was useless, and so I positioned the gun between my knees with the barrel in my mouth to shoot myself using my left hand, but when I pulled the trigger, it failed to fire. It had either jammed, or Lucien had run out of bullets. I shoved the gun into the bushes where it couldn't be seen and fumbled for my L pill in the pendant around my neck. It was then it dawned on me Valerie had been the lucky recipient of that, and I felt a groan escape from my throat at the realisation. I heard a noise behind me and looked up. A large, uniformed man was standing over me, his head framed by the clear moon. He raised his rifle above me and the last thing I remember was seeing it coming down towards my head.

~

I WAS SHAKEN VIOLENTLY AWAKE by the German who'd hit me, and he leered as he dragged me by my hair across the rough ground into the back of the German truck. He ripped at my clothes and raped me on the truck's bench seat; I was unable to defend myself. My right hand was useless, I was still groggy, and I hurt everywhere. I wasn't expecting any help—it was one thing to stop the assault on an innocent girl, but quite another for one they thought was a spy— especially one who had been involved in the killing of their brethren soldiers—no, I was fair game. I knew that and accepted my fate.

The canvas at the back of the truck opened sharply and an officer looked inside.

"Ralf, stop that, we have to get her back for interrogation right now," he yelled.

The leering soldier reluctantly released me, and I pulled my clothes about me with my left hand, trying extremely hard to distance myself mentally and emotionally from what had just happened. I knew I was bruised and damaged internally from the assault, but that was the least of my worries right now.

After what seemed a long and uncomfortable drive, I was manhandled out of the truck by two soldiers. I wondered where I was...near Arlaise? Drayville? Bourselle?? I tried to look for anything of recognition to identify where I was but couldn't see much. I was roughly pushed and pulled into the building along a corridor, where I noticed offices labelled for Gestapo and Abwehr. I was pulled into a dimly lit room and immediately noted what looked like dried blood patches on the bare brick walls and what appeared to be dried excrement on the floor. I was terrified.

There was a large metal tub on one side of the room, with a jug by the side, it seemed so out of place, along with the coat and hat stand in the corner. On the back wall was a badly pinned up swastika flag. There was a desk and two chairs in the centre of the room, and I was shoved onto the nearest one with my back to the door. There was a small window, but it was far too high up to see out of and get any bearings.

I knew I didn't have a snowball's chance in hell of getting away by fluttering my eyelashes at anyone this time. I reasoned it must be about eleven or midnight. I knew I had to last forty-eight hours at least to give the others time to get people away. They would have to change safe houses and pickup sites I knew about in case I told them everything. I ran through my mind the things we'd been taught about interrogation and the experience I'd gone through in train-ing. The first fifteen minutes of torture are the worst; use a method to take your mind off it like counting or reciting poetry or literature. *Oh God help me,* I prayed, *help me. Don't let me say anything. Let it all be over quick.*

47

A VISIT FROM EVIL

A bright lamp was turned on by a young German soldier, which was then directed straight at my face from the opposite side of the desk. He looked so young and fresh faced as if he should be in school. I heard the door open behind me and a man in a very spick and span French uniform came into view with two other Frenchmen, *the French Police.* I gave an internal sigh of relief; I might just get away with this. The one in the important uniform asked me my name and I figured my very first cover story was my strongest, it was one I had memorised well. Once more, I became Evelyn Bouvier and making out I was groggier than I was, I gave him my details. My other ID had been lost during my last escapade anyway.

The French policeman was a short rotund man, reddened in the nose and cheeks, possibly from too much drink over the years. His eyes were set quite close together, and he gave the impression he thought he was especially important by the way he strutted about the room, issuing orders. He seemed to particularly like ordering the young German soldiers about. He got one of them to fill the jug with water from the tub and poured it over my head, washing the blood from my face and 'waking me up.' He took off his hat and sat on the desk in front of me. He slapped my face, which snapped my head to the side. That wasn't too bad, I thought, it was like a woman's slap. Then he slapped me again on the other side of my face and I tasted blood in my mouth. He shouted that I was lying to him and grabbed me around my throat squeezing hard until I thought I would pass out. There were little white lights dancing in front of my eyes, and then he suddenly let go.

As I got my breath back, I sensed someone else had entered the room as the atmosphere changed dramatically. I heard a German voice.

"You were told not to do anything to the prisoner, just to keep her for me to interrogate. This is not a French police matter. Get out," the German shouted furiously. I concluded the Germans won that battle, as the Frenchman got up, picked up his hat and furiously marched out with his two underlings.

The German came into view from behind me, and I recognised him immediately— Schaefer, the officer who had stopped me being assaulted at the cafe. My stomach cramped in fear. I'd heard about this man and what he was capable of. *Had he been Valerie's torturer?* They must have brought me back to Arlaise where I'd worked at the cafe. I knew he had interrogated and killed several agents and resistance and I was terrified. My only hope lay in keeping my cover story going for as long as possible. He knew I'd worked there, and the cafe was known for helping the Germans. I had to think of a believable story, and I came up with one. They had found no gun or papers on me to my knowledge to disprove what I would say.

He sat opposite me and moved the blinding light trained

on my face away. He had his full, pristine Gestapo uniform on, including his hat, an iron cross at his throat, his SS insignia on his collar and a white silk scarf hanging loosely around his neck. He had on very shiny black boots, which I'm sure he didn't polish himself. He was mid-forties, had a hard-chiselled face, military cut blond hair, sadistic blue eyes, and a thin-lipped smile. He was what anyone would think of as the perfect image of an SS officer. He apologised for the behaviour of the soldier in the truck as he took off his hat placing it on the desk.

"You must understand, my little bird, he had not seen a pretty girl for some time to have some fun with, so you must excuse him. I recognise you. Now, where do I know you from?" he said.

He paused for maximum effect, drumming his fingers on the desk, and then pointed at me. "Aha, that's right, you were a waitress at Adelle's place in town."

I nodded, as I desperately wanted him to follow that storyline.

"Now, little bird, what were you doing in that truck?"

My training around this came to mind: don't antagonise your interrogators, be polite but firm. I had a story mapped out in my head and there was no-one who knew me enough to disprove it.

I began confidently, "I was with my boyfriend; your soldiers just killed him. He was supposed to be taking me out for dinner, but he changed plans at the last minute and we ended up miles away, waiting for someone he said he had to meet first. I was cross that the curfew would be missed, and we would be in trouble. I demanded he take me home and then all hell started, someone jumped in the back, and we were being chased. I couldn't get out of the truck as he was driving so fast, and he wouldn't stop, so I lay on the floor. I was terrified and then he got shot and the truck rolled over, and your soldiers arrested me. I haven't done anything wrong."

"I see, what is your name, little bird?"

"Evelyn Bouvier," I replied.

That would be difficult for him to break as I was living as her and had taken on her persona for months. He asked why I'd left the cafe.

"The owner wasn't very pleasant, not like Adelle. He was repulsive and assaulted us girls when we were at work. I just didn't want to work for him anymore."

I watched nervously as he pulled his white scarf from around his neck and hung it on the coat stand with his hat. He came back and sat on his desk in front of me.

"I know you've been flown here by plane, little bird, to spy, and everyone who comes before me talks in the end. It may take some time, but you will talk to me. You will tell me your contacts, your codes, and the safe houses... Oh, they all come in here like you, and stick to their silly stories, trying to be brave, but in the end they all tell me what I want to know. You'd be surprised how much I already know. In my vast experience of doing this, I know bravery always fades. It's just an illusion. It's just a matter of pain to make that illusion disappear."

He then punched me full in the face with some force. I felt the bones grate in my nose and warm blood pouring down the front of my face and onto my clothes. I was groggy and dazed from the unexpected blow and as I reeled back in the chair, I began to swallow my own blood.

He then said to me in an ice calm friendly tone as if we were chatting over tea, "This isn't how it has to be. We are civilised people, and we already know so much that you will just be confirming information, so there is no need for you to go through any of this. Save yourself. This is the time to talk. Do you think anyone in London gives any thought to you? or even cares about you? You're just cannon fodder to them, just a sweet innocent girl they have manipulated to do this. They gave you a poison pill to swallow to kill yourself rather than allow you to live, didn't they? That's what they think of you. I'm your only friend in this because I want you to live. Now tell me your real name."

"Evelyn Bouvier," I replied, trying to stem the bleeding from my nose with my sleeve.

He clicked his fingers. "Bring in our other guest."

A minute or two later, the door opened, and the two soldiers came in with a man being dragged between them. He had been brutally beaten. His face was terribly swollen, his hair was long and matted, he had a beard and was skeletal, but I recognised him immediately. It was Cameron. The man who had made my life an absolute misery. I was stunned at this turn of events. *What were the chances?* Had he been the experienced agent dropped in with Valerie? I showed no recognition of him on my face.

I mentally reached out to him in desperation. "All *you have to do, Cameron, is say you don't know me at all. It's that simple. I have a chance of surviving if this bugger can be made to believe my story. Just say you've never seen me before in your life. That's all, just as you've been trained.*"

Cameron was stood facing me at the side of the desk, held up by two men, he had dried blood encrusted into his beard. His right eye was severely damaged, and he looked finished, broken, and defeated.

"Make your friend see sense, Mr Cameron." Said Schaefer.

Through his blood and spit Cameron pleaded, "Just tell them Yvette. They know everything already. Save yourself.

They'll let you live if you cooperate. Just do it, you're too young to die here. Just do it Devereaux." They dragged him back out of the room.

Shit.

Schaefer returned to his seat and turned the light on my bloodied and battered face. There was nothing he could have read from my expression.

"Ah, Yvette, what a beautiful name. Your friend here was caught by one of our female agents like you. I think in England you call it a honey trap." He offered me a cigarette and I thanked him. Keep it civil, I thought. It would at least take up some time.

"I think we can work something out, you and me. You're a sensible girl, if you just give me your codes as a start, that way none of your friends would be involved, just the codes Mr Cameron says you have."

I said nothing and sat still. The bleeding from my nose was lessening. I watched as he got up from his chair and walked to the metal tub at the side of the room. He unzipped his trousers and urinated in it, the tub already had water in it, and I had an idea what was coming. I had a plan ready, silent acceptance of what was about to happen. Escape.

Schaefer returned to his chair and nodded to the two soldiers in the room who had just returned from taking Cameron back. They grabbed me by my arms and hauled me off the chair to the tub on my knees.

Before they put my head under the water Schaefer said, "Now is your chance, Yvette. Speak up and save yourself. It will get much worse for you if you don't. You have to realise there are no heroes coming to rescue you, I can promise you that."

I said nothing, he didn't realise the mistake he was about

to make. Schaefer sighed. He nodded to the men and my head was put under the foul liquid and held tightly. It was sheer agony and incredibly difficult to do, but I forced myself to breathe in. It caused my nostrils and throat to sting, and I wanted to vomit but managed not to. I didn't struggle at all and after a few more seconds of hell and agony, blackness welcomingly arrived.

I FOUND myself looking down and watching an awful scene unfolding. Two soldiers were brutally drowning a woman and I wanted to stop them but couldn't. I then had the horrific realisation that the woman was me. I was confused and didn't understand what was happening. Not only could I see myself, and what was going on, but I was flooded with the thoughts and feelings of everyone there.

I watched as the soldiers felt my body go limp in their hands and looked at Schaefer in absolute panic. Realising what I was doing, he frantically shouted at them to drag me out.

They laid my lifeless body on the floor; I wasn't breathing, my lips were blue, and my eyes were dead. The soldiers weren't sure what to do. One of them, the young soldier who'd never killed anyone before, was panicking. His thoughts flew at me. This wasn't what he'd trained for; he was meant to be a soldier fighting the enemy not torturing young girls. He felt uncomfortable with what he was seeing and doing. He had only recently been sent to serve under Schaefer and was disturbed by him, thinking he was seriously mentally ill.

I had "died," but Schaefer wasn't going to let his prey go that easily. He ran from his chair and stamped down on my lifeless chest a few times as I lay on the floor. As he did so, bloody, frothy liquid shot out of my mouth and nose and I began to breathe again, dragged back from wherever I'd been.

I came to on the floor of the room, a severe pain spreading across my chest. Some more of my ribs were likely broken. I played semi-conscious as I lay there, mystified at what had just happened. *How could there be two of me? How did that happen?*

I then heard Schaefer say he needed a break and ordered them to take me to a cell. My body was dragged along a corridor past Cameron's cell and placed on the cold concrete floor. In my half-conscious state I heard Cameron sobbing words at me.

"I'm so sorry, Yvette. I shouldn't have given them your name. It's against the rules. Oh God, I've just done it again, how stupid of me. I'm a stupid coward. It was a bloody woman who caught me, a bloody woman. Please forgive me, Yvette. I don't know why I treated you like I did; I was jealous of you. You always appeared unbreakable, not scared like me and putting on an act. I wanted to make myself feel better by making you feel bad and I'm ashamed of myself. Now we will both be dead soon. We're going to die here, Yvette—you and I are going to die, here in this Godforsaken place, we're going to die. This is it for us. But I will make it up to you. Everything I've done I'll put it right. I will never let you down again. Just give me a chance to prove it. I promise you from the bottom of my heart. You must believe me, I'm a better man than this. Oh god, what have I done?"

He cried and sobbed loudly as he said he'd given up information during his torture, which had caused people to die. He knew he would have to pay for that; his soul would be damned. He kept saying "I'm sorry" repeatedly begging me for forgiveness and wanting absolution, which I just couldn't give him.

I continued to hear this drivel over and over and through my own severe pain I just said, "For the love of God, Cameron, just bloody well shut up," as I felt myself losing consciousness going gratefully once again into the abyss, wondering if I would be in or out of my body.

AFTER ABOUT AN HOUR, I was dragged out of my cell and hauled along the corridor by my arms, my heels bumping agonisingly on the bare floor. I was taken back to the room I'd already been tortured in. Cameron had shouted for them to leave me alone as we passed him but was ignored. He'd already given them everything they needed to know about his role, and he was now surplus to requirements. His fate already decided.

They stood me against a wall in the room, with the bright light shining directly on my face. My ankle was hurting like hell, and I couldn't fully bear weight on it. Schaefer came in and once again removed the silk scarf from his neck and returned it to the coat stand. That act became a prelude to pain and suffering, and I started to dread him doing it. It was as if his white scarf could not be tainted by the cruelty and horror that he was inflicting on me, and it was put safely out of the way. I imagined it was a gift from someone special.

What was left of my bloodied blouse was ripped off and Schaefer asked me again about codes I had, and who I knew in the resistance and the safe houses I'd stayed at. I said nothing and started reciting my poem in my head, the one I'd memorised about a girl who told dreadful lies. It was to calm myself during a scenario such as this. He wouldn't use the water torture again; I was sure of that. He put food and drink on his desk where I could see it to torment me further. I was very thirsty now, my throat so sore and dry and my tongue swollen from the drowning episode, and I was in dreadful pain, but I had to somehow survive this and repeated reciting the poem in my head.

This was going to be a battle of wills between him and me. I was determined not to talk and just count down the forty-eight-hours. He was determined I would talk in the shortest possible time. Schaefer said he always got the information he wanted, never failed. His reputation depended on it, and so I knew he feared failure more than anything else. I had nothing to live for and so death held no real fear for me. Men had betrayed me and treated me badly all my life and I was now prepared to die rather than give in to this one. This would be my final act of defiance against this ghastly world and that helped to sustain me as the clock ticked relentlessly on.

My legs got weaker as I stood, my muscles going into spasm. I was punched against the hard bare bricked wall, and whipped with a riding crop, but I still said nothing. I had to watch as he ate and drank in front of me, my body craving just a mouthful of water. I was being treated to the full fury of Schaefer; he couldn't let people see his methods were failing with me, and in his mind at that point they were. He ordered them to sit me back down and tried again to reason with me, using my name over and over to make it more personal.

"All of this could stop just like that, Yvette." He clicked his fingers in front of my face for effect. "There's no need for any of this." He then spoke softly, taking on a fatherly tone. "You're a beautiful young woman, Yvette. You have your whole life ahead of you. You can live a long and happy life if you just talk to me. I will personally make sure you're looked after and returned to your family after the war. Just talk to me. Think of saving yourself, Yvette. No-one else cares about you; you're nothing to them. I'm the only one trying to save you. I'm the only one who can."

I still didn't speak. I couldn't. I had by now firmly set my response to complete silence. I'd also seen what they'd done to Cameron who had talked. There was just no point in continuing with false stories or the agent handbook responses. We had both hardened our positions, our lines drawn firmly in the sand. He nodded to one of the men behind me and I felt my hair being roughly cut off. The hair was then put in front of me on his desk. I had plaited it that morning and it was so strange, this one simple act caused me to feel so violated. It was so irrationally stupid after all I'd been through. *It's just hair,* I told myself, but it was symbolic of me as a person and stupidly affected me like nothing else so far.

Schaefer fiddled with the hair, twisting it around and around in his hands, pulling the plait apart with his fingers, but again no emotion was displayed as I watched.

He then lit up a cigar and took a few puffs and admired it. "There's nothing better than a decent cigar, that's one thing I agree with Winston Churchill on," he said, as he inhaled the smoke and blew it out high into the air. He then ordered the soldiers to hold me tightly in the chair as he began burning my breasts, inner arms, and neck with the lit cigar. I could hear someone in the distance screaming loudly, I then counted between screams, only making it to ten each time.

He attached electrodes to every sensitive area of my body, and I screamed repeatedly, as electric currents jolted through me. I breathed in the smell of burning flesh as the awful sounds of the electric current filled my ears. I left the horror of that place and in my mind went to my bluebell wood. I imagined it as I'd first seen it—the peace, the sanctuary. It was where I desperately wanted to be. But I was dragged back to that grim, dark room and found myself lying half naked on the filthy hard floor, then passed out.

WHEN I CAME TO, Schaefer was back in friendly mode again. He instructed his men to put me back on the chair opposite him.

"You don't think I enjoy this, do you, Yvette? I'm a gentleman and a father to two girls myself and this sort of thing really upsets me. But it's my job, you must understand that. They expect me to get results. Our victory in this war depends on people like me. Your army is losing the war, you do know that don't you? Oh, you didn't? Yes, it will all be over soon as scheduled, we will be victorious and lead a new world order. You will have paid the ultimate price for nothing, so let me help you, Yvette, let me end this suffering."

He continued in an odd, but jolly upbeat manner. He was smiling at me in a way a teacher would do to a well-loved pupil. He slapped his hands down on the desk. "Let's start again, start from the beginning. All of this will go away, the pain will stop, we'll get you treatment at the hospital and let you rest and recuperate. All it takes is just simple cooperation. All the people who have gone before you have cooperated. Look at your fellow agent, Cameron. It took a while, and some ingenuity on my part, but even he eventually saw sense and told us everything, absolutely everything, who his trainers were, where he was trained, his mission, his contacts, and his codes, he even told us about Mr Steadman. He was extremely helpful, and is still being helpful, identifying others we bring in like yourself.

"You help us now, Yvette, and we'll let your family know you're safe. We will soon know where your family are. We have agents all over England to find them, but it would be quicker if you just told us now. Think of your family, Yvette. They must be so worried about you and would want you to stay alive and go home to them."

I said nothing. I knew I was going to die, and forty-eight hours hadn't passed yet, with the clock still ticking. I hoped he would just shoot me out of frustration at me not talking.

The basic wooden chair I was sitting on hurt my spine and ribs badly when I leaned back into it. I had to sit upright, even though that hurt as well. Whichever way I positioned myself it was agony; there were no parts of me left undamaged. He leaned over the desk and took my left hand very tenderly in his, examining it as if it were a precious jewel. He smiled and looked deeply into my eyes, as if searching for something inside. He recoiled at whatever he saw there and snapped back upright in his chair.

He nodded to the soldiers, the older one held my hand down firmly as Schaefer forced small wooden strips under my nails and pulled out two of them with a pair of pliers that he had taken from the desk drawer. Again, I went gratefully into oblivion without saying a word.

He kicked me back into consciousness. They stood me up with my back against the bare brick wall again. My feet and ankles were swelling, and I thought death was close. It was then I began to hallucinate and saw people from my life appearing in front of me.

I saw my father striding towards me, he looked so solid and real. He told me in German that I'd been a burden to him and the reason he'd been poor and had to kill himself. Alfie then took his turn, calling me a whore for sleeping with Americans and now Krauts. "You have no shame," he spat at me. I saw Stapleton in front of me saying how useless I was. I was weak, a feeble woman trying to be a man. "Rules have to be followed; a good agent would have killed themselves rather than be captured."

I saw Ethan come into view. He told me what a fool I was for not spotting he was an agent; he'd never really loved me he said, our marriage was just a cover for him, and he laughed. Steadman was shouting at me for letting him down, his reputation was ruined thinking women could be good agents. Whippet telling me he'd died because of me, and his life, so full of promise was now over and all because I was selfish and weak. Louis blamed me for being slow on the radio, it had got him killed.

Adelle laughed at me, telling me I should have taken her up on her offer when I had the chance. "Look at you now. How sad you are, alone and sad. They took your body by force, and you should have just given it freely in return for nice things." Frosty face sneered: "Once a trollop always a trollop."

Lucien just stood there with blood and brains dripping from his head down his face.

Finally, Cole came in front of me, as strong and handsome as I remembered. I hoped at least he would be kind to me. I desperately wanted him to take me away from all this horror.

He just stood there and laughed in my face. "Look at the disgusting state of you. Who on earth would want you now? You meant nothing to me, don't you realise that? You were just a bit of cheap fun, something to do on a weekend pass, a joke. I could have anyone I want."

Then the faces of the people I'd shot at the farm came into view, as well as Valerie, screaming and blaming me for her demise, telling me I'd killed her when she was going to make up for what she'd done. The Fourniers were in front of me sobbing, telling me they couldn't find their boys.

They all came into view at once, their eyes all fixed on me, circling me, including my mother, calling me selfish. They then started shouting, laughing, pointing, blaming me, telling me I wasn't brave. I lost track of who I was. I couldn't remember. Was I Sabine? Camille? Evelyn? Yvette? Devereaux? Janvier? Ella? Avette? Eve? Bradshaw? Bouvier? It all jumbled around in my head. I was totally disorientated and losing focus. I wasn't sure where I was, or what day, time, month, or year. I held out my hand to them as they circled me, I desperately needed someone to hold my hand to ground me and give me strength or comfort, to be on my side, but no one did. I wasn't being brave. I'd failed. I was useless and worthless, unloved, and unwanted by anyone.

Then an almighty explosion sounded, which rocked me out of my hallucinatory state. The building rattled, and some of the glass in the small window cracked. The figures tormenting me all melted silently away. The fog in my head cleared and I realised it must be seven-forty-five a.m. on Monday morning in Arlaise. *Hector must have just lit up his usual cigarette before entering his cafe*. The gas I'd left on in the kitchen on Saturday night when I picked up my radio had been building up over the last thirty-six hours and exploded, fuelled by Hector's fag. I hoped it was that, and smiled through the pain, but this meant I'd only survived about nine hours of torture so far.

Schaefer looked at me in fury. He wasn't going to be beaten by me, he was never beaten. He left me standing against the wall, telling his men he was going to find out what the explosion was. He put on his hat, took the white scarf, and wrapped it around his neck.

"She mustn't sleep. Keep her awake until I get back. If she closes her eyes prick her with this. Understood?"

He took out a large thick needle from the desk drawer to show them. Both soldiers agreed but appeared uncomfortable with what they were being asked to do.

"Do you understand?" he yelled as he left. Both the young soldier and the older one, who probably had daughters my age, nodded but seemed unsettled and gave each other worried looks. They knew this was wrong and both looked concerned, uncomfortable, not sure what to do. After Schaefer had left, the older one gave me a mouthful of water, sheer bliss to my parched throat and I closed my eyes. They allowed me to rest with my eyes shut and my head hanging down on my chest, while standing against the wall. The relief was indescribable.

THE DOOR OPENED a short while later, and I opened my eyes quickly, not wanting to get these two into trouble, thinking they might help me more later. I saw Schaefer walk to the coat stand, take off his hat, and slither the white scarf from around his neck. In my fearful state it looked as if he was doing it in slow motion and I wanted to scream, as that act sent sheer terror through me every time. It meant pain and suffering were coming and there was nowhere to hide, no one to protect me. He knew I'd worked at the cafe and would know now that was what had exploded.

He stared at me coldly and his mouth twisted into a smile, his eyes like devil's eyes darkened by evil. He purposely walked towards me and began punching me and kicking my legs. He had his boots on and stamped on my bare swollen feet. He must have seen my fleeting smile when the explosion went off.

"I'll wipe that smile off your face, you bitch." He punched the side of my head incredibly hard, snapping it to the side, and blood sprayed from my face onto his white scarf, which was hanging on the stand.

His expression shifted from sheer fury to shock and disgust.

"That was a Christmas present from my daughters," he screamed.

It was then he lost all semblance of control. He punched me to the ground and kicked my body. I tried protecting my head and face as he kicked me. He stamped on my broken ankle, and I felt it give way. He then kicked my ribs and, grabbing my already fractured right wrist, he swung my body around, causing my shoulder to dislocate.

I screamed so loudly. "Enough, please stop, please enough."

But it was too late. He'd gone beyond all reason and mercy. He continued his vicious assault, finally kicking my head against the wall.

Everything slowed down around me, and all the pain just melted away. I had a feeling of incredible lightness. I didn't have a body, but I did. It was on the floor in front of me. I was in two places at once again. It was surreal. I found myself hovering above my body, looking down at me. I could see Schaefer checking my neck pulse and slapping me, but I couldn't feel a thing. It was as if he were hitting an old coat I'd discarded. I saw the young soldier open the door and run from the room. I desperately wanted to get out of this place of horror, and now was my chance. I followed him as he sped down the corridor. I passed Cameron's cell and saw him pacing, still talking gibberish to himself, and apologising for everything, promising to put things right. I wondered how long he'd been captive as his mind had been destroyed, beyond any help now.

The young soldier came running back towards me with another uniformed man from German intelligence. He was a very senior officer judging by his insignia, and as I "stood" there, they ran right through me into the interrogation room. I went back after them, interested as to what was happening. I followed them unseen and unheard and hovered in the doorway rather than be in that room again. The senior Abwehr officer took out his gun and pulled Schaefer away from my body.

"Leave her alone. Stop this right now", he shouted. "If you don't, I will shoot you myself. This girl is almost dead if not dead already, and you won't be able to get any information out of her now, so hitting her is pointless."

Schaefer looked furiously at him and placed his hand over his own gun as if he were going to pull it out but decided against it. I watched as the Abwehr officer, gun still in hand, checked the pulse in my neck and ordered the soldiers to take me back to my cell. They very gently picked up my battered and broken body and carried it away. My face was a completely swollen, cut and bruised mess and I could read what they were thinking. They felt so sorry for what had happened to me, respecting my resilience, thinking they couldn't have done it. They would have been happy to kill Schaefer themselves, thinking he was deranged, but feared the consequences if they did.

I began to feel strangely detached watching all of this from the corridor, it was my body I saw, I know, but it wasn't the real me, it was like a vehicle I'd used and got out of. *Am I dead then?* I wondered. *If so, where do I go?*

I saw Schaefer leaving the interrogation room shouting as he went, "She is my prisoner, not yours, if she's not dead by tomorrow morning, I will come and shoot her in the head myself."

I followed him as he went past Cameron's cell. Schaefer looked at him scornfully as he was apologising and making promises to protect me, telling Schaefer to leave me alone. I felt so sorry for him, and I smiled at him as I went past, but realised he couldn't see me, just as the others couldn't. I saw Schaefer raise his gun and shoot him. Having relieved his frustration by killing something, he walked towards the exit as Cameron slithered to the floor, dead.

I followed Schaefer down the corridor towards the exit door. At one point he stopped and looked over his shoulder, as if sensing there was someone behind him. He turned back, shrugged to himself seeing no-one there and aggressively flung the door wide open.

I wanted to get out desperately now. I felt confined by the walls, which appeared to close in on me, suffocating me. I wanted to be free from this place. I made for the open door when the most amazing light came and filled the doorway in front of me. It was so bright, brighter than the sun, but you could look at it. I was mesmerised and drawn to it as it emanated such peace, such intense feelings of belonging, of pure welcoming love. I could see someone standing in the light and I desperately wanted to go with them. I must be dead, I thought, this is where I'm meant to go. I made eagerly for it.

Just before I reached it, the door slammed shut, the light snuffed out, and I was pulled rapidly backwards down the corridor as if attached to an elastic band. I slammed into my body and the excruciating pain returned.

I was left in my cell on the cold concrete floor for the rest of the day. I had awoken every now and again in terrible pain. Every time I made the slightest move it was agony. I was desperate for water, hungry, and needed the toilet. The two soldiers and officer who had been on duty the night before returned for their next shift and came to check on me. They expressed astonishment I was still alive, albeit groaning in pain and semi-conscious. It must have become too much for them then as their humanity and compassion took over.

I heard the officer order the younger one to get the local doctor who'd been treating injured soldiers. "If he refuses, you have my permission to bring him at gunpoint."

Shortly afterwards, one very cross doctor, who must have been roused from his bed, grumpily came into the cell. I remember him looking down at me in absolute horror. He examined me and told them my shoulder was dislocated.

He gave me a morphine injection, scolding them as he did. "This is meant for soldiers only. You know we could all be shot for this."

They ordered him to get on with it. Once the injection had taken effect, he manipulated my shoulder back into position by putting his booted foot under my armpit and pulling hard on my arm. It went back into place with a sickening thud. I became nauseous with the pain. But once back in place the pain lessened greatly, and I could relax, just a little bit.

He examined me and verbally listed my injuries. "She has a fractured jaw, nose and possibly an eye socket, fractured wrist, fractured ankle, finger and toe-nails missing. Burn marks, cuts, whip marks and bruises over her torso. Broken ribs, with possible internal injuries. Keep her as comfortable as possible." He covered my body gently with a blanket. "She'll be dead by morning."

He got ready to go and said sternly to the three gathered in my cell, "I'm ashamed, as a man, a father, and a human being. Tell me, is this war? Is it? We torture, rape, and kill young girls in the name of war, do we? The world's gone mad. We're all going to hell after this."

With that said, he handed them more morphine injections for me and slammed his hat back firmly on his head. He stomped out of the cell into the night, no doubt to return gratefully to his warm bed.

They lay me on a pile of blankets to raise me off the hard floor, covered me and made a pillow for my head. It was so much better like that. They discussed my situation outside my cell, not realising I was conscious and could hear.

The officer was appalled by what Schaefer had done. "If she's still alive in the morning, he will kill her or start on her again."

I heard the plan they had devised before the next shift came on duty. I was quite impressed with it as the second morphine injection took its blissful effect.

Cameron's body was thrown into a truck along with another male body that had succumbed to torture. They carefully placed my newly morphine-drugged body into the truck next to the two others and passed me off as dead. They handed over the list of the dead prisoners being removed and then drove the truck to the local hospital and took me inside. The Abwehr officer told them I'd been the victim of a motor vehicle accident and was gravely injured and I'd been given morphine already.

"At least here she can die in peace," he told them as he left.

A SMALL GROUP of hospital staff then set about returning me from near death. I could finally fully let go as I put myself in their caring hands. No one knew my name and they deliberately kept me off the records. On seeing the extent and nature of my injuries they had worked out I was a victim of the Gestapo, not a vehicle accident. They bravely took it upon themselves to protect me and give me a chance. They kept me separate from other patients, in a small, locked, back room away from the main wards, nursed on a makeshift bed. I was given time to recover by truly kind and brave hospital staff who put themselves at risk for me. Schaefer would think I was dead when he returned that morning and checked their meticulously kept records. I thought how pleased he would be at that. No one beat him, he was always victorious one way or another.

I was recovering slowly in isolation and had improved enough from the fractures and other injuries after a few weeks to be moved from the hospital, but there was nowhere for me to go. There was no mirror or window in the room I was in to be able to check how bad my injuries were, but I could feel scarring on my face and body, with disfigurement where my facial bones had been fractured. I'd lost a couple of back teeth, my jaw was still painful, and I couldn't eat solid food. I had a weakness on my right side due to what they said was a small bleed on my brain and a limp from my healing fractured ankle, meaning I could only walk very slowly. My body was badly broken, but I was alive.

While in isolation I had ample time to ponder over things that had happened, including being out of my body. The experience unsettled and confused me; I still couldn't explain it. It seemed so real, so clear, but it could have been hallucinations, brought on by almost drowning, severe pain, dehydration and still being able to hear what was going on when semi-conscious. If I'd died, then surely, I couldn't still be here, could I? It changed my view on the possibilities of something after death and questions of why we are here at all. What was all this for? What was the purpose of it? This went round and around in my head and being alone most of the time gave me no respite from the tortured, confused thoughts.

Only a small number of people were looking after me now and I was working hard at my rehabilitation, while trying to plan some sort of escape and life for myself. I could sense the people hiding me were becoming edgy and uneasy as more soldiers were admitted to the hospital. They were concerned at being implicated in working for the resistance if I were discovered. They had families who could be in danger if they were caught and were rightly terrified of the consequences. A few staff stopped coming at all. They had been doing this now secretly for a couple of months and told me they were trying to contact the resistance to come and get me. They had been incredibly brave in supporting me and I was so grateful to them, but knew I had to move on and organise my own escape.

The matter was taken out of all our hands, however, when the Germans raided the hospital and rounded up civilian patients, including me, while I was on my one and only rehabilitation walk in the corridor. As a result of my injuries, I was unable to run the few yards back to the safety of the storeroom. The men were sent to one camp and we women to another. We ended up at a small temporary camp which the Germans had set up in an old French army barracks. This was done to free up beds at the hospital for injured soldiers who were being admitted in increasing numbers. We were herded into the camp with other females, either political prisoners, resistance, or those considered undesirables. I was so shocked that Alice and Stella were amongst them.

At first, we didn't recognise each other in the crowd of women, but after a couple of minutes of guardedly studying one another, they made a beeline towards me and they hugged me so tightly, it was sheer agony. I groaned loudly, and they quickly released me. Stella had been badly tortured and seriously sexually assaulted by a group of soldiers and was not mentally right as a result, her eyes were dead. Alice had lost so much weight following her own torturous experiences that she was just bones; they both had their hair cut very short. Alice had a scar across her cheek going down into her neck as a result of her escape attempt.

The two of them had met each other by chance after being dropped in to work in different circuits as couriers. They decided to work together, believing they stood a better chance that way and had only been working for a short time, when they were betrayed by a member of the public for money. I felt selfish at being comforted seeing them, as they too told their own horrific stories.

We spent every waking minute together after that and slept in the same hut. We vowed to stick together and support each other come what may. We would not be broken by this now and were determined to see the war out and return home.

Despite my physical injuries, mentally, I knew I was in better shape than the other two. I had the strong sense that neither of them could take anymore and were both a hair's breadth from giving up totally. Some women had already committed suicide in the camp, unable to continue with the painful horror their lives had become, when all hope had been snuffed out. I knew we had to just hold on for each other and everything would be okay.

I focussed my energy on helping them get mentally stronger with reminiscences about their lives at home. We had hard labour to do in the camp, and they supported me physically and fought to make sure we had a share of any food that was available. I still couldn't eat solid food comfortably and made do with the soup we were given. We exercised and worked together and gradually, gradually things for all of us started to improve.

49

ONE MOMENT IN TIME

One afternoon, at a rest period from work, we were sitting on old wooden crates we'd fashioned as furniture near our hut. A few other women were milling around the yard area looking hopelessly lost and sad, struggling to maintain their sanity and survive. I always made sure we had a daily positive session and would tell each other what we would do when the war was over, and we went home. We were fully aware the war was escalating now, as we'd seen the increasing number of Allied bombers flying over day and night. The bombing was intense, and the Germans were jumpy and not as vicious as they had been. Their attention was being diverted more to what was going on in battle, giving us more time to rest. My hair had grown a few inches, and I took to styling it back in my old plait fashion, which was cathartic in a strange way. The pain from my injuries was resolving and I began to dare to believe we would see the war out and return home.

I realised for the first time in my life, despite the surroundings, I was genuinely enjoying the company of these women. After everything we'd gone through, we had developed a tight bond. We discussed what we wanted for our futures. Alice wanted to get involved in politics, stop wars starting in the future. Stella wanted to get married to someone with lots of money and a sense of humour. I had to think hard about what I wanted. I knew any hope of marriage and children were out of the question after what had been done to me. My mind as well as my body had been irreparably damaged, and I doubted I would ever get over it. I just wanted peace, just peace, no violence, no stress, or aggressive people around me and to be able to help others in trouble, as I'd been helped.

We teased ourselves about having roast dinners, steak and kidney pudding, fish and chips, and ice cream by the sea. Alice wanted to travel the world, Stella wanted to live near the sea, and I wanted to see America. We were all becoming upbeat about life after the war, we'd made it this far and were optimistic now about seeing it out to the end.

As we sat and chatted, I watched as an open-top car drove up to the large, gated entrance to the camp, with four people in it. The car stopped at the gate for its security check, and I saw a face I knew only too well in the rear of the car—Schaefer. His hat, scarf, and demeanour exactly as I remembered. My gut quivered and every fibre in my being wanted to scream, my already stressed body consumed with terror. Any mental recovery I had made was rapidly disintegrating.

We'd heard rumours we were being moved to a concentration camp in Germany, to make way for German soldiers to be based at this one, and so were expecting upheaval. Having this man come here, to oversee it, made me think any sick women, agents, or those he didn't like, would not be leaving here at all. Schaefer was perfect for this job. Having hundreds of weakened females at his mercy, he would be in his element. The colour must have drained from my face, and I was frozen to the spot in sick fascination, as I watched the security guards check Schaefer's documents and salute him. They started to open the gates to the camp to let the monster in.

Alice noticed the sudden change in me. "Are you all right, Yvette? What's wrong?"

"You must trust me, Alice. Get away from me right now, this minute. Go and hide as quickly as you can. If he sees you both with me, he'll kill you." I hissed at them.

Alice followed my gaze towards the car, and sensing danger, dragged Stella up and walked quickly with her behind the huts, out of sight. I heard her reassuring Stella, who was upset and confused by what was happening. I stood up but knew I couldn't move quickly due to my injured leg and limping away from him would just draw his attention to me.

I was totally and irrationally mesmerised by him and his scarf and stood where I was by the crates at the front of the huts, my attention solely on his vicious face. There were a few other women milling about, either sitting, walking, or standing around and I hoped he would just see me as just another worthless woman in the crowd and pass by. I realised then, to my horror, I was the only one with blonde plaited hair, everyone else around me had dark hair, by standing up I was more obvious. I was making sure the other two were safe, thinking they might just get the chance to hide from him if his attention wasn't drawn this way. Once they were hidden, I turned slowly to walk in a different direction, with my head down, to hide amongst the other women, but it was just a second too late.

I heard a shout, and a car door open and shut. I didn't turn to look, as a voice behind me I knew extremely well spoke, "Well, well, little bird, what a pleasure to see you again and I thought you'd left me." I turned as he smiled at me with his thin lips and shark eyes. "I see you have some reminders of our last meeting. Shall we continue where we left off?"

I really looked at him for the first time since my escape and all fear of him just evaporated. He was just a man, like all the others. I faced him with a defiant look, and for a split second I thought I saw a flash of fear fly across his vicious face. He hadn't broken me. There were no other pleasantries between us as he took out his gun, grabbed me by my newly grown plait, and dragged me stumbling along the ground on my weakened ankle. He took me to the edge of the camp to a barbed wire fence, beyond which was a line of trees. He stood behind me as I struggled to stand up straight. I knew what was coming and I wasn't going to die on my knees.

Strangely, I welcomed death, embraced it even. I'd finally reached the end of any will in me to fight to stay alive. I'd already made peace with myself over everything bad I'd ever done or said in my life as I lay in isolation at the hospital. I was glad I'd given my friends a chance. I was proud I'd never given in to Schaefer. I hoped the Bissett family got away and the German spy in England had been caught before he could wreak more misery on others. Schaefer couldn't take away these achievements if they'd been successful. He had been beaten in that respect.

I remember thinking if there is another life after this, I hope it's a kinder, gentler one than this hellish one. And if there was nothing, well, it wouldn't really matter at all would it? I'd seen what might be waiting for me and I wasn't afraid. My victory over him would be complete, as I would be where he could no longer touch me. He could only kill me once.

I felt and heard the shot through the left side of my head and fell heavily to the ground. I wasn't quite dead yet, and stayed alive long enough to see my blood trickling down the slight slope of earth in front of my eyes, and then this life was over.

I was twenty-one.

50

PRECIOUS REVELATIONS

I felt myself peel from my body and looked down at myself, dead on the ground, this time with total indifference. I watched Schaefer walk away and get back in his car. I stayed by the body watching as they threw it onto a wooden cart, wheeled it away and dropped it in a deeply dug pit with other poor souls. Like rubbish.

Everything then became so crystal clear as if a veil had lifted. I knew everything—past, present, and future. Any question I had was answered in a split second, flooding my thoughts like random little films. Schaefer had only come to the camp to deliver orders and would then leave, so Alice and Stella were safe. I knew they would survive the war but would be separated as they returned to their different lives, which destroyed them both. Stella would die by her own hand just after the war, unmarried, alone, and scared of everything, due to the mental and physical trauma she'd suffered. Alice, battered by her experience, tried her hardest to get into politics but had to settle for a humdrum secretarial job with a politician. She married, divorced, and led a lonely, unhappy life, eventually dying from cancer in her fifties.

As scenes of my life flashed before me, my one experience of love drew my spirit to Cole, and I relived that fateful morning from his perspective.

COLE

THE DOOR to my cell finally opened. I'd been shut in here for hours without knowing why and given no access to a telephone. I'd just asked the receptionist where I could get flowers, when I was pounced on by three British Military Police. I pleaded with them to let me go back to our room, or at least to let me leave a message for my girl at reception, but my pleadings fell on deaf ears.

One of them, who came into my cell later said, "Sorry sir, your arrest was a case of mistaken identity. We were looking for a man fitting your description wanted for a serious National Security matter. You are, however, now free to go. We do apologise, just doing our job, sir. I hope you understand."

I was mad as hell. I didn't understand any of this. It just didn't make sense. What National Security? I didn't argue with them, as that would have delayed me even longer. I asked to hitch a lift back to the hotel and they obliged. I was a bit flustered and desperate to see her, wanting to explain what had happened. I rushed into reception and met the woman who had booked us in last night. She was alone. The last time she'd seen me I'd asked her where I could get flowers for my wife. She told me where a florist stall was nearby and as I was leaving, I was arrested.

"Has my wife booked out of room thirteen?" I asked her breathlessly.

"Yes, the young lady left quite a long time ago now, sir."

"Did she leave any message for me?"

"No, none, sir."

"Did you tell her what happened?"

"That is not something we would talk about in reception, sir. This is a respectable hotel," she replied haughtily.

"Can I have the outstanding tab, please?"

The sarcastic reply came slowly and deadly. "Your 'wife' has already paid."

I made my way slowly to the station, distraught, trying to figure this all out. I wondered what she must think of me. I would make it up to her thousandfold. It then struck me like a thunderbolt—I didn't know enough about her to find her and explain. It was unlikely she would ever come to look for me after this disaster. I boarded the train to my base, gazing sadly out on the English countryside as it flew passed, feeling helpless and devastated at the loss of the only girl I had ever truly fallen in love with. I only knew her first name: Yvette.

~

YVETTE

UNDERSTANDING what had happened was heartbreakingly sad. *Oh, what could have been*. I saw his death at the D-Day landings. At least it was quick.

I saw every betrayal of me as a person in this life and why it occurred. I saw Steadman and the others watching me that day as I tussled with the idea of going to the interview. The evaluation meeting that they had where my fate was sealed by Steadman. I saw Stapleton's betrayal of me in that fateful telephone call to Steadman when I'd met Cole and was going on my date and his intervention with the note under my door before the last test.

I saw my mother, buried in rubble under the community hall after the bomb had destroyed it and saw Alfie in the rubble and dirt, severely injured himself, putting her first for once and comforting her lovingly as she died. He was holding her hand and telling her how much he had always loved her and begging for his Leese not to leave him. Who would have thought it?

I saw Schaefer's death take place a couple of years in the future. He was being chased through the streets like a terrified fox chased by hounds. He was beaten viciously, almost to death, and then hung by local French people as he tried to escape. His body hung there until it rotted. I was there, watching with others he'd killed, as the beings of light encased his evil soul as it emerged from his earthly body.

It was as if my mind had recorded every second of my life, along with the effects of my actions on others, good and bad, and the effects other people's actions had on me. I watched Stapleton when he heard about my death. He felt so guilty he'd played a large part in my downfall and emotional destruction with Cole, albeit he was just following direct orders. His phone call to Steadman about my date set my life path in a terrible direction—and led to my death. It was something he would never get over. He remembered me at every remembrance Sunday, at every nostalgic moment with his daughters, like their weddings, until his death at the age of seventy-four, surrounded by his wife, children, and grandchildren. If he could take back his betrayal of me, and protected me, he would have done so in a heartbeat.

I saw the families of the people I'd killed grieving for them. I saw the lives they would have lived if I hadn't ended them when I did. I watched the arrest of the German spy in England. A group of men were sitting in a living room smoking and laughing with each other. Soldiers marched in and arrested the man I had identified; my message did get through. Under interrogation he buckled within hours. Happily sitting out his time in England, helping intelligence with whatever he knew. His information included a network of German agents already established in England working close to the security services and intelligence.

Fast forward, I saw him living out his life in Argentina. His conscience was clear, he was following orders. But he spent the rest of his days looking over his shoulder, always with a gun, not trusting anyone, paranoid, expecting someone to take their retribution, and haunted by Adelle.

I flew into Steadman's office and watched as several dead agents' files were put in front of him on his desk. His job was to write to their families, informing them of their demise. One of the files was mine. They were now sure I was dead. He now knew I had no living relatives either, there was nothing British about me, as Alfie Bradshaw had never formally adopted me. He pondered for a second or two and then stamped my file to be "scrubbed." No record of me would ever be kept. I had never existed.

My mind then flew on to the Bissett family. I really wanted to know what happened to them and once again fast-moving images slowed and came into focus like a play.

In the early hours of the morning two men hurriedly approached the Bissett farm and knocked the door. Aaron Bissett opened it to see two men there and asked what they wanted at that hour. They asked to come in to speak to him urgently and Aaron reluctantly opened the door. I saw Theo and Mathilda safely hidden with their mother. They told him they'd been sent to pick the family up as they had information they were in danger. The Germans might now know they worked for the resistance, harbouring escapees, and were coming to arrest them in the next few hours.

Aaron was immediately cautious. I could read his terrified thoughts. This could be a trap. If he confirmed he acted as a safe house for the resistance, they could shoot him and his family there and then. If they were legitimate, and he ignored them they could all be captured and killed. He asked who had sent them, and they told him they didn't have time to debate things with him, they needed to move immediately. They firmly told him they had put themselves in personal danger coming after the curfew. Again, Aaron wasn't comfortable; he was in anguish, unsure of what to do to protect his young family and was scared and desperate. I could feel the fear and uncertainty raging in him. I knew he would react like this.

"Look, we've been instructed that if you won't come with us or need confirmation, we are to tell you this order has come directly from Avette not Yvette.

Aaron sighed with utter relief and let out a stifled sob. This was the name Mathilda had called her and no one else apart from Yvette and his family would have known this. It was such a small but important thing and he felt reassured, calling his wife and children out of their hiding place. They quickly grabbed some things and fled the farm.

This was the favour I had asked Dubois for. He now knew it was why I'd made him jump from the truck. I read his mind. *She must have known we stood a better chance if four of us were firing at the pursuing vehicles. But she needed an emergency backstop for this family to escape and I was it. I gave her my word.*

During a full moon, a Lysander came into land in a moonlit field in France, the engine still running as the pilot turned the plane ready for take-off. This was to have been the plane to pick me up. Instead, racing towards it were Aaron, Margot, Theo, and Mathilda Bissett. The plane roared off from the field soaring high into the moonlit sky, to safety.

Madam Blanchard lived to be one hundred and five years old. Spending her later years happily telling anyone who would listen of her exploits in the war, eventually dying peacefully in her own bed, surrounded by family photos and mementoes of her life.

I then saw the end of the Second World War, people dancing in the streets hysterically happy. It was all over, until the next one, terrifying visions of which roared into my thoughts.

I found myself judging myself against my own actions, feelings, and thoughts. It was as if time had no meaning. The past, present, and future were all rolled into one. Time was only an earthly issue. What would have taken days or weeks on earth to review, went by in a flash. I watched this "film" of my last life with every act or omission, and the associated feelings of myself and the others involved. They were jumbled in sequence relating to the questions I had or lessons I'd learned, acts of kindness, or wrongs I had committed.

I sensed an enormous loving presence at my side and was guided by them to see the very purpose of my life, the lessons learned revealed. The existence of so many of my other lives on this earth shown to me. Every life lived has purpose. Our physical brain so limited in its ability to comprehend the vastness of our spiritual existence is there-fore cleared and set as a clean "tape" when we're born, concealing the existence of our true spiritual home and our other lives.

I had been guided to choose this life and the lessons it could teach me, hard though it had been. Planned lives, with specific goals to be achieved, like a contract we sign. This can all get thrown off course because we each have been given free will. Our life plans impacted by bad choices, natural disasters, or evil actions by ourselves and others.

The thought came to me from my spiritual companion that we each have a spiritual flame that burns brightly for eternity. It takes on a physical body to experience a physical existence when it needs or wants to. It is never extinguished but can become dimmed and burn less brightly as this earthly life and problems burden it. Once our physical life is over, we return to our home and natural selves, supported there to "Fix the Flame" damaged by the last physical life, until the next time when we return with more lessons to learn, actions to be taken, experiences to be had or promises to fulfil.

The being by my side was emanating such understanding, forgiveness, love, light, and peace, which then embraced and enveloped me too. I turned to look at the presence with me, and with recognition of that spirit, I slipped softly and silently from this earthly plain. I was going home.

51

ME, MYSELF, AND I

I was in a room watching a man shouting and crying hysterically. The other man with him was counting and talking to a child's body on a chair, shaking her and patting her hand. They were both in a dreadful panic and I didn't know why. The child wasn't dead. The man on the right looked terrified, his thoughts flying at me in waves.

Has she gone into the light? Was she supposed to go into the light? He remembered that he had seen a child going into the light in a movie at one point and he was panicking about that. He was distraught he had badly failed this child. He knew he had a duty to her; he had made a huge promise to her and knew he had failed.

The man on the left was becoming desperate, the child wouldn't wake up. This had never happened to him before; but he had never let a session go on this long with a child. It had been going on for hours. His thoughts were of being arrested, lawsuits, permanent vegetative states, absolute panic emanating from him at that moment, but he was masking it well trying to keep the other man calm.

I wondered what I was doing there. *What has this got to*

do with me? Why am I here? I looked at the child on the chair and focused. Everything about her life shot into my thoughts. A very loved, protected, and nurtured child. I saw her future and it was then, seeing a person I recognised as being a big part of that future, I realised who she was.

Me.

We were one and the same. As this clarity roared in, I knew who the people around me were and how they had been related to me in the past. I knew where I was meant to be, my place in the universe at this time, at this moment, and I willingly returned to "this life."

CHLOE

I HEARD Harry telling me to shut the door of the room I was in and to lock it and to come back to my chair, which I did. He said my legs, arms, and body were getting lighter, relieving any stress in my body and I was then told that he would count to ten and once I heard the word "ten," I would open my eyes and I would feel well. I would forget everything about my bad dreams and any aches and pains I had would be gone.

I listened as he counted slowly to ten, and as soon as I heard it my eyes sprung open. I looked at Harry, who smiled back at me.

"Thank the Lord. Hello, Chloe."

I looked at my dad, who'd been crying. I'd never seen my dad cry before. What had made him cry? We had got here in the morning, and it was now afternoon. I'd slept for hours and hours. I was hungry and thirsty, my throat was very sore and dry, and I needed the bathroom. Harry asked to speak to my dad in another office and got Debbie to look after me. She showed me to the bathroom and got me a drink and a sandwich. She then sat with me, and we talked about London and what she thought I might like to see. I liked her.

Dad came to get me, and hugged me real hard, and wouldn't let go as if he'd been gone for years when it was only a couple of minutes. He held my hand tightly and kept looking at me and Evelyn as we walked back, stopping for ice cream on the way. The others were waiting when we got back.

"Are you okay, Peanut?" they said in unison.

"I'm fine. What have you been doing?

"The London Eye," they said in unison.

"That's not fair, I didn't go. It's not fair. I wanted to do that. You said we'd all do that together," and they laughed. I heard my mom ask Dad how it had gone and saw him look at her as if he didn't know what to say.

After a pause he just said, "Nothing to worry about. It really was just a bad dream from the war films and stuff she'd seen. She'll be fine from now on."

Mom gave a huge sigh of relief. I was a bit upset that I'd slept through the whole thing and missed it all.

52

THE DREAMS BOX- CHLOE

SEVEN YEARS LATER

I had been putting this task off for weeks now, but finally, after non-stop prompting from Mom, I found myself clearing out my closet. It was no longer a walk-in; you had to mountaineer over the old stacks of junk to get in there. I knew it needed doing, it still had my old princess style pink scuffed walls and a stained cream coloured carpet, while the rest of my room was the new teenage me, clutter free, with crisp grays and whites and chrome accessories. I sat cross-legged on the floor sorting through piles of stuff, *this will take me days* I moaned to myself. Ryan was moving out of the house and needed a large suitcase that was buried somewhere in this closet, which added a bit more urgency, and so I got on with it.

Ryan was the last of my brothers to leave home and I gave a loud sigh at the thought as I pulled boxes and bags from the closet. I picked up items from the past, each one holding a memory for me, and then reluctantly placing them in plastic sacks for charity. It reminded me of that old lady telling me, "We don't need things." I was still not totally convinced about that, but some things could go.

I looked through a box of old photographs of me and my family and paused to reminisce. I thought about how things had changed so much, how time just flies by and we can't stop it no matter how much we want to. A photo of me and Rocky made me cry, how I loved that dog. His death had left a large hole in our family. Tearfully I decided to leave the photos for another time. I realised everyone was moving on except me. Scott was now married to Mia; I'd been a brides-maid at their wedding and was now an aunt to a nephew and niece. Mike and Joel had moved away, both in long-term relationships and pursuing careers. Grandad George had passed a couple of years ago too.

Now my funny, loving brother, Ryan, was packing to leave home to move into his first apartment with friends. I felt so sad at the thought of how empty the house would be once he'd gone as well. All these changes had such an unsettling effect on me.

My thoughts were interrupted by a text from Sienna and Scarlett to meet them at the mall on Sunday. I saw them less and less these days, as Scarlett had met the love of her life and was spending every second with him. Sienna was involved in every school debating society and focus group going. "With an eye on being the first female president," I teased her.

I hadn't met any boy I liked enough to go out with on more than a few dates. I'd joined a swimming club, played tennis, and met boys there, but there was always that feeling of something missing. I learned to drive and found that so easy after all the driving Scott and Dad did with me, but I didn't yet have a car of my own. I was going to have to work on Dad for that.

I was also planning my future as a helicopter pilot for the air and sea rescue service or a trauma nurse to help injured people. For as long as I could remember I'd had a deep need to help people who were hurt or in trouble.

I replied to their text and got back to the mammoth task ahead of me, watched over by a now very battered and worn Evelyn, sitting on my dresser.

I found the large suitcase Ryan wanted, dragged it out of the closet, and just tipped the contents onto the growing pile on the floor to be sorted through. That's when I saw the little blue wooden box with the blue and yellow flowers carved in the top. I'd gotten it from the old lady's yard sale. Wow, I'd forgotten about that. It was my dreams box, but I hadn't seen it for years. How small it looked now compared to when I first got it.

I opened the fiddly latch, lifted the lid, and saw loads of small notes stuffed inside, written on my old pink princess notepad sheets. There were badly drawn stick pictures and notes with names and places I didn't recognize, like Shaver, Yvette, Coal, Matilda, Bowman. As I read each one, I was baffled by them. One of the drawings looked like the game "hangman" with a stick man hanging in the air. Another had a parachute and large birds flying around it with scribbled words that looked like "wipe it."

This was all such a mystery. I couldn't remember writing or drawing any of it. I picked up the box and decided to go downstairs and ask Mom and Dad about it. As I got to the landing, I heard their voices below me. They were flirting and laughing like a couple of teenagers. It made me smile. I paused a moment, and as I did, I remembered sitting at this very spot on the landing all those years ago as a child, listening to their conversations without being seen.

I clutched my dreams box, and flashbacks from that dark time when I was troubled by nightmares roared into my head. I couldn't remember the dreams at all, but what I saw in those long-buried memories was the upset and trauma I'd inflicted on everyone with my screaming at night. My wetting the bed, the arguments and conflict between my parents over me, my mother crying into her pillow. The psychic incident and the resulting terrible row. My brothers' worry and feelings of helplessness and despair. My parents even crying on vacation when we should have been at our happiest together. And I was the cause of that to my family who really didn't deserve it.

I remembered our trip to Europe and my dad taking me to see a man named Harry about my bad dreams. A couple of months after we returned from that trip, I recall being sat in this exact place with my iPad when I heard my mom anxiously say to my dad, "Oh, David, it's over now, she's better. That doctor Harry Mayfield has helped her. Whatever was causing her nightmares is over; please let's not keep digging into it. Stop all this relentless researching for her sake as well as ours, please, please, let's just forget it now and move on. You must stop obsessing over it. I can't deal with any more of it and it's making you ill. I just want my husband and family back."

"You're right," Dad said. "I know you're right, I'm sorry, I'm just tormenting myself with it. I've researched so much now about things that I'm confused by everything; I'm not getting anywhere with it anyway. She's not suffering anymore and is back to being our Chloe, it was like that doctor just flicked a switch in her head, it was remarkable. Okay I'll drop it, no more obsessing I promise."

Listening to their laughing and flirting again now, seven years later, I knew there was no way I was going to put them through anymore distress by bringing up those troubled times. As I turned to go back to my room with my dreams box, I heard my dad say,

"I have a confession to make."

I was immediately on interest alert, eager to hear if it was about me. Mom sounded shocked.

"Oh God David, what?"

"When Chloe was a baby and I was watching her, she fell off the sofa onto the floor and landed on her head. I never told you."

"Is that all?" said Mom." You had me worried for a minute. If it's confession time, I have one. Ever since we married, I've checked everything of yours, phone, computer, receipts and wallet to see if you were cheating on me."

"Me too, said Dad laughing."

I heard them giggling like kids and planning a romantic getaway for them both, and smiling I returned to my room. I recalled the way I used to keep this box under my bed, secretly pulling it out whenever I had an important note to add. When we left for our trip to Europe, I'd hidden the box in that old suitcase so no one would find it while I was gone. Then I'd forgotten all about it as I had no more bad dreams to add to it.

My fingers brushed across the carved flowers on the box as I opened it and studied the childishly scribbled notes and drawings again to see what I could make of them. I laid the little pink notes on the floor, trying to piece it all together, but it honestly meant nothing to me at all. I must have just been a weird little kid at the time. I decided to shove the box under my bed and finish the task of sorting through the rest of the piles of stuff from the closet.

As I was sorting through the closet items, my thoughts returned repeatedly to the notes in the little blue box. It was all such a mystery, and I was intrigued by it. I recalled the terrible feelings of frustration and the constant fear that had plagued me back then. I remember I'd kept the notes hoping to try and figure out what was happening to me someday. I'd been frightened and helpless then as a child, trying to cope with it all, pretending everything was alright when it was far from it. Now I was sixteen I knew I could investigate this mystery myself without any fear, and hopefully solve it myself for the last time.

Once the closet was cleared, I knew I had a couple of hours before dinner, so I sat down with my tablet and typed in the name I remembered my mother saying: Doctor Harry Mayfield. In London.

Harry Mayfield was a psychologist, specialising in child psychology. He had written books on his treatment of children with phobias, nightmares, abuse, and trauma. One article I read was about his experience with children recalling past lives. He had written that in a number of cases it appeared possible that a past life had carried over or 'bled' into the child's current life, causing flashbacks and nightmares.

Could that be it? Was that what had happened to me? I had read about other cultures and religions that believed in past lives and reincarnation. Even saw stuff about it in a couple of movies and fantasy novels. But my parents didn't believe in things like this, especially my dad who dismissed it all as impossible nonsense. Once we returned from our vacation, nothing was ever said to me about my experiences again. Our family just went back to normal, and I was so glad about that and didn't question anything at the time. Doctor Mayfield's name was never mentioned and that whole dark time I went through was hidden away like a dirty secret.

I checked on Harry Mayfield's contact details, but his office was no longer listed, his web site had not been touched in two years and he was no longer registered, indicating he had either retired or passed on. He was pretty old from what I remembered, and frustratingly, that avenue of information appeared closed off. I was tempted to ask my dad about my session with Harry, did he have any records of it that I could have? But realised again that risked raking up all the trauma and upset as he would know I was looking for answers.

Both my parents were in a good place now, Dad had been promoted and that meant a bigger salary, and much less travelling. Mom had a part time job at the garden center and surprisingly loved it, they were having fun and enjoying their time as we kids made our own way in life. Mom was so much happier now with Dad here all the time, and she didn't have the daily grind and responsibility of small kids anymore. I was completely torn between raking this up with them and putting their happiness at risk, or just piling it all back into the little blue flowered box and forgetting it. I agonised over it for quite a while and then made my decision.

I pulled the flowered wooden box out from under my bed and opened the little latch, gazing once again at all the little childlike notes I'd written nestled in the dark velvet lining. With a huge sigh of resignation, I emptied them all into a plastic trash bag, one fluttered to the floor. It had Evelyn written on it. My little companion, is that why I had such a link to her as a child? *Was she part of another lifetime?* With a heavy heart I tied the trash bag up and took it outside to the trashcans by the garage. I put the dreams box in a bag for charity in the den, maybe another little girl could make use of it.

WHEN MOON AND STARS ALIGN

Ryan's last night at home was a sad affair, but as usual he succeeded in making us laugh. Mom was a bit upset he was going, but he would be back in a few weeks and Scott was due a visit next week with his kids. There were always comings and goings in our house now, and Mom didn't get so weepy about it anymore.

But I was feeling sad that Ryan was leaving. I'd felt the loss of each of my brothers as I watched them striking out in life. But Ryan was the last to go and that was particularly hard for me.

I imagined myself like a puppet held up by four strings which were being cut away one by one until there was nothing holding me up. I was falling with no one to catch me. The house had become emptier and emptier with the loss of each brother, rooms vacant and unlived-in or turned into an office or gym, emptied of all their personal stuff. They'd always be my brothers, I knew that, and we would see them periodically, but it wouldn't be the same. They would have girlfriends, wives, and kids in tow. It would never be just 'us' again

That night as I lay on my bed looking up at the pristinely white ceiling (I remembered how back breaking it had been removing all those moon and star glow stickers from when I was little) I thought about the things I'd read on my tablet about reincarnation.

I fell asleep and started dreaming. It was a kaleidoscope of images about the words and drawings on my scribbled notes. People and places and things happening—some very terrible things. I also had the old beach dream, with the huge wave covering me. But instead of being frightened, I had a deep sense it had been trying to protect me all along.

As before, I saw a figure at the end and started to run eagerly towards them, but as usual, I couldn't get any closer and just stopped running, I knew it was useless and sadly slumped to the sandy ground. When I looked up, a boy was standing right in front of me, he was like a hologram. It didn't frighten me, and there was a reassuring feeling that we knew each other, and he was looking out for me. He faded away, and as he did, the huge wave receded back over my head and down the beach, leaving me alone.

I half woke up in the middle of the night with such a start in a cold sweat, my heart hammering in my chest, very unsettled. I glanced at the wall mirror across the room, and in my half-awake state, saw a fleeting glimpse of a misty, shimmering image of a young blonde woman with blue eyes reflected. As I looked at her, I recognised her, and everything snapped into place. I realised then that I had been "the lady in the mirror," I saw all those years ago.

And I wasn't afraid.

I then saw myself as a child in my pajamas saying to my father, "But that's it, that's right, that's why you're here, Daddy. You promised me, don't you remember? That's your job this time around."

I sat on my window seat looking out at the night sky, reflecting on an article I read this afternoon that said souls may come back to Earth in groups to live a physical life together again. That where there are unresolved issues between people, they come back to solve it. They might also have to come back to pay debts to another soul that need to be repaid, or to positively intervene in someone else's life. Or they just like each other so much they choose to be together again in this physical life.

I wondered long and hard about that. Was that why I was in this particular 'family?' and met with certain people? Is that why me and Mom had problems early on? I'd also been nurtured and protected by all the males in my life, my brothers, and my dad. I'd had them all to myself and only had to squeak once and they would come running to make sure I was okay. But now their cloaks of support and protection which had covered me were being pulled away. I tried to put a positive spin on it, imagining that having protected me to sixteen, they were now releasing me gently one by one to allow me to be free to fly, to be myself and go into the world to make my own life. Either way it hurt. I knew I was blessed in life to have such a family and friend network around me, but I still had a feeling that something important was missing from my life, and I wasn't sure what.

Unsettled, I rechecked my mirror and just saw me, Chloe Anderson almost seventeen, reflected. I knew I had enough to deal with in this life and decided the best thing for me and my parents would be to focus on the future of this life, and not chase impossible things from the past that I couldn't change. I wouldn't share these thoughts about past lives with anyone either, not even Sienna or Scarlett for fear of them thinking I was completely mad.

I sat back on my window seat and looked out into the

night sky and saw the most beautiful moon. It appeared to be smiling down at me. It had a pink haze around it, and I was mesmerized. I'd always preferred the moon to the sun —moonlight appeared exciting and mysterious as if something were about to happen. The moon had a particularly magical feeling tonight, and it reminded me of an anonymous quote I'd seen:

"The sun loved the moon so much; he died every night to let her breathe."

I loved that. It reflected how romantic moonlight was and fit in with what I believed true love to be. As I sat there, I glanced over at the house next door. It had been left vacant now for quite a while since our old neighbors moved. I wondered who would be living there next, I hoped it would be a girl my age who I could hang out with.

I got back in bed and after a further short burst of sleep, I awoke about four with such a tremendous feeling of loss, like a bereavement. I was distraught, and inexplicably began to gently sob. The notes meant something important, and I just couldn't let them go. I felt a desperate need to hold onto them and panicked that the trash may have been collected already and I tearfully rushed outside to retrieve them. Thankfully, it was all still there, and I rummaged through the bags to find the right one. I then pulled out the dreams box from the charity bag and went back to my room. I lovingly placed the notes back where they belonged, nestled in the velvet lining. I sealed it with tape. I then saw Evelyn my beloved friend and companion on my dresser. Knowing her name was written on one of the notes and must have been a part of whatever had gone on before, I tearfully tied her plait neatly, straightened her little blue dress, kissed her tenderly, and placed her gently on the dreams box. They were stored in the small cupboard at the back of my closet.

It was where Evelyn now belonged, just out of sight, but still here and never forgotten, as I moved on with this life. *One day Evelyn, when the time is right, I will revisit all of this with you.*

As I SAT with my parents and Ryan that morning, I knew my decision to keep things to myself and not raise it again now was the right one. After a joke filled breakfast with Ryan, he wanted to get going to his new home, and we waved him off in his over packed car.

When we went back into the kitchen to clear up Dad stopped in his tracks. "It's just dawned on me," he said. "For the very first time the females outnumber the males in this house—me. God help me."

We all laughed at the change, and me and Mom hugged. It meant we could outvote him on everything from now on, perhaps that's how I could get my car. I was ready for one and was aching to drive myself having been given lifts by my dad and brothers for so long. I got ready for my tennis class, happy to bike the two miles there and back, but I really wanted a car. The promise of independence beckoned.

I kissed my mom and hugged my dad particularly tightly as I left through the kitchen door to get my bike. I put my helmet on and stowed my racket in the bag on the back and set off down the side driveway. As I did, a car came speeding around the corner onto the drive and made me swerve into the hedge, launching me onto our lawn. My wrist felt like it was on fire and my bike was stuck in the hedge, totally mangled. I sat there on the grass, furious at the idiot who had just caused this. I got up and marched around the hedge to confront them.

I was met by a boy about nineteen years old and was instantly unsettled by him. I thought I'd met him before somewhere, possibly at school or at the mall? I couldn't pin it down and place him, but I'd seen his face before, I was sure of it. Maybe at one of my swimming or tennis clubs? He was tall, had brown hair and brown eyes that looked at me as if he could see through my jeans and shirt, which made me blush. I was still angry with him though, and flirty looks weren't going to let him off the hook for this, that's for sure.

"Hey, are you okay?" he said.

I launched a verbal assault at him.

"No, I'm not okay. You have no right to be on this drive. It's ours, and you were speeding. You could have killed me."

"But I have every right to be here. I live here, it's a shared drive," he said. "You were just cycling way too fast on the wrong side of the driveway to stop."

We argued and talked over each other and eventually he put his hand over my mouth and made a shush sign with his finger over his lips. I was furious. I pushed his hand away. If I'd had my tennis racket handy, I would have hit him with it. The more I lectured him the more he smiled and laughed at every word, which was infuriating.

"You're just so obnoxious, and you don't live here, I know that for a fact. The house is vacant. What are you really doing here anyway? Casing the joint probably."

"Casing the joint? So, here I am, not only obnoxious but probably the worst burglar in history. I drive my own car onto the driveway of the house I'm going to rob and, lo and behold, it's an empty house."

I ignored him and realized I was still wearing my helmet and must look like a ten-year-old boy. I felt mortified and took it off, allowing my long hair to fall around my shoulders. There, at least he would know I was a girl.

He then disarmed me further, saying, "By the way, I moved in last night, to check the plumbing and things before the rest of my family comes today. You might want to think about shutting your blinds when it's dark. My room overlooks yours and you gave me a view of what shouldn't be seen until our fifth date, and we haven't even had our first one yet. Just a thought." He winked at me suggestively.

I furiously tried to think what I'd been up to in my room last night before I went to bed. *Oh God, I wasn't dancing around singing, I hoped. Was I wearing nightclothes when I'd sat on the window seat? Oh God, oh God, oh God.* I felt my cheeks burn. I was completely lost for words. I was never lost for words. I wasn't one for blushing like this in front of people either. How embarrassing.

I huffed at him and went to drag my bike out of the hedge.

"Hey, have we met somewhere before?" he called to me, as I hauled my bike out of the hedge. I felt a sharp pain shoot through my wrist and dropped the bike.

"Ouch," I cried out, holding my painful wrist, and looking daggers at him. "I think you've broken it, and I honestly think, with you being so obnoxious, I would remember if we had ever met before."

He moved closer, standing over me, and tenderly took my arm in his hands, examining it. He then looked deeply into my eyes.

"I'm sorry you're hurt, but hey, I can fix it." He walked off to his car. With those words being said, I had the strangest feeling of sadness and hurt evaporating from me. Who is he? *Why is he having this effect on me? Where had I seen him before?*

As he pulled out an Ace bandage from a duffle bag in his car and carefully wrapped my wrist, he told me they were having a housewarming party the following Saturday and practically ordered me to be there. I was still desperately struggling with my feelings for this newcomer. *I'm not going to make it that easy for you.*

"How presumptuous of you to automatically think I would be free. I could have a broken arm and be in the hospital, thanks to you, or I could be on a hot date myself and so I might be there, and I might not be. I will have to see if I'm free."

"You'll be there," he said, laughing at me in my pompous, childish, mode. "Living here is going to be fun. Except when you wake me up going through your trash in the early hours? Is that some sort of local ritual?"

I gave him my well-practiced death stare; he had been watching me last night retrieving my notes when I was in my old pajamas.

"I obviously have a stalker moving in next door to me," I said.

He roared with laughter and swept me up in the humour of it all as my pompous hard-to-get plans fell apart. I knew he was right, and I would be at his housewarming party.

"Alex Millar," he said.

"Chloe Anderson. Welcome to the neighbourhood."

I went to pick up what was left of my damaged bike, which was a struggle with only one useable hand. He moved closer to my side to help me with it, and as he did, it finally dawned on me where I'd seen him. My legs went weak, my heart raced, and I became breathless as images and memories of far-away places and past times fluttered into my mind like butterflies. I just stared at him in stunned surprise. I couldn't take my eyes off him. He was the boy in the tunnel, the boy who had been waiting at the end.

The name Cole flew into my mind just as he said...

"I'm really annoying you, aren't I?" He was smiling widely at me now, searching deep into my eyes, and I just stared back in absolute wonderment.

I had such an intense feeling of déjà vu, and as the world swirled around us, we both said in unison, "But look me in the eye and tell me you don't just love it."

BIBLIOGRAPHY

For further information on the Special Operations Executive in WWII the following books were used in research for this book.

Maurice Buckmaster, *They Fought Alone*. The True Story of SOE's Agents in Wartime France.

Sarah Helm, *A Life in Secrets*. The Story of Vera Atkins and the Lost Agents of SOE.

David Stafford, *Secret Agent*. The True Story of the Special Operations Executive.

Gibb McCall, *Flight Most Secret*. Air Missions for SOE and SIS

Anne-Marie Walters, *Moondrop to Gascony.*

Major Robert Bourne-Paterson. *S.O.E In France 1941-1945.*

Hugh Verity, *We Landed by Moonlight*. The Secret RAF Landings in France 1940-1944.

M.R.D. Foot, *SOE. The Special Operations Executive 1940-1946.*

ACKNOWLEDGMENTS

Writing your first novel is a daunting experience, and I could never have completed it without the help and encouragement given to me along the way.

I would firstly like to thank my wonderful husband Andrew, for being there, and for his encouragement to finish this book. To Steve, for the years we had with you. To my darling daughter Laura, who makes me laugh with the craziness that is her life. To my beautiful grandchildren, Sienna, Scarlett, Dawson, Ace, and Ella, who make my life worth living every day. To my lovely mum, fondly known as Gan, who keeps me fed on Welsh cakes and iced slices. To my sister Carolyn, and Joe and Rachel, always there for me in good times and bad. To my extended family for putting up with me droning on about my book. Thanks to all friends and colleagues, past and present, who have all added to the rich tapestry of my life. A special thanks to all Steve's true friends and to Chris.

Once I'd written the book, I became lost in the ongoing process to finalising and publishing. Two amazing professional people have helped me through that torturous journey; I would like to extend a special thank you to Peter O'Connor from Bespoke Book Covers, who not only designed the most beautiful book cover, but has been so kind, patient, supportive, and encouraging when I was ready to throw in the towel and give up. He has such vast in-depth knowledge of the whole process, and I feel so blessed that as a new writer our paths crossed.

To Alicia Street for her guidance and honesty, and for not laughing and throwing my efforts in the bin when she was sent the very first draft of this book to edit.

Finally, it goes without saying that there should be a special acknowledgement to all British agents in World War II, some paying the ultimate price, to allow us all the freedom we have today. That freedom should never be taken for granted.

Printed in Great Britain
by Amazon

70416148R00251